THE BOOK OF GOLD

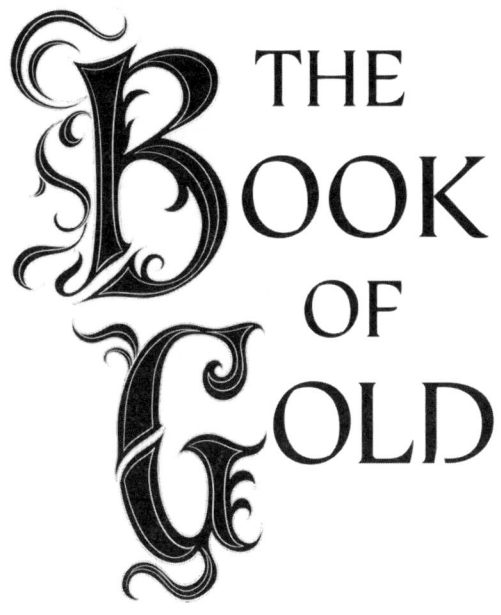

THE BOOK OF GOLD

RUTH FRANCES LONG

HODDERSCAPE

First published in Great Britain in 2024 by Hodderscape
An imprint of Hodder & Stoughton Limited
An Hachette UK company

1

Copyright © Ruth Frances Long 2024

The right of Ruth Frances Long to be identified as the Author of the Work has been asserted by her in accordance with the Copyright, Designs and Patents Act 1988.

All rights reserved. No part of this publication may be reproduced, stored in a retrieval system, or transmitted, in any form or by any means without the prior written permission of the publisher, nor be otherwise circulated in any form of binding or cover other than that in which it is published and without a similar condition being imposed on the subsequent purchaser.

All characters in this publication are fictitious and any resemblance to real persons, living or dead, is purely coincidental.

A CIP catalogue record for this title is available from the British Library

Hardback ISBN 978 1 399 73156 0
Trade Paperback ISBN 978 1 399 73157 7
ebook ISBN 978 1 399 73159 1

Typeset in Baskerville MT Std by Manipal Technologies Limited

Printed and bound in Great Britain by Clays Ltd, Elcograf S.p.A.

Hodder & Stoughton policy is to use papers that are natural, renewable and recyclable products and made from wood grown in sustainable forests. The logging and manufacturing processes are expected to conform to the environmental regulations of the country of origin.

Hodder & Stoughton Limited
Carmelite House
50 Victoria Embankment
London EC4Y 0DZ

The authorised representative in the EEA is Hachette Ireland, 8 Castlecourt Centre, Castleknock Road, Castleknock, Dublin 15, D15 YF6A, Ireland

www.hodderscape.co.uk

*To my family and friends
real and imaginary
And Feral Bob who could be either.*

Se non è vero, è molto ben trovato.
Even if it is not true, it is a very good fabrication.
– Giordano Bruno , Gli Eroici Furori

Bisogna adunque essere volpe a conoscere i lacci, e lione a sbigottire i lupi.
One must therefore be a fox to recognise traps, and a lion to frighten wolves.
– Niccolò Machiavelli, Il Principe

Occasio facit furem.
Opportunity makes a thief.
– attributed to Seneca the Younger

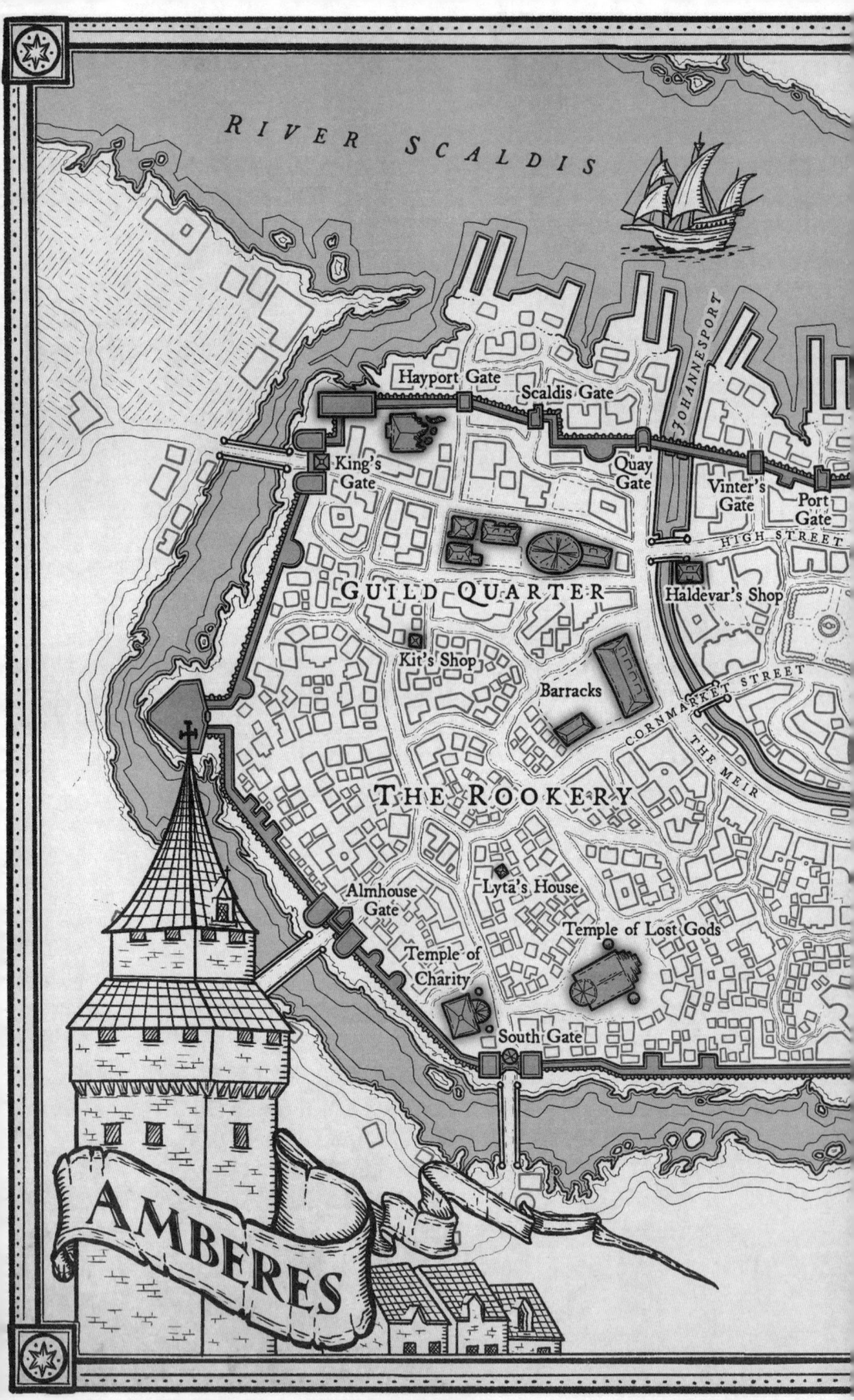

Dramatis Personae

The Crew

Lyta Cornellis – a thief
Christopher (Kit) Cornellis – Lyta's brother, a printer
Sylvian Chant – a captain of the Royal Bodyguards, Lyta's former lover and partner in crime
Frida Elwynn – Lyta's current partner in crime
Beatriz Alvarez – the Lady of House Alvarez
Benedictus (Ben) Alvarez – Seigneur of House Alvarez

Gods

Eninn the Trickster – God of Thieves
Cissonia – Goddess of Commerce, Patroness of Amberes
Kyron – the Warrior, God of Soldiers
Gloir – God of the Forge and the Hearth
Ystara – Goddess of Love
Nimyeh – Goddess of Wisdom
The August Imperator – the Imperator Eternal, the August One, God Emperor of Caput Mundi

Nobility

Francisco – King of Castille, León, Aragon and the Greater Brabantine, the Soldier King, the Golden Lion of Castille

DRAMATIS PERSONAE

Annika – Queen of Castille, León, Aragon and the Greater Brabantine, youngest daughter of the Royal House of Vasa, princess of Geatland
Iseult – Duchess of Montalbeau
Charles – Lord Alderton, a lord of Albion
Carlos V – King of Castille, León, Aragon and the Greater Brabantine, Francisco's father, deceased

Church Imperial

The Magister of the Scholar's Tower in the Brabantine
Frater Julius – Librarian of the Scholar's Tower in the Brabantine

Royal Bodyguards

Elia Vasquez – General
Ivar Torren – Captain
Luca Juárez – Captain
Gabriel Montes – Captain

People of Amberes

Ranulf Wray – master thief, Lyta's husband, missing
Petrus Janlow – criminal gang leader in Amberes
Mattias Haldevar – spice trader, fence, former burglar
Jem Nyati – bookbinder, Kit's business partner
Molly Nyati – their accountant and Jem's wife
Rhea Cornellis – Lyta and Kit's mother, deceased

CHAPTER ONE

Lyta

Lord Alderton's masked ball was practically an invitation to be robbed as far as Lyta was concerned, an open challenge to infiltrate his hallowed halls and make off with whatever shining treasures just happened to find their way into her hands.

The sweet music of a string quartet rippled through the formal gardens, swirled around the ballroom among the dancers and drifted up curved stairways, while the scented air carried rumours of secret liaisons and bitter rivalries. Falconbrook styled itself as the best address within the city walls: the buildings were ornate and beautiful, with gardens sweeping down to the edge of the canal, which wound a circuitous route until it reached the watergates of the Scaldis. The mansion glowed with the light of a thousand candles, and Lyta moved effortlessly through the ranks of the great and the . . . well, she couldn't say *good*. There was precious little good about any of them. She knew that better than anyone.

It wasn't like Alderton and his ilk didn't owe something back to the city, all of them. Amberes was the richest trade port of the western world, the financial centre, the crossroads of civilisation. The great River Scaldis carried galleys, carracks and caravels up- and downstream, bringing treasures and wonders from the far corners of the world. Riches circulated through its canals on punts and barges and set off on carts and wagons through its gates, across the continent. And eventually, in turn, it all came back to Amberes again.

There might be cities with more prestige and honours – royal capitals, holy citadels and ancient foundations – but there was nowhere else like Lyta Cornellis's home. It made the others look like sleepy country villages. So long as it didn't harm trade, you could do whatever you wanted in Amberes. If you were rich enough. Or clever enough.

Except for theft. That was frowned on wherever people had riches. Or at least the kind of theft that stole from them. *Their* particular brand of theft – the one with paperwork and lawyers – that was fine. Her kind, on the other hand . . .

The gown was beautiful, she had to give that to Frida. It hugged her in all the right places and from the lingering gazes of more than a few guests, Lyta had a pretty good idea that the distraction was top-notch. No commoner could look like this – at least, that was what they all thought – and they'd never recognise her afterwards. The delicate mask which covered the top half of her face was like filigree, disguising far more than it revealed. There was just one more thing to do.

Frida wore even more finery, but where Lyta's outfit was elegant and subdued, Frida's screamed wealth like a fishwife broadcasting the daily catch. Her partner had been swanning around as loudly and as ostentatiously as she could all evening, swilling champagne and laughing with all the right people, people far too polite and far too grasping not to pretend they knew her when she was clearly convinced they should. Her luscious black hair was piled up on top of her head around a tiara. She glittered as she walked, the image of a society matron who had risen by wealth alone. 'New money,' they called it, and sneered. As far as Lyta was concerned there was nothing whatsoever wrong with new money. It spent the same way.

As Frida walked by the guards, she reached to the back of her neck as if adjusting the catch of the necklace, released the pin and sent silvery grey pearls spilling everywhere.

The screaming became real.

'My necklace! It's priceless!'

People scattered after the pearls, with shouts of alarm and amazement. Servants, guards, not a few of the guests . . . Frida stood in the middle of the chaos and pressed her hand to her chest, heaving in breath after breath.

And just like that the door was unguarded. All Lyta had to do was put her back against it, shift her weight to lean on it and slide inside, closing it behind her. The arrogant idiot hadn't even locked it. He never did. Bribes to underpaid servants always paid off.

Lord Alderton's study was empty. The only light she had to go by came from the windows, illuminated by the glow of the braziers in the garden. Paintings lined the walls. Only the best. He'd been busy at the art market: De Vos, Key and Pourbus, as well as countless others she didn't recognise. Another show of wealth. The sounds from outside were muffled but she could still hear Frida as clear as day. Lyta could always count on her to be the perfect distraction. She excelled at it. Always had.

'My husband will hear of this. Oh, thank you. Thank you so much. Such a terrible shock. Yes. Oh, look there. Another one went that way. You, yes, thank you, my good man . . .'

The desk was neat and orderly, the papers in piles or filed in the drawers. It only took a moment to pick the locks, not even a challenge. If that was all he relied on, he was worse than she thought. She flicked through the folders. Nothing there. Damn. She knew it was too easy.

Turning around, Lyta surveyed the room with a practised eye. Behind the desk hung a portrait of a slender, handsome man with cold eyes, by Frans Floris himself – or possibly his students if the gossip was true and the old artist could barely hold a brush anymore from tremors. Alderton had made sure to have his portrait painted by the best name in the business. All the better to look down on those who had the misfortune to sit before him here. Lord Alderton liked to drag people through his home before removing everything of value from their lives. Just so they could see what they were lacking.

Rumours flew around him like wasps. He was a spy for the Queen of Albion, or had been sent into exile having displeased her. He was hand in hand with the Hansa traders, the secretive seagoing network scattered around the shores of the North Sea, who worshipped money and brought kingdoms to their knees. He was richer than the Imperator, or he was borrowing hand over fist to maintain this lifestyle. You could take your pick.

The frame was slightly askew, and Lyta tilted her head to one side to examine it more closely. Everything else was perfectly aligned but the frame – the one thing every terrified debtor would be looking at in order to avoid the merciless gaze of the real thing.

A safe was set back in the wall, hidden.

From the sobbing shouts and exclamations outside, she was running out of time. She hadn't reckoned on a safe. They were expensive to install and once a locksmith knew you had one, generally there was hush money involved. Especially in Amberes. This one looked Latinate, metal-bound, with twelve bolts, but only one keyhole. Not so different from a strongbox really, just more modern than she'd expected.

When he was little, Kit would have been fascinated with it. He would have taken it apart and put it back together until he'd had it all figured out. Her brother was good with mechanisms. Now he was a law-abiding and upright citizen, a guild member and a pillar of the community. Her little brother. Too good for his own sister these days.

Luckily, Lyta had always had a talent when it came to locks in particular. Ranulf had taught her every permutation of the locksmith's arts because you never knew when you'd need to open something someone else wanted to keep shut. And this? This was child's play.

Well, it was if you were a child from the gutters of this city.

Lyta pulled a couple more of the picks disguised as pins from her hair and set to work.

Outside, the voices ramped up another notch.

'What the devil is going on here?' Alderton. It had to be. No one else had that arrogance. The accent was distinctive too. Like cut glass about to break.

Frida bawled out an explanation. Lyta could picture her clinging to the tall, slim Albion lordling. 'My husband . . . Oh my lord, he will be furious. Have you found them all? Please, tell me you have them all. Over there. Check over there. You don't know his temper!'

THE BOOK OF GOLD

The safe opened with a *clunk* and Lyta grabbed the files inside, sliding them into the secret panel of her bodice and wrapping the material back around herself so they were securely hidden. Her eye caught on something else: a ring, small and gleaming, white gold, marked with a little sigil of Ystara's star. Her heart stuttered.

The ring. He *did* have it after all.

Kit called it the magpie bit of her brain, the bit that saw something shiny and just had to take it. She called it divine instruction, but not out loud. It didn't do to announce your affinity to the God of Thieves, but Eninn the Trickster had never steered her wrong. The ring was there. Just as promised.

Admittedly the promise had been made in a half-remembered dream, but here it was in reality, so that was good enough for her. Eninn wanted the ring, and if she stole it for him, well . . . only good things happened to thieves who honoured their god. It stood to reason, didn't it?

Lyta could almost hear a voice, like an echo. A chill crept across her skin and the hairs on her arms stood on end. *Take it. Take it and it will help you. Take it and find him.*

She had to. Eninn help her, she needed to find Ranulf. She owed him. And Eninn owed her.

Snatching the ring, she stuffed it down her top, shut the safe, moved the picture back into place and dived for the floor, sliding under the desk and out the other side.

Alderton threw open the door. 'What are you doing in here?'

Lyta scrambled to her feet. Alderton was handsome in that polished way only rich men could be, the lines of his face enhanced by his neatly clipped beard. But the eyes that bore into her were cold and hard. She forced a smile.

'I found it,' she squealed breathlessly. She held out a single silver-grey pearl, flipped her auburn hair and giggled. 'Oh dear me, what must I look like? Excuse me, sir. I'm so terribly sorry.' She danced by him, holding the pearl aloft in triumph. 'Aunt Lucrezia? I found it!'

'*Aunt* Lucrezia?' Frida said, her tone scathing. She set the tankard of ale down on the bar. '*Aunt?*' They sat side by side in the tavern on the old wharf, as the noon bell finished ringing, their borrowed finery returned to Kaisa, the dressmaker, their plain, everyday leathers and cotton a world away from what they had worn last night.

'Some people have young aunts,' Lyta explained, hiding her grin. 'Some people have aunts who are younger than they are.'

'Not aunts called Lucrezia,' Frida grumbled, and drained the last of the tankard.

'Hey, at least he bought it, but it won't be long until he takes a look in that safe and then he's going to raise hell.'

'He doesn't have a clue who we are. And if he starts going around accusing every woman at that fancy ball of his of theft, he's going to find himself shut out of polite society. He's not established enough to try that. I think we're good.'

'Shame about the pearls,' Lyta said. They were expensive, those pearls, and they'd only found eighty-nine out of the hundred.

'Some bugger's made out like bandits, I tell you,' Frida replied with a tone of regret. 'Probably those guards. Or the harridan in puce. She had a light-fingered look.'

True enough. But it was worth it for what they'd got from the safe. Some things mattered more.

They left the tavern, turning down Coopers' Street and joining the bustling crowds outside. Amberes was a riot of colour, noise and smells. All along the quays, the merchant vessels were tied up for the day and the traders were already haggling, while elsewhere cargo was unloaded and carried through wharfside gates and into the streets, or stowed away in warehouses for onward passage. Languages mixed in a cacophony, sounds from all over the known world. Brabantine and Castilian, of course, and Frankish, which Lyta spoke well enough. There was Occitan as well, lyric and fluid and a bugger to learn. The language of Albion was creeping in more and more thanks to Alderton and his countrymen and their trade in wool, linen and lately in print. Kit was already trying to arrange contracts for the printshop. They couldn't get enough of books like the ones he produced so skilfully. Lyta might not spend time with her brother anymore but that didn't stop her keeping an eye on him.

Oxen pulled carts over the worn-down cobbles and bellowed in rage at the indignity, while the nobility, still nursing their hangovers, held small bouquets of dried flowers to their noses. They had to sidestep a gaggle of geese that had escaped their drover. Shops spilled their merchandise on the streets, stalls and trestles inviting further interest, hawkers yelling their wares. There was shit in the gutters, rats in the alleys and fine houses with gated internal gardens side by side.

On the way towards their destination, Lyta paused at the old shrine to Eninn, which was set back into a wall on the corner of Silversmiths' Street, just before the vast space of the Great Market. Lyta pushed a coin into the gaps in the brickwork while a shapeless statue stared down at her like he wanted more. He always wanted more. For a moment she thought of the little ring she'd grabbed, now hanging around her neck, beside her pendant.

She wasn't sure why Eninn wanted it, just that it would help her find out what happened to Ranulf. Her dreams were never clear but she had learned long ago not to ignore them. Her god watched out for her better than most.

Belief died hard in Amberes. Once, there had been many gods, and the traces of them still lingered, their temples and shrines dotted across the city, although most were empty now or used as markets, dosshouses or communal meeting places. But the faithful still came, following gods who no longer showed themselves. Her coin was not the only one. Some did it with devotion, some for luck, some for a laugh. But Lyta couldn't help but take it seriously. She always gave him something.

'I don't know why you still do that,' Frida muttered.

Lyta just shrugged. Not even Frida knew about her dreams. The only person she had ever shared them with was Ranulf, and he had taken them seriously as well. Thieves of his skill knew about stuff like that. He was one of the old guard of the criminal fraternity of

Amberes. 'It's not in our interest to forget Eninn. Never know when we'll need his blessing. Especially in our line of work.'

He'd given her the pendant, a silver disc bearing Ennin's mark, with an off-centre hole in it, the edges not quite round, not quite smooth. She still wore it on an old leather thong, and it was her guide even now.

Frida marched on ahead, her voice drifting back. 'Just don't let the Church catch you outside Amberes worshipping anyone other than their Imperator. A flogging so often offends.'

Like Lyta would be stupid enough to leave Brabantine lands.

In their own territories the Church could flog who they wanted. And worse. But Castille, León and Aragón were pulling away from the Church Imperial and taking all their associated territories, like Amberes, with them. The kingdom wasn't alone. Albion had long since parted ways, a schism which shook the continent. North of Amberes, Gelderland was in turmoil with new ideas. Such revolution made the Church even more strict where it still wielded power. Viciously so. And those places were not so very far away.

They held land only a few days ride from town and had strongholds even closer. There was still an Imperial temple just off New Street, but the aldermen kept close eyes on that, and the acolytes didn't stray far from its grounds.

It left the people of Amberes free to worship as they saw fit. Most of them worshipped money rather than gods anyway.

Lyta blew a kiss at the small faceless sculpture and they headed on their way.

Stalls sprawled across the Great Market, drenched in warm afternoon sunlight, selling everything imaginable. The opulent facades of the guild houses surrounded it on three sides, towering structures topped with painted golden statues representing their trades. The fourth side of the market held the Exchange, where the trade families and merchants met, and deals were done. It was almost as ornate as the Rose Palace, from a time when trade ruled the city instead of the king. It waited, people whispered, like Cissonia, the Goddess of Commerce, biding its time, until the city crowned it again.

Anything was available in Amberes, so long as you knew where to go and didn't care how much you paid. Turn the wrong corner and the deals done could get dark indeed. Although slavery had been outlawed by Isabella the Magnificent a century ago, it wore lots of disguises. Human traffic was cheap here. Lyta glanced into the maw of Cutlers Lane as they passed, catching a glimpse of dull-eyed girls and boys, leaning against walls outside the brothel. They were getting younger all the time. More reputable places, where the prostitutes had a say and a share, were expensive. Not more than a stone's throw from palace and Exchange, Janlow's seedy little empire around Cutlers Lane was not.

Amberes had a criminal underworld underneath its criminal underworld, and Petrus Janlow was the blackest bit of its black heart. He'd always been there, lurking in the shadowy corners of Lyta's life. They had run in a pack when they had just been street kids with no future and nowhere else to be but the wharfs and alleys of the city – Lyta, Sylvian and Janlow. The three of them were inseparable and constantly in trouble. Always a new hustle, a different scheme. They would rule the city one day, Janlow said. But she and Sylvian, stupid and in love, just wanted to get out of Amberes and see the world. One big score was all it would take.

So when Janlow suggested they steal from Gaspar Ducci, the chief crime lord of Amberes at the time, Sylvian had jumped at the chance. Ducci was loaded, everyone knew that. And then Kit, her little brother, had got involved. Because he was just fourteen and he wanted in. He wanted a place with their gang so badly he'd do anything.

Sylvian had promised her – promised on his life – that he wouldn't get Kit involved, that he'd never let anything happen to him. A promise he had promptly broken. So Lyta did the one thing she could.

She'd gone to the watch.

It was a hasty decision that cost everything. Sylvian and Kit were caught before they had even cracked open the window and it had taken every coin she had and all she could borrow to get enough for the bribe to free Kit. Which meant she left Sylvian behind in Old Steen. She had to. It was the last she had ever seen of him.

Part of her still wished there had been any other way. The rest said, 'Good riddance.'

But her problems only multiplied when Janlow cornered her a few days later. In the middle of the market where everyone could see, right where she stood now with Frida. She'd betrayed the gang, he said and Syl, his best friend, strong right arm and the one who brought in most of their protection money, was gone. She owed him now, he said. And he was going to make her pay. On her knees, on her back, whatever it took, first for him personally, then in the brothels. And then Kit as well.

Even now the thought of it made her blood turn to ice in her veins and the sensation of standing there as he leered down at her, dug his fingers into her hip and pulled her against him, the reek of his breath and his triumph choking her . . .

'Enough,' Ranulf had said, stepping out of the crowd of onlookers. 'That's enough. We have a prior debt, Lyta and I. Let her go, boy.' Even Janlow wasn't going to cross one of the old guard, right there in the heart of the city. Not with everyone looking on.

Ranulf had always been part of the landscape of her life too: older, wiser, a master thief with a string of successful jobs under his belt and a bag of gold hanging from it – a legend in the underworld of Amberes. He drank at the tavern where their mother worked back in the day, and she'd taken him under her wing, because she was a kind woman, Rhea Cornellis, looking out for those from the gutters until the day she died. She fed hungry bellies and gave people shelter. She believed in community, even if it was a community of thieves and whores.

Of course, kindness was no protection against the fever which had carried her off. But debts were taken seriously in the city and not all debts were about money.

Ranulf's offer came from the same kindness, rather than love, but it had been the lifeline she needed and Lyta had grabbed it with both hands. At eighteen, she'd married a man almost twenty years her senior. *Let the gossips talk*, she thought. She knew where she stood with him and he had never asked anything of her, never lied to her and always kept his word. Ranulf had been there for her.

Lyta missed her reprobate husband every single day. He had been missing too long now. Nine months, almost ten . . . The ring burned against her chest, along with the unspoken promise that it would help her find him again.

Frida turned away from the market and Lyta followed her, down the labyrinthine lanes of the city, their feet finding their way unerringly where others would fear to tread. They were known here. This was their world.

Haldevar's shop was hard to miss, so stooped that its gable almost kissed the house opposite. The front was shabby and in need of repair, but so were half of the buildings in this part of town. A tiny bell rang above their heads as they entered and Frida closed the door behind them.

The smell of herbs and spices assaulted their senses. Gleaming jars contained every leaf, seed and bark imaginable on the towering shelves surrounding them. If it could be dried and used in any way, Haldevar would have it, from the most common and meagre to the costliest things on the earth. He'd list places that sounded like they came from a dream: Samarkand, Nihon, Calicut, the Americas, Salonika, Kush . . .

All those places Lyta had long ago dreamed of visiting with Sylvian. Those dreams she had given up and now knew for a lie.

'You're late,' Haldevar called from somewhere in the depths of the shop. 'I thought you weren't coming.'

'And miss the opportunity to share these sweet moments with you?' Frida replied tartly. 'What kind of fools do you take us for?'

When Haldevar smiled at Frida his eyes had a familiar flirtation to them. 'The kind of fools who come bearing gifts, I hope,' he said with a wink.

'Should I give you two some privacy?' Lyta asked as she handed over the crumpled papers.

Frida smirked as Haldevar smoothed them out on the counter and peered at them.

He had been Ranulf's right-hand man and sometime burglar back in the day, until he broke his leg in three places during a tavern brawl. That put an end to running over rooftops. Now he had a new line of work.

Haldevar didn't just sell herbs and spices. He sold anything. He bought things too. And if they weren't available to buy, he knew how to acquire them.

'Good,' he said at last. 'I'll take care of everything. Here.' He fished out a weighty pouch and slid it across to them. Frida took it eagerly and counted it while Lyta waited.

'What about the deed?' Lyta asked.

Haldevar pushed a crumpled piece of paper from the pile at her. 'It's just an almshouse, Lyta. It's half-empty. That's hardly the most important thing here.'

'It is to the people who live there.' Like Kaisa's mother. The dressmaker had been desperate for help, which was why Lyta and Frida had become involved in the first place. Everything else was gravy. She took the paper back and studied it, not that she could make out much of the writing, which was small and crabby. Instead she handed it to Frida, who rolled it up and put it in the bag with the money. Frida took care of that side of things and Lyta trusted her completely. There weren't many people she could say that about.

'They don't even have the first clue what you've done for them,' Haldevar said. 'Why bother?'

'We don't need more people out on the street, do we?'

The fence cleared his throat. 'Why does Alderton want property by the Almshouse Gate? That's the question.'

'It's the other end of the city,' Frida replied. 'A world away from Falconbrook and all those fancy mansions with their pretty gardens. There's actually water in the canals up there rather than whatever shit they're clogged with here.'

'Exactly. He's up to something.'

'Does it matter to us?' Lyta asked.

Haldevar fixed her with a stern look. 'It should. It all depends whose behalf he's acting on. Still, if he is working for the Hansa they aren't going to be best pleased, and if it's Albion that wants a foothold down in the shit end of town, well . . . he's fucked there too. The Virgin Queen is not exactly known for her even temper.'

Haldevar snorted and turned away, taking the remaining papers with him. The full repercussions of what she'd lifted from Alderton's office would take a few weeks to ripple through the city. Lyta didn't much care what was in there – blackmail material on half the city aldermen probably – but the main thing was that the almshouse was safe now they had the deed. She had no time for anyone who preyed on the weakest in their society and targeting the almshouse, where those with nothing could be cared for in their old age, had put Alderton right in her sights.

Alderton had swanned into Amberes as if he owned the place, more like an ambassador for Albion than the merchant he pretended to be, with a chest full of gold and a mouth full of empty promises, buying up property where he had no business buying it. He was rich and privileged, and thought the world owed him whatever he wanted. Now, he would learn differently, and Lyta would make sure it was as hard a lesson as possible. Her people might not want a fight – trade and compromise were their forte – but if they had a battle facing them, by all the gods, they went in tooth and nail.

'When's the hearing?' Haldevar asked tentatively.

'The hearing?' she echoed, bemused.

'For Kit.'

That caught her attention. Kit was at a hearing? There was no one more law-abiding than he was. He prided himself on it, and had more than once made it clear that her choice of career was an embarrassment to him, not to mention a professional liability.

His printing business was doing well, last she'd heard. She was proud of that, and of everything else he had achieved, coming from nothing as they both did. He'd turned away from the life of crime that had come so easily to her, preferring hard graft and an honest living instead. And how they had fought about it. His licences were all in order, she'd made sure of that. Of course they were, because this was Kit and it was the law. Printing without one was no joke and likely to end you up in—

'What happened to Kit?' she whispered, her heart lodged in her throat.

'He was arrested yesterday, Lyta.' Haldevar looked uncomfortable. 'I thought you knew. You know everything that happens in this city.'

It was all she could do not to throw herself over the counter and shake it out of him. She couldn't believe it. Kit arrested? Kit wouldn't break the law. He wasn't that stupid and he never caused trouble, not like her. He'd tried it once and that had ended in disaster, so ever since then he'd been a model citizen. He was supposed to be the good one.

'Tell me what happened! Is Kit in trouble? Where is he?'

Haldevar's face had paled. 'Something about printing and distributing a pamphlet. You know how it goes. He's been charged with sedition.'

'He's a printer. He prints a lot of pamphlets. What's seditious about that?'

Haldevar gave her a pitying look. A lot of things could be seditious about a pamphlet, especially now. The King of Castille, Aragón and the Greater Brabantine was in Amberes, trying to assert his authority over a city that didn't want to be under anyone's control. At twenty-six, he was new, young and untried, except in battle. All he knew was violence, and that was how he governed too.

He had arrived in Amberes with fanfares and celebrations, and had promptly dismissed the despised governor, the Duchess of Montalbeau. At first, the people celebrated. There was talk of extra freedoms, of taxes being lifted and a new era in Amberes. But it was the talk of fools. Nothing would change: nobility looked after its own, not the common man. In the king's eyes, all Amberes was good for was money: it was the market of the world. There would be no rights or justice for them. And Lyta had no doubt that was what her noble, foolish little brother's pamphlet was about.

He had put himself straight in the king's sight this time. And Francisco wouldn't tolerate dissent.

Kit had no one of note to vouch for him, no one to stand for him except her. He wouldn't have a chance. They may not see eye to eye and hadn't in years, but that didn't matter. He was Kit.

'Where's he being held?'

CHAPTER TWO

Lyta

Old Steen Prison was a hulking grey block of a building right on the river, wedged in the city walls, with a turreted gatehouse and iron bars as thick as young oaks covering every miserable window. It took Lyta far too long to get there, even though she ran all the way, heedless of anything and anyone in her path. It had been a fortress once, hundreds of years before, foreign armies breaking themselves on its defences, and it retained that reputation for blood and death. She didn't even know if Frida had followed her. She'd just taken off, sprinting through the city she knew like the back of her hand, now made strange and terrible.

Kit was in trouble. Kit, who never did anything wrong. Kit, who she had spent every single day of her wretched life trying to protect.

Old Steen haunted the nightmares of the worst of society. She knew people who'd come out irreparably broken. Others emerged so filled with rage or terror they barely functioned. Torture, disease, misery and despair lingered in every corner of every cell. And that was just for those who left alive. Only the fortress of Montalbeau itself had a darker reputation.

Sedition was a high crime, a transgression against the king himself.

As Lyta reached the desk she was almost relieved to see the man sitting there had a familiar hangdog face: Tijs Straeten.

'Kit Cornellis,' she said.

'They've already taken him to trial,' Straeten told her in what might have been a gentler tone, had he not looked at the duchess's man over her shoulder and stiffened. They were still swarming over Old Steen then, still holding the reins of power here. The king might have armies, but prisons needed guards. The desk sergeant's eyes grew careful. 'Nothing I can do for you. If he comes back it'll be for the noose.'

When Lyta opened her mouth, Straeten shook his head in the smallest gesture of warning. The duchess's guards were on the lookout for trouble and if she was arrested, who would help Kit?

Rumour had it Iseult of Montalbeau served a goddess so dark she didn't even have a name – not one anyone would say out loud. Too many of those called to work for her never returned, and people whispered, in the dead of night, that she bathed in blood to augment her magic. The victims were never named, of course. But they vanished all the same. Especially people who found themselves suddenly on the wrong side of the law. People who had no one to support them, no one to miss them.

Straeten sorted through some papers as if he hadn't a care in the world, but his hands shook. 'Want to take a message for me? There's coin in it for you.'

She sucked in a breath, watching his hands. Words appeared beneath his pen: *Admit bearer to public gallery.*

Straeten handed her the slip. 'Take this. You've time yet but not much. Now off you go.'

Lyta walked out clutching the piece of paper in her numb hand. She passed some royal guards outside, posturing and posing in their newfound position. The fight between the duchess and the king was already spilling onto the streets of her city. It wouldn't end well, and it was the ordinary people who would suffer. Then there were the aldermen, elected by the guilds and ratified by the Crown, who ran the city watch, and just wanted to be left alone to trade and count their money.

Too many forces at odds in one small tangle of a city.

Amberes was a rich purse ripe for picking, and the vultures were circling.

The Rose Palace was a confection of a building, the intricate facade soaring to the sky, the stone carved with lifelike flowers and vines.

Its gutters dripped gargoyles shaped like fantastical creatures of legends, and the turrets were topped with golden spires. The windows glowed with more stained glass than a temple. It couldn't have looked more out of place in Amberes if it tried.

The site it occupied had once been a medieval trade hall, before old King Carlos took Amberes with cannon and sword and claimed the largest building in the city for his new home. He rebuilt it and renamed it. Why 'roses' was anyone's guess.

As a trade hall it had been open to all, and traces of that structure still remained. Half had been kept as civic offices, courts and barracks, while deeper behind the walls, the private quarters now housed the king and his entourage. It had to be a security nightmare.

There was talk of a new civic building, a city hall, to be built in the Great Market, which would dwarf the Exchange and the guild houses, to separate the work of the city from that of the Crown – more to insulate the Crown than to serve the people. But there had been talk of that for twenty years.

Lyta looked up at the imposing gates, decorated with bosses carved with roses and thorns, with crowned lions over the occasional ghost of guild signs or trade-house symbol, in a dizzying riot of imagery. She picked her way through the petitioners and the queues of onlookers swarming the entrance, all shut outside.

The enormity of it settled on her shoulders like a weight. There were too many people here. They wanted a glimpse of the king and his new queen. They wanted to see the duchess humbled or revenged, and to see criminals punished as brutally as possible. They wanted a show. They wanted blood.

Lyta presented her paper to a disinterested guard, who briefly searched her for weapons before letting her inside. She made her way up the narrow stairs to the balcony over the chamber and seated herself on a narrow wooden bench. The gallery was packed but she managed to peer over the heads of those in front of her.

Opposite, she could see the aldermen seated in their boxes overlooking the floor beneath. The Ursels, Van Stalens and Marnixes – all the trade families. De Moy had brought his new mistress. They ignored the sea of prisoners beneath them. De Werve was noticeably absent, as was the Rockox clan. Political lines had already been drawn.

And below them . . .

So many. It stole Lyta's breath. People shackled and herded together like animals. The public crowd in the balcony jeered and shouted. Any of the usual rotten vegetation and other missiles that the good people of Amberes liked to throw at those in the dock would have been removed by the guards, but that was only because the king was present.

Her eyes were drawn to the man seated at the distant end of the chamber, far from the rabble. Stained glass rose like a spiderweb of rainbows behind him. King Francisco himself took centre stage, clad in plain enough clothes given his elaborate titles, and wearing a slender golden crown. The Soldier King, they called him, and the Golden Lion of Castille. A war hero, fresh from victorious battles in Aquitaine, Burgundy and the Breton Marches, although Lyta doubted he had ever been in actual danger, surrounded by his guard at all times, just as he was now. The king was young and supposedly handsome too. She couldn't tell from this far away, but there was something arresting about his dark colouring and intense eyes. He held himself with an air of command, as if he was the centre of the world. The sword across his lap had to be ceremonial. It was huge. And yet, something told her that if called on to use it, he wouldn't be wanting.

Two women flanked him. The Lady Iseult, Duchess of Montalbeau, was a familiar enough sight, dressed in black and veiled in lace, still ostensibly in mourning for her late husband. Rumour was she'd had him murdered or had even done the deed herself. But Lyta knew all about rumours like that and there was rarely a chance they were true. Men died, especially old men. And sometimes they left young wives behind.

The shadow of Ranulf hung over everything in her life. He had left on one last job, one of Eninn's own devising – to break into the most dangerous fortress in the region: Montalbeau. And he hadn't come back.

Lyta had loved him in her way, and he had cared about her. That was why he hadn't allowed her to go. And that was why he hadn't come home again.

Lyta reached for the necklace and squeezed the pendant and the ring through the fabric of her shirt. Eninn had promised the ring would help her find Ranulf. She had to trust in that. But now she needed his help with something far more pressing – Kit.

The other woman beside the king was the dawn to the duchess's nightfall, slender and fair, wearing a gown that shimmered in the afternoon light. There was no doubting her beauty. She radiated it. The queen, a new wife, innately royal in her own right. Annika had come all the way from Geatland in the distant north to Francisco's fortress in Valladolid, right in the southern heartland of his empire, to marry him, the youngest daughter of the royal house of Vasa. Her beauty was famous the world over. They said she was descended from a goddess of love through her mother, a blessed bloodline, full of divine power. Francisco had moved heaven and earth to win her.

A queen like Annika legitimised his reign, young as he was and a second son. The carrion crows had been circling from the moment the crown went on his head, but he'd seen them all off and won his prize as well. Rumour had it that the royal coffers had been bled dry by war, and her dowry didn't do enough to fill them. Geatland wasn't rich. But the king had set any thought of that aside the moment he'd set eyes on Annika. Some things were worth more than money. Her lineage for one thing. And her beauty. Now all they needed was an heir.

Annika looked so slight a breeze might blow her away was it not for the weight of jewels on her body and gown. She was pale as the snowy land from which she hailed, her white-blonde hair like gossamer, held back from her slender face by a white-gold diadem. Her icy-grey gaze travelled over the prisoners before her and for a moment Lyta sensed distress from her. Perhaps even pity.

Behind the royal party stood an array of guards, decked in the royal colours, navy and gold. Armed to the teeth. It was a show of strength. A threat.

A name was called, a man thrust forward, charges read. It was piteously quick. King Francisco listened, his face giving no indication of his feelings. If anything he looked bored.

A hushed silence fell over the chamber.

'Guilty,' the king said, and the prisoner was dragged away.

Another name was called, and another. Some crimes were worse than others. Some made even Lyta shrink inside herself in disgust. But most could have been settled without this showmanship. The duchess must have been saving trials up for the king's arrival, whether to dismay him or exhaust him it was hard to say. Not that it seemed to be bothering him in the slightest. Sometimes the king listened closely, sometimes he appeared to have already made up his mind. No one got a say in their own defence.

Disposable lives, that was all they were.

'When someone shows you what they are, Lyta,' Ranulf had told her once, 'believe them. And when someone puts on a show, ask yourself, why? What do they want you to see? What do they want you to learn?'

What did the king want them to see? His strength. Nothing more than that. His complete power of life and death over each and every one of them.

The crowd in the chamber and in the gallery started to dwindle as the light faded outside. Very few prisoners were acquitted and there was still no sign of Kit. The dull thud of a headache built between Lyta's eyebrows but as the gallery cleared, she was able to make her way to the front and peer over. A youth sat beside her, a boy perhaps fourteen, the same age Kit had been when their mother had died, too young to be watching something like this. But here he was, leaning over the rail as if he was at the theatre. Thin as an alley cat, with mismatched eyes, he grinned at Lyta, a far-too-knowing grin on so young a face, and then shifted over for her to get a better view.

Kit appeared from the pit housing the prisoners, his red-gold hair catching the last of the light as he climbed into the dock, the curls tamed and tied at the back of his neck. Lyta's breath wedged in her throat as she saw the bruises down one side of his face, and her stomach twisted when he turned to look up at the gallery and his blue eyes caught hers. Something hardened in his expression, something she had never seen before. Kit was in trouble and he knew it. And he didn't want her there.

The last time they had spoken it had ended in a fight. He was banging on about natural justice or some such nonsense. She'd told him that he might as well take up farming unicorns. He'd called her a criminal and a liability, and she'd . . . well, she'd said some things she wasn't proud of. He'd finished by telling her he never wanted to see her again. And she had said, fine, he never would. She hadn't meant it. She embarrassed him, she knew that. And because she secretly admired everything he had achieved, that stung.

'The charge is sedition and the publication of treasonous pamphlets contrary to the royal licence,' the clerk of the court's voice rang out. Dates followed, details, a brief description of the raid and Kit said nothing, just held his head up high and looked right at the king.

The others had grovelled and tried to show deference. Not her brother. Lyta had never been more proud of him. Or more afraid for him.

King Francisco leaned forward. He'd barely moved in the last hour. A murmur ran through the crowd. Lyta studied the aldermen opposite her, who were craning their necks too, like vultures.

'Christopher Cornellis,' the king said, his surprisingly melodic voice melting against the senses. 'You're an educated man. Do you have anything to say in your defence?'

'If it please, your Majesty.' Kit's voice sounded strained. You'd have to know him well to hear it. 'All the guilds are asking for is a fair hearing. Taxes are strangling the city. Your people are starving. Rents are increasing, as is crime, and no one is concerned with the—'

That was as far as he got. A club landed squarely in his stomach with a sickening crunch and Kit doubled over, smacking his head on the wooden edge of the dock.

'Bow before your betters, dog,' the black-clad guard sneered at him. Hooting laughter and jeers followed.

Kit struggled up, fresh blood trickling down his face. His hair had come loose, as rebellious as hers, turning dark where the open gash bled on it. He drew in a shaky breath, obviously in pain, and Lyta had to dig her nails into the bench to keep herself still.

'Majesty,' Kit tried again, 'we only want to petition you to—'

Another club struck him, in the back this time and Lyta let out a cry of dismay. She clapped her hands over her mouth, aware of eyes turning towards her.

A cold hand gripped her wrist and pulled her back. The adolescent boy again, surprisingly strong. A shiver ran through her and her stomach clenched. They were going to kill Kit. One way or another, they were going to kill her little brother. She sank down on the bench, waiting for the end to come. *If he comes back here it will be for a noose*, Straeten had said.

No one expected him to be acquitted. Not even Kit. But he was still going to try. He was still going to run his mouth off about justice and fairness, and any number of other myths that nobility hated to hear about. If he was lucky, they'd just hang him.

Lyta squirmed, pleaded silently with her god for help.

The boy beside her squeezed her hand. He didn't say a word. There was nothing he could say.

The queen raised a hand to her husband's arm and said something. His expression clouded and then he nodded. Without warning, he rose to his feet. 'We will resume tomorrow morning. Our beloved queen is unused to such spectacle and wishes to retire. Clear the court.'

And just like that they were gone, sweeping out of the chamber with their guards and retinue following, Kit forgotten.

Lyta shook off the boy's hands and scrambled for the door and the stairs back down, but by the time she reached the doors, there was no sign of Kit. There was no way he'd survive another night in Old Steen.

Lyta couldn't break him out. But maybe she could plead for him if she made a case before the king. Now. She was already in the palace after all and she knew its layout. She'd learned it when Ranulf had planned a break-in years ago. In the end the gang he led had insisted she be left behind and they had almost been caught.

That was when her husband had taken to calling her their *lucky charm*. Blessed by Eninn, his favourite.

But he still hadn't taken her on the last job. And then he hadn't come back. Which she felt proved the bloody point.

Reversing from the main doors, Lyta headed straight for the guardroom. A cloak hung there, in the deep wine red of the city watch, the crest of Amberes picked out in a frayed gold thread, a tower surrounded by fortifications. She grabbed it and swirled it around her shoulders.

Keep moving, always make it look like you know where you're going, like you have somewhere to be. People won't look twice or question anyone who appears to have a purpose.

It was almost as if Ranulf was walking beside her, whispering in her ear. She grabbed the pendant about her neck and offered up a prayer.

The corridor turned left and she saw a flash of movement ahead. The boy, the one from the balcony. How had he got ahead of her? And what was he doing here? He poked his head around the corner and grinned at her, his mismatched eyes gleaming, and then he was gone.

Lyta hesitated. 'Hey,' she called softly. But no one called back.

The door stood ajar at the end of the hall, obviously a servants' entrance from the plain walls and the darkness beyond. She slid inside, pulling it closed behind her and began to climb the stone stairs. Above her she could hear footsteps, quick and light. And for a moment, she was sure there was a laugh, one she almost knew. It lived in the corners of her dreams and ghosted after her sometimes in the alleyways of the city. It sounded like Eninn.

Her skin gave that familiar shiver, as if a breath ghosted over its surface.

Sometimes she just had to trust in her feral god.

Lyta slowed as she reached the first floor where the royal quarters were located. She hesitated, wishing she had a weapon, even though sweat slicked her palms and she would probably drop it rather than find use for it. Then again, only a select few could legally bear weapons in Amberes. Breaking into the royal quarters was bad enough. Doing so with a blade in hand would be an instant death sentence.

Soft carpet muffled her footsteps as she stepped out into the first-floor corridor. Tapestries hugged the walls and she began to sweat beneath the cloak.

As Lyta made her way past a series of formal reception rooms, towards an ornately carved set of double doors which had to be the royal apartment, she heard rising voices from the other side.

'And where have these surplus tax incomes gone, Lady Iseult? We have no records of such rises.' The king's voice, cold and angry, dangerous.

The duchess laughed, apparently unconcerned. 'The people always complain of taxes, your Majesty. It's a fact of life. He's just a troublemaker, from a family well known to the authorities.'

Lyta sucked in a breath and made herself still and quiet. That wasn't good. The idea that the duchess knew anything about her family set every nerve tingling with alarm. Instincts rose in her that would make everything so much worse: to burst in there and defend her brother; to speak up for his good name, which wouldn't do him a blind bit of good. Kit needed her to be calm, to be the voice of reason. Kit *needed* her.

The door opened and Lyta took a step back, slamming into something hard, tall and broad, a solid wall of muscle and armour. She started to turn, but hands like stone seized her by the shoulders.

Instinct took over. She twisted, dropped, her leg lashing out as the figure behind her lunged after her. She felt her foot connect and he grunted. But he didn't let up, taking the blow and still coming at her. She launched herself off the floor, grabbing the nearest tapestry to give her leverage. It came down as she went up, using the wall to hurl herself away.

She wasn't fast enough. He grabbed her out of the air and slammed her on the ground. Before she knew what was happening, there was a foot on her chest and a sword tip at her throat.

Lyta fell still, staring up the length of the blade, straight into the endless black eyes of the man she had once loved body and soul, and who she had betrayed into forced conscription, thirteen long years earlier: Sylvian Chant.

CHAPTER THREE

Sylvian

It should have been easy. It should have been a position of honour and what the general had referred to as 'an easy ride'. He'd gone from conscript, to soldier, to war hero, to royal bodyguard and companion. He thought he'd be in the sun-drenched capital of the southern kingdom, Valladolid, or following Francisco around Andalusia or Navarre, fighting by his side in Aquitaine, Naples or Burgundy. Instead he was back in bloody Amberes again, with the king and the duchess at each other's throats, the queen terrified of her own shadow and, to add injury to insult, now forced to confront the fear-wide, cornflower-blue eyes of Lyta Cornellis.

Lyta, his Lyta, once love of his life, who had abandoned him to the tender mercies of Old Steen. Lyta, who had turned him in and left him to rot. The woman whose neck he would cheerfully ring.

Her lips parted, forming his name, or part of it, but she didn't say it out loud. Just lay there, staring up at him in horror. Well, he was her nightmare, wasn't he? And she was his.

The last time he'd seen her, she hadn't even looked at him. When he'd knelt on the stone floor of Old Steen in shackles and she'd strolled past him and pointed at Kit. 'Him. I'm taking him.'

A gnawing rage ground away inside him, one he thought he'd long ago managed to suppress.

Right on cue, the king appeared, holding an ornate but deadly double wheellock pistol his father had prized, made by the skilled hands of a master gunsmith as a bribe. It might be twenty years old, but it was still in perfect condition, maintained as lovingly by the son as it had been by the father. Light gleamed off the cherry-wood stock inlaid with carved ivory, its steel body overlaid with gold. Just looking at it chilled Sylvian's heart.

'What is going on out here?' Francisco asked.

'Your Majesty—' Sylvian began, but Lyta, still lacking the self-preservation skills most people were born with, spoke first.

'I'm unarmed. I'm here to beg for my brother. Please, you have to listen to me, your Majesty!'

Lyta was here for Kit. Of course she was. The rage sparked up another notch. It didn't matter that this was exactly why Sylvian had been coming to see the king, to beg him to spare the boy. Well, Kit was a man now. But that was beside the point. Lyta had got here first. And Lyta would always do anything to protect Kit.

'Let her up, Chant.' The king sighed and lowered the firearm, returning the lock mechanism to its safety setting. 'It has been a very long day. Torren and Juárez are standing by in the anteroom. If she is indeed unarmed, I'm sure between us we can handle any issues. Or would you rather I summoned the rest of my bodyguards and explain your fears?'

He gave Sylvian a cynical smile and stepped back into the room from which he had come.

'Come in here then,' he called out.

Sylvian couldn't disobey a direct order from his king, so he stepped back, releasing Lyta but keeping his sword blade bare. His left hand itched to pull out the knife at his belt. Once he would have trusted Lyta with his life, but that had been a long time ago. And this wasn't about his life: it was about his king's.

He would do anything for Francisco. He had proved that hundreds of times.

'Really, your Majesty?' The duchess sneered as Lyta passed her. She even took a step back to avoid the thief. 'You're consorting with the scum of Amberes now? You won't learn anything from her. An upstart from an upstart city, one which will still not accept its place.' She looked Lyta up and down as if assessing a pig and shook her head. 'Not the worst they have to offer, I suppose, but there are better whores all over the docks.'

Once Lyta would have lashed out in rage. Now she bowed her head and folded her hands in front of her. The words, however, were quiet, carefully pitched and devastating.

'I guess you'd know.'

An upstart from an upstart city indeed. A long, shocked silence followed. The duchess's face froze in suppressed rage.

From the far side of the room, the queen made a noise like a stifled laugh. She sat with her back to them, gazing at the fire, ostensibly ignoring them. Sylvian knew she was listening to every single word. There was a mirror over the fireplace. She was watching too. Nothing got past Annika.

The duchess's face went even whiter but she didn't look around. She had barely acknowledged the new queen which was yet another snub.

'You should hang them both,' she said in glacial tones. 'You'd only be saving time. With your permission, your Majesty, I will depart. I have a long journey home and I fear the stench is turning my stomach.'

Lyta opened her mouth again and Sylvian took a step forward in warning. She'd only get away with so much and she was already dangerously close to that line. Only the fact that she appeared to be amusing the queen stood in her favour. Sylvian knew Francisco too well. He didn't like to be crossed and the gods help anyone who did.

Luckily for Lyta, all his attention was fixed on the duchess. 'There is still the matter of the book, madam,' he told her. She stopped, and a slow, cruel smile spread over her beautiful face.

'The book? Why, the book is mine, your Majesty. A gift from your noble father.'

The king stiffened, scowled. 'And now your king has need of its return.'

She shook her head. 'I think not. The book is secure, safe within my library. And there it must stay. The Church agrees. It is far too precious a thing to bring forth into the light on the whim of a girl who follows a lost goddess, I think. Not yet, in any case. Perhaps, when the time is right.'

Francisco's voice was the sudden snap of a whip and Sylvian knew this was sliding badly sideways fast. The girl in question had to be the queen, so that was insult enough, but the command had come from the king's mouth. It was not to be denied. 'This is not a request, Iseult.'

She met his gaze, head held high. Her disdain was written all over her face. 'Oh, I think it is. One I decline. Farewell, Lord King. And may you have the joy of Amberes I never did.'

'I have not given you leave—'

But she had already walked away. No one could command the Duchess of Montalbeau. Sylvian had tried to tell him, but Francisco wouldn't listen. People didn't say no to him.

Until now.

Lyta cleared her throat. 'I can get the book for you.' She spoke far too quickly. Sylvian knew that tone. Lyta was desperate and right now she'd do anything, promise anything. This was not good.

Sylvian's heart plummeted. 'Lyta, you have no idea what you're saying. Just shut up and hope that—'

'Enough, Chant.' The king cut across him. His attention fixed on Lyta now, intrigued. Sylvian cursed under his breath. 'I want to hear what this lady has to say.' Lady indeed. If only Francisco knew.

By the antlered helm of Kyron, he could strangle her right now. A hundred times over. And it had nothing to do with their past.

'Majesty, please—' he began.

The king grinned like a boy and Sylvian knew he'd already lost the argument. Francisco's mood had changed again, like quicksilver. 'Put the sword away and introduce me to your friend. Lyta, isn't it?'

'We're not friends,' Sylvian said quickly, at the same time that Lyta blurted out 'He's no friend of mine.'

Well, that was where they both were then. Good. It was better this way.

The king laughed loudly and walked back to the fire and his waiting wife.

'Take off the cloak,' Sylvian hissed at her as they followed Francisco to the seats at the far side of the room. 'You're no more city watch than I am.'

She looked him up and down in far too familiar a way. 'No. You far outgrew that idea, didn't you? No soldier either now. What are you?'

'King's bodyguard,' he growled.

She snorted out the most unladylike laugh. 'Figures.'

The king had taken a seat near the fireplace while Queen Annika perched on the edge of one of the other silk-covered chairs. She helped herself to a glass of the rich red wine they had brought with them from the south, from the royal cellars. They didn't trust anyone in Amberes, with good reason. And while the palace was well secured with Sylvian's fellow guards, the king wanted his privacy. Courtiers got in the way and Francisco believed that a person who couldn't even serve themselves food and drink didn't deserve to be fed and watered.

It was a nightmare.

One that had just taken an even more horrific turn with the arrival of Lyta Cornellis into their supposedly completely secure quarters.

'You know each other,' Annika said, her voice like birdsong. Sylvian had never met a woman quite like the queen. Every sound was poetry, every gesture a dance. And she had a mind like a bear trap. People took one look at the beautiful doll of a woman and completely underestimated her. Even the duchess, who should have known better.

Francisco had been completely smitten with Annika from the first moment they met. Sylvian had seen it in his eyes, could have attested to the moment it happened, the complete and utter surrender to her, right from the start. He'd felt the same way himself. Just a moment in her presence was enough to do it. She had that effect on everyone – everyone except for Lyta, it seemed. And Iseult of Montalbeau.

'I'm Lyta Cornellis, your Majesty,' Lyta answered before he could work out what to say. 'Syl and I grew up together. He was quite the rogue back then. Until he joined the army, we were inseparable. We were going to be married, but he left me behind in Amberes.'

'And the moment I left she married someone else, so she wasn't too heartbroken.' Sylvian couldn't let her have the last word. Not in this. Especially not to Annika and Francisco.

Lyta shook her head and smirked. 'Who mentioned anything about hearts, Syl?'

Sylvian cursed under his breath.

Francisco laughed, his mood softened, amused. Well, it was better than his temper. He wasn't used to defiance and he didn't take it well.

'Cornellis?' he said. 'That was the name of the printer in the dock this evening. The last prisoner.'

'He *is* the printer,' Lyta replied, leaning on the word 'is' and subtly emphasising printer instead of prisoner. 'My brother. I want to beg for his life.'

Lyta, begging. Sylvian had never dreamed of hearing that. And yet, hadn't he come here to do exactly the same thing? Kit had been a good kid.

'And yet you don't seem to be begging very much,' the king said. 'Sylvian, pour some wine. We want to hear what Mistress Cornellis has to say.'

'Mistress Wray,' Sylvian corrected as he moved automatically to obey.

But Lyta had to argue. Of course she did. 'Mistress Cornellis is just fine. Never changed my name and I'm on my own again after all. Just my brother and I.'

That almost made him trip over his own feet. What had happened to Ranulf? He cast her a confused glance, but she wasn't looking at him. She only had eyes for the king, and they were wide and blue and pleading. She was still the consummate actress, playing for sympathy. So helpless and alone, with only her brother, who could be taken from her in an instant, at the king's whim.

'How can you get the book that the duchess denies my lord husband?' Queen Annika asked.

'I have certain skills,' Lyta told her with false modesty.

Sylvian poured the wine and handed it to the king with a bow. As he straightened, he saw the amusement in Lyta's eyes. Oh yes, she'd find his deference hilarious, naturally. He hadn't known what the word meant when they were together. He knew he had changed and he didn't regret a thing. He served the king, for the love of all the lost gods. He'd earned his place, Francisco's trust and all the more besides. And what had Lyta done? 'She means she's a thief.'

Francisco grinned his most reckless grin. 'A very good thief, I presume, to be standing here.'

Lyta had the gall to drop into a curtsey as graceful as any the queen's ladies of the court of Valladolid itself could execute. 'The very best.'

The king was studying her. 'And presumably in order to undertake this task, you want your brother exonerated instead of executed.'

Sylvian expected a trademark Lyta smart answer, but once again she surprised him and just nodded. Maybe she had learned some self-preservation skills in the last thirteen years. Then again, breaking in here, making her way to the royal chambers, putting this offer to the king . . . maybe not.

Lyta lived for risks. Always had. 'I'd prefer him alive and free,' she said carefully, steering clear of his wordplay.

'Well,' the king leaned back in his seat, sipping his wine and still watching her over the edge of the glass. 'That remains to be seen.'

Sylvian's stomach tightened uncomfortably. The king was looking for some sort of entertainment then and for the first time Lyta had not provided it. Now he was sulking. In a regal way, of course, but it amounted to the same thing.

Sylvian loved his king, would do anything for him, had done things he regretted and things he preferred not to think on, but gods, it was so much better when Francisco had a war to occupy him.

'Was this Christopher Cornellis the reason you requested an audience with us this evening, Captain Chant?' the queen asked gently, but knowingly, and Sylvian had to swallow a curse as Lyta's eyes flicked towards him with interest. Queen Annika noticed. She saw everything. She was so much better at all of this than Francisco. 'Presumably you grew up with him as well.'

'I— I wanted to plead his case, yes.' He couldn't lie. Not to them. He'd taken vows of obedience and service. He was bound to the throne. It gave him a certain leniency with them, that and his devoted service. He'd saved Francisco's life countless times on the battlefield and more than a few since. If he pleaded for someone, he would be heard. 'He's a good man, your Majesties. A passionate man, with a pronounced sense of justice. If Duchess Iseult has indeed been squeezing extra taxes from Amberes' – which of course she had been, but no one wanted to admit she'd been skimming the cream off the top for years and nobody had done anything – 'then the city and its people, particularly the common workers, will have been under considerable strain, and Kit is the type of man who would want to see that injustice righted. He was trying to plead his case, and that of the city, in the way he best knows how. Nothing more. I am sure of this.'

For once Lyta didn't look fit to kill him. She swallowed hard, her throat working furiously. Something glistened in her eyes and she turned her face away.

'You care about him?' Annika asked with surprising gentleness.

'Yes, ma'am. He was like a brother to me.'

If he and Lyta had got married, if he hadn't been a fool and got involved in things far out of his depth, if he hadn't let Kit get tangled up in it too, if he hadn't chosen conscription over a prison sentence, if he had made it back just a little sooner . . . a thousand ifs from long ago that had combined to create never ever.

If Lyta had just trusted him. Just once. If she had chosen him.

But that would never have happened.

'An interesting name, Christopher,' the queen mused, almost to herself. 'Unusual, especially here. From the Hellenic language, I believe.'

Lyta stared at her, as if trying to work out how to use this interest to her advantage.

'Our mother liked unusual names,' she said at last. 'Her family came from the Hellenic islands, she used to say. But that could have just been a story.'

Lyta spoke only hesitantly about her mother, a kindly olive-skinned woman who Sylvian remembered with affection. Rhea had died too young, and her family, whoever they were, had never looked for her. Their father . . . well, who knew? To Sylvian's knowledge he'd never come looking for his children. They had all assumed he was dead as well.

'Interesting,' said the queen. 'Hippolyta was the daughter of the Hellenic war god, Ares, did you know that, my beloved? And a warrior in her own right. Or so the stories say. It means wild or untethered horses, or perhaps one who sets horses free . . . something like that.' She sipped her wine, smiling softly at her husband who gazed back at her in adoration. He loved to hear Annika display her knowledge and learning. And when she spoke like that, she calmed him.

The king cleared his throat and shifted in his seat. 'Ares was one of the first lost to the Church Imperial, was he not? Not a very effective god of war then.'

'Forgive me,' Annika said quickly. She even blushed prettily. 'I have a fascination with names, languages and old tales. When someone bearing the name of the child of any god appears before us, my beloved, we should surely consider their offer, don't you think? Even a foreign god long lost to the Nether.' She said it like a joke, but Sylvian could see from the look in her eyes she was serious.

'Very well,' said the king, ready to grant Annika anything she desired, as ever. 'Mistress Cornellis, I will pardon and release your brother. And you will fetch *The Book of Gold* from the duchess's library in her fortress of Montalbeau. Do you agree?'

Sylvian felt his heart sink again.

But before Lyta could reply, the queen spoke once more. The sweet, gentle exterior was gone. 'But it's not enough to just take the book from Iseult. She treasures it, of course. But you need everyone to know that you've taken it from her, that her security isn't what she thinks. She has a fearsome reputation, as does her unbreakable fortress. We need to break both. Shatter them. Otherwise she will always be a thorn in your side.'

Lyta shifted from foot to foot, listening carefully to the exchange, clearly trying to see which way this was headed now. And which way she should run.

'What do you suggest, my beloved?' Francisco asked with all the indulgence expected of a new husband.

Annika smiled, a slow calculating expression that even on her beautiful face made Sylvian's blood run cold. 'We have a thief. We also have a printer. Iseult wants to keep that book all to herself. So we do the opposite. We make copies of her precious book and hand them out to whoever wants one. We get a translator and let anyone who can read the words have access to them. The people can recite on the street corners if they so wish. It will humiliate her. What do you think?'

Francisco's smile of vicious delight should have been a warning to all of them. Sylvian dreaded it.

'An excellent plan,' the king agreed. 'Well, Mistress Cornellis? What do you say?'

Lyta had gone quite pale and Sylvian didn't blame her. Play games with kings, queens and duchesses and it was no secret who would get burned.

But she'd left herself without any choice. Breaking into Montalbeau was impossible. It was a deathtrap. Everyone knew that. Even Lyta. Sylvian watched her pull herself back together and paste a resolute expression on her face.

'Your Majesties,' she said, her bravado shining from her like a beacon, 'you have a deal.'

CHAPTER FOUR

Kit

Kit huddled in the corner of the cell. Everything hurt. Everywhere. Hardly surprising really. He had always known the risk. The duchess didn't take kindly to anyone getting above their station, or what she deemed their station to be, and Kit had been more than just outspoken. He'd been about to accuse her of stealing from the royal treasury, but he never got the chance. Her guards had done all they could to shut him up.

Just a few more minutes. That had been all he needed. But he'd heard Lyta's voice, and looked for her in the gallery, in spite of himself. And his moment was gone. So was the king.

What had she even been doing there? They had nothing to do with each other anymore. He didn't need her in his life. His sister was nothing but trouble. But gods, there had been a moment when his heart had leaped to see her.

Kit tried to close his eyes and get some sleep. He probably shouldn't. From the pounding in his head and the wooziness that came over him in waves, he could have a concussion. If he tried to stand his stomach threatened to empty itself, even though there was nothing left in there. Not a good sign.

Night had fallen. It was black as the grave, and it felt like an old nightmare, a half-remembered memory of long ago, locked up in the darkness, waiting, dreading . . .

He had been fourteen years old and he'd thought nothing could touch him. He was with Syl and Syl wouldn't let anything happen to him. That was the promise. That was how he'd persuaded Syl to let him help on the job, even though Lyta would have gone berserk if she'd found out. Which she did. He had wanted to prove himself, to show them all he was a man now, as much as Syl or any of the others were. There was no one as tough, or as brave, or as wild as Sylvian Chant and Kit wanted to be the same.

It had all gone wrong, of course. They hadn't even made it inside the house. The watch was waiting for them and pounced the moment they reached for the window, and they'd ended up here in Old Steen. The guards had taken their time flogging Syl, just for the hell of it, and every time they seemed about to stop and turn their attention to Kit, Syl would say something and they'd start in on him again.

Syl couldn't let them have the last word, even if they beat him to death. That was just who he was. Kit hadn't realised until later that every time he did, he stopped them turning their attention to Kit.

And then Lyta had come. She'd come for him and she had left Sylvian Chant behind to his torture and had never spoken about him again.

Kit had blamed himself for years . . . when he wasn't blaming her.

No one was coming this time. Even thinking about that nightmare sent panic spiralling through his body. He had to force his breath to calm. It was going to be different this time. He wasn't a boy. He wasn't helpless.

He just had to get through tonight. Tomorrow he'd be up in front of the king again and this time he could make his case properly.

Because the king had to know that people were starving, that the taxes were bleeding them dry and that the punishments for non-payment far exceeded the legal bounds.

But there were meant to be other representatives of the various guilds there as well. Not just him. He'd never intended to stand there as a prisoner, alone. They'd assured him he wouldn't actually be arrested, let alone arraigned before the king. And yet . . .

Co-conspirators. That's what they'd be called. They turned out to be made of smoke and shadows. De Werve, Van Stalen, Jansen . . . not even Jem had come to support him.

Just Lyta. Of all people. He had spent his whole adult life trying to sever any connection with his sister, trying to be a law-abiding citizen. As Lyta had careened down a path of crime and mayhem, following Eninn and revelling in it, Kit had learned a trade, built up his business, paid exorbitant taxes, made connections with guilds and traders and kept himself meticulously on the side of law and order.

And in the end, she was the only one that had turned up for him.

He could have wept with the irony of it.

Kit sighed, trying to shift his weight so that the shackles didn't drag quite so much. The movement made them clank and one of the prison guards glanced over his shoulder into the cell. He looked away just as quickly. No one wanted to be associated with anyone accused of sedition, which was far too close to treason for anyone's comfort. Kit stared at the corridor beyond, the way out. It was a world away.

And then she appeared, like a dark shadow on the edge of his vision, beyond the bars of his cell.

'Cornellis,' she snapped, and the guards stiffened to attention. Fear came off them like a stench.

'Inside, your Grace.'

She lifted her veil and peered into the darkness, her face a pale sculpture, her eyes like stone. Though objectively a beautiful woman, she carried an aura of nightmare and Kit couldn't help but shrink back. He'd all but accused her of cheating the king. She'd been sitting right there when he said it.

'Captain, bring him,' said the Duchess of Montalbeau and turned away without even waiting to see if her orders were obeyed.

Within a few moments her guards were dragging him out of the cell, while the other prisoners scrambled out of the way, into the stinking depths of the shadows. Kit had no way of escape and no defence.

The door at the other end of the corridor was thick wood, studded with iron, the kind of door that opened like a mouth and swallowed people whole. Whatever happened, he didn't want to go in there. Whatever happened . . .

He wrenched himself free. Just for one brief moment, he tried to run. This wasn't meant to be happening. He hadn't been tried yet. There had been no verdict. The king hadn't passed judgment. None of this was meant to be happening.

The guards seized him and slammed him against the wall. Air burst from his lungs as fists landed deep in his stomach and his solar plexus, one after the other, driving all fight from him with brutal efficiency. He couldn't breathe, couldn't think, couldn't function. He wasn't a fighter. He never had been. And now he was wounded, beaten and outnumbered, dragged to the other end of the corridor and thrown inside the interrogation chamber.

That ominous door closed quietly behind him with all the finality of a tomb.

Kit lay on the floor, aware that this could be the last anyone ever saw of him. No one would ever know. Not Lyta, not the guilds, or the aldermen, not his employees at the printing house. His heart thundered out of rhythm. Someone lit a glow ball, filling the room with a reddish light, like a brazier. Kit had never seen one close up before. They were alchemical devices, and they rarely got out of the hands of the richest or their guards. Once he would have given anything to examine one up close, to figure out how it worked. Now he couldn't risk so much as a glance at it if it meant taking his eyes off her. Not that he would have been able to focus on it anyway. His vision blurred, his head pounding. Was it blood or sweat in his eyes? He couldn't even catch his breath.

'Well,' said the duchess, standing over him, a slim knife in her hands. Its blade shone silver in the light, and the reflection bounced into his eyes, dazzling him. She had removed her veil entirely, leaving it draped over her captain's arms. 'What on earth did you think you were trying to tell the king, Master Cornellis?'

There were times for valiant defiance, times to stand your ground and speak your truth. Kit knew that this was not one of them. He swallowed hard on the lump forming in his dry throat and said nothing.

The duchess made a curt gesture to the guards. They seized him again, dragged him onto his knees and held him there before her.

Nowhere to go. No way out. Just that knife, glinting at him.

'What am I going to do with you?' she asked sweetly.

Whatever she wanted. There was nothing he could do to stop her.

One of the guards pulled his arm forward and jerked up the sleeve of his shirt, exposing the skin beneath. His pulse raced and somewhere inside him a scream was building, one he couldn't let out.

A smile flickered over her full red lips, as if she was amused by his silent distress. 'Captain, what is the punishment for those who bear false witness? For printers who print lies? For those who slander their betters?'

Her captain had the face of a hungry dog. 'Mutilation, your Grace.'

The duchess met Kit's terrified gaze. 'Mutilation,' she repeated. The way she said it sent chills through him. 'So many choices in that word, aren't there? So many variations. Ears, eyes, fingers . . .' Her gaze went lower. 'And the rest. It can take such a long time as well. Nothing fatal. Not at first. If only we had the time, Cornellis, I could show you wonders of agony.'

'Please—' He didn't know where the word came from. It was stretched thin and desperate. Her smile widened and knew he had to keep going. Because she couldn't think he— She couldn't— Tears burned his vision away. 'Don't—'

'If only we had time,' she repeated, merciless to the last. She leaned down, cupping the side of his face with her cool, soft hand, like a mother comforting a child. He was frozen. Trapped. 'But the night is drawing in and I have miles to travel yet. Perhaps one day. Poor sweet Christopher.' She leaned in closer, whispering fondly. 'I met your sister this evening, and that's why I'm here. To see you. Such a delightful puzzle, the pair of you. I'm going to delight in taking you apart. Listen to me. Listen closely. When you get out of here – and you will get out of here – it's because I've allowed it. And because of that, you owe me. I will know what you know. Don't fight me. It'll be quicker if you don't. Blood brings power and blood binds. Blood is power. I won't lie though. It will hurt.'

He stared up into her eyes, like grey crystals bearing down on him, consuming him.

'You belong to me, Christopher Cornellis,' she whispered and something inside him turned to stone. It was the way she said his name, like he was no more than a pet. The knife bit deep into his outstretched arm and this time he did scream. He couldn't help himself. His voice broke on the ceiling over him, on the pitiless stone walls, as her blade dug deeper and deeper into his skin and muscle, as if boring down to the bone beneath.

The darkness that swamped his mind was a blessed release and when the floor hit him, he wept with relief. But the burning inside his arm went on and on. Released by the guards, he curled in on himself, sobbing as the acid touch of whatever she had done, whatever magic she had wrought, ate through him.

Her footsteps echoed after she left, but no one came for Kit. Alone in the dark, he had no way of knowing how much time had passed.

He was back in Old Steen, lost in his deepest, darkest nightmare.

Eventually Kit found the strength to drag himself towards the door, but pain made him slow, and long before he reached it, he heard an unexpected voice ringing against the stone.

'Kit!'

Kit slumped, defeated and broken. Lyta. How was she here? He covered his face with his hands, wishing he could keep her from seeing him like this. Again. But here she was, cursing and swearing, and trying to drag him up from the ground while no one did anything to stop her.

When you get out of here – and you will get out of here – it's because I've allowed it.

The words echoed in his head. She had come to find him because of Lyta. Why? What had his sister done this time?

Lyta was many things – a force of nature, a gifted thief, his champion through thick and thin, whether he wanted her to be or not – but even she couldn't command the prison guards. Not in Old Steen.

Except once. Once she had come for him in a cell very like this, had dragged him out of the darkness.

'Him,' she'd said. 'I'm taking him.'

He'd thought that was the worst moment of his life. He'd been wrong.

His sister framed his face with her hands, far less gently than the duchess had, and studied him, assessing the damage. She clearly didn't like what she saw, and Kit groaned. He was never going to hear the end of this. Lyta shook her head, lips tight, then glanced over her shoulder. Her expression was strained, as if she'd been up all night, as if she had not slept a wink. Which was probably the case.

'Did they do this to you? The guards?'

He shook his head. That wasn't quite true, but it didn't matter. They'd enjoyed roughing him up when he first arrived, sure. But the worst of it? No. He tried to speak, but the words wouldn't come out. His forearm was a mess of blood and torn flesh. It still burned with an unholy fire.

Lyta glanced over her shoulder and her voice hardened dangerously. 'If I told you to kill them, would you do it? For old times' sake?'

Kit couldn't see who she was talking to. His vision wouldn't focus on anything further than an arm's length. But then the shadowy figure behind her spoke, his voice deep and strangely familiar. 'No. But I can have them up on so many charges they're going to wish I could. Does that help?'

Kit frowned, setting off another explosion of pain in his head. 'Is that Syl?' he tried to ask, but his own blood choked him. He spat it out, and Lyta growled something barely coherent.

'It's a start. Come on, Kit, we're getting you out of here.'

She began hauling him to his feet and Kit had no option but to let her. The strength had left his legs, but his sister managed to manhandle him into a mostly upright position and started dragging him towards the exit.

Sylvian followed them silently, and Kit could only imagine that Lyta had somehow blackmailed him into helping. He certainly didn't look like he wanted to be there.

Who would?

And what was Sylvian Chant even doing back here in Amberes? He was taller and broader than Kit remembered. Older, stronger, harder.

'Lyta? My arm, she—' Kit stumbled and a lance of pain shot through him, like ice inside, so cold it burned. It stole his voice again, smothered what he wanted to say about the duchess and what had happened.

'Shh,' she said. 'It's over. I've got you. We're going home, all right? Just let me deal with it.'

There were stone steps and another corridor. He could hear people sobbing and calling out. So many people locked up here, awaiting trial at the king's pleasure. Or their deaths. The stench choked him, as it had all those years ago. He had thought then he'd never get rid of it. He'd scrubbed his skin raw for weeks afterwards, and still did sometimes, when the nightmares were bad.

More stairs, more cold stone flags beneath his stumbling feet, and a series of oak doors studded with iron. They flowed past his unfocused eyes as Lyta held him and kept whispering encouragement.

'Just a bit further, Kitten. Just keep going.'

Gods he wished she wouldn't call him that. He wasn't a child anymore. He just wanted to sob like one. Especially when she used their mother's pet name for him.

And all the time Sylvian followed them. She hadn't left him behind this time.

As they reached the outer gates of Old Steen, dawn's light hit Kit's face, blinding him as the sun rose over the grey horizon. When had that happened? How? Had he spent the whole night on the floor of that wretched, filthy room? Kit wilted against her and felt her stagger as she took his weight. He had to be twice her size and he couldn't walk without help. What little strength he still had was almost gone. One of the city watch made to stop them, and Lyta all but snarled, struggling to keep them both upright.

'I have his pardon. Talk to him.' She jerked her head backwards, indicating Sylvian, who was still following them like the Ghost of Vengeance.

'Let them pass,' Sylvian echoed, his voice cold. He had sheathed his weapons, but no one who faced him would have wanted to cross him. He had been imposing when Kit had known him as a boy, no stranger to using his physique as a threat. Now there was something else as well. Sylvian Chant looked like he had killed lesser men with that glare alone. 'Lyta, you can't carry him the whole way and he's not going to manage himself. Let me—'

'What? You'll carry him? We don't need your help, Syl.'

He raised an eyebrow, his meaning clear enough. He was here, he'd come with her. She already had his help. And she had needed it too, whether she wanted it or not – or was willing to admit it.

'I was going to arrange a ride,' Sylvian told her, his tone still icy. 'That would help, wouldn't it?'

'Yes,' Kit cut in before Lyta could start yet another argument and make life even more impossible for them both. Because that was what she did. Everything hurt, body and mind. Everything. 'Yes, get us a ride. Please. I want to go home. Thank you, Sylvian.' He was babbling and he didn't care. He just needed to get as far away from Old Steen as he could.

That, at least, shut her up. Lyta frowned and then nodded at Sylvian. 'Do it,' she agreed. She held Kit closer. 'Let's get you out of here.'

Kit hadn't talked to her in weeks and the last time they had spoken he'd more or less told her he never wanted to see her again. He hadn't really meant it, but it was so easy to lose his temper with her.

And yet here she was anyway. Rescuing him. Again.

He was never going to hear the end of it.

But it wasn't actually a rescue, was it? The duchess had let him go. And he had no idea why.

CHAPTER FIVE

Lyta

Planning any job took time and resources. How long before a king got fed up waiting? Irritating royalty was not a good idea – even the dogs in the street knew that – and Lyta could already tell that Francisco would not be a patient man. She'd seen the look of dismay on Sylvian's face when she agreed to the deal.

Perhaps she should have thought about it for more than a second, but she was desperate. And she had a plan for this, all ready and waiting. Ranulf's plan. And Ranulf had been the best. The moment the king mentioned Montalbeau, the pendant had warmed against her skin and she'd known it was meant to be. Eninn wanted her there. He'd led her there. And that was why.

Her god would lead her if only she would let him. He had never failed her yet. She'd done what the God of Thieves wanted in stealing from Alderton, and now he was rewarding her. Had to be. She was going to find Ranulf. Or at least, find out what happened to him. That was the deal.

Despite his protests, she took Kit to the house on Larch Lane that Ranulf had bought all those years ago. It wasn't much. Narrow and neat, two rooms up and down, with an attic, which had been Ranulf's room.

She could still remember the feeling of Ranulf's calloused hands covering her eyes gently as he ushered her inside that first day.

'It's yours. All of it. The papers are all drawn up. You just sign them.'

She'd never had an actual home before. He'd moved her in, found Kit his apprenticeship and given her a room all to herself. That night, she'd waited in her new bed for her new husband, old though he was, and when he hadn't come, she'd swallowed her fear and gone to him. She didn't love Ranulf, not like that, and she certainly didn't desire him. He was old even then, thirty-seven years old. But she'd heard enough stories about duty and honour, and he had asked nothing of her when he saved her and her brother.

Lyta knew all about sex. She didn't know a thing about marriage though.

But when she opened his door, she found the room empty, the bed neatly made. She'd been so confused she just sat there alone, until the morning when he returned, with his clothes still dishevelled and the sated eyes of a man who had found pleasure elsewhere. He froze at the sight of his very young wife perched on the end of his bed, panic in his eyes.

'That's not—' he said, guilt and dismay written all over his face. 'I'm not— I don't like—'

The pieces clicked into place: he didn't want her. He didn't want any woman that way. But he was kind and she had been in distress. He thought he owed Rhea, so he'd done the only thing he could think of to save her daughter from Janlow and the clutches of men like him. He tried to explain and Lyta, who had lost all dreams of romance to Sylvian, finally understood. He'd married her for pity. Maybe for guilt that he hadn't stepped in sooner. Not for anything else.

But he taught her. He became her mentor. He gave her and Kit security and stability, the kind they'd never had before. He'd saved them.

Lyta didn't know where he was now, but she feared the worst. He might be a master thief, but there was every chance she would never know what had happened to him. He'd gone after an impossible prize. Fortune and glory were all very well, but Ranulf should have known better. He should have taken her with him.

The cart Sylvian had hired – or possibly commandeered – pulled up at the end of Larch Lane, half-blocking the street. Someone started yelling at the driver, but he just yelled back and then glared at Lyta expectantly. If he was looking for money he was sorely mistaken. When Lyta went to wake Kit, he startled as if she was attacking him.

She struggled with his flailing arms. 'Stop! Kit, it's me! Stop, you're safe. I promise, you're safe.'

He stared at her as though she was a stranger and then his face crumpled in tears. Lyta pulled him into her arms and held him as tight as she could. Their driver took off without a word as soon as Kit's feet touched the ground, clearly desperate to be rid of them. Lyta couldn't blame him, given the state they were in. She slung Kit's arm over her shoulder again and guided him inside.

Sylvian had offered to come with them and help. She'd told him where he could go and he just snorted as if he'd expected as much and left them there. She kind of regretted dismissing him now. Kit was heavy.

The stairs were too much for the moment, but she managed to prop him up on the window seat in the front parlour before closing the door on the noise outside. The light inside was dim, illuminating the dust in the air. She hadn't been back in days and it smelled stale and airless. Once she and Ranulf had kept it spotless, wood polished and a fire always ready in the grate instead of the old ashes that filled it now. The simple furniture was hardly used these days. She covered Kit with a blanket. He closed his eyes again, face pressed to the shutters, creases lining his brow, his blood dripping onto the floorboards.

Lyta went back outside and found one of the local kids who she sent for the healer and then for Frida. If she was going to break into the fortress at Montalbeau, she would need someone she could trust.

Frida arrived first, bustling through the door when Lyta was trying to get Kit to drink some brandy. That was meant to help, wasn't it? Ranulf had always sworn by it. If her friend had questions, all but one died in her throat when she saw the two of them.

'Sweet gods, what happened?'

'Old Steen happened. Give me a hand. I need to get him to a bed.'

Between the two of them they hauled Kit up the stairs and Frida went back down for water and bandages. As Lyta worked to make him comfortable, he opened his swollen eyes and tries to focus on her.

'Just rest,' she told him before he could speak. 'It's okay. I'm here and you're safe.'

For a moment she thought he'd argue, and then that he'd cry, but instead he let his head fall back. His hand closed on hers and she felt his trembling, but he didn't say anything, just clenched his jaw. Frida arrived with the supplies. She stared at the two of them for a long moment.

'I'll go and get the healer,' she said. 'He should be here by now.'

The wound on Kit's arm was the worst, still bleeding with no sign of letting up. Lyta staunched the flow as best she could with a cloth, cleaned it with more brandy which made him curse and try to pull away from her.

She schooled her voice to patience. 'Let me see, Kit.'

Reluctantly, he unfurled his arm. The wound wasn't straightforward. It wasn't a cut the way she knew them, not a slash or a deliberate stab. If anything it looked like a symbol had been carved in his flesh. She hissed though her teeth.

'Don't,' he told her, wrapping his entire body around his forearm defensively when she lifted the brandy bottle.

'Come now, Kitten.'

Their mother had called him that, when he cried in the night when he was young. But if anything, the name sent Kit into an even tighter ball.

'Lyta, I'm not a child.'

'Then don't act like one. I have to make sure it doesn't get infected, Kit.'

'When did you become a healer?'

'When did you become a criminal?'

He looked up suddenly in shock and stared at her, unspeaking, perhaps unable to speak at first. That didn't last, of course. He was still a Cornellis.

'I didn't break the law, I just—'

Lyta glared at him as if she could see through ever lie he had ever tried to tell. Which she had. 'So why were you in Old Steen then? What was going on in that courtroom? Theatricals?'

'I— I just— Someone had to say something, Lyta. Someone has to care.' It clearly hadn't occurred to him that he'd broken the law, that he was in real trouble and she could still see it written all over his poor battered face. He thought he was doing something noble or righteous, didn't he? Of course he did. But that didn't matter to the authorities.

She turned her attention back to his arm, wrapping it tightly in a clean bandage as best she could.

'Who did this?' she asked, ready to murder whoever he named.

'It doesn't matter,' he said at last. She could see the lie in his eyes. He wanted to tell her. But he wouldn't, or couldn't, do it.

She would find out. Eventually. If she knew one thing in life it was how to wear her little brother down. Lyta promised herself this was not over yet. But not now. She couldn't pester him now.

'Where's Frida with that healer?'

'She's probably robbing him,' Kit said with a sigh. Which was not an impossibility, if Lyta was honest. Kit knew Frida as well as she did. She almost laughed and Kit smiled through his pain. The smile faded quickly enough, replaced by something soft and earnest. 'You came for me.'

Lyta pulled his head against her shoulder, holding him close. 'Of course I did.'

'How did you get me out? Sylvian?'

Kit had idolised Sylvian, following him around, looking for his attention, mimicking him in every way. Just like any kid with a hero. Even a shit one like Syl. He couldn't believe it when Syl left. Of course he wanted his hero back again.

Lyta brought her mind back to the present. She sighed and steeled herself. She might as well tell him what she'd done. She was going to need all the help she could get. 'I made a deal with a king for you, little brother. Fought a royal bodyguard,' – no need to say she hadn't exactly won, or who it had been – 'charmed a queen and faced down a duchess.'

His whole body stiffened, and he jerked back, cradling his arm again. 'You what?' The words came out between clenched teeth.

'It's all right. Really. Just . . . just let me handle it. You can go back to your upright and honest life.'

He barked out a laugh, such a harsh and un-Kit-like noise that she shied back from him in shock, and that was when Frida arrived with the healer in tow, his arm clamped in her fist. She looked like she had grabbed him off the street and frogmarched him over.

'Dear gods,' the wan little man said looking at the damage. 'What happened to you?'

'Old Steen,' said Lyta and that was enough. He set to work, largely doing everything Lyta had already done. When he took out a needle and thread and called for boiling water, Lyta lurched to her brother's defence. And that was when the trembling little grey-haired doctor turned on her, like an old dog with a pup to defend. 'Out,' he said. 'You, take her downstairs.'

Lyta stared at Kit, who had gone a peculiar shade of pale green. He stared at the equipment and swallowed hard.

'Go on,' he said at last but held out his other hand. 'You can leave me the brandy.'

Frida led her downstairs and Lyta found herself following like a lamb when every instinct told her to run back up there and stop the butcher in disguise. 'Want to tell me what happened?' Frida asked.

So she did. Everything, from Kit's trial, to seeing the king, to Sylvian, to offering to steal the book, to getting Kit out of Old Steen. By the time she had finished, Frida was sitting perfectly still at the other side of the table, staring at her as if she'd just finished some kind of tale of terror for the Darkest Night.

'Do you have a plan?' Frida asked at last.

'I have Ranulf's plan. The best there is.'

'Ranulf vanished. He's probably dead. You know that, don't you?' It had to be said. And she was probably right. Lyta nodded solemnly.

'You aren't going in there looking for him, are you, Lyta? Because that's a fool's errand and you know it.'

'I do. And I'm not.' It wasn't entirely a lie. Not really. 'In and out, I swear it. Simple as. So, what do we need?'

Frida shook her head and exhaled slowly, choosing to believe her, for now anyway. 'We'll need a map of the area around the fortress, floorplans, several experts, a heap of muscle to back us up and . . . gods and goddesses of old, I don't know . . . a bloody miracle?'

'No,' Lyta said. 'We need someone who knows as much as possible about old books.'

Few people in Amberes could get difficult-to-acquire information as quickly and as quietly as Haldevar. Plus he would do anything for Frida. So that was where Lyta went the next day, once she was sure Kit was on the mend.

He'd insisted on getting up this morning, which was just as well because he'd woken up screaming three times in the night. He refused to talk to Lyta about it. But he was always her little brother and perhaps that was part of the problem as well. She wondered if they were the same bad dreams that had tormented him when she got him out of Old Steen all those years ago, or if they had taken on a new dimension this time around. They seemed worse and he was even less willing to discuss them. Pride was always his problem.

The shop was closed when Lyta arrived, which was odd. It was only late morning. She frowned in through the windows but couldn't see anything. Haldevar's was never shut, not as long as she'd been coming there – she'd be surprised if he'd ever taken a day off.

'He isn't there,' one of the neighbours told her, popping her head out of the next doorway when Lyta knocked. Lyta knew the woman to see, a bit of a busybody, but good at heart and fond of Haldevar in her way. 'Left this morning just before a couple of Janlow's heavies called around looking for him. Must have had word.'

If Janlow was sniffing around that could not be good news. This new day was going from bad to worse.

With Haldevar gone, she needed a new plan. If he was avoiding Janlow, he would have been thorough in covering his tracks. She took another look up and down the alleyway, but the cold stone walls yielded no new clues. There was nothing else for her here.

Lyta wandered back towards the market wondering what she might be able to do to persuade her brother to stay a little longer.

The Great Market sprawled over the open area in between the Exchange and the guild houses. It was the usual carnival of noise and colour. Anything and everything was for sale here, fresh off the ships or straight in from the countryside. Everything which hadn't already been bought up in the Exchange, by people who didn't have to sully their feet with these cobbles. Livestock made a racket, which meant everyone had to shout over them. There were linens and silks, every kind of food, raw, cooked and still alive. Artists and musicians had been pushed to the edges these days but still added to the chaos. Over by the gates of the Exchange a speaker was railing against the taxes again, and the city watch were getting ready to clear him off. On the other side some kids were watching a puppet show with a knight and a dragon. It was a whirl of movement and she fell into it with ease. It was home. Her natural environment. She knew how to move with its currents, flow with it, sense the moods of her city.

'Just don't go there, that's all I'm asking,' a mother told her daughter as they inspected eggs for sale.

'But there's good money to be made. I can cook and clean. Better there than here.'

The woman dropped her voice to a hiss of concern. 'People don't come back from Montalbeau. And she's angry since the king took over. Be sensible, love. Stay here.'

The name of the duchess's fortress sent a chill through Lyta and she moved on quickly. Two young apprentices who should have known better lifted the purse of an oblivious out-of-towner. Normally she'd have left them to it. Fools and their money were easily parted, but they laughed about it so unpleasantly once out of his earshot that her hackles rose. They had their livelihood secured if they didn't mess up: training, good jobs, a future. There was no need for theft.

Eninn hated a sore winner more than a sore loser. It only took a few moments following them to arrange an accidental collision.

'I'm so sorry,' she stammered, bowing as if to great lords. 'Please do forgive me, masters.'

They blustered a bit and made some threats but she was gone back into the crowd long before they realised that she had deftly taken what they had stolen, with interest.

She caught up with the fresh-faced farmer just as he was patting down his clothing, turning red with embarrassment as he tried to pay for his purchases. He even tried to reward her when she handed his purse back, so she knew Eninn was smiling. She'd put the rest in the poor box and a coin on his shrine later on.

That was when she realised she was being followed. A hulking figure shouldering his way through the crowd, made straight for her without any hesitation. He wasn't even subtle. Cursing herself for her inattention, she ducked down a side alley towards an abandoned temple to some old fertility god, still decked with faded wreaths and garlands of straw, and came out beyond the civic gardens, hoping that was enough.

No such luck. Two of them now, built like brick shithouses and just as ugly.

'Fuck it all,' she murmured and dodged down the road which led back towards the docks through a warren of tiny lanes. Down there it should be just chaotic enough to give them the slip.

Lyta ran. She didn't hesitate or look back, just flat out ran, taking every twist and turn of Amberes' labyrinthine streets, ducking past the porters and their carts as they tried to force their way through the riverside gates, leaping over the bollards at the end of the quay and ducking down into the alleys that backed onto the warehouse district. That brought her back to the far side of the market where the crowd should have done the final trick.

Just when she thought she was in the clear she skidded to a halt. Petrus Janlow lounged on a seat outside the Byzantine coffee shop on the edge of the Great Market, basking in the warmth of the sun. He had a couple of empty glasses, a steaming jug of warm cream and one of those elaborate silvery coffee pots in front of him. His grey eyes locked with hers and he lifted his hands in a slow clap.

Lyta felt rather than saw his men fall in behind her. Smelled them too. Heard their heavy, irritated breath. She had to fight to keep her shoulders from tightening.

'You're getting predictable in your old age, Lyta,' Janlow sing-songed. Old age indeed. He had no more than a year or two on her.

'Nice to see you too, Janlow,' she lied, careful to keep her own tone fluid and even. 'Now what do you want?'

'Sit down,' he replied. 'Have something to drink. The coffee is good.' He pushed a small glass towards her. Since when had Janlow become the would-be sophisticate? The coffeehouse had only opened a few months ago. Two brothers had arrived from Venice with sacks of the stuff and, some rumour had it, a couple of the much sought after plants as well. They were making an absolute mint from it. One of them had had the bright idea of mixing it with cream. Half the aldermen were already addicted and all of Amberes would follow them. Janlow took a sip. 'We have some shared business interests.'

They didn't. They really did not. She made absolutely sure of that with every single job she took.

But she didn't have a choice but to hear him out. Not with the twin mountains of sweat looming over her.

So she sat, one hand on her thigh near where her belt knife hung beneath her jacket – she'd picked it up this morning on a whim, or perhaps an instinct. She tended to credit Eninn with impulses like that. With good cause.

'A certain gentleman is annoyed to find someone was rooting around in his private papers,' Janlow said, leaning forward conspiratorially. He was a handsome man if you didn't look beneath the surface, high chiselled cheekbones, sallow skin and a sensual mouth. Not her type, of course, but she'd never been attracted to psychopaths. He had the voice of a lover, the eyes of a seducer and the mouth of a courtesan. That was how he'd started out, he used to say.

A lover, not a fighter. Another lie. She knew he fought like an animal if it came down to it.

'What gentleman?' she asked. As if he'd know one. Not unless it was through blackmail.

'Oh you know full well who.' He smoothed his fingers against his neatly trimmed beard. 'The theft he might be able to forgive . . . if a certain item is returned.'

Alderton. Had to be. Fuck!

'That's out of my hands, I'm afraid,' she said. 'I don't have anything I shouldn't.'

When your god directed you to something, it was meant to be yours. Even if he was a god of thieves. It was always easier to deny all knowledge.

Janlow laughed, a slow, lazy chuckle that made her stomach plummet. 'I sincerely doubt that, my love.'

That word did it. She froze. Couldn't help herself.

'I'm not your love.'

'You'll always be mine, Lyta,' he purred. 'Bought and sold, remember? Inherited, even. It's just a matter of time before I collect.' He reached over to touch her face.

She had the knife out before she knew what she was doing. Janlow didn't hesitate. He grabbed her wrist and slammed it onto the table, pinning her hand there with the blade underneath it.

The mask he wore cracked. 'Don't cross me, bitch. Now, this gentleman wants his property back. And he'll get it back. Even if I have to cut you into pieces to find it, understand? Either you have the ring or Haldevar does, and whoever hands it over first . . . well, they'll be the lucky one, won't they?'

The ring. What was so bloody special about that little ring? Eninn wanted it, and it was going to help her find Ranulf somehow. But she hadn't imagined a reaction like this over a scrap of washed-out gold. Why was it so important? She could feel it now, digging into her skin where it hung from the chain around her neck, tucked safely under her jerkin. Any second now he'd search her and find it.

Don't say a word, Lyta. She imagined Ranulf's voice, soothing her, helping her keep her cool. *Don't offer up anything you don't have to.* Or maybe it wasn't Ranulf, not quite. Part him, part something else. But Eninn sent dreams. He didn't speak to her like that. Her skin shivered, hairs rising in response to something *other* that seemed to pass over and through her. Call it the numinous, call it instinct.

It wasn't fear. It definitely wasn't fear.

Janlow held her gaze, a small smile hovering at his lips. He was waiting for her to struggle, waiting for her to crack. But she wouldn't give him the satisfaction.

'I don't even know what you're talking about. And I haven't seen Haldevar in days. I've been busy.'

'I heard as much. Poor Kit, getting in such a state. Not the first time.' Janlow's cold fingers traced patterns on the back of her hand. 'Maybe I'll let you work off your debt another way. You can still be mine, love. Just like you were meant to, before Ranulf interfered. But the old man is gone now, isn't he? No one to look after you now. Our mutual friend might enjoy that as well. And once we're done with you, I know several others who'd love the opportunity to—'

A shadow fell over the table and they both looked up at the unexpected interruption. Janlow's expression faltered from irritation, to surprise, to fear.

Syl drew back his arm and punched him full in the face.

CHAPTER SIX

Lyta

One moment Janlow was pinning her arm to the table and the next he was staggering off his seat, holding his face and roaring. One punch. That was all it took. A single punch.

And Sylvian wasn't finished. Janlow went nowhere without his heavies and today was no exception. Lyta had only seen the two who herded her back here. Now others poured out of the corners of the Great Market, as the crowd scattered back from the first signs of trouble. Some of them were new, some were old hands. Some of them even recognised Syl. They were the ones who hesitated.

Probably saved themselves a lot of grief with that, Lyta thought.

Having recently experienced Sylvian on the attack, it was quite something to sit back and watch him in action. She didn't mean to. She couldn't help it. She couldn't seem to move. It was like watching a whirlwind. Syl was violence in motion, a swirl of limbs. He'd always been graceful and fit, but now there was skill and an ease with what he did that he'd never had as a young man. The aggression was focused, precise and calculated. He knew exactly what he was doing, where to hit, how hard, how much damage to inflict.

She was so captivated by him, she didn't notice Janlow until he lunged at her again, perhaps intent on dragging her off while Syl was occupied. Lyta twisted aside, snatched up the knife again and brought it between them without hesitation. She'd use it and he knew it. Janlow swore at her, blood dripping from his nose, and backed away. Always the coward when it came down to it.

The guards were arriving now, city watch from their cloaks, but seeing Sylvian's uniform they hung back, unwilling to get involved. It wasn't like he needed their help. They'd mop up later.

Just like that, it was over. Janlow vanished into the crowd that had gathered around to watch from a distance. Always the first to weasel his way out of trouble. His men, the ones still standing, melted away too, leaving the rest to their fates.

Sylvian stood in the middle of a jumble of groaning or unconscious figures, turning in a circle as if looking for someone else to take on.

'Syl,' she called.

He fell still at the sound of her voice, his chest heaving, and he stared at her like he would consume her. As if the fight had released something inside him, something that had been trapped, caged. And it wanted more. Far more. That was the Syl she had known, but she could see he had changed. Purified, refined and turned into a living weapon. Not just Syl. Captain Sylvian Chant. He hadn't even drawn his sword. He'd taken them all down with his bare hands.

Lyta tried again. 'You all right?'

He blinked, drawing a shield of control around himself even as she watched, and gave a curt nod. 'You?'

That was it. One word. He said it as if even that was a huge effort.

A watchman came forward, nervously. 'Captain, we're here to offer assistance.'

'You're a bit late,' Lyta told him. The guard didn't so much as glance in her direction. She couldn't blame him. No one sane would take their eyes off Sylvian right now.

'Unnecessary,' Sylvian hissed. 'But you can take this lot in.'

The guard squirmed. 'On— on what charges, sir?'

Sylvian let his head fall back, a great beast stretching, and Lyta was sure she heard something crack in his neck. He sighed, done with this, all of this. It almost sounded like a growl. 'For questioning. Lyta, with me,' he barked. And then he walked away.

Lyta froze, mouth open. The attention of every single guard was trained on her now and that was never good. Dignity could do one; she ran after him.

'Sylvian? Syl?' She caught his arm as he turned the corner into Mill Lane, with its pretty little artisan workshops and pots of flowers, a few steps and a world away from the market. He tensed, every muscle turning to steel. Rethinking her actions at once, she released him carefully. All the same she fell into step alongside him. 'You didn't have to help me,' she told him.

'And miss all that?' he replied, completely deadpan. He didn't even glance at her.

'Were you looking for me?'

'Whatever gave you that idea?'

'Sylvian?'

'I was sent to find you.'

Oh, that sounded ominous. 'That's the same thing,' she replied, trying to brush the feeling of foreboding aside.

He cast a scathing glance her way and increased his pace. 'It really isn't.'

'Why are you so angry with me? I didn't do anything. I was just trying to go home when Janlow—'

He growled again. Definitely a growl this time. It made her stomach tighten and she wasn't entirely sure why. 'It's not about Janlow. Janlow is nothing.'

Janlow would love to hear that. And it hadn't seemed like nothing when Sylvian punched him full in the face. No, that had seemed very personal indeed. Which, given their history together, was fair.

Once upon a time, she knew, Syl had thought that Janlow would do anything for him. Turned out, not so much. She wasn't the only one who had left him to rot in Old Steen.

'So where are we going so fast now? I thought you were looking for me.'

'Did you always ask this many questions?'

Of course she had. He used to tease her about it. Back when he used to tease her, when they used to laugh together, when everything was different.

The thought of how much had changed sent a pang through her, one she had never expected to feel again. She'd put it behind her. She hadn't had any choice.

'Right then,' she announced, as firmly as she could and stopped dead in her tracks. He kept going, long legs sweeping him away down Cornmarket Street, towards the shrine to Gloir, where the Blacksmiths' Guild made their headquarters. The smell of their furnaces already hung in the air, the sound of their hammers ringing out. Lyta just watched him go, unable to help admiring his frame, his gait, the way he moved. He was angry with her. Perhaps he always would be. But he was still beautiful.

Eventually he realised, either from the silence or the lack of footsteps, that she was no longer trotting obediently alongside him. He turned back, searching for her. Lyta folded her arms in front of her and waited.

It was somewhat gratifying to see him forced to retrace his steps. He towered over her, but she didn't care. She'd had enough of this. Sylvian Chant had never intimidated her. She wasn't about to let him start now.

'We don't have time for this.'

'For what, Syl?'

He winced. 'Please don't call me that.' So he didn't like to be called Syl anymore. That was a useful piece of information. Sometimes you needed to know which buttons to push.

'Captain Chant.' Lyta grinned at him and the scowl deepened. Oh, this was far too easy.

'The king has decided to help you and found a scholar to advise on the book itself. You do need help there, don't you, unless you've suddenly become an expert in translating ancient manuscripts? So we are going to see someone who can help with this ill-advised mission you got us into.'

'Us?'

Sylvian exhaled slowly, as though seeking patience. 'Yes, *us*. His Majesty has decided I should . . . what was it? *Supervise?* Obviously,

I'm thrilled at the idea. I always thought returning to a life of crime would be the perfect crown to my otherwise exemplary military record. And I might have known you'd be the one to lead the way.'

'You aren't supervising me.'

'No,' he said coldly. 'The words he used were "take command." He was very clear. Are you going to argue with him as well?' He gazed at her for a long moment and then shook his head. 'What am I saying? Of course you are. It won't do any good, Lyta. Our king is a man who knows his own mind. He doesn't take direction. So, are you going to come with me or not?'

'Where?'

She didn't like any of this. And while Syl of the past might be up for a bit of casual law-breaking and general mayhem, this one was almost a stranger to her. She hadn't considered how much he might have changed. Rigid, rulebound and angry about everything. Not just her, she realised. The king he seemed to worship. Amberes. His whole life, probably.

'I can't tell you.'

Of course not. She scowled. 'Well your answer's no then, Syl. And anyway, you don't get to tell me what I can and can't do. You gave up the right to have any say in my life when you abandoned me to Janlow.'

He looked at her like she was delirious. She didn't like it.

'You were the one who did the abandoning as I remember it. You turned me in and then walked out with your brother.'

Lyta couldn't do this. Not here. Not now. 'We remember things very differently then.'

She marched off, this time without looking back.

How dare he? How dare he turn up here and try to just take over? King or no king. She wasn't having it. She would run this job her way or not at all.

Admittedly not at all probably wasn't much of an option just now. She'd made a deal with the king, and you didn't go back on things like that.

She had almost reached her house when she smelled smoke and saw the crowd gathering. Up ahead she could hear shouts, alarms being raised, and bells beginning to ring.

Panic snaked its way through her. She'd crossed powerful people, she knew that. Janlow had told her Alderton was looking for reparations. And Sylvian had humiliated his former friend in front of the city while she looked on. And now . . .

Lyta didn't have time to think. She broke into a run, sprinting towards the fire. The whole neighbourhood was out on the street at the end of her narrow lane, some trying to fetch water and organise a chain to douse the flames. It wouldn't be enough, she could tell that right away.

Her house was already in flames. The next two either side were catching. It was an inferno, spreading fast. Too fast.

And she'd left Kit in there.

'Kit!' Someone tried to grab her as she ran forwards. She wrenched herself free. 'Get off me! Kit!'

He couldn't be in there. If he was, she had to get him out. Her little brother had always been her life. Now he'd be her death as well. Lyta threw herself into the burning building.

CHAPTER SEVEN

Sylvian

Sylvian stood in the middle of Cornmarket Street, the porters, wagons, carts, livestock and other traffic diverting around him with curses, jeers and shouts, feeling as if the air had just been kicked out of him. Even the blows from Janlow's heavies hadn't struck him as hard as Lyta's words.

'We remember things very differently then.'

Lyta had turned him in and bargained away his freedom for her brother's. And fool that he was, he'd still believed she'd come back and break him out. They'd always promised they would come back for each other. But she didn't. Janlow had arrived instead. Janlow, who had told him what she'd done, rubbed it in his face while he was half-mad from torture and pain.

He hadn't meant to say it but the words slipped out anyway. And Janlow's little eyes had shone like he had just won every single game of cards ever played. Sylvian didn't want to remember that. Janlow had been his friend, or so he thought. But then Lyta had been his lover and Kit the little brother he'd always wanted. In that moment he'd lost everything.

In Old Steen hope was hard to come by. They'd offered him conscription, a young strong man like him, a fighter. A way out. But Sylvian had come back. First chance he got. Of course he had. That had always been the plan. He had never intended to stay with the army or make it his life. It had been a way out of jail. Nothing more. He'd finished the basic training, got his leave and come straight back here to find her. There would be an explanation and reconciliation. He knew that. He was prepared to forgive her and Lyta had always been there for him.

But Lyta had married Ranulf and never wanted to see him again. Every dream he'd once had about their future was as much ashes as paper in a fire. He'd left Amberes, returned to the encampment before his leave was even up, walked into the general's tent and signed up then and there. And that was that. Sylvian had thrown himself into war, expecting to die every day. He still didn't know why he hadn't.

For years, the fight was all he wanted. To burn the feelings out of him. It had worked. Or so he thought. Francisco had saved him, in so many ways, on countless battlefields, sure, but afterwards as well. When the king had offered him a place in his personal guard, it had been like a resurrection. He had survived all the mud and blood and shit, to be born again, a new man, a better man. There was nothing the king could ask that Sylvian would not do. His king trusted him, gave him purpose and all Sylvian had to do was obey. He loved him for that.

Resisting the urge to put his fist through the expensive panes of glass of the shop window behind them, Sylvian took off after Lyta, determined to have it out with her. To tell her what he'd done and why. To clear his own name. Just for once, he'd make her listen.

None of this was his fault.

Why did no one believe that? This morning, when he'd arrived with the other bodyguards for duty Francisco had looked at him like he'd turned up drunk.

'What are you doing here?'

'Your Majesty?'

Montes had the effrontery to wince but the king ignored that. His ire was fixed wholly on Sylvian. 'You should be protecting my interests, Chant. What's to stop your thief making off with her brother and not fulfilling her part of our bargain? They could be miles from Amberes already.'

He could have said Kit was in no fit state to travel when he last saw him. Or he could have explained that Lyta would never leave the city. The very idea was impossible to imagine. She belonged here and so did Kit. Leaving Amberes would be like cutting off a limb.

But that wouldn't wash with Francisco, would it? He didn't want excuses. He expected results. It was one of the things Sylvian admired about him: a man of action, a king who had cemented his initially fragile rule first with the sword and then through marriage and peace.

'You need to make sure this mission is a success, Sylvian. Take command of that woman. Now.'

Take command of Lyta. Well he had just seen how that idea had gone down. The very thought . . .

Up ahead, alarm bells started ringing and he stopped, smelling smoke on the air. A group raced by from the canal with buckets, shouting at others to help. Even the great bell at Cissonia's temple was sounding now, and when that rang out, all the city responded.

Fire in a city like this could be devastating. It spread too quickly in the poorer districts, where galleries jutted out over the street, cellars were extended at whim, where thatch and wood were always cheaper than slate and brick, and costs had to be cut.

Syl broke into a run, following the group, and as he swung around a corner, a woman lurched at him, grabbing his arms, frantic. Frida, who had always been Lyta's friend, had always been part of her life and had never approved of him.

'Sylvian!' she shouted, her face white. 'I couldn't stop her. She wouldn't listen. She went in after Kit.'

'Where's Kit?'

'He's not there. He went home earlier. Must have left a candle or something in the grate. I don't know! But she just—'

She went in. That was all he needed to know. He tore off his cloak and mail, but left the leather jerkin on. He'd need the protection. He pulled the length of scarf from his throat and wrapped it around his face.

Grabbing a bucket from one of the would-be firefighters, he doused himself and then plunged in after Lyta.

The heat was like a solid wall. The fire was everywhere, consuming everything. Syl had seen it move that quickly before, but only in war when naphtha or pitch were used. The smoke was thick and black, blinding and suffocating at the same time. He could hear the beams above him creaking, ready to give and saw the shadow of Lyta ahead, trying to reach the stairs which were already wreathed in flames.

She stumbled and called out for Kit, her voice barely audible. Coughing seized her and she staggered up one and then two steps, picking her way through the inferno. She'd never make it.

Syl didn't waste his breath calling her name, but plunged towards her. As he reached the stairs, they came down with a crash, sending sparks, flames and smoke billowing out in a wave. He grabbed Lyta as she fell and even then, she struggled, trying to tear herself free. There wasn't time, or breath, to explain. Smoke almost blinded him now. Without hesitation, he slung her over his shoulder, still kicking and writhing.

He could hear her sobbing, could feel it against his body, but he had to harden his heart. If she got away they were both going to die. He wouldn't be able to leave her in here. And there wasn't time to search any further. He had to trust that Frida was right, and Kit had gone before any of this started. A terrible creaking sounded overhead, and he knew the ceiling was about to give in. Anyone up there was dead already.

The fire moved like a living creature, a monster ready to consume them both. It rippled up the walls and over the ceiling.

Flames filled the doorframe by which they had entered. It blazed bright, blinding him, but it was the only way out left to him. Everything here was gone, consumed, but out there, on the other side . . .

The groan above them reached a crescendo and the fire roared in triumph. Sylvian leaped for the door, still clinging to Lyta, who had gone limp against him. He burst through the inferno, flames licking against his skin, singeing his clothes.

Sylvian wasn't quite sure how he did it. He staggered out into the street, flinging himself across it, barely feeling the hands reaching out to help him, people pulling the two of them clear. He dropped to his knees, cradling Lyta in his arms and staring at her soot-covered face. Too still, too pale. His heart stuttered inside him. She was never this quiet. Lyta was life and constant energy, always fighting, always moving. Lyta was fire itself.

Then she coughed. It was violent and racked her whole body. Her eyes flew open, and she instantly tried to launch herself up again. Ready for her this time, he wrapped his arms around her and brought her to the ground.

'Kit!' Her voice was a hoarse croak of pain.

'He's not there,' he yelled at her. She had to listen. 'Frida said he left. He's safe, Lyta.' He hoped to all the old gods that he was right. She'd never forgive him otherwise.

Who was he kidding? She would never forgive him for anything he'd done. Lyta could lose every memory she'd ever had and still recall her grudges. But this would be so much worse.

Slowly the words permeated her panic and, as she fell back, Sylvian became aware that he was pinning her to the hard cobbles of her street, their bodies pressed intimately together. Around them people were trying to quell the fire and the bells were still ringing. The fire brigade had finally arrived and were pumping water onto the collapsing structure and those to either side. Sparks lit up the sky and smoke shrouded everything.

He released her carefully, afraid she'd take off again.

'Are you sure?' Lyta whispered. She pushed herself up onto all fours and from there to her feet. Wrapping her arms around her body she looked in horror at her home. At what was left of it. Frida arrived at her side with a blanket, wrapping it around her against the shock. She glared at Sylvian. Great, he could run into a burning building after Lyta and Frida would still blame him.

All that could have happened to her raced across his mind's eye again.

'What were you thinking?' he snapped.

'That my brother was unconscious up there,' she croaked and began to cough again with the effort, doubling over, straining to draw breath.

Sylvian's temper slipped loose of every control he'd ever managed to put on it. 'And you were just going to get yourself killed going after him? You're so bloody reckless, Lyta. You throw yourself at the world, no matter how awful, and gods help us all if it doesn't get out of the way. You could have died in there, and for what? Nothing.'

'Syl,' Frida tried to interrupt. 'This isn't the—'

'Not nothing.' Lyta bared her teeth at him. They were very white in her soot and tear streaked face. She could barely force the words out. 'Kit.'

Damn it all to hell. She wouldn't listen. She never listened. 'Kit wasn't even there. You didn't let Frida tell you. You just barrelled in, like always, completely heedless.' He grabbed her shoulders to shake some sense into her, but he couldn't. He just held her there. 'I could have really lost you this time!'

She stared up at him, her eyes bloodshot, the blue bright with pain. And she looked so scared. Scared of him. Of life. Of everything. She wheezed in another breath, a huge effort, and then she wilted.

'Lyta!' Sylvian lunged forward as she folded up and dropped. Her head lolled back as he caught her.

She wasn't breathing. Why wasn't she breathing?

The world pitched inside him from rage to terror. The smoke. She'd inhaled too much smoke running in there, screaming for Kit.

'Lyta,' he whispered, trying to shake her awake. 'Lyta, please. Breathe!'

For a moment there was nothing and his chest hollowed out, sucking away his last remaining hope. As if the fire had taken the air from him as well.

And then she moved, her lips parting for a weak, fluttering breath that sounded like agony. The words were so faint he could barely make them out, but he heard. They were precious as life itself and he made sure he heard.

'Don't order me around, Syl. Doesn't work.'

Then she slipped into unconsciousness again. Panic boiled back up from the pit of his stomach like acid. He moved, driving himself up and forwards.

'Where are you taking her?' Frida yelled, running after them, of course.

'To get help. I'll send word. Make sure Kit's all right.'

CHAPTER EIGHT

Lyta

The sunlight was too bright against her eyes. The whole room was too bright. Lyta lay on soft sheets and as her eyes opened, her whole body ached.

But her lungs felt clear again. The dreadful weight that had settled on her chest after the fire had gone, and her eyes didn't burn anymore.

She tried to sit up and someone caught her, pushing her back down unapologetically. The grip was strong and unyielding. She didn't stand a chance.

'Don't move. Don't try to—Just rest, Lyta. It's all right. You're all right.'

Sylvian. What on earth was Sylvian doing here and why did he sound terrified? She was used to angry, or frustrated, or even exasperated, but not this.

She tried to focus on him, but the room was still too bright and he was a shapeless blur. She blinked furiously and some of her vision returned. It was Syl, all right, still looming over her. Still ordering her around.

Lyta struggled to pull herself together.

'Get off me,' she snarled.

He drew back. 'Thank the gods,' he murmured. Well, the gods were going to be his only hope if he carried on like this.

'Where am I?' Because this airy room with its fine furnishings and luxurious bedclothes was not her home. Her home . . . a pang of something unexpected shot through her. Her home was gone. And Kit had been . . . 'Kit!' she shouted and sat bolt upright.

'He's fine. He wasn't there. Frida went to tell him.' Sylvian yelled it all so quickly, she slumped back onto the mountain of soft pillows behind her in shock at the volume and the panic that riddled his voice.

Kit was safe. That was all that mattered. A house was just a house. She'd worry about that later. It didn't matter that it was her home, that Ranulf had given it to her, that it was all she had of him. It couldn't matter. She pushed those feelings aside. She'd find somewhere else to live. And when he came back . . .

If he ever came back . . .

Where was she?

She lay in a four-poster bed, on rich cotton sheets. Someone had washed her, tended her. There were bandages on her hands and she could smell a sweetly scented salve beneath them. Her hair was even clean, soft and fragrant against her face.

'What happened?' she asked, her voice still hoarse and painful. At least that meant it had been real and not a nightmare. It felt like a nightmare.

Sylvian sat back in the chair beside the bed. He'd washed too, but he didn't look like he'd slept. Dark circles under his dark eyes gave him away. 'You're in the house of Beatriz Alvarez, First Lady of the House of Alvarez. I presume you know who she is?'

Of course she knew. Finding her mouth suddenly hanging open, Lyta shut it. Beatriz Alvarez was probably the richest woman in Amberes, richer even than the duchess, richer than the king. Than several kings. She was also known to be a kind and generous benefactor to the poor and those in need. She was, by all accounts, a living saint. People loved her – at least, those who didn't attempt to cross her in business. They tended to hate her with the fire of a thousand suns.

She had pitched up here about a year ago, buying the house on Crescent Street outright and settling in, her businesses instantly thriving.

Her money came from trade, banking and a lineage longer than most monarchies. House Alvarez was famous across the Castilian empire. She lived a life more enlightened and cultured than many of the other so-called nobility could ever hope or aspire to enjoy. She sponsored artists and musicians, and funded public works. People flocked to her house with petitions and proposals. There were several prominent artists who claimed her as their patroness. She had a rather public argument ongoing with the Imperator of the Church in Caput Mundi over something or other, and was present at various shrines and temples every day for the celebrations, even the ones which ostensibly had no gods anymore.

'Did you bring me here?' Lyta asked Sylvian.

'Yes. Kit's fine. He's at his workshop and Frida's with him. I sent word.'

At least there was that. Kit was fine. He knew where she was. 'How long was I out?'

'The fire was yesterday. We tended you through the night. Lady Beatriz is a gifted healer, but even she needs to rest. I'll have to fetch her. She'll want to see you now you're awake.'

'I do indeed.' A voice came from the doorway behind him, fluid like music, rich with the accent of Andalusia far to the south. 'I thought we might lose you. The human lungs are delicate things. Damage can be swift and irrevocable. But Fortune smiled.' The woman who stepped into the room might have been in her late twenties, or anything up to her forties. It was impossible to tell. She moved like a dancer, her simple blue gown falling over a profusion of underskirts of various shades like the summer sky, the bodice embroidered with small gold flowers which glimmered in the light streaming through the windows. Her hair was a mix of the darkest browns threaded with strands of gold that fell like silk across the olive skin of her shoulders. She wasn't veiled and she didn't tie her hair back. Another rebellion against the expectations of high society.

'Lady Beatriz,' said Sylvian in a suddenly reverential voice and Lyta felt an unexpected lurch of jealousy. She frowned. She had no right to feel that, and no reason either. The past was the past and better left there. 'It is an honour to be here. Thank you for your aid.'

The woman laughed good-naturedly. 'There was not much choice in that, my dear captain,' she added.

'There seems to be a lot of that going around,' Lyta muttered. Choice seemed to be in short supply when kings were involved. Or Sylvian.

The man himself stiffened in indignation and Lady Beatriz Alvarez finally looked at her.

Her eyes seemed ancient. Or rather ageless. And they saw far more than Lyta was comfortable showing.

'Indeed. Well, when you meddle in the affairs of kings that happens. You must be Lyta Cornellis, the printer's sister.'

Lyta tried to hide her surprise. 'You know me?'

Sylvian cleared his throat. He'd told this woman all about her. Now she looked like an idiot, as well as the kind of fool who ran into burning buildings.

'I know of you and of your brother. In my business, I make a point to know who people are in this city. I have a great interest in printing. It's an area I am considering investing in soon. The future, I think. A way to bypass those who would lock away knowledge and keep it for themselves. An enlightened population is a tricky thing to manage, but oh, it offers endless possibilities.' She sounded like Kit, talking like that. 'Now, move aside, Sylvian. Let me examine our patient.'

He stepped back dutifully, an ominous statue. If Lyta hadn't seen the way his hands clasped together behind his back, she would have thought he had no feelings whatsoever. But his knuckles were the colour of bone.

Beatriz quickly examined her – asking Lyta questions, getting her to breathe out and cough – and seemed pleased.

'An excellent recovery. Are you feeling strong enough to rise? We should talk, all of us. The king was most insistent, and it doesn't do to ignore him. You know how he is.' Lyta didn't, but from their brief acquaintance, she could guess. Beatriz Alvarez spoke of him like an old friend. Or a troublesome child. 'Take your time. There are

THE BOOK OF GOLD

clothes in the cabinet over there which will fit you. Your own were so damaged. I hope you don't mind my replacing them. Sylvian, with me, if you please. Give the lady some privacy.'

He followed with obvious reluctance and Lyta had to smile. He looked so awkward. Not the great Captain Chant right now. Or perhaps it was Lyta being called a lady that perplexed him so.

For a moment Lyta had dreaded what she might find when she finally managed to open the wardrobe – gowns and kirtles perhaps, totally impractical for her – but instead well-crafted leathers, a fine cotton shirt and a jacket of Albion wool, coupled with a thick functional belt, awaited her. The boots were wonderful, soft but sturdy. Everything a woman could need in Amberes. Well, a woman like her. Her coin bag and her belt knife were there too. Those were all her belongings now.

She wondered what she was going to have to do to repay this kindness. Then she recalled what Beatriz had said about the king being insistent. Perhaps everyone was following orders after all.

Not something she herself was good at. Sylvian could have told them that. But time was she would have said Sylvian was just as bad and look at him now. Tamed. Tempered. Controlled. The king had sent him to find her. To watch her. To make sure she did as she promised. He was like a dog on a leash.

Beatriz led them into a large well-lit sitting room on the first floor, with huge windows looking out over the gardens behind the house. Beyond it lay the walls, part of the city defences, but the house and grounds were arranged in such a way that the fortifications couldn't be seen. Great ships slid along in perfect view, carracks and galleys, stately as swans on the water. Lyta took a seat opposite the lady, while Sylvian stood behind her, as if he was guarding her now. From what though? He'd brought her here. A fire crackled in the fireplace, unnecessary given the warmth, but then Beatriz was from a far warmer climate than Amberes. Maybe she felt the cold constantly here.

Nervous, Lyta fiddled with her charm to Eninn through the material of the shirt and saw Beatriz's gaze light on the movement. She noticed everything.

'I read the letter his Majesty sent,' Beatriz told Sylvian. 'He is so fond of demands, isn't he? But if he agrees to my condition, which serves him as well, then we will help you in your escapade.'

There was an unnerving quality of stillness about her. Especially when she turned her gaze on Lyta. It was like Beatriz was staring into her heart of hearts and Lyta really didn't like it.

'Can we go back a little way first?' Lyta said. 'Would someone like to explain to me who you are? And what you want out of this?'

'You need an expert in ancient manuscripts. My brother is the finest scholar in the western continent, perhaps in the world. There is not a language he cannot translate, no script he cannot read. You need him.'

She was right, of course. In order to steal *The Book of Gold* they first had to identify *The Book of Gold*. Ranulf had enlisted a scholar of Louvain who had fallen on hard times, but one who he believed could do the job. Whether he did or not was anyone's guess. He hadn't come back either.

'And he would help us, would he?'

'He can be persuaded,' said Beatriz. 'But first you would need to fetch him here. And that is more difficult than it might appear.'

Of course it was. Lyta leaned forwards, watching the woman carefully. She was leaving something out. It niggled at the edge of Lyta's sense, as did the idea that Sylvian also knew there was some kind of surprise on the way and that she would not like it.

'So where is he?'

Still Beatriz didn't answer directly, which just made the feeling of unease worse. 'You understand the love of a sister for a younger brother, and mine is in a dark place. I want him home, that is all. Francisco has agreed, finally, to support action, or at least to turn a blind eye. Our beloved king has spent far too long sitting on that particular fence. My brother will come home. And then he will help you carry out Francisco's plan. He will be useful to you.'

Francisco's plan, Lyta thought. *Sure.*

Beatriz was right, she did understand the love of a sister for a brother. She had almost killed herself for Kit. Twice in recent days alone. In reality, more times than her brother knew or would ever know. She had given up everything for him. Including Sylvian.

'Where is he?' she asked. 'Your brother?'

'In the Scholars' Tower, to the south-east of Amberes, on the road to Luttich, under the direct supervision of its magister.'

Ah, that made things complicated.

'He's a priest? Of the Church Imperial?'

Beatriz shook her head. 'Not yet, though they would make him one. They would scrape him out and fill him with their lies, and use him in every way possible. And as I have explained to our king, this cannot come to pass. That is not and will never be his fate. I want him back. I moved everything I have here for that purpose alone. And you will get him for me. If you do that, you will have all the help you could possibly need. Information, money, whatever it takes. And Ben, his knowledge, his abilities, everything he can do for you. I promise.'

'I don't understand. Are they holding him against his will?'

Beatriz shook her head.

So, this was something else. Lyta frowned. 'If he's studying to be a priest of the Church . . . Are you asking me to kidnap him?'

Sylvian groaned. 'That's exactly what she's asking. Demanding, in fact. Is that not right, Beatriz?'

The Lady of the House of Alvarez shrugged so elegantly it was hardly the same gesture Lyta knew. 'If that is what it takes. We all have prices, Sylvian. I am a business woman after all and— And Ben should never have entered that terrible place. It will destroy him. That man is a monster.'

'What man?' Lyta asked.

'The Magister. He has twisted my brother's mind and made him think— Well, it doesn't matter. Bring him back to me. I will make him whole again, if stepping beyond the Magister's influence alone doesn't do so. And he will help you, this I promise. No one knows the matters of ancient texts like Ben. No one. Without him, you will never hope to find exactly what you are looking for. He alone can identify it and translate it. So really you have no choice. You need him. And I need you to rescue him.'

They did need a scholar, Lyta thought. One in their debt would be best of all. But still . . . she didn't like the sound of any of this.

A banging from outside made all three of them jump and they heard the rush of footsteps as the servants ran to answer the main door. It was followed by raised voices, voices Lyta knew too well.

'Where is she?' Kit shouted and Lyta cringed inwardly, glancing at Beatriz. The woman's beautiful face was calm and placid, all too knowing. Speaking of brothers . . .

'We were told he brought her here last night,' Frida joined in. Because of course she did. They were both here, barging in on this deal at a most delicate moment, which was unfair because this was normally what Lyta did to Kit.

'Let us in.' Nothing was going to stop her brother this time. That much was clear.

'You had better let them see that I haven't murdered you or something,' Sylvian growled and stalked back to the window as if it offered an escape.

Beatriz smiled. Lyta did not.

'Show them in here,' Beatriz called, and the next thing Lyta knew she was swept up in Kit's arms and crushed into his broad chest. When had he got so big? And so demanding?

When had he last hugged her like this?

It took her breath from her.

'What happened? Are you all right? The house, Lyta . . . Frida told me about the fire. I'm sorry. But I swear to you I didn't leave anything lit or—'

'Of course you didn't,' she said, extricating herself reluctantly from his embrace. 'Janlow was too eager to keep me from getting home, wasn't he? It had to be him. Probably on Alderton's orders.'

'Alderton?' Frida looked instantly sketchy. 'Why?'

'Should I know about any of this?' Sylvian asked, suspicion darkening his voice. The two women glared at his interruption. 'Obviously not then.' He turned his back again and stared out of the window. Lyta wasn't deceived. He'd be listening to every word.

'Where is Haldevar anyway?' she asked Frida, but her friend just shrugged. 'You haven't heard from him?'

'Made himself scarce by the look of it. I don't blame him if Alderton is resorting to arson. He's no fool, my man.'

Lyta pulled her aside. Frida was the only one she trusted, and the only one Haldevar would trust. 'Find him for me. We need to make sure he knows. Whatever the fire was – a message, a warning – Alderton's the least of our problems but he could—'

'Lord Alderton?' Beatriz asked. 'Dear me, Mistress Cornellis, not a man to make an enemy of lightly.'

'What have you got yourself into this time?' Kit murmured darkly to his sister. He seemed to take in the luxury of their surroundings for the first time and he looked distinctly uncomfortable. Especially when Beatriz turned her attention on him.

One problem at a time. 'What do you know about the Scholars' Tower, Kit? Because we've got to get inside.'

CHAPTER NINE

Kit

Lyta had been explicit with her instructions, but Kit didn't like any of this. He didn't feel safe in the house overlooking the river. The woman who lived there, beautiful and kind as she appeared to be, made his skin itch. She watched them all too closely. Sylvian seemed enchanted by her and even Lyta had cast aside her usual suspicions, waving his concerns away. He didn't like the way Beatriz seemed to be pulling his sister's strings all of a sudden.

'It's just business, Kit,' she said. 'She wants something that will help us. So we're going to get it for her.'

The fact this this *something* was a person made it worse. He'd tried to explain that too. As usual, Lyta wasn't listening.

But what else could he do? Lyta had never needed him before and he owed her. She'd got involved in this in order to rescue him and now her house was gone. No matter what she said, he was convinced it was his fault. He'd left that morning, locked everything up, but he hadn't checked as thoroughly as he might have. He'd been eager to get back to the printshop. He had an order almost ready and needed to complete it.

The very order that was now in his cart, two days later, a consignment of books for the Scholars' Tower. The Magister had been away for a few weeks and there hadn't been much of a rush. Once he told Lyta that nugget of information, their fate was sealed.

He was her way in.

The tower was just over an hour's ride outside the walls of Amberes, on the road south-east towards the border. The city had not allowed the Church to build any of their fortified residences within the walls. The aldermen didn't trust those who would set up their own strongholds, who lived by rules other than those laid down by the city and the king. And, as the oldest empire on the continent, the Church Imperial loved its own rules.

The walls were thicker and more heavily fortified than those of the city, which frankly, Kit thought, had seen better days. Not these ones. They dominated the landscape, threw down a gauntlet to both Amberes and the king. He shuddered as they entered the long shadow the tower cast over the plain, austere and threatening. You could see it for miles and it always made Kit feel cold and dead inside, like all hope had been drained out of the air around it. There were none of the pretty estates and villas of the rich which dotted the countryside around the rest of Amberes. The farmers who had once called this land their own had moved away rather than live in its shadow. The Scholars' Tower controlled everything in its vicinity.

And the Magister controlled the Scholars' Tower. The Magister who was currently far away in Caput Mundi at the heart of the Latinate states. Kit had hoped that might make security a little more relaxed – that with their master not present, they might let their guard down a little – but it didn't look that way. They were stopped at the main gates like everyone else by the red-liveried church militia and the cart searched.

Lyta sat beside him, looking for all the world like an apprentice there to help him lift the cases and learn her trade. He wasn't quite sure how she did it but perhaps she should have been on the stage. She'd tied back her hair and sat with her shoulder slumped and an insolent expression on her face which made her look for all the world like a boy who would rather be anywhere else.

They moved onwards, through another gate, and then they were inside. Everything was as bleak and grey as he remembered. Gods, this place . . .

They waited in the outer courtyard for the captain on duty to check with the librarian's office, or whatever else they had taken themselves off to do.

'So you're seeing Sylvian again?' he asked, mainly to distract himself and take his mind off what they were doing, not to mention all the possible consequences. And maybe to needle her, just a little. She seemed too calm by far.

'No. I'm working with him. I wasn't given any choice in that.'

'They said he ran into the fire to rescue you and carried you to the Alvarez woman's house unconscious. You don't do that for a mere colleague, do you?'

She cast him a blank look. She clearly didn't want to entertain any of this. 'You'd have to ask him. Maybe he needs me. I have no idea why he's agreed to this, but the king sent him. So he doesn't have a choice either. He's a royal bodyguard, sworn to Francisco. Maybe he just has to obey and that's that.'

Francisco. The fact his sister was referring to the king, of all people, by his first name should have been worrying enough.

'How did he get to be a royal bodyguard?' Lyta shrugged, ignoring his question. But Kit wasn't going to be put off quite that easily. He knew his sister too well. 'Did you tell him what happened? Did you tell him about Janlow and—?'

The words were clipped and irritated. 'It didn't come up.'

Kit exhaled slowly, counting in his head to keep his temper. 'Liar,' he said at last.

But that really was that, because the captain of the militia returned and waved them through the gate. Lyta sat back on the cart, gazing up at the walls, the guards, with assessing eyes.

'Just remember this is my livelihood, will you?' Kit warned her. But she wasn't listening. She never did.

The second courtyard opened up before them and he saw the librarian's familiar face already waiting for him. He looked eager to see Kit and his precious cargo. Mainly the books, Kit thought, knowing him.

The books were simple prayer books. They were a new format, small and compact, for the personal use of the upper ranks of the

Church, the Patricians and their guards, the militia, perhaps a few scholars. Their followers would probably never get more than a glance at one, but since most of them couldn't read, that hardly mattered. They would listen, as they always did, dutifully memorising passages to repeat at the services in praise of the Imperator Eternal.

Despite embracing the new printing technology in Amberes, the Church seemed to have no interest in changing its ways. They still didn't allow printing presses on church lands, sending their commissions to the godless cities where the trade thrived. That was what the librarian had told him, with an entirely straight face, as if Kit didn't come from one such godless city himself. Scribes and illuminators would still have employment, scholars would still translate and interpret works from across the world, while the Church published only what fitted in its narrow world view, filtering out anything else. And knowledge would still be hoarded away in places like the Scholars' Tower. All for the glory of the Church Imperial and the Imperator.

It wasn't right.

But that was an argument for another day.

'Master Cornellis,' the librarian, Frater Julius, greeted him, immediately launching into an enthusiastic monologue about the books and his sheer delight to see the delivery arrive. He looked older than the last time Kit was here, a little more frail, even though it had only been a few months since he'd placed the order. The years were catching up with him, but his enthusiasm was undimmed. Kit and Lyta opened the box so Julius could inspect one of the volumes. While he was distracted, Kit asked his question.

'I believe one of your scholars and I have a friend in common. I wanted to ask him if he might help me with a project. Benedictus Alvarez? With your permission naturally.'

The librarian, still captivated by the book nestled in his hands, barely looked up. 'Alvarez? Yes, he should be around here somewhere. Hardly ever out of my library. He doesn't report to me, but to the Magister himself. He's on a path to be a Patrician, that one, perhaps even an Inquisitor, if the Magister has any say in it. Which of course he does. Benedictus is his special project.' There was an undertone of distaste in the way he said it and he seemed to catch himself. The old man gave Kit a conspiratorial nod. 'Don't tell anyone I said that, Kit.'

Kit smiled his broadest, most honest smile. 'Said what, Frater Julius?'

'Come with me and we'll find him. Your boy can carry the box, yes?'

'I can do that,' Kit said and Lyta glared at him. Right. She was meant to be his apprentice. When he rolled his eyes, she stuck her tongue out at him. Something in Kit's chest went cold. She took such risks.

'Nonsense. What's the point in having an assistant?' the librarian said. 'Besides, your arm is injured. What did you do to it?'

His forearm was still bandaged. Though the bruising everywhere else had largely faded, his arm ached, the stitches itched and the wound was not healing properly. Kit instinctively brought it to his chest, as an image of the duchess's gleeful face flashed in his mind unbidden. He shuddered before he could stop himself and felt Lyta's hand press his back, her touch reassuring and warm.

Had he missed that? Her support, her presence in his life? Something so simple?

'An accident at work.' He dredged the answer from somewhere. He had never been able to lie with the ease of his sister. 'Nothing serious. But yes, my apprentice can carry the box. That's why he's here.'

It wasn't like it was that heavy. And if it was, well, that was Lyta's problem now. She'd insisted he bring her in here with him, potentially jeopardising his business and his contacts. But damnation, she had got herself into this mess because of him in the first place.

They followed Frater Julius inside, Lyta carrying the box with apparent ease, until she relinquished it to the librarian's assistant who spirited it off to an office. Then she stood there, looking in wonder at the library of the Scholars' Tower. Kit had seen it any number of times, and it always impressed, but Lyta, he realised, had never been here before.

Part of him, the cynical portion of his brain that knew her of old, worried what she was planning to steal first, but even he couldn't deny the expression of amazement on her face. For a moment she was just his sister.

No one could deny that the library was beautiful. Galleries stretched up to the painted ceiling far above them, crammed with shelves full of books, parchments and scrolls, materials gathered from all over the world to fill this place. Amberes' trade routes made it easy. Julius would go into excruciating detail if asked, which Kit had learned not to do. Not if he wanted to get anything else done with his day. There were items in here older than the city, older than the protectorate or the duchy itself, certainly older than the kingdom.

In front of them sparse workbenches stretched out, populated by men in drab robes, with an air of detachment, heads bowed, focused on their work. Even the arrival of the librarian and two strangers didn't interrupt them. As they passed, a few glanced up, but most kept on working. At the far end of the room, a young man in his early twenties sat on his own. Dark hair fell over a delicately boned face. When they stopped in front of him and he finally raised his hazel eyes to look at them, Kit felt something catch in his chest.

The light fell from the windows high above them and illuminated him, lending him an ethereal quality. Someone so beautiful belonged in paintings, in stories, in legends, not here surrounded by dust and drabness. He had the same dark colouring and slight build as Lady Beatriz, but where she had been formidable, magnificent in her beauty, Benedictus seemed strangely vulnerable and just a bit lost.

'Master Librarian?' He spoke in low and careful tones, hesitantly forming the words as if he didn't have occasion to talk very often.

'This is Kit Cornellis, the master printer. He has some questions for you. Can I leave you to it? I want to get these books processed. Out of the library itself, if you please, scholar. Don't interrupt the others. Take care, Kit. We'll talk soon.'

He scurried away like a miser presented with a treasure to hide.

Benedictus looked so confused it was almost comical. 'Um, yes, of course. A pleasure to meet you, Master Cornellis.' He closed the book into which he was diligently transcribing a text and tucked it into a pocket in his robes. Laying down the quill he had been using, he sealed the pot of ink and then rose. 'We can talk in the gardens.'

He hesitated as he made to leave, glancing back down the length of the library as if looking for someone or checking that they were not observed. Whatever he saw did not seem to satisfy him entirely. He beckoned the two of them to follow and walked quickly through a small door near his bench. The corridor beyond was dimly lit but soon opened out into a cloister surrounding a garden filled with regimented box hedging and a pitiful array of dull flowers.

For all the spectacle of the Scholars' Tower, beyond the library it seemed a bleak and hopeless place.

Benedictus walked to the far side of the garden and sat down on a bench in the shadows of the column, waiting for Kit and Lyta to join him before he spoke, his soft voice tinged with wariness.

'Did my sister send you?' he asked. 'I told her, I'm fine. I wrote to her.'

'That was more than a year ago,' Lyta said with surprising gentleness. 'She came to Amberes when she didn't hear from you again.'

'A year?' He looked so confused, like a child waking from a dream. Kit frowned. Something was wrong here.

When Benedictus turned those eyes on him, like a kaleidoscope of autumn colours, all he wanted to do was find some way to help.

'The rest of her letters never reached you?' Lyta was asking.

'No,' Ben frowned. 'No letters.'

'But you said you wrote back to her.'

He frowned again, a crease forming between his eyebrows. 'Yes. I— I mean, I thought . . . But we don't get letters. I wrote to tell her I was fine and she . . .' Something passed through his eyes, like a shadow dimming their light. 'We don't get letters in here. The outside world is a distraction. The work is what matters.'

Lyta seemed at a loss for a moment. Her eyes flicked towards Kit, as if to ask him what to do next. There was something about the tower, something which set his teeth on edge, an instinct for wrongness perhaps.

'What work?' Kit asked. What work could be worth cutting yourself off from the world so completely, from friends and family, from everything? He and Lyta might not always see eye to eye, and she might be an absolute liability when it came to his business, but all the same, they were family. No matter what he might have said in the past, he would never cut her out of his life completely. She'd never let him, for one thing.

Ben opened the book he had been writing in earlier, unexpected passion firing in his face. 'I'm translating some of the earliest texts on humanity and divinity. The nature of the chosen and Aspects of deities, and of course the nature of the Divine Nexus. There's more, so much more. Look, this is—'

Just like that, letters, their other questions and Ben's sister were forgotten. So was the curious gap in his memories. All that mattered were the words in front of him. Kit watched him speak with a creeping dread. He was gone again, as if their earlier conversation had never happened.

'We really don't have the time to go into it all now,' Lyta interrupted him, and Kit saw his face fall. 'Later maybe. I'm sure Kit would love to hear all about it later on. Wouldn't you?'

'Yes, absolutely,' he said. And he wasn't entirely lying. He wanted to know about translations and early scripts. He wanted to know what they had hidden away in here and all the things this brilliant man could tell him. He wanted to know it all. But not here, not now. Right now, he wanted to get out. It felt like the atmosphere of the tower sucked all life and joy from a person, distracted them from what was important by convincing them that their work mattered more. He could almost feel it, gnawing at the edges of his mind.

'Come with us to see Beatriz, please?' Lyta continued. 'Just to put her mind at ease. If you don't want to stay no one will make you. She wants to see that you're safe. Ben, please?'

Ben. It was the name that did it. Not Benedictus, but Ben. He shivered and then slowly, he nodded. 'But I can't leave the tower. It's forbidden. The militia won't allow me passage to Amberes.'

They had hoped he'd be happy to go and talk to Beatriz, that they could escort him there and back, or at least take a message to the woman. But now that didn't seem likely. And leaving him here alone felt very wrong.

'Just for a few hours, Ben.'

Ben wrung his hands together, his nails digging into the skin. 'You don't understand. The Magister will know. He's due back today. He'll be furious if I'm not here to greet him. He'll—'

Lyta swung the heavy cloak off her shoulders. 'Look, you wear this, and give me your robe. You go out with Kit, as his apprentice and I'll stay behind. No one will know.'

'Lyta,' Kit warned but she wasn't listening. When had she ever listened? 'Lyta, I'm not sure this is a good idea. If they catch you in here—'

'No one catches me, Kit.' And she grinned as if it was all a game.

'We had a plan,' he argued. They were just meant to talk to him, get him to visit his sister. Not this. At least, that was what Kit had thought. Now, of course, he knew Lyta had other ideas.

'We still do. This is the plan. It's just different. Plans change. If I'm not back outside when we said, you fall back to the city and wait. Trust me, little brother. This is what I do.'

And that was what he was afraid of.

It was a matter of minutes and there wasn't time to argue. They left Lyta sunning herself in the cloister garden, acting as if she hadn't a care in the world, while they made their way back through the library. They were almost at the main doors when the librarian emerged from his office.

'Master Cornellis!'

Kit stopped, his heart hammering in his chest. His arm burned as he plastered a smile on his face. 'Is all in order, my friend?'

'Of course. I just wanted to catch you before you left and thank you. The work is exemplary. Truly exemplary. We will have new requests of you soon, I am sure.'

Ben stepped in behind Kit, ducking his head. Ben was a little taller than Lyta but had the same slight build. Nevertheless, at any second

Kit expected someone would pull back the hood and denounce them both. And Ben's obvious nerves weren't helping.

'I'm sure we'll be able to arrange a generous discount for repeat orders,' Kit found himself saying, as smoothly as if this was a completely normal business exchange. 'In honour of the Imperator naturally.'

The librarian's eyes rounded with delight, the apprentice forgotten. 'That would be most agreeable. The Magister will be delighted to hear of your devotion, Master Cornellis. I will tell him of it directly.'

'Directly? He's here?'

Ben let out a small noise, which he quickly turned into a soft cough. A very unconvincing cough. And Kit had thought he was the worst actor in all of this.

'His advance riders just came in. He's due at any moment, returning from Caput Mundi. Would you care for an audience? I'm sure he'd be delighted to grant you the honour, if you would be willing to wait.'

Shit. Kit scrambled for an answer, keenly aware their slapdash plan was on the verge of falling apart already. 'It would indeed be an honour,' he said, 'far too great an honour for a humble printer. Alas, we must return to our labours. I have other orders waiting for delivery and only myself and the boy here to do it. We wanted to make sure yours had priority. Please forgive us. Perhaps another time.'

He grabbed Ben's arm and steered him towards the door. This was bad, very bad. Kit forced himself on. He just had to get Ben out and hope to all the gods that Lyta could escape by herself. There was no way he could come back for her. Not without returning Ben, which he would not do. Not now he had realised how truly terrified Ben was of the Magister.

Kit remembered that feeling all too well.

A carriage had pulled into the inner courtyard and people were already gathering around it. Ben froze at the foot of the steps, staring like a frightened rabbit before a snake, as the door began to open.

A man stepped out, dressed head to foot in scarlet robes. He was hawkish, sharp-featured, with pale wispy hair cropped close to his skull. He had eyes like a predator.

Fuck!

Still moving, Kit pulled Ben towards the hired cart and donkey, which were waiting where they had been left. 'Get up on the cart,' he hissed, but Ben faltered.

'I— I can't. What if—?'

There was nothing for it. Kit had already been at the mercy of the judicial system of Amberes twice and he bore the marks to prove it. He didn't want to discover what the Church would make of him as some kind of heretic. Kindling, probably.

He cuffed Ben over the back of the head and gave him a shove to drive home the point. 'Get in the cart now, boy. We're late. And we're in the way.' Julius had followed them, and was watching from the foot of the steps, so Kit cast him an apologetic smile. 'Honestly, my cousin's boy. I'd fire him but I'd never hear the end of it from the family. You know how it is.'

Maybe he was more like Lyta than he cared to admit. Or maybe just in the moment of his greatest need something in their shared blood came through. The lie danced for him, just for a moment. Maybe Eninn was with him after all.

Julius nodded distractedly, still staring at Ben's hooded figure. Understanding flickered in his old eyes. Kit held his breath.

'You should . . . Yes, the Magister is clearly very busy. Many will want to see him on his return. You should go. Now.'

The urgency in his voice told Kit that they were out of time and this was the only chance he would get. He jumped up on the little cart and seized the reins as the donkey lurched into motion, turning towards the gates with the steady determination of an animal intent on home and food.

They passed through the outer courtyard in silence. Inside, Kit was a mess. Lyta was still in the tower and he had no idea how to get her out. The Church might talk of mercy, but it had little to offer, especially not to thieves.

And she was, in every way, a thief.

So was he. Here he was, stealing a person. Kidnapping. Whatever you called it.

Rescue. It was a rescue. He had to remember that.

Fuck it, just get out.

The outer gate stood open and the militia, in their red uniform and shining armour, waved them through. Just like that. They had other things to think about than a tradesman going in the opposite direction to their master.

They travelled in silence down the road away from the tower until the sunlight finally broke through the clouds overhead and the air felt fresh again.

'You all right?' he asked Ben.

Ben had curled in on himself, huddled under Lyta's shabby cloak. With a wave of guilt, Kit remembered how he'd manhandled him, cuffed him. 'I'm sorry, if I was rough. I just . . . We had to . . .'

Ben didn't answer at first. Instead he was studying Kit's arm, the bandaged one, his eyes sharp and incisive. Any trace of his earlier confusion was gone. It seemed Beatriz was right: outside the tower, the malign influence drained away.

'What happened to your arm?' Ben reached out a trembling finger and traced the edge of the bandage. There was no way he could know, no way he could see what lurked beneath it. And yet . . . 'Master Cornellis? Who marked you like that?'

CHAPTER TEN

Lyta

It was quiet in the garden and peaceful. Not like home. Lyta was used to the constant noise of the city, even in the stillness of the night. To sit here, in sunshine and listen to just silence . . . She was tired, she realised. It had been non-stop since she'd found out about Kit's imprisonment. Perhaps she could just rest here for a little bit, just relax.

No, that wasn't right. That wasn't the way she thought. There was something insidious about this place, sapping away any sense of independent thought. It set off every nerve in her body.

She needed to find her way out. The sooner the better.

She made her way back to the library and pulled out a few scrolls, unrolling them to study the bright colours and elaborate scripts. There were manuscripts here that looked as if they might fall apart if breathed on too much, so she left them well alone. Kit would never forgive her if she destroyed them by poking too hard. But the library was no place to hide so she carried on until she found the main staircase, and from there the oratory. The marble figure of the August Imperator dominated the sanctum, his arm raised as if addressing the crowd, dressed in ancient military garb the Patricians still mimicked.

Offerings of grapes had been laid out at the back, so she covertly helped herself to a few. They popped between her teeth and their sweet illicit juice filled her mouth. *Eninn would love this*, she thought, stealing from the Imperator's own offerings. Oh, he'd laugh. She could almost hear him, but of course he had no power in here.

There were a number of people at prayer, all kneeling in silence at the front of the chamber, so she took a place in the very back and watched while she tried to figure out her way of escape. Life in here, she decided, mostly consisted of boredom. No wonder they looked so miserable all the time.

But Ben hadn't just been miserable, he had been dazed, as though he was constantly waking up from the deepest of sleep. The more Lyta thought about it, the more uncomfortable she felt. What could cause that to happen to someone? She reached for her pendant and the little ring dangling next to it, and offered up a prayer to her own god instead.

As the prayers finished with a half-hearted exhortation to obey the Imperator and serve him in all things, a high-pitched bell rang out in the central courtyard. Everyone stood at the same time and Lyta had no choice but to fall in with the group filing outside. There were no other women, she realised. Not a single one. The Church didn't allow women to be scholars. They didn't allow them to do much of anything.

There were always the kitchens though. People were always coming and going from kitchens, weren't they? The Church still relied on women to do the tedious work. Things like food preparation and laundry, menial tasks that most people didn't want to bother with. That sort of place. That was where she could vanish and that would be her way out.

A narrower corridor led towards a nondescript staircase that had to be for servants so she made for it, turning away from the crowd heading outside.

'Stop! Where do you think you're going?'

She kept walking, pretending she hadn't heard or that it had nothing to do with her, putting her head down and picking up her pace a little. If she could just make the narrow stairs leading down, she was pretty sure—

A hand grabbed her shoulder and pulled her around. Her hood fell, revealing her face.

'I've found her,' the guard shouted. 'She's here!'

Lyta flung the robes up, tangling them over his head, and dropped out from underneath them. She rolled on the ground, righted herself and bolted for the stairs. The shouts behind her turned to alarm and she was out of time.

She should have moved earlier. She shouldn't have taken so long. She'd been enjoying herself, far too cocky by half, tempting fate and now her luck had run out. Completely run out.

Options. She needed options.

At the bottom of the stairs she rounded the corner and ran straight into three of the militia. They were armed and she didn't stand a chance. Not head on.

She scrambled back up the stairs, but it was too late. Someone grabbed her leg and she went down, catching her head a glancing blow off the stone step above. Everything turned black and white, with flashes of fire.

Time was up.

They dragged her outside into the courtyard. She almost slipped free but one got in a kick to her stomach which left her winded. And then the world slid by her, blurred and incomplete. Stone steps, stone ceilings, walls as cold and heartless as the statue of the Imperator she had already disrespected. Eninn would never be so petty over a few bloody grapes. But she'd had to push it and now she was paying the price.

A brief rush of air as she was dragged through an open courtyard gave her a moment of hope and then darkness closed around her again, along with the heavy scent of perfumed incense.

She was thrown down on an elaborate mosaic floor, an image of a scarlet and black eagle with outspread wings under her. Strange how she could focus on that, but the rest of the world was achingly bright. The symbol of Caput Mundi itself. The heart of the old empire.

'What is *that*?' The voice was scathing.

'The thief, Lord Magister. We caught her trying to escape.'

'There's been a mistake,' she tried to say, but what came out was a strangled wheeze. 'I'm not a thief. Just lost. First day. I was looking for the kitchens.'

The Magister was clad in long scarlet robes, silk if she was any judge. The colour was meant to show he would shed his blood for the Church, but looking at his narrow, vicious face, she knew at once that the only blood shed would belong to others. He'd do anything if it furthered his grim religion. But aside from the luxurious fabric and the jewels he wore, he was the picture of austerity personified. His hair was a shock of white locks, swept back from his brow, but his skin was unlined. His eyes were grey as steel. Merciless.

He smiled, a slow, mocking smile but didn't speak, just studied her.

'Oh, she's our thief all right,' said a far-too-familiar voice from behind her. 'One of the most notorious in the city. I did warn you, Your Eminence.'

Lyta fought to twist around. He was standing behind her so she couldn't see him. But she'd know his voice anywhere.

Sylvian!

The guards held her down on her knees while the Magister watched her, as he might a dangerous animal brought to bay. Sylvian's boots rang on the mosaic floor as he approached with unhurried footsteps. Beneath her the mosaic eagle seemed to laugh at her. The walls were decorated with frescos in the Latinate style depicting great battles of the Imperators past, the moments of their apotheosis, the conquered lands and all the slain gods which had brought them such power. The Magister's audience chamber. This had to be it. Right in the heart of the Scholars' Tower.

Sylvian didn't pay her any attention as he passed. Why would he? She was a thief and he a royal bodyguard. Dutiful as any acolyte, he knelt in front of the Magister and bowed his head.

The Magister stared at Lyta, but rested his hand on Sylvian's head and murmured a blessing. A huge ruby gleamed on his finger. The money that would fetch could feed half the city, if you could find a buyer crazy enough to take it. Lyta tried to focus on that instead of Sylvian's back. And the exact spot she wanted to bury a knife.

The Magister waited until Sylvian rose and stepped to one side.

'And what was a thief trying to steal from us, Captain Chant?' the Magister asked.

'Anything you haven't nailed down, I would suggest. But it doesn't look like she had the time. You're fortunate your militia are so good at their jobs.'

They aren't, she wanted to say. They just got lucky and you tipped them off, you shit. But instinct stopped her tongue.

Besides, Sylvian wasn't really her problem right now.

The Magister hummed, his eyes still on Lyta, analysing her, studying her. Her skin crawled under the calculating intensity of his gaze.

The Magister had ultimate power here. He could do whatever he wanted. To anyone.

'And how should we deal with such a thief?' the Magister asked at last.

'I can take her into custody right away,' Sylvian offered cheerfully. The utter bastard.

But the Magister raised a hand. 'The Church takes care of its own problems, captain. And this is not your jurisdiction.'

'She is wanted on a number of matters, Your Eminence. His Majesty is most eager to see to her questioning. You know how kings are.'

Those serpentine eyes closed for a moment, then opened, piercing and terrible, fixed on her and Lyta froze. Like he was seeing into her. Pulling out her secrets, her lies, everything she had ever smothered down inside her. Her pendant tingled at her throat as if even Eninn himself was squirming to get away. This was not good. Not good at all.

'Please,' she whispered. Pathetic was the way to go here. Men like him lapped it up. 'Please, my lord Magister, I didn't take anything. I swear I didn't take anything. It's all a terrible mistake.'

He leaned forward. 'Are you trying to confess, child?'

'I don't . . . I don't have anything to confess.'

A slow smile spread over his lips. 'We all have things to confess, my child. What brought you here? Abandonment or neglect? Led down the wrong path? Forced into a life of crime?'

Was he mocking her?

'My lord Magister—' Sylvian tried to interrupt but the Magister waved his bejewelled hand and the militia holding Lyta tightened their grip. Others moved to block Sylvian coming to her aid. He didn't like that. It was written all over his face.

Too bloody bad. If he hadn't tipped them off, neither of them would be in this mess.

Lyta couldn't worry about him right now. She was in enough trouble of her own.

'I was—' Lyta gulped out the words. 'I *was* abandoned, betrayed, by the man I thought loved me.'

No, she didn't want to admit this. Not in front of Sylvian. But the words kept coming and she was helpless to stop them, as if something had reached inside her and pulled them out. And damn him! If he was just going to stand there doing nothing, he could listen. He could hear all the ways he had ruined her life.

Her eyes burned with tears she had never shed before. She'd been too proud, too angry at Syl to let them fall.

'He was meant to keep my brother safe, but he didn't. Got him involved in crime. He almost got him killed.' Her voice wobbled. She fought to keep it under control. She couldn't seem to stop talking. Was the Magister doing this to her? Was this the power he wielded? 'I had to save my brother. He's family. He's blood. And he was only a kid. One who idolised a fool. I had to put him first.' She didn't want to talk about Kit, she realised. She didn't want the Magister knowing anything about her brother. Desperately she scrambled around for something else to say. And the worst part came out. 'I went back to save my lover, as soon as I could. I went to get him out of jail as well. I was ready to break him out if necessary. I never intended to leave him there. But then, I heard . . .'

She had stood there in the corridor of Old Steen, her back pressed to the cold, damp wall, its icy touch creeping through her skin, listening to Janlow tell Syl how she'd betrayed them, how she'd sold him out for Kit, and listened to Sylvian, her beloved Sylvian say those terrible words.

'You're welcome to her.'

She wanted to look at him now, to see his reaction, but at the same time, she couldn't. It was the last thing she wanted to say.

She opened her mouth for an icy breath and the words slipped out.

'I heard him say that his whoremonger friend could have me.'

The Magister steepled his fingers together, considering her tale.

'And did he claim you?'

They had views about whores in the church lands. She knew that too. Not pleasant ones.

'No,' she snapped, because she would be damned before she let anyone think she had given herself to Janlow, not even a fucker like this one. 'A friend of the family saved me. He offered me marriage to keep me away from them. He was older but he was good, and we were happy for a long time – years – until he vanished. Just gone one day. And now my house, the only thing left, the only thing I had of any value, is gone too, burned to the ground.'

'And what were you after in my tower?'

Lyta tried to force her lips closed. She couldn't tell him that. Ben was safe with Kit and she needed to keep it that way. What else could she say? Why had she agreed to any of this? Not really to get Ben, not quite. That was what Beatriz wanted. But for her, for Lyta Cornellis, thief and conwoman . . .

She finally glanced at Sylvian, who stood as still as a statue, his eyes hooded, his face unreadable. He wasn't giving anything away. No one would dream she had been talking about him. He didn't even seem affected by her revelations.

'It was . . . It was just . . . no one else had done it. Made it in here and out again. I just . . . It was a test, that's all. I wasn't trying to steal a *thing*. I just wanted to do it, as a test, to see if I could.'

And maybe it was true. Had Beatrice been testing her? Had she been testing herself? Because the fortress at Montalbeau was going to be so much worse than this. Everyone said that. It had taken Ranulf, for Eninn's sake.

And she hadn't stolen a thing, not technically. A person was not a thing. And really, Kit had stolen Ben Alvarez, not her.

The Magister sat back, his games apparently over for now. 'A test. How quaint. Who knew thieves took tests?'

Someone laughed, but the Magister's expression didn't so much as flicker. He beckoned over a red-clad soldier, who stood stiffly beside Lyta and gave a stilted report.

'Nothing is missing from the library and our strongroom remains unbreached. She was in the oratory but never near enough to the altar to take any of the treasures or relics. It seems we intercepted her in time.'

'As the captain said, exemplary work.' The Magister nodded solemnly and a look of relief spread over his soldier's face. 'Very well, Captain Chant, you may take her with you. We have no further need of her here.'

The militia released her and she almost fell on her face. Sylvian hauled her up, never making eye contact. He spun her around and tied both hands behind her back, far too tightly. Lyta hissed as the cord bit into her skin, but he shoved her forward onto her knees again.

'You should thank the Magister for his mercy,' he growled in a voice that didn't sound like Sylvian at all.

'Th— Thank you,' she babbled, too shocked to say anything else. And afraid. Was she actually afraid of him? Of Sylvian? Was that this feeling? Because he didn't look like Sylvian anymore. Not in this moment. He was justice and judgment bound in muscles and armour.

He knew now. Knew she really had left him to rot in Old Steen. Knew she'd heard him give her to Janlow.

The Magister rose gracefully to his feet and held out his ruby ring to Sylvian. Lyta watched in disgust as Sylvian bowed and then pressed his lips to the jewel. 'Send our blessings to the king and tell him to judge this poor woman fairly but not too harshly. Taking her hand will surely stop her falling into such ways again. We can do it now, if you prefer.'

One of the militia drew his short flat-bladed sword.

'Your Eminence is too kind,' Sylvian said a little too hastily. 'But the king does enjoy bearing witness to the punishment of the guilty.'

The Magister nodded. 'Such is the way of the worldly.' To Lyta's horror, he stepped up close to her, so his crotch was in front of her face and tilted her chin up so she had no choice but to look at him. Her throat went dry and she tried to keep the fear from her eyes. Tried and failed. 'A pretty face. One might even say beautiful. Such a shame. But the blessings the Imperator Eternal bestows are only ours for a passing time anyway.'

He held out his hand and one of the militia passed him a short knife. With far too much ease, he drew a sharp line of fire along her cheek.

Lyta hissed in pain, taut with thwarted rage. She couldn't move. She couldn't let herself move.

'Remember our mercy, little thief, and the mercy of the Imperator to transgressors of all kinds.'

Their escape was lost in a blur, as Lyta's mind whirred with shame and misery, and her cheek stung, adding injury to the insult. She longed to shrug off Sylvian's hand as he marched her to the gate, but his grip was too strong.

A horse was tethered there, waiting for him. Before she could run, Sylvian had slung her across the saddle like a sack of wheat and mounted behind her.

'They're still watching, Lyta,' he said, his voice gruff. 'Stop drawing attention to yourself. You aren't going anywhere unless it's with me, understand?'

She hated him. She wanted to scream with it. But she could do nothing except lie there, limp.

She closed her eyes, trying to block the journey out. They reached Amberes just before nightfall. She was finally able to dismount as Sylvian returned the horse to the barracks stable by the Bluetower Gate, and for a moment she thought she'd give him the slip. But her hands were still tied behind her back, which meant every guard in the place was looking at her. She had nowhere to go.

Sylvian led her away through the busy streets, marching her so fast she barely had time to think. They were almost in the centre of the city when he finally slowed, shoving her along in front of him and steered her into one of the laneways off towards the old laundries. The air smelled of ashes and urine, of the lye they mixed with fat to make soap. He untied her hands and then pushed her back against the wall before she could bolt.

'Are you all right?' he said, his voice harsh. He pulled out a small square of cloth and dabbed at her cut, as if afraid to touch it too much. 'I'm sorry, Lyta. I couldn't stop him. I couldn't interfere. If I'd known he'd do that, I would have thought of something. I would have—'

She grabbed the cloth in shaking hands and jerked it free of his grip. Then she pressed it hard against the wound, hoping it would staunch the blood flow.

'Well you didn't. What were you doing in there anyway?'

'You didn't come out with Kit as planned. I waited like we arranged but you didn't appear.'

'You were only meant to back us up, in case it all went wrong.'

'Lyta,' he growled her name, 'it *did* all go wrong.'

'I would have found a way out.'

'But you didn't.'

'Because suddenly they were looking for a thief!'

He fixed her with the most obstinate glare she had ever seen. 'I had to get you out of there somehow. I thought it was the best way. I thought—'

'Maybe you should leave the thinking to me in future, Captain Chant. I never took you for a rat.'

She knew as soon as she said it that it was a mistake. Sylvian had never ratted out anyone. She, on the other hand . . .

For a moment he just stared at her. She ought to be thanking him. Even she knew that. But she couldn't. The moment dragged on too long. Then he snarled in frustration and turned away. 'What do you want from me, Lyta?'

'I don't know. Nothing. I want nothing from you, Syl, and I haven't for a very long time. I thought you were gone forever.'

'I promised to come back. And I did. Even after you turned me in. Even after you left me in Old Steen. I loved you, Lyta. I'd have done anything for you.'

Her throat closed on the words she'd been about to say. He'd loved her. She'd loved him. And look where it had got them. Her cheek burned and she was back on her knees with that son of a bitch pressed up against her, cutting her, telling her to be grateful. And Sylvian had just stood there.

She could still hear his voice, all those years ago, broken from pain, stretched with torture, spitting words formed of venom. *'You're welcome to her.'*

He'd loved her? He'd handed her over to a psychopath. He'd abandoned her.

The world spun around Lyta, before jolting to a dizzying stop. She drew in a breath and let it out in a rush.

'You loved me? You never kissed me with half as much reverence as you paid to that bastard's ring.'

Before she knew what was happening, Sylvian was cradling the back of her head with one hand, his thumb stroking her uninjured cheek and she could feel the heat of his body against hers, pinning her to the wall. It radiated through her, consuming her. For a moment he went no further.

His lips brushed against hers, featherlight. 'That's it, is it?' he asked, his voice like distant thunder. 'That's all you want?'

She froze, memories washing through her along with a wave of desire she'd thought she'd forgotten. With everything that lay between them, all the anger and blame, the kiss should have been rough and bruising, a rushed clash of teeth – but it wasn't.

It was Sylvian, his lips on hers again at last, and it was perfect. He cupped her face, holding her in place, but she couldn't have torn herself free if she'd wanted to. Every inch of her yearned for him, for his touch. They hurt each other, that was all they did. And yet, she couldn't resist him.

Her fingertips brushed his skin where his shirt had pulled free, his muscles like iron covered in silk, and it was enough for his whole body to shudder against her. He made a noise, deep inside his chest, something that spoke of surrender and abandon, and the kiss deepened, half-teasing, half-tormenting. Lyta groaned into his mouth. She wanted this, wanted him, wanted nothing else. For years, he'd been everything to her. No one else, nothing else, came close to him.

And he wanted it too. She knew he did. Every taut muscle in his body pressed so intimately to hers screamed it.

Slowly, he pulled back, his dark eyes even darker, the pupils wide, hungry for more, for her, for everything. She could see her own dazed face reflected as if she were all that remained in the world.

Then his expression went cold.

'Reverent enough for you?' he asked.

And walked away.

CHAPTER ELEVEN

Sylvian

What had he been thinking? He'd just wanted to make a point and he'd almost lost control of himself. Lyta was his weakness. His addiction. His obsession. Always had been and always would be. She haunted the darkest corners of his dreams and that was where he should have left her. Just like she had once left him to be beaten and tortured in the dark, and sold into the army.

She'd heard him with Janlow. That was what the Magister had forced her to admit. Those darkest moments, when he would have said anything. She'd heard.

Yet the feel of her mouth against his, his hands holding her, the sounds she made as he claimed her mouth, consumed him. Her body fitted with his as if she belonged there, lighting a spark deep within. His body yielded to hers in a way he had never experienced before or since. And he'd kissed her as if he had never experienced anything like her. Even after so long. Because he never had.

He shook himself. He needed to get control of himself again.

But he'd seen her on her knees in front of the Magister, seen the blade cut her skin and he'd almost lost his mind. He would have committed murder for her there and then, damned his own soul and anyone in the vicinity to save her from that.

And much thanks it had got him.

He couldn't have got her out of the tower in any other way. She hadn't been able to rescue herself. What was she doing in there anyway? With or without him they would have captured her and if he hadn't been there . . .

She was beyond the power of the city, far outside the world she knew. She had no fear, that was the problem. And she never thought things through. Not when it mattered.

The Magister, a devout servant of the Imperator, would flay the sin out of anyone who crossed the Church. Inside the tower his word was law. And the tower broke people.

Only the rumours about the Duchess of Montalbeau were worse.

Sylvian stalked up the Meir, a wide, elegant street that swept past the palace gardens, heading blindly toward Beatriz's house. He didn't check to see if Lyta was following. He couldn't bring himself to.

Because if she wasn't, that would be his fault too.

And then he'd have to go and find her again.

Everything had been fine until Francisco ordered him back here. Sylvian had been fine. The army had honed him, remade him. He'd had a purpose, a role, a life. He didn't break the law, or lie, or pretend to be anything other than he was. It had come as a shock to him to realise how much he loathed the life he used to lead. Always on the make, always owing something – a favour, payback, an actual financial debt. Always watching his back even among his so-called friends. The big man in the gutter, Janlow's right hand, the brawn to the bastard's devious brains. He'd thought Lyta and Janlow were the only two he could really trust and look where that had landed him. Oh, the violence was worse in battle, no doubt, but at least it felt . . . *honest*. Life here had been a struggle, a pissing contest, a war of its own kind which he could never hope to win. He'd put that behind him. Put *her* behind him. All his debts were square, wiped out, that was what he'd told himself, real and imagined. In service of the Crown.

And now here he was, days after meeting her again, and everything was falling apart. He was falling apart. His years of training, his code of obedience and the self-discipline that had got him through everything from wars to courtly intrigue – all gone. And he didn't know how to get them back.

As he made his way into the quieter Lombard's Street, with its upmarket shops and artists' studios, he could hear her following him. He breathed a sigh of relief, but then again, where else did she have to go? Her house was gone and her brother's life was only safe so long as she kept her end of the bargain. Now Kit had hopefully returned Ben to his sister, they had the last piece of the puzzle they needed to plan the heist in earnest. And once they had the book, Sylvian would never need to see Lyta again. He could return to his new, orderly life. Which was what he wanted. Wasn't it?

It was dark by the time they reached Beatriz's house, clouds scudding across the moon, windows aglow with light. Sylvian waited at the wrought-iron gates of the entrance until Lyta joined him, but neither of them spoke.

There was nothing to say. Nothing good. He had well and truly screwed up their wretched reunion as well.

Beatriz's servant led them inside, through the inner courtyard to the first-floor sitting room with its metal-framed lanterns, overflowing bookshelves and huge windows that looked out over the Scaldis, a picture of understated opulence. Kit was examining a book, his fingers running down the spine as he turned pages and tested their edges. He looked up as they entered, and a shadow crossed his face.

'Thank the gods, Lyta,' he gasped, but his words failed when he took in her face.

He always could read his sister better than anyone. That hadn't changed. The glare he directed at Sylvian was far more threatening than the boy he had known would have been able to produce. But Kit was no longer a boy and he had probably seen just as much darkness as Sylvian had growing up in the shittiest parts of the city. Especially if Janlow had been sniffing around.

Lyta hadn't been lying, had she? He knew that. It left icy cold claw marks inside him. No one lied to the Magister.

'There you are,' said Beatriz brightly. 'Excellent.' She seemed positively jovial, aglow, illuminated by the fire behind her.

'Is your brother all right?' Lyta asked. It was the first thing she'd said since the alleyway. She hadn't so much as glanced at Sylvian. All her defensive walls were up. He didn't blame her.

'He is. He's resting. But—' Beatriz swept forward and, much to Lyta's evident surprise, embraced her. She pressed her hand against Lyta's bloody cheek and within moments the cut had healed without a trace. 'He's home with me again. I cannot thank you enough, Lyta Cornellis. Kit told me about the risk you took. Thank all the gods you're safe. It's a miracle that brought you here. My thanks, my eternal thanks. Now, Kit has told me everything. I have had rooms made up and anything you could ask for will be yours. It is the least I can do. And you too, Sylvian, of course.'

He shook his head. 'I need to go back to barracks. They'll want a report on our progress.'

The king would want to know everything. And Sylvian didn't want to spend a night so close to Lyta, perhaps with only a wall between them.

He had no place here and no desire to linger. He'd spend the night in the barracks and return tomorrow to nail down the next stage of the plans. Now, he felt wrung-out. Exhausted.

The sooner this mission was over the better.

He didn't make it far before Kit caught up to him.

'Syl?' Kit was framed by the filigree iron arches of the gallery on the south side of the courtyard. The rising wind tousled his hair and Syl could smell rain in the air. Lanterns swung beneath the balconies, casting a dizzying pattern of light across the ground.

Sylvian swallowed a curse. 'Kit,' he said, slowing his step without stopping. 'It's late. I got Lyta back to you. I have to go.'

'I just wanted . . .' Kit sounded hesitant. 'I wanted to thank you.'

Sylvian sighed and turned back to face the boy. No, the man. Kit was a man now. Thirteen years was a long time, especially in Amberes. 'I'm sure she would have managed to rescue herself. She usually does.'

Kit shuddered. 'They hurt her, didn't they?'

'She put up a fight. I'm sure she did some roughing up of her own.'

Kit laughed, a brief sound, more like a sigh. 'She *always* does.'

An understatement of understatements. 'I'm aware, believe me.'

'Including with you?' Kit said, his tone sharpening.

Sylvian was not getting into this. Not now. And especially not with Kit. 'Don't, Kit. It doesn't matter. It's ancient history. And I have no interest in Lyta.'

Kit's gaze turned incisive. 'Yeah, that's why you went in there after her.'

'I went because you asked me to. She made her decisions long ago and I respect them, and her. Now, if you're finished, I need to be somewhere else.'

But Kit wasn't finished. Not nearly. 'Syl, what happened?'

Enough. That was enough.

'I'm not Syl anymore, Kit. Haven't been for years. And Lyta and I are done. She made that perfectly clear, then and now. So I know exactly where I stand.'

A lifetime ago, Sylvian had broken a promise and Lyta had left him to rot. She'd taken Kit and turned her back on him. Forever, he thought.

He hadn't known she'd come back. Hadn't known that while he was feeling all the pain of betrayal, while Janlow had taunted him, Lyta had been listening.

And he'd said those words. He had to own that. So maybe she was right, after all.

Kit's voice went icy. 'It wasn't just her you handed over to Janlow, you know. It was both of us. That was what Janlow said. Lyta first. Then me. Without you to bring in money he was out of pocket and Ducci wanted reparations or there would have been blood in the streets. I'd failed him as a thief, so maybe I'd be better as a whore.'

He raked a hand through his hair, like he was shaking off a bad dream. Sylvian could just imagine the demands. They were both beautiful, the Cornellises, and Kit had been young and untouched. Not even sixteen. The brothels' best customers would have swarmed around them, offering anything. The worst too. Those who liked breaking young and beautiful things. And Janlow had always wanted Lyta, willing or not. Sylvian had thought that he could protect her, get the three of them out of Amberes. But in the end . . .

'When they found out she had snitched, everyone turned on us – everyone except Ranulf. He was the only one who stood by us. Who saved us. If it hadn't been for him, we would have ended up—' Kit's voice broke and he took a moment to gather himself to go on. Sylvian didn't interrupt, didn't dare. 'That job I was meant to help you with? They sent someone else a few weeks later, because Janlow wanted to make a point. He was always bloody-minded that way. Still is. They were so sure that Ducci and his men weren't there that they hoisted another kid through the same window I was meant to go through, only he got beaten to death for sport. That would have been me. She saved my life, probably both our lives. So if Lyta isn't exactly delighted to see you back after all this time, dredging up all these memories, you can understand, can't you?'

He spoke calmly, but Sylvian could hear the quiver of anger in his voice. Lyta wasn't the only one who blamed him.

And why shouldn't he? Sylvian had promised to protect them both, had promised to be there for them. And he had failed them spectacularly. Sylvian stared at Kit's solemn face, helpless, just as he'd watched as the Magister dragged Lyta's secrets from her. He hadn't moved to help her. Then he'd kissed her, blamed her and thrown it all back in her face. That was the kind of man he was.

Still a bastard through and through. No better than Janlow. He'd tried so hard to leave it behind. To be better. But it had all been for nothing.

It was all might-have-beens and what-ifs. It didn't matter. Not now. Regrets would bring them nothing but pain.

He needed to keep both the Cornellises as far away from him as possible. Fine then. He could be a bastard. Easily. Especially if it meant keeping Kit safe.

And safe clearly meant far away from people like him.

'I'm not here for old times' sake myself. But I serve the king and obey his command.'

Kit had the gall to give him a look of pure pity. 'You can't trust kings, Syl, no more than you can trust people like Janlow. Haven't you figured that out yet?'

Sylvian bristled. 'You don't know anything. He found me and gave me a purpose. He saved me.'

But Kit just barked out a hollow laugh. 'He used you. Found you desperate and broken, bought you with blood and gold, and gave you a lie to live, a master to serve, whether you wanted to or not. That's what kings do. But only while you're useful, Sylvian. After that . . .' he shrugged. 'Not so different from Janlow really.'

With that, he headed back inside to the others.

Sylvian flung the gate shut behind him as he left, the iron slamming into the frame until it shook. He didn't care. He wouldn't allow himself to care.

The night bell was tolling, the sound of great Cissonia echoing softly over the sleeping city. A misting rain had settled over Amberes, blurring its sharp edges. It was later than he'd thought, the time of mud-minders and tenants of the cesspit, the unfortunates who cleared the streets at night and made sure the sewers didn't overflow. He pulled his cloak around him against the chill. At least in the barracks there would be something hot to eat, even if it had been sitting on the stove for several hours. He couldn't remember when he'd last had food of any kind. This morning probably. Barracks porridge, thick enough to stick to the ribs.

The weather got worse as he walked, the water pooling underfoot, whipped into his face by the wind. One minute Sylvian was turning a corner, his vision obscured by the rain and his hood, and the next there was a bag over his head, a rope around his neck and what seemed like twenty hands on him. His arms were twisted behind his back with brutal efficiency. A punch in the guts winded him, another to the kidney debilitated him and they dragged him into the echoing darkness of a large, empty space. Off the street. Out of sight.

Sylvian struggled to catch his breath and willed himself to move. Rain thundered on the roof high above him but he had no idea where he was. He lashed out, his legs connecting with someone's ankles, making a very satisfying crunch. A man shouted in pain and seconds later they laid into him again. Coshes, heavy and unyielding, fists wrapped in chains and what felt like a plank of wood rained down on him, beating him to the wet ground again. They weren't giving him a second, not one single second.

They knew who he was, what he could do. They had come for him and they had come prepared.

'Enough,' said an all-too-familiar voice. 'I want him conscious for this.'

Janlow ripped the bag off his head and Sylvian tried to focus on him. His one-time friend's face was bruised, the nose clearly broken and Sylvian felt a small surge of satisfaction at that.

The hollow and faded splendour of a temple spread out around him, scattered with abandoned crates. Anything of value had been stripped from the walls. Frescos remained, the colours running and smeared with damp. There were holes in the roof high overhead and rain poured through, forming great dancing pools on the ground. On the far wall, in the sanctum, the half-destroyed horned figure of Kyron the Warrior glared down at them.

'You shouldn't have come back to Amberes, Syl. Don't think that uniform protects you. Not from me.'

Sylvian sucked in a pained breath. Something was broken inside him, he knew that. Several somethings. Not good. Not good at all.

'I'm going to send her a message so she can be the one to find your body,' Janlow went on. 'So she knows. Not just for old times' sake either. Your girl has something I want, something important. You're a reminder.'

'What?' Sylvian wheezed and then coughed up blood. He spat it out. *There, Kyron, an offering for you, help me out here.* 'What on earth could Lyta have for you?'

'Something precious to my associate. Something she took. And if she doesn't know where it is, she'd better find it fast.'

'That scared?' Sylvian managed to say. He had to buy time. He had to keep the bastard talking. 'Never could take me on your own.'

If he could goad him into a one-on-one fight he might still have a chance. Otherwise he was dead. There were too many to fight as a group and his ribs lanced with pain on every breath.

On the far side of the temple, behind a rats' nest of old sacking, Sylvian saw movement. Just for a moment, just a flash. He tried to focus on it, but his vision swam sickeningly.

Someone grabbed a fistful of his hair and jerked his head back. The noose tightened around his neck. This couldn't be happening. Not like this.

Movement again, just catching his eye, way over in the darkness.

He couldn't see, not clearly, but he knew. Somehow he knew every detail.

Someone was hiding in the shadows. A teenage boy, no more than fifteen. He had a riot of curls and mismatched eyes, which were fixed solemnly on Sylvian's face. Eyes that had seen far too much. He knew to be silent, to hide from men like this. He was too pretty for someone like Janlow not to take an interest in. And too jaded not to have had that bitter experience by now. Like Kit. Too much like Kit.

The boy lifted a finger to his pursed lips. Kit had been that age when—

Janlow stepped back into view, sneering at Sylvian as he punched him in the face, just as Sylvian had punched him the other day.

The pain was blinding. Sylvian's nose crunched sickeningly, spraying blood everywhere.

'Payback's a bitch, Syl. And I don't need to take you on by myself. I have an army of volunteers who would kill for the chance to fight the king's dog. If only I had time. We'd make a fortune. Just like the old days.' His voice hardened. 'String him up. Let's see him dance.'

And just like that, he was out of time.

Behind him the gang heaved on the rope and he was hoisted up by his neck, kicking and twisting as the noose closed on his throat. He could hear laughter and blood roaring in his head, and his own desperate gasps. He couldn't get his hands free, not that it would have helped much. But it would have been something.

He wasn't even far off the ground. He didn't have to be. It was enough. And Janlow wanted to watch.

He stood there, his bruised bastard face just out of reach as Sylvian tried to struggle free. He knew it made things worse, but he couldn't help himself. His body was reacting, his primal instincts, not his rational side.

Then, from nowhere, a wave of calm spread through his mind, darkness rising up from inside him like tar, swallowing his panic and fear. Leaving him empty. His struggles lessened as the strength drained out of him.

And with it came a prayer.

Not a prayer, not exactly. A plea. A bargain.

'I'll make sure she finds you.' Petrus Janlow, who had once been like a brother to him, leaned in close. 'Eventually. Maybe when you're good and ripe. It can be a surprise. She used to love it when you surprised her, didn't she? You should have just let me have her, Syl. It all could have been different. You and me, we could have ruled this town. Instead . . . well, I'll just have to do it myself, won't I? But your girl is going to be mine, whether she likes it or not.'

Sylvian gave one last violent twist and kicked Janlow square in the temple. He sprawled to one side and, as his vision darkened, Sylvian felt that one last glimmer of satisfaction as Janlow's heavies had to carry him out.

Then everything went black but for brief snatches of breath, his eyelids too heavy to open, his mind drifting in a body too stubborn to give up entirely. It wouldn't last. His own muscle mass would kill him. It was inevitable now. Time passed in blinks, stilted gasps and the creak of the rope.

Lyta would never forgive him. Then. Now. But he wanted to tell her. He'd done it for her, for all three of them, for a future. He'd never have let anyone hurt Kit, but he knew why she'd turned on him, why she'd picked her brother, why she'd married Ranulf.

And then he heard footsteps, running footsteps. Not the boy. Someone else. Not big or heavily built, so not one of the gang. Frantic. Desperate.

'Here! He's here!'

Lyta? No, that wasn't possible. Why would she be here? She didn't know where he'd gone. And Janlow wouldn't have told her already. He'd want to make sure Sylvian was dead this time. He'd want to gloat.

'Get his legs, Kit!' She sounded like she was far away, or under water. Not here with him.

But he was barely here himself. He was reaching for the old gods, and Kyron was reaching back for him from the temple wall, holding out his gauntleted hand. There was light, so much light, and he could hear the clash of weapons growing louder, smell the blood and the acrid stench of war.

But he didn't want to go back to the battlefields he'd left behind him. He was sick of them.

The world dropped back around him. Or maybe it was him falling. Strong arms seized his legs, holding him up, but the noose still bit into his throat, cutting off his windpipe.

Freezing hands pulled at it, dug in under the rope to loosen it and free him, hands as dexterous and determined as Eninn's own.

'Syl, talk to me. Please. Syl!'

It was Lyta. Her voice, her hands. His Lyta.

All he could manage was a groan, but it seemed to be enough for her. For now. She sobbed something incoherent and pulled him into her arms, his head on her chest. Her clothes and hair were wet, soaked to the skin, but he didn't care. Not now. Slowly, she rocked him as the world went dark.

CHAPTER TWELVE

Lyta

Beatriz didn't bat an eyelid when a rain-soaked Kit and Lyta dragged Sylvian's unconscious body into her beautiful mansion. Perhaps, Lyta reflected, she was used to such scenes. Sylvian had brought Lyta here only the other day in similarly dire circumstances.

Well, no, not as bad as this. Nothing could be as bad as this.

But Beatriz Alvarez was a healer and that was all that Lyta could think of right now. Sylvian needed help.

She'd only reached him in time because of the boy. He'd turned up at the house in the rain, asking for her.

She didn't know what he'd said. She couldn't even remember what his voice had sounded like. All she knew was that Sylvian needed her. Sylvian was going to die.

She'd been so desperate to find him before it was too late, she hadn't even realised she wasn't alone. When she reached the abandoned temple, the boy had vanished, but Kit was right behind her, and she'd never been so grateful to have her brother there. He had followed her. Somehow he'd known too and come after her.

It was only when she dropped to her knees at the side of the chaise longue they'd lain Sylvian on that Lyta realised she'd seen the boy before. The same feral adolescent, all lines and angles and mismatched eyes. In the Rose Palace, when she had prayed for help to save Kit. He had led her to the king. And to Syl.

Eninn, she thought. It had to be him. Whatever he was up to he wanted Sylvian involved and would do whatever he could to ensure it. There was no sign of him now. Just her and Kit, and Beatriz, who was bending over to examine Sylvian. Her Sylvian.

Did that mean he was safe? Did that mean he'd live? He was bleeding all over the priceless damask upholstery, his face swollen beyond recognition.

'Can you help him?' Lyta asked.

Beatriz pressed her hand to Sylvian's forehead in silence and closed her eyes, entirely focused on him.

The door creaked as Ben slipped inside. Lyta spared him no more than a glance, but noticed the comforting hand he had placed on Kit's shoulder, the way Kit stared back at him, suddenly relieved.

Then Sylvian's chest heaved with a fitful breath, distracting her.

His hand slid off his chest, where she had placed it, and Lyta caught it, holding it in both of hers like it was something precious.

His palm was calloused under hers, his fingers long and scarred. The rope that had bound him had cut into his wrists and left raw red gouges in his skin.

'Be careful, Beatriz,' Ben warned.

Careful? Why would Beatriz need to be careful? What was she—?

Soft golden light suffused the room, flowing like molten honey over every surface. The fire in the hearth grew brighter and each lamp took on the warmth permeating the air. Lyta's chest grew light in response, buoyed by joy and hope. Her heart beat more fervently than before, her aching battered heart which didn't know how it went on loving, and sometimes didn't know how it went on beating at all. She drew in a breath of wonder as her gaze fell on Sylvian again, and on Beatriz, still bending over him.

The light came from Beatriz and it flowed through her into Sylvian. It rippled through his long limbs and under his skin. Lyta could feel it pulsing in the hand she held so close to her heart, wrapped in her own.

Janlow had almost stolen him from her. Again. Tears stung her eyes but she blinked them away, focusing instead on Beatriz.

'Oh, Sylvian Chant,' Beatriz murmured softly, her attention fixed entirely on him. 'What has been done to you?'

She moved her fingertips down his body, letting them drift over his clothes until she reached the exposed skin of his other forearm.

There were scars there too. So many scars. Sylvian's whole life was laid out in marks on his skin. Some Lyta knew but so many more were new.

Beatriz lingered on his wrist and Lyta watched in amazement as the rope burns healed, leaving silver-white lines behind them. Beatriz glanced at her and Lyta found herself unfolding, offering Sylvian's other arm so she could heal that as well, just with her touch and her glow.

Heat suffused the room and from the walls, from the floor and ceiling, from the air itself, Lyta heard a heartbeat. Her own strained to match it, to join it. Those threatened tears welled up in her eyes as desire coursed through her, the urge to fall at Beatriz's feet and worship her. The need to do whatever she asked. To love her. To serve her.

'I can't fix everything. There are marks on him beyond even me.' Beatriz sighed at last and pulled back. The light faded. The room grew pale and dark, a faded woodcut of a world that had moments earlier been painted in brilliant colours. The fire crackled in the hearth and Lyta realised her clothes and hair were dry as well. So were Sylvian and Kit, as if they'd never set foot in the rain.

'These . . .' Beatriz trailed her hand up a series of faint scars that ran up the insides of Sylvian's forearms, where the skin was palest. 'These are old. And deep. But the rest . . . He'll need to sleep now for it to work. He won't wake until morning. Not properly. He'll need watching.'

She stepped away and stumbled. Fragile, like a wilted flower about to fall.

Ben reached her first, moving on silent feet, wrapping his arms around her. He looked like a giant beside her, despite his slender frame. He manoeuvred her into her chair by the fire and pulled a throw around her shivering shoulders.

'You do too much, Bea. When will you learn?'

Lyta trembled. She felt bereft, as if something vital had been ripped away from her, something she needed. It came from Beatriz Alvarez, whatever it was.

'What did you just do?' Lyta asked. No one answered. She wasn't even sure she'd said it aloud. 'What was that?'

Beatriz slumped back in her seat, her skin grey with exhaustion, her hands trembling. Ben fussed over her, pulling a blanket up over her lap. 'I'll have the cook prepare something for you. A tisane perhaps? Or something stronger? What do you need?'

'What the fuck was that?' Lyta's voice shook as if the storm of earlier raged in her now.

Ben glared at her, as though his sister were under attack.

'Lyta,' Kit said, his admonishment making it worse. How could he be so calm? Hadn't he just seen what she'd seen?

Ben answered for his sister. 'The divine. She channels it, and not without great cost. This is how you are still with us. Beatriz healed you. And now she's healed him. She can't help herself. She reaches out even without thinking to those in pain, easing suffering, healing ills. It's in her nature. You are already very demanding on her energies, all of you.'

'I've asked for nothing,' Kit protested.

'You don't have to ask, Kit,' Beatriz murmured.

Kit shuddered and dropped his gaze, wrapping his hand around his injured arm guiltily.

'How?' Lyta went on, unrepentant. She wanted an answer.

'What do you know of the old gods?'

She shifted, not sure she wanted to answer that. 'Just stories. Most of them ran away or hid, but a few made a stand against the Church Imperial. They were defeated. Those that weren't killed and fed to the Nether were bound. Locked away. The gods of Amberes for example. All except Eninn.' She grabbed her pendant and held it close. Eninn the Trickster had been the only one to escape, or so they said. She didn't know how or why. '*Ystara threw her light into the sky and lit the far north for a single moment but only Eninn escaped with his heart and his wit.* That's what everyone says.'

THE BOOK OF GOLD

Ben brushed his slender hand over his sister's hair. 'Eninn escaped with his heart and his wit,' he echoed. 'It's actually as simple as that, and of course, so much more complex.'

'You're not Eninn.' She couldn't keep the scorn out of her voice. She knew her god too well to miss a connection like that. She had seen him just tonight and there was no resemblance to either of the Alvarez siblings. They held no trace of him as she knew him. And she did know him.

Ben barked out a bitter laugh. 'Not at all. We're as human and as mortal as you and Sylvian are. But he guides us. We can sometimes touch his power. Or are touched by it. It fills us. There are few gods left to us these days, so we know him. We are called *Aspects*, those who can embody a god, or a piece of their power. Their shadows, or echoes. Their memories made flesh. Once we were their priests, druids or emissaries, their acolytes and some even thought us their incarnations or avatars. But we are very much human. More than chosen, but far less than gods. Anyway, most of the gods are gone these days. The Church saw to that. A thousand-year crusade to wipe them out and steal their power. Caput Mundi will not rest until the August One is the only god left, and all serve the Imperator. But there are still a few free gods in our world, or gods who can still reach us. Eninn is one of them.'

Kit interrupted. 'But you were in the Tower. *You* served the Imperator.'

Ben froze and a shadow passed over his face, memories of something terrible evident in his eyes. Then he scowled, chasing them away. 'Not willingly. I went in looking for secrets and I got myself tangled in his web. They wanted me to join them. He wanted . . . The Magister is . . . He has powers gleaned from years of study, gifts from the Imperator. He's stronger than me. Much stronger. He said I had potential to be more and I listened. I shouldn't have but I . . . I got lost for a time.' Doubt seeped back into his features and then he shook his head. Whatever had happened to him in there, it had left deep scars. Lyta had seen that look before, often on those who had got out of Old Steen, or had served in Francisco's wars in

Aquitaine and Burgundy, or on some of the poor broken souls from the brothels. She swore under her breath, and Ben smiled and waved his hand, as if trying to cast off concern. 'We're not all-powerful. We have limits. So do those gods we can contact. They were beyond count once, now . . .' He shrugged. 'Beatriz has done much for you in the last few days, both in healing you and showing you the truth. She's even providing a roof over your head, Lyta Cornellis. And look at the cost.'

Beatriz gave him a hard look of her own. 'I'll be fine. I just need a moment.'

'It'll take you days to recover and you know it. It's not like you're going to strengthen yourself by stealing power through blood. Or is that why you wanted me back?'

'Ben!' Beatriz's eyes widened in horrified outrage.

The priests of old spilled blood at the blink of an eye, or so the stories said. And worse. Sacrifice or vengeance or any excuse really. Many of the old gods had been hungry and more than a few people suggested that their demise had not been an entirely bad thing. But the Church Imperial had written those histories, told those tales. Lyta had always thought they had to be an exaggeration. Now she wasn't so sure.

Beatriz smoothed down her skirts like a bird trying to straighten ruffled feathers. 'I would never do such a thing and you know it. You're angry with yourself. Not me. And not them.'

But Ben wasn't finished. He looked like Kit when he was upset with Lyta, when he accused her of trying to run his life or disrupt his business. Oh, she knew that particular expression too well.

'Why, Beatriz? Why bother with this? This is a fool's errand for a king who wants a trophy. And even if we get what he wants, he won't thank us. He probably won't let us near it. You know it as well as I do. He's using us. Or someone is.'

Before he knew what was happening, his sister pulled him into an embrace.

'That's my fierce little brother back again,' Beatriz murmured. 'I thought I'd lost you. I missed you, Ben. So much.'

Ben groaned in protest, but didn't pull away from her.

The moment was interrupted by Sylvian's low murmur as he opened his eyes.

'Where's the boy?' he tried to say. His voice came out as no more than a guttural croak, half the sounds smothered in pain. He sounded broken. And so tired. But she couldn't miss the last word.

'The boy?'

'Temple. Boy.' He tried to sit up, but she pushed him back down with a terrifying lack of effort. He slumped beneath her hand and his eyes drifted closed again.

'The boy who led us there? Did you see him, Syl?' He couldn't have known Eninn, could he?

But Sylvian was gone, slipping back into Beatriz's enchanted sleep. Slowly, Lyta turned her attention back to the Alvarez siblings. Beatriz was smiling gently, exhaustion still lining her face. 'He turns up from time to time,' she said fondly. 'When he's needed. Just a nudge or a prod really. A guiding hand. He can't do much more.'

The pendant bit into Lyta's hand. 'That boy was Eninn.' It felt wrong to say it out loud, to admit what she knew. It had always been her secret. That was their deal, their agreement. He guided her; she kept quiet about him.

'Why not?' asked Ben. He stood behind Beatriz now, his hands resting on her shoulders, his frustration apparently gone again. 'He's a god. Not a very powerful one, but still a god. He does as he wills. But it drains him, appearing in the mortal world. After this we won't see him for . . . I don't know. Years probably.'

'For this mission,' Beatriz reminded him, 'nothing is too much. It means more to him than we can know. He has plans within plans, and I think he is already doing far more than any of us realise. He always provides for those who are true to him. Now, it is late, and I truly am tired. And, no, Ben, I will not turn to the bloodthirsty ways of our forebears. Rest, good food, sunshine and light exercise will do instead. Rooms are ready for you all, so please, make use of them. Let Sylvian rest here and my servants will watch over him tonight. Ben, if you will?'

She extended her hand and her brother helped her from the room without so much as a backwards glance.

Lyta watched them go, saw Kit positively fold himself back from the door to get out of their way. He was spooked, like a colt ready to run at any minute. Gods. Magic. Anything of that sort had always freaked him out. She didn't blame him. Kit liked what he could see, touch and know to be real.

'A night's sleep is a good idea,' she said, glancing at Sylvian. His eyes were closed again but he was breathing evenly now. 'You head up. I'll watch him.'

Kit raised an eyebrow without saying a word. He hadn't moved from the doorway.

'Leave off,' she warned him and to her relief she was rewarded with a half-smile. 'You heard what Beatriz said. He has to sleep. Whatever she did will see to that.' The flicker in his face again, that disquiet, discomfort. 'You don't like them.'

'It's not that,' he said. 'I don't . . . I knew there was something off about them. All that talk about blood, sacrifice and power? Don't you feel it? How can we trust them? They're nobility to start with. We're already disposable to them, without the rest of it.'

Perhaps it was just her own exhaustion – the last few days had turned everything in her life on its head – but she didn't have the strength to argue with him.

'I feel that way about everyone except you and Frida, so I'm not the best judge.'

'And him? You trust him now?'

Her lips twitched into something like a smile. 'Definitely not him. I'll be careful, Kit. I promise.'

'It didn't look that way earlier, Lyta.'

'I'm right here, you know?' Sylvian whispered from the chaise longue. Lyta scowled at Kit and finished that line of conversation. So much for enchanted slumber then. He was fighting it. Typical.

'So you are,' she told Sylvian. 'I almost forgot. You were so quiet for a change. You're meant to be asleep, Beatriz said.'

'Not a child,' he replied, sounding for all the world like an exhausted toddler and she grinned.

'So why keep looking for trouble?'

He let out a heavy sigh and his body shuddered. Beatriz may have healed the worst, but she hadn't managed everything. He was wrung-out and his voice still sounded like he'd been swallowing nails. 'That's your job.'

'It's both of yours,' Kit interrupted curtly. 'Are you really sure about this, Lyta?'

Lyta pulled over a chair and started settling herself for the night.

Sylvian's eyes opened again and fixed on her. They were so beautiful, his eyes. Dark, with lashes a courtesan would kill for. Gods, she'd managed to erase all thoughts of him like that before he had showed up in Amberes again. And here he was, turning her world upside down. Just when she thought she had finally managed to get over him.

But when she'd seen him hanging there . . .

Lyta winced and saw him frown, as if he was reading her mind.

'I'm sorry,' he whispered. 'I'm sorry for what I said. What I did. Sorry for everything. Should have said that . . . a thousand times.'

Perhaps he even meant it. The words set something barbed spiralling in her chest. She wanted to believe him. Oh Eninn knew how much she wanted to. But she didn't dare.

His eyes closed again as he drifted back to unconsciousness and Lyta finally let the tears lurking behind her eyes spill out. She looked up as the door closed and realised that Kit was gone. All she could do was wait here, wait for Sylvian, make sure he was all right.

When the servants came in, she sent them away.

The night dragged onwards, the fire died to embers and still he slept. His breath grew deep and even and she watched as pain played over his features, the echoes of a nightmare. He stirred and Lyta reached out, pressing her hand to his forehead.

'I'm here, Sylvian,' she murmured. 'Just rest.'

At the sound of her voice, at her touch, he settled again, but the moment she moved away, he made a noise that sounded like fear.

She'd never thought to hear that, not from him. The Syl she had known wasn't afraid of anything. But this man was not the same. He'd seen things.

His hand closed on her wrist, encircling it entirely, as strong as any manacle. Lyta tried to pull back, but he didn't let her go, and the moment she moved, fear bled into his face again.

She couldn't leave him. Not like this.

Carefully, she shifted closer and sat on the edge of the chaise longue beside him, stroking his midnight hair with her free hand until he quietened again. But he didn't let her go.

Eventually her own tiredness overcame her. She lay down beside him and he shifted, curling around her, holding her against him.

She was just doing it to keep him quiet, she told herself. Just helping him fight his demons, to calm him and soothe his nightmares. So he could rest and recover. So Beatriz's magic could work properly.

It wasn't because it felt good to lie like this again, to feel him stretched out along the length of her, his body moulding to the curves and hollows of her own.

Lyta closed her eyes and dreamed of things for which she had long ago given up all hope.

CHAPTER THIRTEEN

Kit

It was easier to slip away. Kit knew how this was going to turn out and he had no wish to see his sister plunge herself into the hell of her grief again. It had been hard enough on her losing Sylvian the first time. And now the stakes were so much higher. She'd made a deal with a king.

Nobility were not to be trusted. Why did no one understand that except him? The duchess had never looked after the city, just herself and her own pockets. Why would the king be any different? Kit had been an idiot to think otherwise. Standing there in that courtroom, hoping to plead with him, to convince him that the city needed his help – he had been a stupid, naive fool. They'd dismissed him, just like that, and left him to the tender mercies of the duchess.

Kit closed the outer gate behind him and stepped into the night. Into the early morning really. The first knell of Cissonia sounded as the light began to change, illuminating the wet streets. Not even proper sunrise, not yet. But cities like Amberes didn't just run by daylight. Business began long before dawn and continued far into the night. It never stopped and Cissonia oversaw it all. He wondered absently if the goddess the bell was named for had ever been as dutiful as her namesake.

Down at the labour market, men would already be gathering in hope of work, either on the ships or in the warehouses. They would shuffle around in the cold, their breath misting in front of their faces, waiting until those who might hire them roused themselves from their warm beds and arrived to make their choices. Goddess help the worker who wasn't there before them.

It was bitter and hard, vicious, dog-eat-dog.

Kit hated it. Hated the system under which the city operated, hated the high taxes imposed on everyone, no matter what they earned or how they made a living. Unless they were the ones setting those taxes. Hated the way the guards periodically swept up the homeless and destitute and herded them away. Even the way they took men like Sylvian from the jails and conscripted them into the army. It could have been him too. Or something far worse.

But what could he do about it? He'd tried and failed. It had cost him. It might have cost him everything.

He rubbed his arm where it was still bandaged, the skin itching like fury. He didn't know what it had cost him. Not yet. Not really.

All Kit wanted was to make his world better. But everything conspired against him. Every single time.

'Master Cornellis?' The voice calling him was accompanied by footsteps, hurrying down the road behind him. Kit spun around to find Ben running after him. The last thing he wanted. All that talk of gods and power, whatever Beatriz had done to heal Sylvian, and apparently Lyta as well, after the fire . . .

Ben had powers too. He had to. That was why the Magister wanted him. As a tool, as an oddity, as something to study. Perhaps that was what Kit sensed in him. Nothing else. Maybe that explained the pull he felt towards him.

He wanted to put as much distance between himself and the Alvarez siblings as he could, so he clenched his teeth and kept walking. That didn't deter Ben though, who fell into step beside him moments later.

Where had the timid scholar gone? In rescuing him, they had created a monster. A persistent, determined, beautiful monster.

'Where are you going?'

'Home.'

'Oh, I—' Ben faltered and then tried again. 'My sister offered a room for the night. For the duration of this mission. Perhaps you misunder—'

'No.'

Why wouldn't he take the hint? Kit wanted nothing to do with them, or their mission, or whatever Lyta had got herself dragged into. A mission! It wasn't a mission, no matter how many times they said it. It was a heist. Or a con, if Lyta was involved. It had to be.

It was also none of his business. Even if it was his fault.

He shook that thought away, but it wouldn't let him go. It was all his fault. Lyta wouldn't have offered to help the king if it hadn't been for him. And all it had got them was misery. Janlow had almost killed Sylvian. If they had arrived even seconds later . . . Kit put his head down and walked faster.

Ben didn't stop or turn back, simply sped up his pace to match Kit's. It was deeply annoying. Almost a Lyta-level of irritating. Worse, because Ben had no call to be there, none at all.

'You didn't live with your sister then?' he asked. 'I thought her house—'

'I have a workshop and a room above it of my own, down between Book Alley and Preachers' Street. And I guess I'll have to find somewhere for Lyta now. I don't know.'

'She's very welcome to stay with us.'

Kit snorted out a laugh. He couldn't help himself. 'Yeah, for now.'

'No, Beatriz would never cast someone out. Not when they were in need.'

'In need? Oh, Ben.' He couldn't help but laugh. 'Lyta will never be in need. She will always fall on her feet, usually in new boots. Besides, this is a business arrangement, isn't it? It'll come to an end one way or the other. Everyone involved has been put in play by the king. Except me. And I want no part of it. You'll be glad to be rid of us. Everyone is, eventually.'

'But what if we . . . what if we *need* you?'

Kit stopped so fast that Ben kept going a few strides ahead of him. When he turned back, Kit had already folded his arms, doing his best to look as physically intimidating as he could. He was a big man, he knew that, broad-shouldered, muscled from hard work.

He had faced down pushy clients, cheating suppliers and any number of rebellious employees over the years.

Ben's hazel eyes grew large in his delicate face. He pulled his cloak a little tighter.

'You don't need me,' Kit told him firmly. 'You have Lyta and Sylvian. And now they have you, to do whatever you do.' He didn't mean it to sound so scathing, but Ben winced and Kit ploughed on, trying to ignore that. 'And I'm sure Frida will be involved in whatever scheme my sister concocts with yours. She usually is. Nothing comes between the two of them.'

'You were the one who got me out of the tower though.' He whispered the sentence, so softly that Kit wasn't sure he heard him correctly at first.

'What?'

'You made me leave. If you hadn't, I'd still be there. Still . . .' Ben drew in a shuddering breath. 'I can't describe what it was like. I was lost in there. I went in to look for a particular copy of the *Corpus Hermeticum*. I had to get the permission of the Magister to access it of course, and we ended up discussing so much of the hidden learning before he let me have even a glimpse of it.' His eyes shone with the wonder of whatever he'd read. 'It was wonderful, Kit. So fragile and yet so beautiful. The colours, the gilding and the secrets hidden there. And then I thought I'd just study some of the other texts held there when they offered, and then I just . . . I couldn't seem to remember that I could leave. The Magister was insistent that he needed my input. He always wanted . . .' Words failed him for a moment and Kit wondered what he was trying to hide. Nothing good. 'There was always something else to read, another manuscript, and so many books thought lost or forgotten, or a discussion with the Magister. I started a study of the Divine Nexus and—' His face flushed, and he turned away.

Kit frowned. He'd never heard the term before, but it meant something to Ben.

'You mentioned that before, when we found you. What is it?'

Ben took the olive branch offered with enthusiasm. 'It's a kind of Aspect, one which draws gods, like a lodestone. I was making a study and the Magister said—' Ben's shoulders trembled suddenly and he went pale, his eyes misting with dark memories. 'That's not the point. He was using my studies to lure me in. I was an idiot. It was an enchantment.'

An enchantment. As if he'd had no choice. What had happened to him in there? Kit forced himself not to think about it. Ben clearly didn't want to.

'And you couldn't break that? If you and your sister have the powers, you said—'

'*She* does. Not me. I'm just . . .' Ben trailed off and Kit felt an unexpected wave of sympathy. 'I'm just good with words.' He winced. 'Sometimes. Not now, obviously.'

Kit took pity on him, swinging the conversation back to where Ben was comfortable, more at ease. 'A Divine Nexus? How does that work?'

'There's a story, a prophecy. The Divine Nexus is something or someone which draws gods to it, which can harness divine power. The Church is obsessed with it. They want to use it in their crusade. The Magister seemed to think it related to me somehow. It's more likely to be Beatriz, of course, but he can't conceive of a woman wielding the type of power my sister does. And I'd rather keep it that way. It's safer for her. He pinpointed Amberes as the location, the place where the last gods still linger.' Ben frowned. 'Why do you keep changing the subject?'

Because he wanted Ben to leave him alone. Kit shook his head and started walking again. 'I'm just trying to go back home. I have work to check on, things to do. You have Lyta. You don't need me. My sister and I are nothing like you and Beatriz.'

'I think you are,' Ben said, still following him. 'Lyta raised you, didn't she? They're strong, the two of them, and determined. They've done everything to keep us safe all our lives. And we had to be just as strong, and even more determined if we wanted to get anywhere. They want to protect us but sometimes . . . it's too much. They made us what we are.'

There was a thought. One Kit did not want to entertain. Ben sounded so sincere, as if he wanted it to be true. But Kit had spent years pulling away from Lyta, from the chaos she chose. From all the consequences of her actions.

When they reached the printshop everything was in darkness. Kit unlocked the door and lit a lantern. The presses stood like great scaffolds in the shadows and the cases of letters had been neatly put away, all the drawers closed. Kit could always rely on Jem and the apprentices to keep the place in order. Jem had been a journeyman bookbinder alongside him, before he branched out into printing, and had stuck with him since he'd taken over from Master Yellen. Together they had made this place a success after the old man retired and it had gone from strength to strength in a few years. Add to that the financial acumen of Molly, Jem's wife, who acted as their bookkeeper, and the printshop was thriving. They'd need to move somewhere bigger soon, somewhere more respectable like Lombard's Street or Brewers' Gate.

If truth be told, Kit sometimes feared they needed him in name only. The sign of *Typis Cornellis* on the books was becoming a mark of high quality and good content. Master Yellen had transferred the licence to Kit's name when he stepped down and Jem had been fine with that. He didn't need the responsibility if something went wrong, he said. Prescient words.

As it promptly had gone wrong last week. Pamphlets questioning the new taxes the duchess had imposed, to pay for the reception of the king, had been printed here and bore Kit's mark. And even though Kit agreed with every word, he hadn't known about them until it was far too late.

He still needed to have that out with Jem. But his arrest and everything else had got in the way of that conversation.

It might not even have been Jem. It could have been one of the boys. It could have been a dare, or a bribe. It could have been a competitor, because industrial espionage was rife in Amberes. And it could have been a trap for Kit himself.

He could have turned one of them in, or at least cast suspicion elsewhere. But he'd never do that. He could have pleaded innocence but who would listen to him?

No, he'd assured the guildmembers and the lesser aldermen who had supported him at first, he'd stand there and speak for them. All they had to do was be there to support him. He had been so stupid.

Not one of them had spoken up on his behalf. He'd stood alone, for the brief while he'd managed to remain standing. Only Lyta had come. How she had found out he didn't know, and though he would never admit it to her, he'd never been quite so glad to see her face.

Kit stood in his workshop, holding the lamp too tightly, and fought back the moments of terror that had haunted him ever since.

Blood brings power, the duchess had said. *Blood binds. Blood is power.*

Ben himself had talked about the old ways of blood Beatriz could have used to strengthen herself, or steal power from someone else. Ben had sensed that something was wrong with Kit's arm from the moment they met. And then there was Beatriz and the way she looked at him, the compassion in her eyes bordering on pity. That strange uncanny feeling that came over him when she was near.

They knew. He knew.

'Are you all right?' Ben asked. He took the lamp from Kit's now unresisting grip, and Kit closed his fingers into a fist instead, dropping it to his side. He couldn't raise it against Ben Alvarez. Not if his life depended on it. He couldn't say why.

'I'm fine.' He felt taut as a bowstring. Something hitched in his throat.

Such a terrible liar, Kit, Lyta always teased. She would know.

Ben closed the door behind them and stepped into Kit's workshop, the look of wonder on his face illuminated by the lamplight.

'It's beautiful.'

Beautiful. Not a word anyone would normally use about the printshop. Except for Kit himself. For everyone else it was work, an income, a steady and reliable job. A place of toil and sweat. Behind it, the other room formed the bindery and the air there hung heavy with the scent of leather and beeswax. But the print room, not so much. The ink was acrid and sharp, the cotton-rich paper carried a fresh, almost vanilla smell to it. And vellum of course was something else, animal skin treated with lime, and that carried distinct odours of its own.

They were his life, his livelihood. He breathed them in as he breathed in the air itself.

The wooden frames of the printing presses – only two of them for now, but one day he would expand and there would be more – were oak, great beams of it taller than he was, bolted to the floor and the ceiling, so they wouldn't move. Each stood like a door frame with a press mounted in it, over a tray in which the galleys would be set. Little metal letters on the moveable type squares could be arranged in any way imaginable, and he had collected a large number of different typefaces. He even had new ones being made right now. When he had decided on the text, he set the type in order in galleys, rearranging them until they were perfect. He agonised over it. The right words, the right font, the right layout. Everything told a story.

When the galley was complete, it was inked, the paper was placed over it and the press lowered by a lever which turned a huge wooden screw. It worked just like a press for wine or oil, pushing the paper to his studiously arranged and inked galleys, creating the pages. Then another sheet of paper, then another. They printed multiple pages onto each sheet so they could be folded into quires, ready to be sewn together and bound. Each copy as crisp and fresh and identical as the last. He made sure of that. The finest paper, the best quality ink, all the care and dedication that led to their reputation for craftsmanship, as one of the best in Amberes and far beyond.

People from all over the world sought out his books. Typis Cornellis meant something. It stood for something. Something good.

Ben ran his inquisitive fingers over the wooden frame, almost like a caress. He peered at the screw controlling the press and the lever controlling the screw. Kit could see his mind working, his eyes bright with interest and unspoken questions.

But instead of asking, Ben put down the lamp and turned his solemn gaze on Kit. What he said was unexpected and the worst thing Kit could possibly imagine.

'Let me see your arm.'

Without knowing why, Kit backed up against the door. But Ben had closed it already and there was nowhere to go.

'There's nothing—'

'We both know that's not true.' Ben advanced on him, holding out his hands. 'Please, Kit. It's important. I don't know who marked you, but I think it's dangerous. There's magic tangled around you, dark magic, blood magic. Bea sensed it too, but you won't let her near you. Why is that?'

Kit squirmed. 'How do you know any of that?'

All the same he didn't pull away when Ben took his hand, lifted it and then turned it over so the back of his forearm was exposed where the shirt rode up. The bandages came apart under his insistent fingers and Ben gave a small hiss of distaste.

The scar that had formed was still red and pronounced in the dim light. It looked like a letter in a language Kit couldn't hope to read.

'Well, I didn't know. Not for sure,' Ben murmured, peering closer at it. 'But I do now. I told you. I know words. Can you feel it? Does it hurt?'

'Yes. Sometimes. When your sister's around mostly.'

Ben nodded, still studying it. His fingertips brushed lightly against Kit's skin, sending shivers like electricity running through him. 'She would reach out to try to heal you, I think unconsciously. She can't help it sometimes. And this—' He touched the scar tentatively, as if poking a wasps' nest. 'This would fight back.'

The cold snaked up Kit's arm and he tried to pull away again. Ben didn't release him but looked up into Kit's eyes and that was that. Kit's breath caught in the back of his throat.

'Who marked you, Kit?' Ben asked it in a kindly tone, but there was an insistence behind the words, a determination that would not be denied.

Kit swallowed, tugged his arm free, but there was still nowhere to go. Ben was standing right up against him, their bodies almost touching. The door was hard and unyielding behind him.

'I— I— She—' The words wouldn't come. Why wouldn't they come? What was wrong with him? What was the mark and what was it doing to him?

Ben moved, his hand soft on Kit's cheek, so gentle, the fingertips a torture. Did he even realise what he was doing? He looked completely oblivious to the effect he was having on Kit, and it wasn't fair. Kit was just a puzzle to him, something to be solved.

Why was he even thinking like this? They barely knew each other. And Kit wanted nothing to do with him or his sister and their weird magic.

Kit wasn't a stranger to desire, but relationships were beyond him. He'd seen what love did to Lyta and Syl all those years ago, and wanted no part of it. Sex was one thing, but never more than a drunken fumble and a quick goodbye. He didn't trust anyone. He didn't have time. His work was everything.

'Kit,' Ben whispered, dragging his spiralling thoughts back to the here and now, quelling his panic. 'Just breathe. It's going to be all right. I promise. I'll figure it out. Just breathe.'

Air filled his lungs and he felt dizzy with relief. The words, Ben's words, gave him hope for the first time in days. A desperate thought filled his mind: maybe Ben really could help.

The door bucked behind him and someone cursed, shoving harder. The force flung Kit forward into Ben and the two of them toppled to the ground, tangled together. At the last minute, Kit braced his arms and stopped himself from crushing the scholar completely. He hung there, staring down at a pair of hazel eyes that stole all his common sense and a pair of lips he could never, ever kiss. The man was nobility, everything Kit despised. He was some kind of source of magic, a channel to the gods, if he was to be believed. No, he could not kiss Ben Alvarez. But gods, he wanted to. And more. So much more.

'Kit?' Jem said from the now open doorway, his voice full of confusion. 'What are you—?'

Kit's face flamed hot and his stomach contorted. He scrambled up, refusing to look at Ben again.

'It's all right, Jem. We just— I came in early to check things.'

There was a long and painful silence 'Things?' Jem said at last, eyeing Ben curiously. His accent still carried the lilt of Mwene we Mutapa, even after so many years in Amberes, the same way the burnished-bronze tones of his skin would never fade, even under the pale Brabantine sun.

This was not what Kit needed at all. His friend would never let him live this down. And he'd tell his wife who would be all questions. She was determined to see Kit settled down with someone. Man or woman. She didn't care. Molly loved to matchmake and lately she'd been eyeing Kit as her one great failure.

'This is Ben,' Kit said, flustered. 'Ben, this is Jem Nyati.' What was he saying? He sounded like an infant, an idiot. 'My bookbinder. This is Ben, who's my . . .' *Not my anything. He's not mine.* Gods and goddesses of old, what was he doing? 'A family friend.'

Ben half-smiled at him, as if harbouring some secret joke. It was stupidly attractive and Kit didn't know where to look, so he stared at the ceiling and tried to stop his face going scarlet by sheer will alone. Ben turned on the bookbinder with a smoothness Kit wouldn't have thought possible. 'I'm a scholar. Kit was good enough to show me the premises. We're considering working together on some translations of older manuscripts.'

Jem huffed out a sound Kit couldn't interpret, but he sounded satisfied enough. 'We could do with a few more experts around here, that's for sure. You all right, Kit? After all the—' He waved his hand in the air.

'The what?' Kit asked, mystified. At least his heart had slowed down again.

Jem looked uncomfortable. 'The arrest?'

'Oh, yes. Yes, fine now. We've . . . that is, Lyta sorted something out.'

The bookbinder laughed as he wandered off to set up the bindery before the apprentices came in. 'Oh yeah, she would. That's good news. We still have a licence then?'

'I guess so,' Kit replied. To be honest he had no idea anymore, but now was not the time to tell anyone they could all be out of a job.

'Better get to work then.'

Jem closed the door somewhat pointedly, leaving Ben and Kit alone again. For a little while at least.

'What is it?' Kit asked, once he was sure Jem had gone. 'The mark? What does it mean?'

'That someone tried to bind you to their will with some powerful magic. Blood magic. Ancient runes. But it isn't fully active. Not yet. It's just a link. It's stopping you naming them maybe, but I should be able to find a way to neutralise it. If you want?'

What a thing to ask. 'Of course I *want*.' The word caught in his throat. He wanted a lot of things. But nothing could come of it. Nothing good. Ben came from a noble line older than kingdoms. Kit came from the gutter.

And Ben didn't know, clearly, the effect he was having on Kit. He couldn't. He just nodded slowly, as if turning the problem over in his mind.

'I'll help. But I want your help in return. I'm not going to Montalbeau without you. You're needed too.'

'How am I needed? I'm not a criminal. Lyta's world isn't my world and . . . I'm a liability, Ben.' How could he go right into the stronghold of the woman who had done this to him? Especially when he couldn't seem to tell anyone what had happened, never mind who had done it.

'No, you aren't. I don't know what you are. Not yet. But I don't think you should be on your own. Just in case.'

Ben dug out the notebook from his pocket. He slid a graphite stylus from the loop on the edge and began to make notes, wandering over to the corner as if Kit wasn't there anymore. He settled himself down to work, his back to the wall and his legs stretched out. Almost like a cat. Sitting where he would, minding his own business, ignoring the rest of the world.

Somehow the decision had been made. Kit didn't seem to get much of a say in it.

Since Ben wasn't going anywhere yet, Kit might as well get started on his own job. The conversation was clearly over. He'd have to work around him.

Not that he was in the way.

In fact, he slotted in here very comfortably. As if he belonged.

No. Stop it, Kit warned himself. But his eyes strayed back to the scholar, worrying the end of his stylus with those lips. Easier said than done.

Kit's mind remained a jumble of emotions, of which the object of his attention was entirely oblivious. This was stupid. *He* was stupid. He had to put Alvarez out of his mind as firmly as possible.

And fast.

CHAPTER FOURTEEN

Sylvian

Sylvian dreamed of long ago, of war and murder and death, of blood spilling on the ground. Of kneeling on the cell floor, the lash burning his back. Of Lyta turning away.

Him. I'm taking him.

Of the initiation into the royal bodyguards, swearing his oath and shedding his blood. Of the battles and the assassination attempts and all the nightmares in between.

Her hand on his face, her touch. Something else from long ago. A dream he had never quite shaken off. Her scent, her warmth. The thing that had kept him going, through all the times his nightmares became real.

He wrapped himself around her, pulled her against him and inhaled her.

Lyta. It was Lyta. All was Lyta. She was all he needed. All he had ever needed. His Lyta.

Even though she'd forgotten him and married Ranulf. Even though she was far out of his reach. Even though . . .

He closed his arms and there was a body, her body. He opened his eyes to see a blur of auburn hair and her soft sleeping form.

Like he'd conjured her out of all those fervent dreams. Like he'd somehow wished hard enough to make her real again. And put her in his arms. Beside him.

Wrapped in his embrace.

Lyta stirred, murmuring something and Sylvian drew back, detaching himself from her as carefully and as gently as he could. He had to.

He recognised the room. They were in Beatriz's house, in the room where he had carried Lyta after the fire, when he first brought her here, the parlour overlooking the river with its fireplace and its expensive furniture. But he didn't remember how he'd got here this time.

The temple. Janlow. And the rope around his neck. Choking. Kicking. The darkness closing in on him.

And then . . .

As he sat up, careful not to disturb her, his head swam, his body still aching. But he had to get up. He had to get himself away from her. He couldn't risk staying there.

Not so close to her. Not now.

Sylvian slid to the end of the chaise longue and bent forward, his head in his hands hanging down between his knees.

Lyta shifted and he forced himself to his feet.

She rolled over in her sleep, her red hair spreading out across the expensive fabric. She had never looked more beautiful. There was a strength in her face now that hadn't been there all those years ago.

A hardness too. Had he put that there?

No, not just him.

She'd come to save him last night. He hadn't deserved it. He had done nothing but cause her pain and suffering. He'd just hurt her over and over again.

But she'd still come. She'd held him. Comforted him.

He remembered now.

It was enough to send him fleeing down the stairs to the courtyard and freedom. He should go far away. Back to the barracks. Back to the palace to plead with Francisco, to grovel and beg him for release from this mission.

Even though he knew his king would never do that.

'Captain Chant?' Beatriz's voice called from the courtyard as he entered it. 'Sylvian? Are you feeling better already?'

He wasn't. He really wasn't. But that wasn't what she meant. She was talking about his health. He knew that.

She sat in the sunshine, surrounded by leafy ferns and flowering plants in brightly coloured pots, like a blossom herself. Her breakfast had been served on a small enamelled table: delicate little pastries and fragrant mint tea in jewel-coloured glasses.

There was nothing he could do but stop and bow. Every duty and every rule of chivalry and hospitality demanded that he do so. Beatriz looked as beautiful as ever, her skin aglow in the morning sunlight.

'My lady,' he said, as calmly as he could. 'I believe I owe you thanks for saving my life.'

'I believe the person you should thank is still in the parlour,' she replied, with an arched brow. 'I didn't want to disturb you this morning. Perhaps a bath and a change of clothes is in order?'

He winced. He probably stank. And his clothes were more than a day old now. 'I need to go back to my barracks, report in and—'

'Running away already?' she said with a soft laugh. 'Of course, off you go. The gods forbid you should fail to report back. You know, eventually, you will have to talk to her. Have an actual conversation. You *do* know that, don't you?'

He did. Of course he did. But enough things had been said already and he didn't know how to make it right again. Because even after everything he'd said to her, everything he'd done, she'd still come for him and saved his life. When he truly needed her. She might have left him in Old Steen, but now he knew why it was hard to blame her. And that was his fault too.

Beatriz waved him away and told him to come back when he was more fragrant and in a better mood. It felt worse than being dismissed in disgrace by the general, but he took the opportunity to flee while he could.

Morning in Amberes was as loud as ever, a circus of trade and negotiation, of barter and arguments, of cargos being transferred and wagons rolling out in every direction, of ships setting sail, heavy-laden. The temperature had dropped with the night's rain. Sylvian picked his route with some care, far more than he had taken last night and kept his wits well and truly about him this time. But the walk was uneventful and the barracks guards greeted him smartly as he entered.

'What happened to you?' Torren said as Sylvian tried to slip past them, but his brothers-in-arms were not to be ignored. They were clearly enjoying their morning off-duty, sprawled on benches in the mess hall with a greasy fry-up each. The food turned his stomach and Sylvian pushed by them, which inevitably brought all of them after him.

'Chant?' Montes reached him first, the dark-skinned soldier from Cordova frowning at him. 'You look like hell.'

'You should see the other guy,' he replied, hoping to bluff it out. It didn't work. Of course it didn't. They knew him better than anyone. They had been through hell together more times than he could remember – at the siege of Vermand, where men had run savage and set the city aflame, and again at the battle of Gravenenga, pinned under heavy cannon fire, bogged down in mud and fighting hand to hand to defend Francisco, all while they strove to secure their king's throne in the Brabantine and beyond. They had lost friends closer than the blood they shed together.

'What in the name of the lost gods—?' Juárez grabbed his shoulders, stopping his retreat. 'Did your lady love decide to finish the job she started when you left this shithole?'

'She's not my—' The words stuck in his throat. 'I wouldn't be here if she hadn't—'

The others exchanged a knowing look. He hated them for it.

'Go clean up,' Montes told him. 'I'll fetch a healer.'

'I've seen one. I'm fine. Please, just leave it.'

He pulled free, stalking away from them, relieved they appeared to let him go on alone. He fled to the communal bathhouse, which at this time of the morning was blissfully empty. Quiet and the sound of moving water swept over him, soothing him. He closed his eyes and breathed.

For the first time in days, he felt the knots in his shoulders beginning to untie themselves a little. Here, he felt safe. He tossed his clothes in the laundry and stepped into the pool, sinking up to his neck in the warm mineral-rich water. He sat back against the patterned tiles and closed his eyes.

'What were you doing?' General Vasquez's voice boomed out, a voice far louder than anyone would guess could come out of her slight form. It didn't pay to underestimate her, he knew that. They'd gone straight to her, his so-called brothers-in-arms. They'd run straight to the only mother figure who would acknowledge any of them. The bastards.

Sylvian shot to attention. But the general, her face like stone, hardened from years of battle and war, didn't even react to his naked body jolting from the water.

'General,' he barked.

'Report, Captain Chant.'

Here? Now? Like this? But he had learned not to argue with her. It never ended well.

'I'm under orders from the king. A special mission. I'm to report to—'

'I am aware of that. I want to know what happened to you. Look at yourself.'

If she thought this was bad, she should have seen him last night. But he didn't have the nerve to say that to her either.

'There was an altercation with a group of local thugs. I knew them back in the day. Old grudges. It is dealt with, ma'am.'

It wasn't – not yet – but it would be. He'd see to that. He was going to relish pounding Petrus Janlow back into the gutter where he belonged.

Vasquez scowled at him, disbelief written all over her face. 'I see. This wretched city is a wild horse chafing at the bit, just waiting for a chance to bite the hand that holds out the apple. Much like you. I want their names and descriptions. I want everything you know about them. I'll deal with this myself.'

'Ma'am, there's no need to—'

'An attack on one of my officers is an attack on us all. I will not have it. Especially one on a mission from his Majesty. Do you need backup?'

Sylvian shook his head. 'No ma'am. I have backup.' Lyta could be described as backup, couldn't she? Sort of.

She had saved him last night, his treacherous mind whispered.

The general huffed out a dismissive breath. 'I heard about your *backup* in excruciating detail. Don't look surprised, Chant. Do you think I'd let you just go off with a woman like that, with your history together? But the king has made his opinion clear. He thinks she's a marvel. I think she's a nightmare. And I can see exactly who is right. You've been to a healer, Juárez said. At least there's that. Maybe you haven't lost all sense. Get some clothes on and follow me. Now.'

There was nothing he could do but obey, even if the only thing available to wear were the basic bathhouse clothes, loose pants and a lightly tied robe designed for movement between areas. It would have to do.

The general stalked down the corridor and up the stairs, Sylvian trailing in her wake, aware of the fascinated and confused gazes following him. Rumours would no doubt be flying around in no time. They always were. Guards gossiped like market traders. Vasquez reached the door to her office and the men on duty outside it stood sharply to attention, eyes fixed on the far wall.

'Inside,' she snapped, and waited for him to go in ahead of her before she closed the door.

A man was sitting at her desk, leaning back in the chair, looking at a pile of papers. Not just a man. The king.

'This fortress design is beautiful, Vasquez. In the Latinate style. Practical and striking. Who was the architect again?'

'Pietro Tagliapietra, your Majesty, of the Vitruvian Academy in Urbino. It's a bastion fort. Very secure.' The anger drained from her voice. That tone was just for Sylvian it seemed. This was the most eager Sylvian had heard the general sound about anything in years. She really wanted this fortress built. Amberes could do with a citadel. Defending it otherwise would be a nightmare. There were too many points of entry. Take even two of the gates and you controlled a portion of the city.

Francesco smiled at the plan. 'Looks like a star. I imagine the queen would like that.' He finally deigned to notice Sylvian. 'Oh good, you're here. I believe you've had a near-death experience already and you haven't even gone near Montalbeau. Bravo, Captain. Really.'

Sylvian dropped to his knees. It seemed the safer place to be.

Francisco put the paper down and a slow smile spread over his face. 'That bad, is it? Something must have really fucked up somewhere. Want to explain what's taking so long?'

Barely a week if you counted today, which wasn't fair because it wasn't even midday yet.

'These things take time, your Majesty.'

Francisco picked up the letter opener from General Vasquez's desk and began to poke under his pristine fingernails with it.

'The Magister is not happy, Sylvian. It really doesn't do to piss off the Church. Not even I can get away with it. I may not like them, but they are powerful. He wants Alvarez back.'

Sylvian cursed silently. 'What if he doesn't want to go back?'

'That's hardly our problem, is it? Oh, don't look at me like that. Of course I'm not planning to hand a member of House Alvarez to the old fundamentalist if he's unwilling to go. But we need to tread carefully. You're my sworn man, remember? Don't let me down.'

Let him down? Sylvian couldn't do that. It was written in his blood to serve his king, carved into his bones.

'I would never do that, your Majesty.'

Francisco tilted his head to one side like a cat. 'I know, Sylvian. Now, it's time you got dressed in some proper clothes.' His gaze flicked up and down Sylvian's robes disparagingly. 'And time you took your little friends and went to fetch that book for me. No more dilly-dallying, Sylvian. The Church are starting to take notice, and the duchess can hardly be taken by surprise if she sees you coming a mile off. Basic tactics. I want that book, no matter what it takes.'

The king's tone was hard. Sylvian knew him – had seen him at his worst, drenched in blood, roaring out his rage in the middle of a battlefield, blind drunk mourning his brother and his fate, sleeping with half the court in Valladolid – and he knew that when Francisco was in a mood like this, there was no point in trying to argue.

A chill travelled with the thought, something dark and terrible, something that came from far away, that wound itself around the base of Sylvian's brain and squeezed. He didn't have a choice. Francisco knew it and so did he. *Bound to serve* was more than a phrase. So was *no matter what it takes*. 'As you command, my king.'

The king dismissed him with a gesture, no indication that he'd even heard. 'General, I want a word.'

They would be on their own then, once they set off on this forsaken mission. No support from the Crown, or the army. The king could disavow all knowledge of them without blinking an eye. And if it came down to it, any one of them could be sacrificed so long as someone brought him back the book.

Sylvian couldn't leave the room fast enough.

His own clothes felt strange in the place of his uniform. Sylvian made sure he had his weapons on him. He wasn't stupid, and he didn't feel dressed without them. The laws in Amberes were strict on who could bear arms within its walls. If he was stopped by the city watch for carrying weapons without cause, he could send them to Vasquez if he couldn't cow them himself. It was a risk he was willing to take and he had a feeling he was going to need everything he could carry. He took one of the pistols from the armoury, tucked away out of sight, a small plain wheellock far more functional than Francisco's prized weapon, and a pouch of powder, along with another full of lead balls. The leather jerkin had seen better days but was still in good condition. It wasn't armour, but it would do. Slipping into it felt like slipping on an old skin: that of an Amberes lowlife, all swagger and barely suppressed violence.

Which was what he was. Deep down. Even if he'd tried to forget. Even if he'd thought he might become something else. Something better.

The walk back across the city didn't seem to take anywhere near as long. The gate to the Alvarez house opened without a sound and there she was. Lyta, leaning against the wall just inside, watching him. Like she'd been waiting for him.

'About time you got back,' she said. 'We have a plan. If you're coming with us, you might want to hear it.'

Her voice was cold and it took him aback. He thought she'd have questions for him, want to know why he left, or where he'd gone. Might even want to say something about last night.

'Lyta, I—'

She lifted her hand. 'I don't have time for this, whatever you think *this* is,' she told him firmly and walked away.

So that was that then.

It shouldn't have hurt. And she was right. He had a job to do. They both did. There was no room for complications in either of their worlds. Once this job was finished, if they made it back, he would never have to see her again. It was better that way.

When he entered Beatriz's elegant parlour, plans of the fortress had been spread over the table. Kit and Benedictus were already studying them. Beatriz stood by the window, watching with an anxious air while Lyta had joined Frida on the far side of the room beside the bookshelves. As far away from him as she could get.

Sylvian nodded a brief greeting to Frida, who just raised one side of her mouth in a sneer. Well, he'd never liked her much either.

'Can you get him up to speed?' Lyta asked Frida, before turning her attention to the plans and pointing something out to her brother.

Frida looked drawn, not her usual sullen and belligerent self. 'They found Haldevar in the Scaldis.'

'Dead?'

'No, having a swim,' Frida snapped. 'Of *course* dead.' There was pain in her eyes. He knew that look. Damn.

'Who did it?'

'No one knows. It's a mystery. But considering who tried to kill you last night, and probably burned down Lyta's house, I could hazard a guess. Can't you? Thought you were a guard now. Aren't you meant to be out solving mysteries like this?'

A memory stirred. Janlow had mentioned that Lyta had something, something an associate wanted back. Something she'd stolen maybe? Something she might have given to Haldevar. They'd burned down her house. Murdered the fence.

'Not that kind of guard,' he told her, distracted by his thoughts.

'Not much use then, are you?'

He sighed. 'Good to see you too, Frida.'

'Sucks to see your ugly face. But as we can't get rid of you, Lyta has a plan. Ready to do as you're told for a change?'

For a change? When did he ever do anything else? Sylvian nodded anyway and joined the others around the table, ready to hear how Lyta was going to pull off this miracle.

Because that was what it was going to take, if they were going to break into the impregnable fortress belonging to the Duchess of Montalbeau.

'What kind of plan?' he asked.

'Technically, it's Ranulf's plan.' Lyta smiled.

'Ranulf? Ranulf Wray, who's missing and presumed dead?'

'My husband,' she added curtly, as if he needed reminding. 'The greatest thief Amberes ever produced. He had this lined up for years. His biggest heist. His masterplan.'

Sylvian shook his head. He should have known the old man was behind this, but it didn't feel like any kind of comfort. They'd known Ranulf Wray as a kind of legend when they were kids. In the cheapest dockside taverns and the dodgiest alleyways, his exploits were legendary. Lyta had idolised him, Janlow had wanted to emulate him in the laziest way possible, but Syl . . . He'd never had the same faith in Ranulf that Lyta had. If he never saw the old bastard again it would still be too soon. And now something struck him about why Lyta had volunteered so quickly. 'That's why you told the king you could do it. Because you already had a plan?'

She laughed. 'Part of it. Like they say, the gods and goddesses will provide. Maybe they set this up in advance for us. Eninn always loved Ranulf, and he loves me even more. We know he's with us on this. Are you ready? Pay attention, Syl, because we have to get this right.'

CHAPTER FIFTEEN

Lyta

'No,' Ben and Kit had said in unison. Lyta glared at her brother and he flushed red, a beetroot hue that started at his chest and flooded up his face, clashing with his hair.

'It isn't up to you,' Lyta said to Kit.

Ben glared at her. 'Well, I'm pretty sure it *is* up to me.'

'Ben, please,' Beatriz cut in. 'We discussed this.'

Ben rounded on his sister, who had retreated to the window. 'Having just saved me from the clutches of one monster you want me to walk straight into the arms of another?'

'I'd stay out of her arms if I was you. Bad things happen to her lovers,' said Sylvian drily. Lyta scowled.

'I have a plan, you know,' she offered, but she wasn't sure anyone was listening.

'That's what he's afraid of,' Kit piped up.

Lyta rolled her eyes. Since when was Kit so protective of anyone other than his employees and his partner at the printshop?

'Let's start again,' she explained, as patiently as she could. 'The duchess has long wanted a translation of *The Book of Gold*. Ben is the foremost expert in the region.'

'She practically begged him to come in her letters,' said Beatriz, a little smugly. Ben gave her a sour look.

'And what does she want it for?' Kit cut in.

'Shut up, Kit,' Lyta said. 'She's invited him and Beatriz has written back to accept. He's just going to look, give a brief assessment.

No one is making any promises and no one is sticking around for more than half an hour.'

'Won't she get suspicious if it takes him that long?' Kit asked archly.

'I like to double-check everything,' Ben said, smothering a smile, but not quite so quickly that she didn't see it. It was a beginning anyway.

'Ben has an open invitation to visit Montalbeau to examine the book,' she went on. 'That's his way in. They'll search him on entry and exit though because she's not an idiot. She guards that library like a dragon.' Kit opened his mouth to argue again and Lyta ploughed on. 'Ben will be safe because Sylvian is going to go in as his bodyguard, appointed by Francisco himself. She'd recognise you anyway, Sylvian, so it fits. This way it looks like Francisco is sending Ben as a gesture of reconciliation, even if he would never admit as much. Is everyone fine with that?'

Sylvian raised one hand to argue. Lyta turned her back on him and stabbed a finger at the architectural plans. Montalbeau was a maze of tunnels, servants' corridors running behind the main chambers, and layer after layer of cellars – and no doubt dungeons as well.

Years ago, Ranulf had walked her through this plan. Just her. It was his dream heist, and he'd wanted to share it with her, so she could marvel at his cleverness, his audacity maybe. She didn't know. He didn't tend to tell anyone about his plans, and he had a million of them. Some never came to pass, but this one . . . He should never have gone without her. And now he had vanished, swallowed up by this fortress of nightmares.

If he was dead, she'd finally find out what happened to him. That had to be enough. Because she couldn't believe that he wouldn't have come back otherwise. But she needed to know.

And if she didn't tell the others that this was where he had gone . . . well, no one wanted to follow a plan that had got the last team killed, did they?

This time it was different. They had Ben, for one – with his knowledge, expertise and open invitation – and they had her. And with her, Eninn's blessing.

That had been Ranulf's mistake, not taking her with him. He'd had an expert – some scholar from Wittenberg down on his luck and just desperate enough – but he hadn't had Lyta.

The keep operated on three levels. The duchess's accommodation, reception rooms and a great gallery occupied most of it, all on the upper floors. That was where her library was too, right in the middle, accessed only by permission and heavily guarded. Below that, on the ground floor, were the everyday facilities, the kitchens and guards' rooms. Underneath that she had dungeons, notorious for their bleak and desolate nature. No one left them.

Lyta wondered if that was where Iseult of Montalbeau bathed in the blood of her supposed many victims, or if she had it heated and carried to her private chambers first.

Below stairs was a world unto itself. Getting in there, that was the trick. Getting in there unseen would be the miracle.

But no one looked at servants, not in a place where no one intended for them to be seen. Staff corridors were well hidden, but they ran all over the fortress. Even behind the walls of the precious library.

The plan was actually very straightforward, if they would ever stop bickering long enough to let her explain. Sylvian would escort Ben to the library where he would examine the book. While he did that, Sylvian would open one of the hidden doors. Meanwhile Lyta and Frida would disguise themselves as servants, bribe their way inside and wait on the other side of that same door.

'And how will you get in?' Kit asked. He was full of bloody questions today. She should have sent him back to his printshop but he'd probably just refuse to go.

'Frida? Want to take that one?' said Lyta.

Frida rolled her eyes. Since Haldevar's disappearance she hadn't been herself, but there was still no one else Lyta would have at her back. 'The master of the household has a weakness. I'm going to exploit that shamelessly. He'll let us in, don't worry. And he'll hold the way open for us to get back out again.'

'And you trust him?' Sylvian asked. His expression already told them what he thought of that.

'*No*,' Frida replied as if talking to an idiot. 'Of course I don't trust him. But I do trust greed. It's amazing what people will do for something they really want. It's fine, Sylvian. I have it sorted. You do your bit and we'll do ours.'

'My bit?' he growled.

Frida scowled and bunched up her shoulders in near perfect mimicry of a soldier. 'Just glower at everyone and look like you'll beat people up, Sylvian. What you do best. If it comes down to it, you can always punch someone as a distraction.'

Lyta thought of the punch he had dealt Janlow in the market. Pretty good distraction really. But it hadn't ended well for him, had it? Only Eninn's intervention and Beatriz's healing abilities had saved him.

Sylvian knew better than to pay Frida any mind. 'We shouldn't split up,' he told Lyta. 'That never ends well.'

'It's the only way,' Lyta assured him. 'We'd never all get into the library. A bodyguard would be fine, but a group? Not a chance. And as for getting the book out through the front door? No, Frida and I will go in this way.' She traced her finger along a narrow line in the plan. 'Servants' corridors. They run right up here behind the library, and there's a door. It can only be opened from the library side though. Her Grace has to summon them and let them in. Security. Here.' She tapped it and then looked up at Sylvian across the table. 'That's what I need you to do. Open that door. Ben finds the book. We swap it out for a copy. We take the original back through the servants' corridors and you two leave by the front door. Simple.'

She had hoped for some kind of acknowledgement, maybe a small round of applause. There was silence.

'What?' she asked when no one said a word.

'It seems . . . *very* simple,' said Kit, with that dubious tone she knew too well from him. 'What's the catch?'

'There is no catch. In and out. Simple plans are the best plans.'

'And what if you run into trouble below stairs?' Kit asked. 'Sylvian won't be there to look after you. I should come with you.'

Lyta stared at him, mouth open. 'I don't think so.' But she already knew she was going to lose that argument. She could see the mulish look in his eyes. What was he even thinking? 'Kit, you don't do crime.'

He glowered at her. 'Maybe you're rubbing off on me again. And I'm sure I'm as good at punching people as Sylvian is.'

Well, that was arguable, having seen Sylvian fight and Kit rescue spiders from his workshop. But one look at him told her it was not the moment to have that discussion. 'Yeah, but—'

'I'm coming with you,' was all he said and that, apparently, was that.

Montalbeau lay almost half-a-day's ride from Amberes. A bleak fortress on a low hilltop, overlooking a miserable village and a collection of sparse fields. Lyta wondered if the clouds ever lifted, if the sun ever broke through, if anyone ever smiled.

She doubted it.

Frida had scouted it out and made the contacts they needed. She was good at that. As they parted company several miles back, Sylvian didn't look too happy about it but then again, he didn't look happy about bloody anything at the moment so that was his hard luck. Lyta put him out of her mind. She had to if she was going to get through this.

The fortress stood on a low man-made hill, built on the bones of its many predecessors, and ringed with a series of defensive walls. One had to pass through several gates to reach the inner courtyard by normal means and even then, Montalbeau was a rabbit warren of a place. This route would drop them right behind the kitchens. The duchess didn't like to see menial things like deliveries or servants. Because of this there was a hidden entrance. It was guarded, naturally, but once through it, they'd be in the heart of the stronghold.

So here they were, the three of them, sitting on Kit's cart, lurching towards the hulking shape of Montalbeau. Frida had tried to crack a few jokes and put them at ease, but it wasn't working.

'Supplies for the kitchen,' Frida called out as they approached the gate. It wasn't the grand entrance to the fortress itself. This was low and squat, perfectly defensible, with an open portcullis and a very well-designed kill zone immediately beyond that. The walls rose around it like cliffs.

The guards looked bored and cold. Miserable. The best kind.

'Three of you to haul supplies? What's her ladyship planning, a royal banquet?'

His companion barked out a laugh. 'Not likely. Not unless she can personally spit in the royal couple's dishes.' But he lowered his voice as he spoke, just in case.

Frida gave him a broad smile. 'Perhaps she's ordered everything they're known to hate. Can't take fish myself. Gives me such a dicky stomach I could be in the privy for days after just a mouthful. Imagine his royal Majesty on that throne.'

The first guard laughed this time as well.

'I don't know you,' the second one said, peering at her. 'Where are you from?'

'The new merchants at Eel Bridge in Amberes – Wijen and Sons.' She reached back and fished out a package from her sacks. 'Now, don't go telling anyone but these are fresh in from Burgundy, and they are fine.' The cured meat rolls she pulled out were fragrant with garlic and Lyta could see the guard's faces light up as they took them. 'And you'll want something to wash it down. Where's that wine?'

Lyta pulled out the bottles as prepared and handed them over.

'So, things go smoothly, you know?' Frida was saying. 'We're hoping for lots of repeat business as we've got the best imports in the city right now. My boss says anything her ladyship wants we'll get. And if you wanted some other items slipped in, well . . . just let me know.' She winked at them extravagantly.

'You're wanting Master Desidero,' the second guard interrupted them. 'He'll sort you out. You can wait in the kitchens. Someone will send word.'

And just like that they were past the first hurdle. The cart trundled through the gates and into the narrow courtyard beyond. From there, they were waved through a second gate.

'Do you have a plan for getting out again?' Kit asked.

'If all goes well, we just ride out again, remember? No need to worry.'

'I do worry,' he said.

'Just let us do our job,' she whispered. 'That portcullis hasn't closed in months and if they drink that wine as fast as I think they will they'll be sound asleep in no time. Besides, you can always fight our way out, if needs be, can't you, against that pair? Weren't you assuring me you could punch someone as well as Sylvian back at Beatriz's?'

That tripped up her train of thought. No one was like Syl. Of course, there wasn't. There never had been. And Kit was her little brother. He shouldn't be here at all.

'Lyta,' he began reluctantly.

She took pity on him. 'They'll be fast asleep, Kit. We put a shit-ton of poppy tears in the wine. They'll be out like a candle. Trust me.'

He did, that was the problem. He trusted her to get him in and out, to get all of them out. And she had a suspicion he was really here just to make sure no one got left behind this time.

The cart lurched to a halt and they jumped down, ready to meet the master of the household who was already striding towards them. Frida clapped her hands into his and talked expansively about her wares until every other interested eye grew bored. She brought out a sack, one about which she'd been extraordinarily tight-lipped. Lyta trusted her implicitly. They had worked together for years now and Frida always came through.

This time was no exception.

'It's all here, Des,' she said in conspiratorial tones. 'Now, we still have a deal, right?'

His hands tightened on the sack as if it held his first-born child. 'I can . . . I can only cover for you for about an hour, Frida. She's entertaining guests. But if she takes it into her head to—'

'Des, my love, I went out of my way for you. Trust me. I won't let on. I'll be as much in the shit if anyone finds out and you know it, bringing that here. An hour is more than we need.'

'I . . . I don't know.' He hadn't given up the sack though. Whatever was in it, that was worth everything to him.

'I can get it again, you know.' Frida tilted her head to one side. 'Whenever the shipment comes in from Piedmont. My cousin is handling all their official paperwork and they've got to pay him off with something. Come on, Des, we have a deal, remember? Screw me on this and that's going to be the last time you taste it until you drag your sorry arse home again.'

'All right,' he gasped. 'All right. Inside, quickly. And don't draw any more attention to yourselves.'

As he ushered them inside, he clutched the sack against his chest.

'What's in the bag?' Lyta asked as she and Frida entered the storage room beside the busy kitchens. She thought of the poppy tears Frida had produced for the wine, swirling the tiny bottle around with a flourish like it was a party trick. 'What on earth did you get him?'

Frida grinned at her, a manic look in her eyes. 'They're truffles, this big fungus, from Piedmont. That's where Des is from. And believe me the Piedmont Court does not let them beyond the borders for anything. They go mad for them. It's like an addiction. In fact, it might *be* a real addiction. You saw his face. They have to be smuggled in and they cost a small fortune on the black market. If you don't know the right people you won't get a sniff of them before they're gone.'

'How *small* a fortune have you spent?' Lyta asked, dreading the question. The king might reimburse them for some of this, but she wasn't holding her breath. She might be able to get some money from Beatriz, but given everything else the Lady of House Alvarez had done for her, she didn't want to ask.

'It's like you don't know me anymore,' Frida scoffed. 'Nothing. The captain of the *Merry Wanderer* owed me.'

'Deals on top of deals?'

'Always. Now, we need to get going. An hour's not long. Stage two. And pray the others don't fuck up.'

Lyta nodded and glanced around. They were inside and safe, so far. Desidero had everyone else busy far away from them. There were no guards. Nothing. Just a deserted corridor leading down into the darkness.

'This way,' she told the others. She sounded far more confident than she felt. It was Ranulf's plan, she reminded herself. And by all the old gods, that man could plan. But if that was the case, her treacherous brain asked, where was he? And where was Eninn, for that matter? She should be able to feel his presence, but there was nothing. Maybe Beatriz was right and helping her rescue Kit and saving Sylvian had used up all his meagre godly powers. Maybe they were on their own after all. Or he had no more power in here than he had in the tower. 'Kit? Take the rear. If anything happens you get the hell out, all right?'

She had studied the map of the fortress. She knew what she was doing, where they were going. In theory anyway. Lyta had memorised it. But now, heading down the corridor into the lower levels where she knew the duchess kept prisoners, torture chambers and the gods knew what, now she didn't feel half so sure of herself.

The door ahead of them opened onto a staircase. They descended in silence. Lyta took the lead and Kit followed behind.

'This is far too easy,' he muttered. 'Should we be going down? I thought the library was on the upper floor?'

'It's getting out we have to worry about,' Frida told him without irony. Lyta forced herself to ignore them. Her own nerves were bad enough. She couldn't take theirs on as well.

'Eninn's watching out for us,' she told them, even though she wasn't so sure of that. 'Now shut up.'

The next floor was the prison level and Lyta knew for certain she didn't want to be poking around there. But she had to. There would be other staircases heading back up. She could picture them, just a little further on. But first . . .

The door there was heavy, wooden and bound in iron. It was also locked.

Frida stepped by Lyta and pressed her hands to it. 'This one's for you I think,' she said, glancing over her shoulder. Lyta already had her tools out ready to go. 'Keep watch on the stairs,' Frida added to Kit.

The lock was old and not exactly challenging. It relied on the strength of the wood and the iron. And on the palpable aura of fear that permeated the ground here. Lyta could feel it drenched into the stones, filling the air.

Her hands trembled. No, that wasn't right. For a moment she didn't know if she could do this. The doubt that assailed her made her pause. But she had to go on. Ranulf could still be in here somewhere. And this was her chance to find out.

'Lyta?' Kit murmured, the concern in his voice breaking through whatever dark mood was settling over her. 'You all right?'

'Yes,' she said quickly, too quickly. Her brother's hand closed on her shoulder, squeezing gently. He knew. He understood. Maybe he felt it too. He'd always been the sensitive one. But his support was everything.

Her pendant tingled against her chest, a single pulse of reassurance, a message from her Trickster god. It had to be. He was with her after all. The sheer relief made her breath catch in her throat. She had to be on the right track.

She set to work.

CHAPTER SIXTEEN

Sylvian

Ben produced the letter of invitation, scrabbling in the leather pack he carried. The guards stared dumbly at it, their eyes flat and uninterested, while the horses whickered and fussed at the hitching post. Even they hated the atmosphere of this place. Strange that even a hired horse would have better instincts than Sylvian.

'We're here at the request of the duchess,' Ben said hesitantly. 'My man and I. He's to guard me on the road. I'm . . .' He swallowed hard and then ploughed on. 'I'm writing a treatise on Trithemius and your lady has a collection of his works which is unmatched for hundreds of miles. She even has a full copy of the *Steganographia*, all three volumes. The third in particular is incredibly rare. He taught Agrippa and Paracelsus and his influence—' One of the guards cleared his throat of a large amount of phlegm, which he spat to one side. Ben faltered, as if realising no one listening shared his enthusiasm. 'In return I am to examine a book for possible translation for her Grace. I— I was told to present myself to the seneschal and—'

The guards at the main gate wouldn't have gotten past Vasquez's inspections, Sylvian thought. And while the fortress itself loomed over them, a mass of grey stone that seemed designed to drain all hope, the manpower was thin on the ground, which meant she had to have other guards stashed out of sight. Because nothing could be this easy.

'Stay here,' said the first guard and nodded to the second, who retreated through the gate.

Again, stupid. Sylvian narrowed his eyes and looked around covertly, noticing the slits in the stonework above them and the glint of light on metal on the walkway above. There they were. Waiting. Watching.

At least he looked the part of a mercenary hired for protection. They were a common enough sight on the roads outside the city, free of the restrictions the aldermen placed on arms. And they were necessary because you could never tell what trouble you could run into outside the city. He'd be expected to accompany Ben here and wait until he was finished.

This was already taking too long, he thought. He didn't like that the other three had gone in separately. He didn't like any of it. He wondered where they were, if they were inside already. The thought of Lyta just brazenly wandering about in there made a chill creep down his spine.

But he had a job to do and that was that. He was already in it all far too deeply, and if he didn't get Ben out safely Beatriz would never forgive him. He didn't fancy being on the wrong side of her.

The man who emerged from the gatehouse wore much finer clothes than the guards, a deep green surcoat over mail. But he had the same dead eyes, which flickered over the letter more closely.

'Follow me, both of you. Turn out your bags. You'll have to leave your weapons here.'

Sylvian made no move to comply.

'He is my bodyguard,' said Ben in that slightly outraged tone only a nobleman could truly pull off. 'He wouldn't be much good unarmed. If you read the letter, the duchess guaranteed—'

The senior guard looked Sylvian up and down and clearly decided not to contest the matter. Perhaps they thought they could take him. Perhaps they thought he actually needed his weapons. Sylvian kept his face completely impassive. No one moved. Perhaps this was going to be over before it began.

'Very well,' the guard muttered. 'Follow me. Keep your hands in view.'

Vasquez would have had words about that as well. They were arrogant here. Still, Sylvian didn't fancy the thought of fighting their way out. He glanced at Ben, slim and delicate. No, he didn't fancy the thought at all.

The outer courtyard was well-kept and neat, hardly any sign of the usual life he'd have expected. The keep towered over them, grey and imposing, and when the guard led them inside, the doors closed behind them with a terrible finality. The reception room was richly furnished but felt hollow and empty. The guardsman spoke briefly with a liveried man of middle years. He had the thin, drawn look Sylvian was beginning to associate with Montalbeau.

'My Lord Alvarez, you're most welcome,' he said, though he didn't sound convincing. He sounded like they had turned up in the middle of his dinner or dragged him away from his lover. 'Please, follow me. I'll show you to the library.'

'My . . . my thanks,' Ben managed to stammer out, and then seemed to remember himself, that fluid arrogance of nobility flowing back into his voice. 'And you are?'

'Her Grace's seneschal,' he replied, with a hint of a sneer that didn't quite seem to fit his face. 'She has been waiting for your reply for some time, Lord Alvarez. We did not expect you to come in person without advance notice.'

When in doubt, say nothing, Lyta had instructed Ben. It was a good rule in general, Sylvian thought, and not one Lyta herself ever followed. Thankfully, the scholar did that now, adopting a distant and austere expression which Sylvian wondered if he had learned in the tower.

With no reply forthcoming, the seneschal led them down a series of corridors and up flights of stairs. Carefully, Sylvian kept track of the route, judging that the circuitous way he led them through the keep was designed to confuse.

Finally, he showed them into the library and as Sylvian stepped inside, he felt like something had pushed all the air out of his lungs.

It wasn't as large as that in the Scholars' Tower, or the royal library in Valladolid. But it was crammed with books and manuscripts, scrolls and parchment. They were piled on shelves and stacked on the floor. This was a library that was lived in, worked in, constantly added to. There was nothing orderly about this place. It didn't have any sense of structure or any obvious way of keeping track of what was in here.

They were never going to find a single book in here.

In the middle of the room there was an enormous oval mirror set on a gilded stand. In front of it stood a large lantern and the flickering light reflected in the surface illuminated the room. The only windows were high overhead and small, letting in little natural light, and offering no means of escape.

The whole place felt like a cage.

'If you don't mind waiting,' said the seneschal and closed the door behind him.

Sylvian checked the door which was firmly closed but not locked. Ben was already at the nearest shelf, examining the contents. He flicked through one book after the next, opening them, scanning a single page and putting each one back exactly where it had been.

'Frater Julius would have a fit to see this,' said Ben crisply, the shy and bumbling scholar act evaporating like morning mist.

'What?' was all Sylvian could manage.

'Find the door and open it for the others. I'll find the book.'

Sylvian gestured around the cluttered room, shelf after shelf stretching back into the recessed shadows. 'How?'

'Don't worry about that. We won't have much time. No one in their right mind would leave a scholar alone in a library like this for long. Find the servants' door and open it.' He had already moved on to the next shelf, his hands never pausing. It was almost as if he was searching for *The Book of Gold* by touch alone.

Sylvian shook his head and set to work. Lyta had given him directions as to where the servants' door should be, tucked away in a corner, discreet and made to look like part of the panelling. The problem was, he couldn't see any panelling and half the walls were covered in shelves and bookcases.

He pushed his way to the closest wall and ran his hand down the surface. There were heavy gilded leather panels fixed there, decorated with ferns and birds. When he knocked on one the sound was dead and solid. He moved on, finding another gap but there was nothing there either. He had to keep going, had to find it. Somewhere behind the walls here, Lyta should already be waiting. Maybe she would even knock back.

'I think this is it,' said Ben from somewhere behind him.

At least there was that.

He knocked on the wall again and it returned a hollow echo that made his chest tighten. But there was no sign of a door, just a narrow gap between bookshelves. On the ground, he could see scratches on the floorboards, fresh ones. This had to be it.

'Over here,' he called to Ben, and grabbed the edge of the bookcase, pulling it back from the wall. He could see the lines of the door behind it in the leather panelling. He knocked again but there was no reply. Where was she?

The latch however was right there, right where she had said it would be. Sylvian lifted it and pushed. It opened silently, but beyond there was only darkness.

'Lyta?' he whispered into the empty space. Why could she never be where she was meant to be when she was meant to be there? Why couldn't she, just for once—?

Behind him, Ben made a choked noise, somewhere between shock and alarm. Sylvian darted back to the centre of the room, where the lantern blazed in front of the mirror, and Ben stood with his back to him, struggling against something unseen. The mirror reflected him, holding a book with an ornate gilt binding in one hand, the other pressed to the open page. Smoke spooled out between his fingers, coiling around his body.

'Stay back, Sylvian,' he gasped, trying to pull himself free of it, but some force was holding his hands on the book as if glued there. The smoke turned thicker, darker, moving like a living thing, tightening its grip on him. 'This isn't the book. It's . . . I don't know what this is.'

A low laugh rippled through the still air of the chamber, silencing Ben. White-faced, he looked up, his eyes widening, and Sylvian drew his sword to face this new threat.

Everything about this felt wrong. Everything about this room felt like a trap.

Because it was a trap.

'Well,' said the Duchess of Montalbeau, pale and beautiful and wreathed in darkness. She emerged from the recesses of her library, from the deep shadows where things rustled and shifted in her wake and her voice sounded hungry. 'Here you are at last, Seigneur Alvarez. I have been waiting for so long to get you here but the Magister just refused to let you go, didn't he? You have a good eye. That's almost *The Book of Gold*. But not quite. A decoy, one might say.' She smiled broadly. 'Or bait.' As Sylvian surged forward she held up one hand and it was as if he had slammed into a window. The air thickened around him, alive with shadows. 'Stay where you are, Captain Chant. I won't warn you twice. You're expendable. I suppose that's why that buffoon of a king gave you the job.'

He moved anyway, he couldn't help himself, pushing through her spell. Black tendrils of smoke twined around his limbs, holding him in place. But they didn't feel like smoke. They were smooth and hard as glass, except that when he tried to cut them, his sword passed effortlessly through.

'What are you doing?' Ben exclaimed. 'This is dangerous magic.'

'Oh absolutely.' She sounded unbearably pleased with herself. 'My goddess has given me more powers in her service than you can imagine, Benedictus. I feed her the sacrifices she needs, and she gives me the secrets of *The Book of Gold*. She's going to love you two.' She reached out, brushing her cold hand down the side of Sylvian's face. He flinched, but couldn't get away. He couldn't even move his arms now. She took his sword from his unresisting grip and with a mocking smile, slid it back into its sheath. 'All that pain, all that suffering, so much blood on your hands.' She let out a low, sultry laugh and Sylvian saw in her someone who loved to toy with those they

THE BOOK OF GOLD

destroyed. He'd met her like before, but he'd never felt so helpless. 'Oh yes, you're perfect. She'll swallow you down whole.'

'How did you know?' Ben was still fighting the enchantment too, Sylvian could see that, trying to rip himself free. Like Beatriz, Benedictus was powerful. But not powerful enough.

Iseult of Montalbeau pushed past Sylvian. 'I've been watching,' she purred. 'All this time. Waiting. Poor things, should I just show you?'

With a wave of her hand, the mirror rippled and the reflections changed. Before Sylvian's horrified gaze, Lyta opened a door into darkness. He watched her step inside without a backwards glance and—

'It's Kit,' Ben hissed. 'You were the one who bound Kit.'

She smiled triumphantly. 'Not much. Just enough to see through his eyes, hear what he heard and to bind his tongue. He doesn't even know what I've done to him, poor pet. And until I tighten the noose, he won't. I thought he might come in handy but I never dreamed of this.'

Sylvian couldn't tear his eyes off the mirror, from the image of Lyta in it. There were cells on either side of her. The dungeons. What was she doing in the dungeons? They were meant to be up here, coming this way. She didn't seem confused or in a rush, just walked on, that familiar determination on her face, while Frida and Kit followed. And in the black depths of those cells, something moved, something growled. Eyes glinted like silver coins.

'The hunt is on,' Iseult of Montalbeau murmured. 'They're on the right path, you know. That's the funny thing. They might just have stumbled onto *The Book of Gold* by accident. So close to the vault and yet a world away. They might even see it before the end. Just a glimpse. If my dark lady allows it.' The duchess gave a contented sigh. 'She's going to be so happy, so grateful for this bounty. She's been so hungry and the dregs of Amberes are hardly enough. She chews them up and spits most of them back out as wild things, savage and mindless. But an Aspect like you . . . oh yes, she will be pleased. She will feed and feed on the power in your veins. Once you're more agreeable, my dear Benedictus, I'll fetch *The Book of Gold* from the vault and you can translate it for me. So it all won't have been in vain.'

'No,' he replied, and from somewhere the Lord of House Alvarez appeared again. 'I won't give you such power.'

Her laugh mocked him. 'You won't have a choice. You'll beg me to let you serve when I'm done with you. You,' she poked his chest with an exquisitely manicured finger top. 'And my darling Christopher, and even the stalwart and true Captain Chant here. You will serve me eventually, faithful to the end. I may even send you back to the king, Sylvian. You can wait until the right moment and when I command it, you'll slaughter your precious Francisco for me.'

Never, he thought. That he would never do. But the duchess smiled at him as if she knew better and that chilled him.

'Poor captain,' she murmured. 'You have no idea, do you? A man can be made to do anything with the right pressure. Surely your king taught you that. He's certainly made use of you. There are so many ways you can be useful to me. Both of you.'

The duchess didn't mention Lyta or Frida. She didn't mean for them to survive whatever she had in store. Sylvian wrenched himself forward, one step and then another. But it was like wading through stone. The duchess watched him, tilting her head to one side, and her eyes gleamed with something like pride in his meagre progress.

'Don't fear, Sylvian. You'll be bound, in the darkness, drained and remade. You'll be better than ever. All your past, all your sins, washed away. And your little guttersnipe friends will be joining you soon enough.'

She waved her hand again and the darkness swept up like a wave over Sylvian's face.

CHAPTER SEVENTEEN

Kit

As Lyta worked, all Kit could do was stand there, listening to his own thundering heartbeat.

He couldn't shake the feeling of something crushing down on him, or pushing out from behind his eyes. A cold ache had wound its ways into his bones, especially his wrist where he bore her scar. He needed to tell them, to warn them. He knew that but the words stuck in his throat like a fishbone. Why couldn't he speak of it?

Ben had said he was marked by magic, and now he was deep inside the stronghold of the person who had performed that spell. It couldn't be good. But Ben had also promised him it wasn't active, that it shouldn't have power over him. Gods and goddesses of old, Kit prayed that the scholar was right. Because something felt very wrong.

A dull clunk echoed around the antechamber and Lyta made a small sound of triumph, grinning up at him as the door swung open to the deepest darkness he'd ever seen. There was no natural light in there. Nothing. With the door closed they'd be blind.

Frida was ready for it though. She rummaged in the bag on her back and pulled out a small round ball, shoving it into Kit's hand.

'Shake it,' she told him. He did as instructed, bemused, and to his amazement the ball began to glow with a pale watery light. She handed another to Lyta and kept the third for herself. For a moment he studied his, trying to work out what it was, how it did that. Not magic. There was a scent of something almost familiar.

Then he remembered. The duchess had had such a thing – only it had been red. The memory of it made his stomach clench.

'Try and stay together,' said Frida. 'Don't wander off. Who knows what's in there.'

'Where did you get these?' Kit asked.

Frida grimaced. 'Oh, you really do not want to know. There are a number of alchemists who can make them for enough money. Just put the right potions inside and when you mix them up, it's like magic. Except it's actually reliable and you don't need to do any deals with gods. Now, are we going to stand here chatting or are we getting on with this? We don't have all day and I for one don't want to be stuck in there when these things run out.'

Neither did Kit.

Kit followed his sister and Frida brought up the rear this time. They descended into the darkness below Montalbeau.

'These aren't servants' corridors,' he said warily.

'No, those are cells,' Frida replied, her voice suddenly cold. 'What are you up to Lyta Cornellis?'

'There are stairs up at the other end,' Lyta said lightly. Too lightly.

'Up where? What servants come down here?' Frida could ask but Kit already knew the answer. The type of servants who had been with the duchess in Old Steen, for example – her most trusted guards.

But the cells were empty. Somehow that didn't feel any more comforting. They pressed onwards, Lyta checking each cell as they passed, looking for someone, he realised.

And then it came together. Why she was here. Why she was *really* here.

Because they never left one of their own behind, not if they had a chance to get them out. Ranulf had taught them that.

'Lyta, what have you done?' he whispered, the sound far too loud in the darkness.

The guilty look she shot him as she reached the last cell told him everything. So did the devastation lingering behind it.

'What?' asked Frida.

THE BOOK OF GOLD

'He isn't here anyway,' Lyta muttered to Kit, realising that he had figured it out. 'Look for yourself.'

Of course he wasn't here. Had she actually hoped he was?

'Ranulf's dead, Lyta.' He hadn't meant to say the words, not out loud and certainly not before she admitted it herself. But Ranulf *was* dead. He'd gone off on another heist and never come back because that was what happened to people like him. And like Lyta. Sooner or later everything caught up with them. Like Haldevar. They all ended up dead.

But clearly Lyta refused to believe it. Because that was why she was here. Not for the book. Not to save him.

She was here to find Ranulf.

'Eninn said,' she whispered brokenly. 'He showed me. Ranulf should be here.'

God, she didn't even look like herself. A girl stood there, wide eyed, desperate. Begging him to say he was wrong and she was right, that everything was going to be fine. It was like a punch to the guts. Lyta, strong, determined, belligerent Lyta, who always had a plan, who always knew what to do and went straight through anything that got in her way . . . she looked so lost.

'Lyta,' he murmured and she jerked from him as if he'd scalded her. And kept backing up.

Her expression changed, from lost to horrified.

'Run,' she said, grabbing his arms and trying to drag him with her. 'Quick, run!'

Something slammed into Kit's side, taking his legs out from under him. He heard a snarl too close to his ear and spit hit the side of his face as clawed hands scrabbled at him. Too many hands.

Frida shouted something but he couldn't make it out. Twisting desperately, he kicked out with both legs and felt them connect with the shapes swarming over him, their weight lifting momentarily.

Lyta pulled him after her as he scrambled away. They sprinted, glow balls illuminating the way jerkily, like drunks at a carnival. Behind them he caught glimpses of emaciated forms clad in rags and filth, mad eyes gleaming like silver, reflecting the scattered light.

Frida laid into the nearest of them with a leather cosh, taking the first down and driving the next back with a blow to the head so hard its head snapped to the side with a sickening crack.

'Let's go,' Lyta yelled, still pulling him after her. 'Frida! Now!'

The door at the far end of the rows of cells stood open and they threw themselves through it. Lyta slammed it closed behind them, using her body to hold it there. Kit grabbed a huge wooden bar and slid it across the frame to secure it.

On the other side, emaciated bodies slammed themselves against the wood, snarling and growling like thwarted wolves. The door bucked and shook, but it held. Then it went abruptly quiet.

'What the fuck was that?' Frida yelled into the silence.

'Her prisoners,' Kit replied. 'What's left of them anyway.' They had been more like rabid demons than human. He tried to catch his breath and make his racing heart calm.

'And why are we even down here, Lyta?' Frida went on, as if she hadn't heard him. She hadn't realised yet, Kit thought. And when she did, she would be furious. You never told a partner only half the plan, even he knew that. 'I thought we were heading for servants' corridors. Not the dungeon.'

Lyta had doubled over, her hands on her hips, as if she might vomit. She was breathing hard, fighting for control of herself. She looked up through the fall of her hair, the glow ball's light from where she held it against her leg making her eyes too bright, almost mismatched.

'You thought he'd be here, didn't you?' Kit asked. 'Ranulf? Is this where he went? His last heist? Sweet goddesses of old, Lyta, you could have told us.'

Frida sucked in a breath as everything hit home at once.

Lyta's words came out in a rush of grief. 'You wouldn't have believed me. Everyone said he was dead and no one gets out of Montalbeau. But Eninn *promised*.'

'Oh, you and that little bastard of a trickster!' Frida snarled. 'You promised *me*, Lyta. You said we were just following the plan, nothing more, that you weren't going to look for him. In and out, you said. What about Sylvian and Ben? Where are they? Wandering about up there waiting for us?'

Lyta straightened, something of her old bravado seeping back in. 'I factored in the time. I had to know if he was here and if he was, I had to get him out. He'd have helped us. You know that.' Frida scowled at her, unmoved. 'Kit, you understand, don't you?'

Kit took a deep breath. The urge to scream at her, or throttle her, died away as he saw again the desperation in her eyes. And this was Ranulf they were talking about. They owed the old man everything, owed him in more ways than they could possibly ever repay.

'He wasn't there,' he whispered, almost like an apology. And if one of those things back there had once been Ranulf . . . well, he wasn't going to be the one to say it. It was better not to know. 'So we need to get going now. We have to find the others and get out of here. Which way?'

Lyta nodded, perhaps understanding, perhaps just grateful he wasn't picking a fight as well. Frida didn't seem so easily mollified though. Still cursing under her breath, she followed them, holding her glow ball out so she could see further into each shadow, her cosh at the ready in her other hand, just in case.

But the tunnel they followed didn't seem to be going up. Rather it led slowly and steadily downwards. They didn't meet any steps, just a long spiralling slope, which made him think of a throat, swallowing them up. At last, the tunnel led them into a high-ceilinged room, domed and circular. It was deep and old. Kit ran his fingers along the carvings decorating the wall, picked out in the watery light. They almost seemed to move. Figures carried treasures and offerings, and sacrifices, he realised. Some screamed and wept, some danced and celebrated, some were obscene, and some . . . some weren't human at all. Or rather not human anymore. He thought of the lost souls behind them and shuddered, pulling the glow ball away.

A chill crept up his spine and he felt the scar on his arm like icy needles under his skin.

'Where are we?' Frida asked. 'It's like standing in a tomb.'

Or a temple, Kit thought, a strange and absent thought that hardly seemed to belong to him. An old one, for a dark and bloodthirsty deity. The kind their distant ancestors worshipped in.

'The stairs are just through there,' Lyta said.

'You'd better hope they are, Cornellis.'

'I'm sorry, Frida. I had to. And I memorised the map.'

'Ranulf's map? A lot of good that did him. You should have told us. If I'd known we were following the plan that got him killed—'

Kit saw the moment his sister snapped, turning on Frida, torn between rage and grief, and he stepped neatly between them. Lyta froze against his back.

'Frida, enough!' he thundered. His voice, which he normally kept soft and careful, echoed off the domed chamber's cold walls, silencing them both, cutting off arguments and recriminations. For now anyway. There wasn't time for this. They couldn't turn against each other, not here and now. The only way they were getting out was together. Carefully, he lowered his tone again, so as not to disturb this place, temple or crypt or dungeon – whatever it was. He had a sense of something sleeping here he really did not want to awaken. 'Let's find the others, get this done and get out. Agreed?'

Ben and Sylvian were up there somewhere, waiting on them to swap out the book. They just had to get there. They would find the way back up and rendezvous as planned.

And get out again, a mocking voice whispered in the back of his mind. He pushed it away, which just seemed to amuse it more.

There were three doors off the chamber, all closed. He shuddered, the now familiar feeling that they were being watched making his skin crawl. Especially around his wrist.

'Can you smell that?' Frida asked.

'What?'

'Like . . . like copper and salt. But foul, like rotten meat. Like . . . I don't know.'

There was an odour. Something familiar and yet strange too. Out of place. It hung heavy on the air.

'Like an abattoir,' Frida added darkly. 'This isn't good.'

'It was never going to be good,' Lyta agreed solemnly. 'Let's keep going.' She headed across the chamber for the far door. As she reached the middle a cold spear of premonition passed through Kit.

'Lyta, stop!' he yelled.

He was a moment too late. The floor wrenched open beneath her feet. She staggered on the edge of the newly made abyss, her balance teetering.

Frida reached her first, grabbing Lyta's arm. The ball tumbled from Lyta's other hand, plunging into the darkness below. With a jerk, Frida pulled her back and Lyta sagged in her friend's grip. The two of them stared at each other, argument forgotten for now, while Kit's heart battered helplessly in his chest.

'I'm fine,' Lyta said, her voice shaking. She scrabbled at her neck, where her necklace had swung out from beneath the collar, that little disc with the symbol of Eninn he knew so well, and something else, a white-gold ring he hadn't seen before.

Frida released her. 'Where did you get that?' Her voice sounded like breaking glass.

'This?' Lyta shoved it hastily back under her shirt. Too hastily. 'Ranulf, of course. Ages ago.'

Kit knew when she was lying. So did Frida. But this was neither the time nor the place and Lyta clearly didn't want to talk about it. What else wasn't she telling them?

Oh they were going to have words after this. And that was nothing to what Frida was going to say.

Kit drew in a shaking breath and looked over the edge and into the pit.

The glow from the ball lit it up only weakly, but it was enough to see that it was deep and at the bottom there were spikes daubed with dark splashes of old blood. Among them he could see shapes, and he didn't want to look any more closely.

'We knew she might have traps,' Lyta said. 'We can jump that.' The two of them looked at her as if she had finally lost her mind entirely, anything else forgotten. 'What? It's not far.'

Kit's voice shook. 'It may not be far but it's a long way down. And I'd like to draw your attention to the large array of pointy death at the bottom.'

'Our mother didn't raise cowards, Kit.'

'She didn't raise fools either.'

In the back of his mind, he could hear laughter again. He knew it wasn't real, or rather that it wasn't happening here. But all the same, he knew someone was laughing at them, watching them, enjoying this.

And then, as he listened, he heard something else, just within earshot, the pounding of feet in the corridor they'd just left. The prisoners, or whatever they were, had broken through the door.

And they were cornered on the edge of the pit.

'This way,' Lyta said, making for the door on the left.

'What's in there?' Kit asked, not trusting anything about this place. 'Quickly Kit, before they get here. We're using one of the oldest tactics there is.'

'What's that?'

She grinned at him as she opened the door and slipped inside. 'Hiding.'

Everything was telling him that this was wrong, that it was a bad idea. It might work. If they were lucky.

But when were any of them ever lucky?

Frida and Lyta were already inside. What choice did he have? Stay out here to face what sounded like a small army of feral prisoners? Give himself up to the mercy of the duchess again?

No. Not while he could still breathe.

'Hiding,' he said firmly. 'Right. We're good at that.'

He hurried through the door and caught a glimpse of a sculpture carved on the far side of the dark room, arms spread wide, hair flowing like gold down her back, a rapacious smile on her face. She seemed to emerge from the wall itself. The carvings on the outer walls had all been pointing this way, a ceremonial procession. To this room, he realised. To her.

The door shut behind them with a very final click. No sooner had he inhaled to warn the others than the world slid around him, twisting, becoming something else.

Soft light spilled across the bed through the gap in the curtains. A man was stretched out beside him, tangled in rumpled sheets. Kit lifted his head, blinking sleep from his eyes, and stared at Ben's sleeping face.

It was his bed. In his home. Perched above his printshop. He could hear the noises of Amberes outside, the morning business trundling away, shouts and laughter, wagons and all the things familiar to him. He was home. Safe.

He was lying beside Ben. A very naked Ben. He felt loose-limbed and content: warm, and soft and sated. Happy. At peace. Perhaps for the first time in his life.

Kit had never brought anyone back here, especially not someone like Ben.

Ben's eyes fluttered open. 'Kit,' he murmured sleepily and reached out his hand, smoothing it down the side of Kit's shoulder, making his skin shiver with desire. He frowned a little, studying Kit's expression and reading something there to concern him. 'Are you all right?'

'Yes,' Kit replied. Maybe Ben thought he was having doubts. He wasn't. This was . . . this was everything. 'I was . . . I think I was dreaming.'

'A good dream?'

Kit shook his head, his red-gold hair spilling about his face. It was loose, hanging in thick curls which reached his shoulders. 'A nightmare.'

'I can chase nightmares away,' Ben told him with a teasing smile and pulled him in for a soft yet demanding kiss which claimed Kit's mouth and his body. Not to mention his soul. 'Trust me.'

'I do,' Kit answered, moving against his lover with languid ease he'd never managed with anyone before. Ben was special. Ben was magic.

Magic. The word snagged in his mind like wool on thorns. There was something about magic. Nothing good.

Ben pushed him onto his back and rose over him, straddling him, pinning him there with a strength Kit would never have thought the slender scholar could possess. He smiled, his hands roving over Kit's chest, admiring the contrast between their pale and darker skin, before taking Kit's wrists and lifting them up over his head.

A pang of concern made Kit squirm. He blinked and the scene seemed to shift, blurring at the edges. He couldn't move. His arms were tangled in something, held firmly in place above his head. Like they were manacled.

The smile on Ben's face broadened and it didn't look like Ben's smile now. Not anymore. He'd seen it before somewhere, recently, carved in stone.

'You belong to me, Christopher Cornellis,' he whispered, the grip tightening to iron on Kit's wrists. It wasn't his voice and those weren't his eyes. Kit stared up at Ben, trapped by him, pinned down, but it wasn't Ben.

Kit's skin burned, his bones ached and he wanted to cry out, but something smothered his voice. Panic made him buck, trying to twist free, but the power the duchess possessed was far too strong. Because he knew it was her. Her and her nameless goddess.

Not Ben. This was not Ben.

'Please,' he whispered, not even sure what he was begging for. The smiled broadened further, stretching grotesquely on Ben's beautiful face.

'Did you really think it would be that easy? You are mine. And you always will be. Now I'm going to teach you how to obey.'

The light filling Ben's eyes burned brighter and he bent down to kiss Kit. His mouth was savage, vengeful and Kit was helpless, trapped by her spell, by the magic she'd carved into his skin and his bone.

And there was nothing he could do about it. Nothing at all.

'You belong to me, Christopher Cornellis.'

CHAPTER EIGHTEEN

Sylvian

Once upon a time, Sylvian had believed in happily-ever-afters. Quite a feat for someone who grew up on the streets of Amberes, where the only fairy-tale endings were dark and stained with blood. But deep down inside him an idealist had always lurked, sure that if he found the correct path, everything would work out in the end. If he was just good enough, he could make things right, make something of himself, find the perfect life. Of course, he never shared that with anyone. Not even Lyta. He'd always been afraid to look like a fool.

Light blossomed out of the darkness, the bright hot sun of Valladolid like molten gold, and he stood in a royal audience chamber, waiting to formally swear his fealty to the king, waiting for his life to finally change for the better.

'Syl?'

He ignored her voice. He didn't want to hear it now. Lyta had given up on him. So he had given up on her. Fair was, as they said, fair.

'Syl, please.'

He closed his eyes and tried to concentrate on the here and now, on where he was. The air was unexpectedly cold. But when he opened his eyes again, he could see the sunlight streaming through the open windows.

And yet, something was wrong. Something didn't fit.

Lyta stood behind him. She wore a gown the like of which she'd never had the ability to buy or even borrow. Jewels clung to the bustline like a sprinkling of frost. The cream silk shaped itself around her body. A court gown, fit for a lady-in-waiting.

'What are you doing here?' he asked, and she smiled.

'I'm here for you. I always was. You just wouldn't see it. Syl.'

'Syl's gone. I'm Sylvian Chant now, a captain of the King's Bodyguard, sworn and bound. Please, Lyta. You have to go.'

Lyta reached for him, her hand pressing to the shoulder of his scarlet uniform, softly for a moment, then harder.

Why was it so bloody cold? It was never cold in Valladolid. That was one of the most annoying things about the royal city. The temperature in Castille soared until the air was like a stew, and they still lit fires in every room.

He turned on her so quickly she jumped back like a startled cat, closing her arms around her body. Where she touched the dress, she left a smear of red. The red of his uniform.

But the uniform he wore wasn't red. The royal bodyguards wore blue and always had. He shivered, glancing down, then back at her.

Lyta's dress was smeared with blood, her palm scarlet with it.

And he was drenched in it, the material soaked through, blood dripping from the hem to splatter on the priceless carpets beneath them.

'What did you do?' she whispered, horrified.

What hadn't he done? For the king, for the realm, for his own survival. Lyta was no wilting violet by any means, but even she would be horrified if she knew everything.

He'd thought pledging himself to the king would lead him into noble service, but instead he was awash in death and blood. How many friends had he lost fighting the vassals of the Church Imperial, while they tried to crown a new king and the rest of the so-called nobility used the chaos to grasp for scraps of land? He hoped never to see that kind of brutality again. As a commander, Francisco had been effective and destructive, but as a king securing his rule, he'd become remorseless. He'd sacked cities, executed prisoners, burned temples to the ground. They had done such things . . .

The fear on Lyta's face now . . . perhaps she guessed. Perhaps she knew. She had never looked at him that way. Never.

There was a knife in his hand. He could feel the weight of it, the ice through his skin. Sylvian took a step towards her and Lyta pressed back against the wall. The last time he had kissed her mercilessly. This time—

No, this wasn't happening. It couldn't be happening.

'Kill her,' said a voice behind him. 'Kill her and free yourself from the past. You know that's what you want.'

It sounded like the queen. Sylvian turned around and the royal court was gone. Instead, he was back in Gravenenga, where the screams of dying men and broken horses rent the air while the miserable little canalside town burned. Strategically important and wealthy, everyone had tried to take it, so Francisco had razed it to the ground instead. If he couldn't hold it, no one would have it.

Sylvian dropped to his knees, mud and blood sucking at his aching body. Cannons thundered over his head and he crawled towards his men, huddled together in the lee of a rock outcrop.

'Report,' he barked. The blond lieutenant lifted his head, his eyes hollow and desperate, terrified. Just as Sylvian had seen him the last time. Before . . . before . . .

When Vincenzo opened his mouth, blood and maggots spilled out instead of words.

It was a nightmare. It had to be a nightmare. This was years ago. Vincenzo was dead. A mercenary from Galicia had torn his head from his shoulders in the fifth campaign. Francisco had hunted the bastard down and returned the favour.

'He was one of mine,' the young king had raged as he hacked through the Galician's neck with his massive sword and raised his head up like a trophy on a pike. 'No one takes what's mine.'

Sylvian tried to breathe through the panic racing through his brain even now, like an out-of-control horse. This wasn't real. It couldn't be. But what was it?

His worst nightmares. All the things he had tried to push down and forget. All the moments—

No, not all of them.

The weight of the irons on Syl's wrists and ankles. The rasp of his breath and the way the lash marks crossing his back opened again with every inhalation. He lay on the ground, in the piss and dirt of Old Steen.

Kit had stopped sobbing, sinking into an ominous silence that meant he was on the point of breaking, no choice but to watch what they were doing to his friend, his so-called protector.

They would turn their attention to him any second. Sylvian could not let that happen. He forced himself back up onto his knees. 'Is that all?' he drawled, swallowing down the blood and bile. The guard raised the whip again.

The door scraped open and everything went quiet. The guards stepped back as their commander entered, taking in the scene without comment.

'Well, there you have them,' he said to his companion. 'Like I promised. Take the one you want and get out.'

Sylvian forced his eyes to focus and knew. He just knew.

Lyta's face was thin and pale. Her eyes bored into him like she was trying to fix him in her memory, like she was trying to tell him something she couldn't say out loud. So this was how he'd got here. This was how they'd . . .

She swallowed. He watched her throat work, saw the pulse point where he'd kissed her a thousand times, made her shiver beneath him.

'Him,' she said, pointing at Kit. 'I'm taking him.'

Sylvian's world shattered around him. But all the same, he knew.

The scene twisted the way nightmares did, like a smear of blood on stone.

Petrus Janlow smiled, that lazy, evil little smile. 'She betrayed you, mate. Betrayed all of us. So, here's the deal. Are you listening? You're leaving me with a lot of debts, Syl. Some embarrassing reparations too. And she's going to pay. And keep on paying, for as long as she's able. Can you imagine what people are saying about what your beloved did to you? Life's about to get very hard for her and her brother around here.'

The pain was swallowing him up, fever racing through him, rage and fear and everything else a maelstrom of emotions. 'You're welcome to her,' he hissed, and he meant it. Hated himself for it, but meant it.

Outside, in the corridor, a world away, someone made a sound of dismay and hurried away.

Lyta, he realised now, a lifetime later. It had been Lyta.

Sylvian wrenched himself free, plunging into something else, anything else. He hadn't meant it. He'd never meant—

The man at the bar didn't look up as Sylvian took a seat beside him. He glowered into his tankard, and it was all Sylvian could do not to lash out at him then and there.

'You listen to me, you sad old—'

'No,' Ranulf replied, his voice cold. Around the bar, chair legs scraped on stone as men rose to their feet, surrounding him. Ranulf's men. Ranulf's friends. 'You listen. She's safe. I won't have you coming back to destroy everything for her all over again. Do you understand me? Janlow can't touch her. She's under my protection. It's shit for you but that's too bad. You didn't see what you did to her, Sylvian Chant. You didn't rescue her and the boy. You weren't here to comfort them, to build them back up again. We are not going through it all again. Leave Amberes. Or we'll help you leave. Get it?'

Sylvian chewed on his lower lip. Ranulf was right. And while he wanted Lyta – dear gods and goddesses, he wanted Lyta – he had almost destroyed her once already. Her and Kit.

And she had left him there in Old Steen.

'She entered into this willingly?'

'Of course she did. I wouldn't have done it otherwise. More willingly than she would have gone to Janlow and his crew, and she wasn't going to get a choice there. She didn't deserve that. No one does. And yet you offered her up.'

'I didn't.' The lie sat on his conscience like a stone.

'We heard different. She turned on you, you took revenge. The easiest explanation. Besides, people do strange things under torture, Syl. Just to make it stop. We know the truth. Sometimes just the need for survival makes us monsters.'

THE BOOK OF GOLD

He wasn't a monster. He wanted to tell Ranulf that, but the words wouldn't come out. Then again, there was a darkness within him. He'd sunk so deeply into it during the wars that he barely knew what light looked like anymore. He had told Janlow he was welcome to Lyta. And she had heard. He deserved this.

It was as if Ranulf saw it in his eyes. 'You survived, that's the main thing. Now fuck off and leave her alone. Let her have a life.'

Lyta deserved a life. Lyta deserved everything. The ache inside Sylvian ripped itself open again, a raw and bloody wound. All he had done to numb it, all the ways he had tried to smother his feelings, were for nothing.

'Chant, on your knees,' Francisco snapped. Gods, there were times Sylvian hated that voice. But what could he do? Even as he heard the shout, his knees were already bending, his head already bowing. 'What do you offer, soldier?'

'My life, my loyalty, everything.' He had nothing else. And no one else to give them to. He stretched his arms out, wrists turned up and rested them on the block between them. Some men swore they could hold still, that nothing would make them pull back. Blood had stained the wood beneath his arms black, and as the restraints closed over him, the urge to wrench himself free was so strong that he knew they all lied. But there was nothing else for him now, nothing but this.

In a blood-soaked courtyard of the broken fortress of Vermand, with the smoking misery of battle still clinging to the air, Sylvian said the words that would bind him to the service of the king. And the king produced a knife that gleamed wickedly as it cut into his skin.

He must have screamed and the scene disintegrated around him. Francisco laughed about it later.

'But at least you didn't pass out. Or throw up. You have no idea how the biggest of men will weep before it's over. Hand me the wine.'

They sat side by side in a luxurious corridor of the Valladolid palace, drunk and stinking with it, swigging wine straight out of the flasks they had seized from the cellars.

'Don't you have a new wife waiting for you?' he asked the king.

'Technically. And she is the light of my life but I can't give her what she wants. What we both want. She says you can. You want her, don't you?'

He did. You'd have to be made of stone not to desire Annika. But he could never say that. This was another test. And Francisco was an utter bastard to pull it. Sylvian stayed quiet, because he knew to admit his attraction to the queen could be a death sentence.

Francisco cuffed his shoulder. He was trying to look on this politically, like a battle or a treaty. He was hiding behind bravado, because Annika was everything to him. And whatever Annika wanted, he would give her. Even Sylvian. 'Serve her as you have served me, Sylvian. Make me proud.'

At the end of the corridor, the door to the queen's bedchamber loomed over them both. Sylvian wasn't drunk anymore. He was sober. He'd bathed. There had been perfumed oils. The king had insisted. He'd bloody supervised.

And Lyta stood like a ghost, watching them in disgust.

'You aren't here,' he told her, revolted with himself, with the king, with all she was seeing.

'I'm always here. With you. You know that. Just never took you for a whore. I thought that was the plan for me, not you.'

Sylvian lunged towards her. Instead of recoiling, she pressed her hand against his face. Her gentleness undid him.

'Lyta,' he whispered. It wasn't real. None of it was real. He only wished this part was, that she would touch him like this again, that she would say his name in that way she used to. Before, before . . .

'Come back to me, Sylvian.' Her lips didn't move but he heard her voice. It was everywhere, rippling through him. None of this was real. None of it could be. 'Come back, my love, my heart. Please. You don't belong here. This isn't you.'

But it was. It was all him. All the terrible things he'd done.

The moment he'd broken his promise to never involve Kit in anything criminal, everything had gone wrong.

'Lyta, I wish . . .' He closed his eyes and felt a wash of cold sweep over him again. Someone was sobbing. Kit. It sounded like Kit.

THE BOOK OF GOLD

Sylvian opened his eyes.

He stood in a small, round chamber. Across from him, a statue of a goddess seemed to drag itself from the walls, reaching for them with a ravenous expression on her beautiful, terrible face. Shadows coiled around him like vines, twisting from the ground and plunging into his skin. He tore himself free and they flailed before dissolving into the darkness around him. It was cold, his breath misting before his face, and the only light came from the glow ball in Frida's outstretched hand, trembling with her fear. Kit was on his knees moaning, while the shadows tightened their grip on him, the other ball clenched in his fist, and beside him, Ben was curled into a foetal position, making no noise at all. Tremors quaked through him and the shadows twisted like wire against his skin, digging their way into his skull and filling his open mouth, silencing a full-throated scream.

And Lyta. Lyta stood like the statue, her arms spread apart, tears silvering her face, her eyes wide but unseeing, her mouth a thin, hard line as she fought whatever demons this cursed place had conjured up from her past. Around her feet and calves, the vines had turned hard and shone like polished armour that was even now crawling higher up her body.

The statue carved of white stone looked like a ghost, mirroring her, looming over them all, drinking down their suffering.

Sylvian didn't think. He couldn't. He surged towards her and pulled her into his arms, shaking her, calling her name, tearing those shadowy things off her. The shell clinging to her body cracked and disintegrated like black ice. The shadows faded with his touch, leaving nothing but a trace of frost on her skin and clothes.

Lyta blinked, staring into his face as if seeing him for the first time in years. Her mouth worked, but no sound came out. Then, to his horror, she buried her face into his chest and a sob wrenched its way out of her.

'Lyta, it's all right. I'm here. It's over.' He held her tight, trying to quell the pain and fear. He couldn't guess what she'd seen, what she had endured, but given what he'd experienced, he knew it was bad. 'It's just a nightmare. Just a bad dream. It wasn't real.'

'I had to.' One fist thudded against his chest. 'Damn it, Sylvian, I had to. You— I had to save Kit. They said just one of you— and I— I had to pick him.'

Of course she'd had to choose Kit. He would have done the same. He had been trying to save him in his own way. And she had come back for him, only to hear him give her to Janlow. It wouldn't have mattered whether he meant it, whether he was delirious, whether it was the torture talking. He'd said the words. But he had never thought of what it had done to her. He had never thought she knew.

He wanted to whisper that he'd never hurt her. Except he had. Too many times. The words failed.

'I know,' was all he managed to say.

Lyta drew in a shuddering breath and he felt her pull herself together and withdraw from him again. 'What happened to you? How are you here?'

He winced and glanced around for Kit. 'She was waiting for us. The book's in a vault, not in her library. That was a decoy. She planned all this.'

Lyta pulled free. 'We have to get the others out. It's a trap. A bastard, vicious trap. Help Frida. I've got to . . . Oh gods, Kit!'

Kit. How did he tell her about Kit? That the duchess was using him, that she'd been watching them through him. Because someone had to.

She dropped to her knees in front of her brother, trying desperately to wrench him out of the spell. Because it was Kit. And she'd always choose him. Sylvian didn't blame her. Not now. Not then. Couldn't. Kit was far better than either of them. Always had been.

Frida snapped out of it fighting. Sylvian had to duck the cosh she lashed at him before she even knew it was him. She gasped for air and then doubled over, retching into the darkness. He didn't dare ask if she was all right, let alone what she had seen. Too much, too personal. Like his own nightmarish visions.

Ben was less simple. He was still curled into a ball, the vines twisting like a crown around his head. He'd been there longest and the duchess, or her dark goddess, wanted control of him most of all. Every time Sylvian tried to pull them away, more appeared, plunging beneath his skin and making him whimper with agony. They filled his mouth, pushing deeper down his throat, relentless.

'Let me.' Kit looked ragged and desperate as he shoved Sylvian aside and pressed his hands to either side of Ben's face.

Lyta helped Sylvian to his feet. 'How did you get out of it?'

'It was you,' he told her, distracted. Something like suspicion passed over her features. 'You told me . . . It doesn't matter. I realised it wasn't real. That it couldn't be. Just a nightmare.'

She shuddered, wrapping her arms around her body. 'Just a nightmare,' she echoed, as if unable to believe such words were possible. 'We need to get this over with and get the hell out of here.'

Kit had managed to get Ben back on his feet, though the scholar leaned on him heavily. His hand closed on Kit's wrist. The panic filled Kit's eyes and Ben frowned. 'You have to tell them.'

'There's nothing to tell,' Kit replied stubbornly. But he didn't pull his arm free.

'Kit,' he murmured, turning his name into an admonishment. He sounded tired, exhausted, but he didn't release Kit's arm. Right where he'd been hurt. Right where the duchess had carved her mark into him.

'She's watching us,' Kit blurted. 'She's . . . she's watching us. Using me. She did something when I was in prison. I . . . I don't know what.'

Frida frowned. 'She bound you? You let the duchess carve her mark on you and you didn't tell us? Damn it, Kit. What is it with you Cornellises?'

'It wasn't consensual,' Kit said, pulling himself free of Ben.

'Why didn't you say something?' Sylvian asked, trying not to make that an accusation as well. But someone had to ask.

'She bound his tongue,' Ben said, leaping to his defence. 'I can try to peel back the spell but she's strong and skilled. You know that. More so than we imagined. It's not his fault.'

Lyta wrapped her arms around her brother's shoulders. 'Of course it isn't his fault. I'm sorry, Kit love. I should have known.

I should have guessed. I was so caught up in everything else. I knew you were hurt. I just didn't think to ask how.'

Kit shook his head, clearly wishing he was anywhere but here. 'I couldn't have told you anyway. She made sure of that. I'm her eyes and ears, she said. Bound to obey.'

'But you aren't. Look at me, Kit.' He did reluctantly. She was his sister. He trusted her like she trusted him. But the shame in his face made Sylvian's stomach twist. 'She used you. She doesn't control you. You're here, with us.'

Sylvian spoke up again. 'Because maybe that's where she wants him. Here, so she can watch you. She had a mirror in the library. She was watching every step of the way.'

'I'm blocking it,' said Ben. 'She can't hear us or see us, not for the time being.'

'How?' Lyta asked protectively. She looked like a lioness. 'How can you block it, Alvarez?'

'Let him do it,' said Sylvian. Lyta swung her glare to him. 'No one should be enthralled to that harpy. She has got away with her dark magic for too long.'

'What do you mean?'

'You hardly think your brother is the first. Why do you think so many of her guards follow her with such fanatical loyalty?'

'And the king knows this?'

'Of course he does. If she was just creaming money off the top of his revenues, he wouldn't pay so much attention. No, he came here to stop her specifically. And get the book back. That's how she knows how to do it. That . . . whatever that is.' He gestured at the statue. 'And the book.'

'The book?' Lyta asked. 'The book we're stealing? And you want to give that sort of power to the king?'

Sylvian cast her a bleak look. 'He doesn't need it for that. He has people to do that kind of— It doesn't matter. He just doesn't want *her* to have it.'

Ben looked up from his study of Kit's arm. 'Sylvian is right. She's serving a dark goddess.' He glanced at the statue, as if afraid it might move. 'She has learned things from the book: secrets, magic, blood rites. She may even have used it on the king's father and his brother, thinking Francisco could be more easily manipulated. Royal blood is said to be the most powerful of all, except perhaps for that of Aspects like Beatriz and me. But now we finally have a chance to take it from her.'

He didn't look away from the statue, though he gently rubbed Kit's arm, as if trying to offer comfort.

'Who is she?' Lyta asked.

'I don't know. I don't recognise her. One of the lost ones maybe? One of the ones we turned away from. She's dark and she's dangerous and feeds on fear and suffering. And she's made Iseult strong.'

Sylvian shook his head. 'Not so lost if her power can do this.'

'Why do I feel like a huge lump of information has been kept from me?' Lyta asked, glaring at Sylvian. She was one to talk. What had she been playing at, telling him one plan and then haring off to the dungeons? She carried on, heedless of how she sounded. 'Frida, do you have anything to add? Any dark secrets you need to get off your chest all of a sudden?' Frida had recovered herself enough to be scouting the room for another way out and had found one. She stood by another door of heavy oak crossed with iron.

She eyed each of them coldly, even Lyta. 'Pretty sure you know all my secrets already, Lyta. Seems I'm the only one *not* hiding things here. Want to tell the boys why we're really here? Lyta's looking for her missing husband. We're all second to that.'

Sylvian froze. He couldn't help himself, spitting the words from his mouth. 'You're *what?*' And at the same time . . . *Of course*, something bitter whispered in the back of his mind. *Of course.*

Lyta raised her hands, obviously defeated, denying nothing. She'd come here for Ranulf.

Never leave one of your own behind. That was her creed.

Of course she'd done all this for Ranulf. Sylvian sucked in a breath and felt the stab of betrayal all over again. Because he didn't count in her equations. He never had. But everyone else did. Kit, and now Ranulf.

He stopped himself, grabbed those emotions and pushed them out of sight and out of mind. Out of reach, where they could do no more harm.

There wasn't time for this. They needed to get out. 'There's a door,' he said gruffly. 'Open it.'

Lyta looked like she wanted to explain but then gave up. She pulled out her lockpicks again but this time there was no need. Frida turned the handle and pushed. It swung aside and a soft, warm glow spilled out. The remaining nightmare vines recoiled, slithering back into the darkest corners, pooling beneath the feet of the forgotten goddess.

CHAPTER NINETEEN

Lyta

No one moved. The outer chamber they had come from must be swarming with the prisoners by now, and in here the statue still leered at them, hungry and patient. But ahead was unknown, and after their last experience no one was as keen to rush forwards, Lyta least of all.

The light flickered like a flame, beckoning them in.

'Right,' Lyta said.

But Sylvian was there ahead of her. 'I'll go first. Stay here.'

She hadn't expected that. She'd seen his face when Frida mentioned Ranulf, just for a second seen that stab of punctured faith once again. She had used him. Shit, she had used them all. She'd even used the king. And all for nothing.

But Sylvian pushed that aside, a professional to his core.

He stepped through, sword in hand and Lyta followed him, ignoring his instructions as usual. She let her eyes adjust to the new light. This room was ten times the size of the last, and around the edges statues carved from black obsidian stared sightlessly forward. There was nothing to distinguish one from the next, and no sign of the unsettling face of the goddess. Behind them, bookshelves curved around the walls. Wrought-iron pedestals were dotted at intervals between the statues and the centre of the room, forged to look like human arms reaching upwards, each one cradling an open book.

'What is this place?' Lyra asked.

Sylvian glanced at her. 'I don't know. You're the one with the map in your head.'

But the floor plan she had seen had shown nothing like this. This wasn't Ranulf's plan anymore. Everything here felt like a trap.

If the duchess was watching them, what did she want to see? Lyta didn't want to think about that. She just prayed Ben was right and he could block the spell on Kit. And find a way to peel it back.

'This shouldn't be here. There was no other door marked and no room like this. But it looks like a library, doesn't it?'

'This is her vault,' said Ben suddenly. He stared at the room in wonder. 'It has to be. She said you were close but you'd never make it. Right next to the temple and part of it. That has to be what she meant. Guarded by her goddess.'

Frida cleared her throat. 'So, magic boy. You know this stuff. Where's this book the king wants?'

'That's it,' Ben said, pointing to the middle of the room.

A wooden platform rose from the floor, gilded in intricate patterns, flowers and circles of leaves gleaming in the rich mahogany finish. At its centre another pedestal held a book open for inspection and display. That shifting golden light, which was illuminating the room, came from its pages.

Again, far too easy. It was all too easy.

Ben moved before any of them could stop him.

'Ben, wait,' Kit called. 'It might be another trap. It might be—'

As soon as the scholar's foot struck the first step, the door behind them slammed shut. The noise reverberated around the room, louder and louder as it built on its own echoes. Lyta covered her ears but saw Sylvian tense, weapons ready.

The black statues around them lurched into life.

Lyta scrambled back as the nearest figure lunged at her. It was swift with fluid movements, not like a statue at all.

She twisted to avoid the hand reaching for her. Sylvian's sword was a blur, his body burning with life and death. Ben threw himself at the book, the light illuminating his face with an unholy glow. Frida cried out in alarm and Kit took a blow to his face which sent him flying across the room.

'Kit!' Lyta yelled, but he didn't move. No, this couldn't be happening. She dodged another of the grasping figures, and slid under its legs, using her feet to trip it.

It fell with a clatter. Lyta stamped hard on the small of its back before kicking it in the head until it went still. They weren't armed and for that she thanked the old gods. But they didn't need weapons. They were weapons.

Five were closing in on Sylvian. They would tear him limb from limb given half the chance. He was the greatest threat here and they all knew it.

Frida had seized one of the iron pedestals and was using it like a mace on the one coming at her, trying to force it back as best she could. The final one bore down on Kit and Lyta threw herself at it. She leaped onto its back, clawing at the mask covering its face as it spun around trying to dislodge her.

'Ben, do something!' Lyta screamed. 'Help Kit!'

Ben looked up from the book. He seemed dazed, as if he had been a million miles away. But when his gaze fell on Kit, he tore himself away, pulling Kit onto the platform beside him, away from the statues – who didn't follow. Why didn't they follow? They hadn't gone near Ben, not once he was at the book. They'd attacked everyone else but not him.

Ben held Kit and rage passed over his normally gentle face. But then the book pulsed with unnatural light, as though it was calling to him.

'What are you doing?' Lyta yelled. 'Get him to safety. Please!'

But he didn't. Instead, he let go of Kit, stood up and placed both hands on the pages of the book. Light exploded everywhere.

Lyta's eyes burned and she had to shut them against the brightness. When her vision finally returned, the entire platform was gone.

The guard beneath her spun around and she had to cling on as he pitched forward, trying to dislodge her. As they came up, she saw

Sylvian had despatched all but two of them and Frida was laying into hers with a fury.

But Kit and Ben . . .

Sylvian took the head off one in a spray of bright red blood. The statue fell to the ground, still twitching.

They weren't statues, Lyta realised. They were people. They were people who had been trapped by the vines, just as they had almost been. Trapped and enchanted and . . .

'Sylvian! Stop!'

Oh, gods and goddesses.

But Sylvian didn't stop. He couldn't. He probably couldn't hear her and even if he had . . . He was a warrior. He fought to kill and he was lost in a blood rage, like one of Kyron's own chosen.

The last of the enchanted prisoners fell to its knees in front of him, Sylvian's knife buried hilt-deep in a chink in the armour. The one under Lyta reversed course and charged backwards, slamming her against the bookshelves. The air went from her body and something inside her cracked, followed by a spear of pain that made her release her grip. She slid down as the figure turned, towering over her. It reached down to seize her by the throat, lifting her with ease in spite of her feeble struggles.

She gagged and tried to shout but it was useless. Her neck was caught in a grip of stone, cold and implacable, crushing the life from her.

Except it didn't crush her. It held her, almost as if it was studying her. The head tilted to one side in a familiar way. She knew him. She was sure she knew him. And he knew her. The broad shoulders and a too familiar bulky frame tensed for a moment and then he began to release her.

Frida slammed the metal pedestal against the side of his head, sending him sprawling onto the floor, and Lyta fell with him, landing heavily at his side, gasping for breath.

'Syl, finish it off!' Frida yelled.

The mask had cracked and fallen away revealing most of his face. *His* face. His pale eyes blinked at her and she could see the recognition in them. Confusion, pain, agony . . . but recognition.

She knew him. How could she fail to know him?

Sylvian stepped over him, sword tip poised at the back of his neck. One swift movement and it would all be over. His face was hard as stone. Judge and executioner. He raised the sword, ready to bring it down.

Lyta threw herself across the body. Sylvian pulled back, staring at her.

'What are you doing?'

'You can't. You can't kill him. It's Ranulf!'

CHAPTER TWENTY

Kit

Light spilled around him, bright and beautiful, more than sunlight, more than fire. It flickered and danced on the stone-vaulted ceiling. For a moment Kit feared he was back in the nightmare, trapped again. But this was no dream of his. Kit's head pounded and he could taste blood in his mouth. When he tried to move, he let out a weak groan which echoed back at him.

But at least he could move. And feel. That had to count for something. Even if all he felt was pain. Never mind he was feeling far too much of it. He tried to force his blurred vision to focus and pushed himself up on his elbows, looking around.

Ben stood over the lectern, his hands pressed to the book. Slowly, he turned the pages and the glow lit his face in an infernal light. There was nothing else. No sign of the others or their attackers, just this tiny windowless, doorless room and bare stone walls.

'Ben?' Kit's voice grated against the inside of his throat. 'What happened? Where are we?'

'We're safe.'

'And the others?'

Ben didn't answer. His eyes flickered back and forth as he read, his brow furrowing.

Kit pulled himself up on all fours and clambered to his feet. His head swam sickeningly, as if he'd been drinking for days, and his stomach threatened to empty itself. This was not good. Not good at all.

Two years ago, he'd been knocked out when the shelves had come down in the workshop, falling in a shower of metal-type pieces and wooden trays. Jem said he'd been lucky they hadn't killed him. This felt worse. Like he'd run headfirst into a wall. Which given what had attacked them did not feel far from the truth.

They were alone in the silence and the eerie light. There was no obvious way in or out.

'Ben, where are the others?'

'I need to focus on this.'

He barely sounded like the timid scholar Kit had come to know in so short a time. There was an ice in his voice that hadn't been there before. He sounded . . . wrong.

'Ben?' The glare Ben shot at him stopped him in his tracks. He looked wrong too. Furious, dangerous, *other*. 'What have you done?'

Ben slammed down one hand on the pedestal and sparks flew from his skin. That's when Kit saw it. The light was running through him, and with it words, unreadable and ancient – the words of the book.

Iron negated magic, Kit remembered from something he'd read. Or printed. One of those old texts. So the magic of the book flowed through Ben instead.

'I can't . . . I can't focus. You have to . . . You have to let me . . .' His voice shook and he frowned. His voice softened and he stared around him as if seeing the place for the first time. But his hands didn't move from the book. 'Kit, there's so much . . . so much in here. And it . . .'

'This isn't right. Ben, please. Stop.'

'I can't. I have to do this. I have to. It's all in here. They're here. I just have to . . .' He gave a gasp of pain. Like he was struggling to breathe.

Kit edged towards him. He reached out, his hand closing on Ben's shoulder. The scholar sagged a little against his touch. As Kit glanced down at the book he saw that the pages Ben had already read were blank.

Ben turned another page and his hand shook.

'What are you doing?' Kit asked.

'What I have to do. What I came here to do.'

'I thought we came to steal the book.'

Ben glanced at Kit. A bitter smile flickered over his mouth, so close to Kit's own. 'That's what I'm doing. I have a way with words. I told you.'

'Magic? Like your sister? But you said you weren't an Aspect.'

'I'm not. I'm something else. Kit, please . . .'

'Did you lock us in here? You said—'

Another voice came from Ben's lips, lips that were no longer smiling, and Kit recoiled at the change, before he even figured out the words. 'Yes, *magic*. Call it magic. Fine. It's simplistic and stupid but call it that if it helps. We're safe for now, if we're quick. Now let us work.' It didn't sound like Ben at all. It sounded ancient, short-tempered and exasperated.

Kit didn't know what to do, what to say. Logic screamed at him to let go, to leave Ben to it and back away as far as he could. It was either magic or the scholar was possessed. Or perhaps it was even worse than that. How was he to know? He was just a printer. He worked with his hands, with paper and ink. With real and tangible things. Not this. Whatever *this* was.

Besides there was nowhere to go. The tiny room pressed close around them. There was no way out except one that he hoped Ben could provide. Or whatever was using Ben.

'Who are you?'

Ben scowled, and then his expression was wiped away and his eyes grew round, their many autumnal shades aglow from within, like stained glass.

'Please, there isn't much more and precious little time. We won't hurt him. He's going to be fine. We just . . . we need him. He's ours. Always had been. Our Nexus.. Made for us. Please . . . Just a little more.'

Again, not Ben. Kit knew that instinctively. This one was gentle at least, pleading. But so very alien. And talking to the strange voices coming out of his friend didn't seem wise. At least this last one said 'please'.

'Can you take much more of this, Ben?'

Name him, something was screaming in the back of his mind. *Keep using his name. Remind him who he is.* Otherwise, Ben could be swept away altogether and Kit could lose him.

Him. The voice had referred to Ben as *him*. Not *me*. It had said *we*, not *I*.

There was more than one of them, whatever they were, and they were not Ben. They were using him.

Ben turned another page. A sob burst through his lips. Shivers passed over his body. Tears slid down his face and glowed as they hit the pages of the book.

Kit wrapped his arms around him and Ben's legs gave out. He slipped forward, his strength almost gone. Still he clung to the book, and light and words slid up his skin, vanishing inside him.

'Kit,' Ben whispered, and this time it was Ben. No doubting that. 'I'm scared.' But he didn't stop. Not for a second. 'Help me, Kit. Please. We've got to do this. We can't leave them here. This is the only way.'

The memory of the nightmare of Ben bearing down on him reared up in his mind. Panic raced along every vein in Kit's body, and then rage followed. Rage and fury such as he had never known. He needed to stop Ben, to throw him to the ground, grab the lectern and smash his head . . .

Kit recoiled from the intrusive thoughts. That was not him. It would never be. Maybe Ben wasn't the only one possessed.

You belong to me, Christopher Cornellis.

Ben had never said that. It had been the Duchess of Montalbeau. And Ben had never looked at him with such malevolence. Concern, gentle amusement, perhaps even desire, but not that. If he wanted to belong to anyone it was to someone like Benedictus Alvarez.

Holding him close, Kit tried to breathe calmly, softly, silently offering him the strength he needed. At the same time, he assessed their surroundings again. There was nothing to help him here and the oppressive feeling was growing.

The duchess was angry. And if she couldn't make Kit obey, she'd try something else.

Another sound was bearing down on his senses now, a low grinding noise. It wasn't Ben's laboured breathing or his own hammering heart. It wasn't the rustle of the pages.

It was coming from the walls. The walls which were not as far away as they had been. The room, which had been small to begin with, had shrunk by a good yard already.

'It's closing in on us,' he told Ben.

'I know. I can't hold it all. I have to keep her from you. Her magic is too strong, Kit. She's defending the book. She'll kill us and destroy it rather than let it go.'

There had to be something he could do. Walls didn't just move. Something had to be driving them.

Think, Kit.

He handled machinery all the time. He was good with it, could work out problems and kinks, the logic of them singing to him. The wooden floor wasn't being destroyed. The walls were moving over it, which meant . . .

'Ben, just hold on,' he said. And then Kit addressed the things within his friend. 'You, whoever you are, if you hurt him, I will hunt you down. He needs your help if you want him to finish this. He needs your strength, or none of us are getting out. Understand?'

Silence fell around them, as if something old and vast was considering his words. Kit could feel them studying him. He felt like he'd peeled back the veil of the world and was witnessing something else, something ancient and powerful and *other*. And he'd just given it an ultimatum.

'And what will you do?' asked the gentle voice.

'I'm going to find us a way out. Or at least a way to stop us being crushed to death. Because I imagine if you're determined to stay in Ben, you're just as vulnerable as we are.'

There was another long pause.

'Proceed,' said the older, harder voice – the one Kit was really starting to loathe. 'We will support Benedictus and lend him strength. But there will be a price.'

'Fine. A price. We'll pay a price, right Ben? But later.'

'Later. It is agreed.'

Gods and goddesses, Kit hoped he was doing the right thing.

Ben stiffened and began to turn the pages even more quickly, his attention entirely focused on the book. His breath hitched but he didn't seem to notice. The walls were still closing in. And Kit was running out of time.

He had to find some way to stop the machinery. His eyes fell on the lectern, the only thing other than the two of them and *The Book of Gold*. Iron. Thick and heavy.

'I need that,' he said and ripped the metal stand out from under the book. Impossibly the book itself hung in the air, the golden light coiling around it like a living thing. But what was one more impossible thing right now! His world, which had seemed so solid and secure and real was full of them all of a sudden.

Kit lifted the pedestal. The bottom was square, a block with sharp edges. Exactly what he needed.

He brought it down on the wooden floorboards, raised it up and struck again. A second time. A third.

'What are you doing?' Ben asked. Or someone did. He forced himself to ignore the question. The walls were getting too close, hemming them in, forcing him back.

He hefted his makeshift tool again, bringing it down with a shout. The floor splintered. Twice more and he'd made a hole big enough to peer through. Without pausing, he lay the pedestal down lengthwise, hoping that it would slow the walls on either side once they reached it, and peered into the darkness beneath. He needed more light. Then he remembered the glow ball. He'd stowed it in his pocket when they'd entered the previous room. It gave him only a wavering light to work by, but it was enough.

Cogs turned a long metal screw, tightening either way. He just needed to wedge something in there that was solid enough to stop it, or at least slow it down. The lectern was too big. He'd have to widen the hole and there wasn't time. Besides, the walls had reached each end of the pedestal, and though their approach had stalled for now, even the iron was not going to last forever. He could already hear it straining and starting to give. Maybe the walls would go first. It was a toss-up really.

He couldn't risk moving it.

Above him Ben slammed the book shut and it dropped to the ground, all the magic drained out of it. Just a book bound in good, strong leather on wooden boards, pages made of parchment.

Kit didn't think. He didn't have time. Grabbing the book, he shoved it through the gap, deep into the mechanism.

For a moment nothing happened, but then everything ground to a halt with an agonising groan.

Ben slumped down beside him, eyes closed, skin pale and washed-out in the flickering light of the glow ball, their only remaining source of illumination.

'Fuck!' Kit snarled as he struggled to stand. The space was barely wide enough for both of them. 'Ben, talk to me. Are you all right? Ben!'

No answer. Ben was breathing but in fitful starts and that couldn't be good. They needed to get out of this miserable oubliette, or it would all have been for nothing.

Then he heard it. A noise overhead, a scraping of stone on stone. A gap appeared, and then an impossible, wonderful face.

'Stop loitering down there with that boy, Kit Cornellis,' Lyta yelled, unaccountably delighted with herself. It made him want to slap her if he was honest, a feeling that was at least familiar. 'We're getting out of this shithole. Do you have the book?'

Kit winced and looked at Ben, lying there, no longer glowing, no longer covered in floating words, no longer speaking with all those other voices.

'It's a long story,' he said.

He only hoped he was right.

'Oh, you just wait for a long story,' she replied, and he stared, the joy in her face impossible to explain.

He hauled Ben up, shaking him awake. He seemed dazed and delirious but then his eyes fixed on Kit and he smiled. Really smiled. Except it wasn't his smile. 'Thank you,' he said. And passed out again.

Cursing, Kit manhandled him upwards and let Sylvian and Frida lift him out. Beneath him he could hear the gears grinding again. He was running out of time. Sylvian's arm reached down and Kit had to leap up to grab hold.

As he sprawled on the floor of the room above, littered with black-armoured bodies and blood, he heard everything underneath give way in a crash of wood, metal and stone. Still swearing to himself, and at himself, he sat up, looking for Ben.

He had to tell them what had happened, what Ben had done. The magic, the voices, everything.

But the impossible sight of Ranulf Wray stole whatever words he had been trying to form and the thought was lost in his shock.

Lyta had been right. She'd found him.

CHAPTER TWENTY-ONE

Lyta

Had Ranulf been there all this time, locked in a spell and unable to break free? Lyta would have sworn that no jail could hold the old thief, but it looked like he had finally met his match in the Duchess of Montalbeau and her cursed magic.

'How long?' he said again and his voice shook. She didn't like it. He sounded shattered. This wasn't the Ranulf she knew. He'd been unbreakable. Everyone said so.

'What happened?' she asked, instead of answering.

'There were three of us: Anover, Daimon and me.' He glanced at the bodies. A shudder ran through him, and he turned his face away. She didn't ask who the others were. Maybe they'd been here longer. Maybe they'd come afterwards. 'Should have been easy.' Lyta thought of the ring on her necklace, the one her god had insisted she steal. He had guided her here, but that was to get Ranulf, surely. But why would he have abandoned Ranulf here in the first place? 'The next thing I knew I was stuck in that thing, trapped in nightmares, and had no control over what I did anymore. Damn it, Lyta. I could have killed you.'

'But you didn't. And you're all right now. We're getting out of here. Do you remember the plan?'

He frowned, staring at her and she thought for a moment that he looked far older than she remembered. Older than his years. Something – that spark, that rebellion, whatever it was – that something was gone. Stolen. Carved away by the duchess.

THE BOOK OF GOLD

'The plan's out the window now, pet. Those maps were lies, all of them, part of her trap. She likes to watch us run around in this maze, likes to see who dies first, who gives up, who breaks down. She feeds our pain and suffering to that bitch goddess of hers. This place moves and changes all the time. But I can still get you out, Eninn willing.'

Eninn willing. He'd always said that. Well, Eninn hadn't been much bloody help when he'd got himself trapped in here, had he? And where was the little demon now when a bit of divine help would come in handy? Eninn didn't have any power here, she realised. Not in the temple of another god.

Frida and Kit were still trying to revive Ben. Whatever had happened down there in that hidden room, Kit looked stunned. Seeing Ranulf had almost brought him to his knees.

The old man wrapped his arms around her brother and held him close for a moment. 'It's all right, son. It's over.'

'We thought you were dead,' Kit mumbled into his shoulder. He had dwarfed Ranulf for years but still reverted to an awkward teen with him, folding over him as he hugged him, all limbs and elbows.

Ranulf gave that familiar gruff laugh. 'You know me better than that. Now get that boy up on his feet or we're going to have her guards to contend with. Not to mention what else she can throw at us. Sylvian's good with a blade, but not that good.'

Sylvian eyed him warily. He was splattered with blood and looked half-animal. He hadn't sheathed his weapons yet.

'What happened to the book?' Lyta asked. Kit frowned.

'It's gone.' It was the worst thing she could have heard. They'd come all this way for nothing? 'I destroyed it. But I think Ben . . .'

Ben had finally opened his eyes and he blinked, staring around him as if seeing them for the first time.

'Ben?' Lyta asked.

'I've got it,' Ben Alvarez told her and tapped his head with a trembling hand.

'You memorised the book? The whole book?' She could do that with a map or an architectural plan, but not an entire tome. Lyta thought of Beatriz's insistence that Benedictus join them. 'I get the impression that you and your sister have plans of your own, Alvarez.'

And if those plans involved double-crossing her or her brother, she could happily leave him to rot down here.

Ben eyed her warily. 'I swear to you, by Eninn and all his brethren, I will transcribe it for you when we're out of here. But we need to move.'

'On that we agree,' Sylvian chimed in. 'We can't stay. I can't fight off an army.' And clearly he didn't expect anyone else to be any help.

Lyta scowled at him, and he returned the new stony expression she was growing used to now.

'I've had enough of this box of tricks anyway,' she told them. 'Let's go home.'

Not that they had a home anymore. They had a pile of smoking rubble. She ached at the thought of telling Ranulf. He moved stiffly, his feet slow and heavy, forcing himself on with a grim determination. Making for one of the bookshelves he traced a line along the topmost one and then down to the left. A panel slid open, the shelves moving to reveal another doorway.

'She needs a way in to admire her treasures. And her—' He glanced back at the obsidian-encrusted bodies. 'Her trophies. Come on. It isn't far. And the others won't be long behind us. We can slow them down though.'

The others. Lyta thought of the dungeons and their inhabitants. Was that who he meant?

He stepped inside, with Frida and the remaining light close behind him. Kit slung Ben's arm over his shoulder and the two of them followed. Until finally only Lyta and Sylvian were left.

'Lyta,' he said in a low, dangerous voice. 'Be careful. There's something more going on here.'

Thinking of Ben Alvarez, she nodded. 'A lot more.'

'The chances of that being Ranulf, of him surviving . . .'

'It's Ranulf,' she told him, more certain of that than anything else. 'But he isn't telling us everything.'

'How do you know?'

She gave a brief laugh. 'He never did before. I'll watch him, Syl. I promise. Just watch my back for me, all right?'

'Did you know he was in here? Was this why you said you'd do it?'

There was an edge to his voice she didn't like. Something like accusation. But what did it matter now? She'd done what she had to do. That was all. She always paid her debts.

'I had an idea. I hoped we'd find him. I didn't know if he was still alive, but Eninn—'

'Eninn the Trickster? How can you trust a trickster?'

She gestured to the place Ranulf had vanished. 'He hasn't let me down yet.' And she prayed he wouldn't. There was always a first time and they were not out of here yet.

Sylvian narrowed his eyes, studying her, but he didn't pursue it. She wasn't sure what that might mean. Finally, he nodded grimly and waved his dagger towards the open doorway. 'Why aren't you ever properly armed?' he asked, as if it was grave oversight.

'I am.' She pulled out the stubby little belt knife she used for everything from food to forcing things open that wanted to remain closed. He eyed it in such disbelief she thought for a moment she ought to be insulted on its behalf.

'That's not a weapon. It's a tool, barely more than a toothpick.'

Lyta shrugged. 'Never needed a weapon before. They're illegal in Amberes for people like me. Besides, confrontation isn't my style.'

Janlow had taken that very same knife from her in seconds. She just wasn't very good with weapons and didn't really like them. Not that she would ever admit that, especially not to Sylvian.

'I think styles have changed, Lyta.' With a swift movement he flipped the dagger around and handed her the hilt. It was heavy in her hand, the grip still warm from his skin. Comforting.

'I was afraid you'd say that,' she sighed and slid it under her belt. There was no point in arguing for once. Sylvian barred the door behind them and they followed the others.

Ranulf wasn't wrong about being followed. As they hurried down the passage the sound of pursuit grew, savage snarls and, behind that, the sound of armoured men. Soon they were running blindly. They came to a narrow door which they poured through, slamming it behind them. Ranulf and Sylvian lifted the bar across it.

'You think that'll slow them down?' Sylvian asked. Despite his words of warning, Lyta noticed how well they worked together. In another life they would have made a good team.

'A bit,' Ranulf said. 'Not much. But it'll take time to get through, especially in numbers. And from the sound of it they have numbers. They aren't stupid, or mindless. Just possessed or driven insane. Hard to say.'

'I'll stay here, stop them as they come through.'

Ranulf shook his head. 'Not here. You'd be fucked. Further up. There's a perfect place.' They took off again as something thudded into the barrier behind them.

'Do you know where we're going?' Lyta asked

'Not far now,' Ranulf called back. 'The way splits ahead: one way up to her private chambers and the other out to the back courtyard. You'll have to run for it but once you're clear of the gate it's a straight path.'

'Why? Why build this?' Kit asked, always with the questions.

'She wants her own way out if it ever comes down to it, doesn't she?' Up ahead their way was blocked by a heavy portcullis, oak and iron, but Ranulf didn't hesitate. He reached into a gap on the left and pulled the lever there. Slowly, the portcullis dragged itself up. Breathing hard, Ranulf clung to the lever and ushered them through. 'It drops fast,' he told them. 'So get moving.'

'How did you know that?' Kit demanded. 'How did you know where to go? What to do?'

Outside. Lyta could smell air. Blessed, fresh air.

But Kit didn't move. Lyta stopped beside him. Something was wrong here. Desperately wrong. Her hand closed firmly on the knife.

'What aren't you telling us?' Kit growled and Ranulf gave him a small, sad smile. 'I'm used to Lyta keeping things from me, but she learned it from you. What are you up to?'

'You always were the brightest, Kit, my boy.' He pressed his hand to Kit's face and his ragged sleeve fell back around his arm, exposing the livid red marks. Kit jerked back and Ben gave a hiss of recognition.

The same mark as Kit wore. The cuts the duchess had given him when she bespelled him and formed the link that Ben had broken. Or at least dampened.

Something else to work out, Lyta thought bitterly. Ranulf turned his other hand over, exposing the forearm and the same mark repeated. Old and deep. 'I can feel her, just like you can. A link works both ways. And I've had a lot of time to figure it out. Time when I couldn't do anything else. Locked in nightmares. You don't want to find out, Kit. Get to safety. Go on.'

Kit swallowed hard, clearly wanting to say something more. But in the end he nodded, hurrying for the light with Ben limping along between him and Frida.

Ranulf didn't move. And he wasn't going to, Lyta realised.

The portcullis was a heavy, fortified barricade, a way to close the passage completely and trap any pursuers behind it. It stood open now, but only because Ranulf had reached it first. Release the handle and it would drop in seconds, sealing off any hope of escape. And there was no way to hold it open without someone standing there. No way to open it from the other side.

'Get out, Lyta,' he told her firmly.

'I'm not leaving you here. Ranulf, I can't just—'

His face fell and he looked so old as he tapped his head. 'She's in here, love. And she's been here for too long. I'm not going to get rid of her, not now. But payback is a bitch, just like she is.'

Sylvian stared at him, as if seeing more than Lyta could. 'Why?'

Ranulf glanced down, and Lyta let her gaze follow his. At his feet, the obsidian shell had started to climb back up, covering him as far as his calves. Shadows were already moving higher over his skin, binding him in stone. 'She's been busy while we've been chatting. I'm not going anywhere. And I don't want to live like this, not again. Understand me now?'

Sylvian just nodded, once, and before Lyta could argue he plunged into the guardroom, emerging with a small barrel and an assortment of weapons. He handed Ranulf a sword and several knives. The barrel he rolled down the passageway behind them while Lyta tried to persuade Ranulf to run.

'We can't just leave you. We have to do something.'

'Not this time. It was my fault back then. I should have stepped in so much earlier as soon as I realised what Janlow was planning. If I hadn't lied to protect you all, well, things would have been different.'

'What lies?' Lyta asked.

'Too many. He came back.' He nodded at Sylvian who watched him with a face of stone, giving nothing away. 'I never told you that. I was the one who got him conscripted, because otherwise he was going to drag young Kit down the same path as himself. And you too probably, once he got out again.'

'Ranulf,' Lyta whispered, taking a step back. He'd lied to get her to marry him? Why? He hadn't even wanted her. 'Ranulf, what did you do?'

'Too many things, pet. I told Syl he'd be okay if he took conscription for one thing, and I'm sorry for that. Then I told him you hated him. And after that scene in the jail cell who wouldn't believe it? Even though I knew waiting for him was tearing you apart. I told him to leave you alone, not to even try talking to you. And was the army the making of you, Captain Chant?'

Sylvian shook his head, his mouth a hard line. 'You don't know the half of it.' That didn't sound like confirmation.

'Fucked one way or the other. Story of my life too. But I had to look after her. Eninn had said so and that was it. But I would have done it anyway. I'd do the same thing again.'

The two of them looked at her, then at each other. Their eyes met in a shared understanding and Lyta knew she'd lost. She hated it. Hated both of them. But they were never going to let her stay with them. Sacrifice themselves sure. But her, never.

'Here,' said Sylvian, handing Ranulf a slim pistol, the kind assassins used. 'You know how to use this? It's primed but you'll only get one shot.'

THE BOOK OF GOLD

Ranulf nodded. Sylvian took the remaining glow ball and rolled it back down the tunnel. It clinked as it hit the barrel and lay there, softly illuminating the floor.

A crash told them the guards had broken through the door. They were out of time.

The obsidian was up to Ranulf's thighs now.

'I'm not able to go anywhere, love, and we both know it,' he said in that gruff, gentle voice.

Lyta stepped in close. There wasn't time. She couldn't say what needed to be said. Couldn't do anything but what Ranulf wanted. She had to leave him. She hated herself. Hated him. Hated everything.

'Ranulf, please . . . I came for you. I don't care about the book. Eninn sent me here for you. I can't—'

Ranulf wrapped his hand around hers. 'You can and you will. And Eninn doesn't give a damn about me. It's you he's watching over. Always has. I'll hold the way long enough for you and I can take some of those bastards with me – release the wretched creatures.' His expression softened. 'The best thing I ever did, pet, was look after you and Kit. But I did a lot of ill too – to you and to Syl. And I'm sorry for that. Hold on to him this time, Lyta. Don't fuck it up.' With that he pushed her beyond the portcullis. She staggered, trying to find her footing. Sylvian caught her, holding her there.

The portcullis came down like a headsman's axe, cutting them off from Ranulf.

Lyta flung herself against it, but it wasn't going to budge. She could hear the inhuman wave of creatures coming. Too many of them. Pouring down the tunnel in a fury. They sounded ferocious, animalistic, whipped to a frenzy. Behind them, driving them in a stampede, the duchess's guards followed.

'I'm coming back for you.' She reached through the gaps. 'I'll find a way.'

'There's no way back from this, Lyta love. If they take me, she'll make sure that next time I'm locked in her enchantment for good. I know her, remember?'

'I will find a way.'

'And I'll be long dead – if I'm lucky. Now,' Ranulf hissed, clenching his teeth and raising his weapons as he turned to face the oncoming horde. 'Go!'

But Lyta couldn't move.

Sylvian seized her, throwing her over his shoulder. Ranulf aimed the pistol and fired. Up ahead the barrel ignited, gunpowder inside it exploding to screams and shouts, but still they kept coming. As Sylvian carried her away, Lyta saw them for a moment, illuminated by the fire, a sea of monsters. Throwing knives flashed through the dark and the sword rose as Ranulf faced the onslaught. The obsidian held him upright and he met them like an Aspect of Kyron himself, ready to fight until the strength drained out of him with his blood and his life. And all the time the shadows climbed higher.

Frida drove the wagon straight at them as they emerged into the shabby courtyard. Sylvian threw Lyta into the back, leaping in after her. She could hear Kit calling her name, asking her what had happened, where Ranulf was, but she couldn't find her voice to answer.

They thundered away through the outer gate, where the portcullis stood open and the guards were passed out against the wall, exactly as she'd predicted – perhaps the only thing that had actually gone to plan in the whole disaster.

Lyta curled her hand around the pendant and the ring dangling around her neck and cursed the little god who had sent her here for nothing.

CHAPTER TWENTY-TWO

Lyta

Lyta didn't remember how they got back to Amberes, or back to Beatriz's house. Perhaps it didn't matter. She'd got Ranulf back, only to lose him again. She had never believed he was dead, not really. But now she did.

She had loved him. Not in a romantic way, but like the father she'd never known. Like a friend, a mentor. Like the one person in the world she knew would never let her down.

And now he was gone.

The plan lay in tatters. There was no book and she severely doubted Ben's claim that he had the whole thing memorised, because who could do that? Kit had been jabbering on about magic and voices all the way back, trying to explain what had happened when they vanished.

Lyta had hugged her knees to her chest and tried not to listen, not to feel, to block it all away. Because the moment she dropped those walls . . .

'Lyta?'

Sylvian's voice was hesitant and unsure. Lyta had stumbled into the bedroom while Beatriz assured her that baths were being drawn and that they would be cared for in every way possible.

The necklace around her neck felt unbearably heavy, as if the thong would cut through her neck. She pulled it out and stared at it, at the silver pendant Ranulf had given her when they wed, and the ring she had stolen from Alderton's safe because Eninn wanted it. Because it would help her find her husband.

She had failed Ranulf. And Eninn had failed them both.

'Lyta, please, talk to me.'

Sylvian again. She frowned and put the necklace away. 'About what?'

Sylvian knelt down in front of her. He'd shed the leather jerkin and wore only a clean loose white shirt over his breeches. He'd washed, his hair still wet and falling in black locks over his forehead. He smelled of honey and lavender.

When had he had time to wash?

'Have you been here since we got back?'

She was sitting on the floor at the foot of the bed, her legs splayed out in front of her. When she'd made it to the quiet of the room she had tried to sit on the end of the bed, but had slid down to the plush carpet, unable to stand. She knew she'd wept. Now she ached with emptiness.

'Sylvian?' she whispered.

'Yes. Come on. You can't stay here like that.'

Like what? And then she realised she was still covered in blood and dirt, still stinking of sweat, still wearing the clothes she'd worn when Ranulf—

Sylvian lifted her and carried her out of the room, and this time she let him. The bathing room smelled of scented oils and the warm air wafted around in a fragrant mist. Lyta closed her eyes, letting her head rest on his shoulder as he gave someone instructions about fresh hot water, towels and a change of clothes.

'It doesn't matter,' she tried to tell him.

'Yes, it does.' It was a voice that would brook no argument.

If she looked at herself she'd see the blood and she'd remember all over again.

'I never hated you, Sylvian. And I never wanted to betray you.'

Sylvian sighed, the world-weary sound of someone who knew far too much about battle and death. And betrayal.

'No one said we were too bright back then.' When she opened her eyes, his dark gaze was fixed on her, and his eyes were full of ghosts. 'Can you undress yourself? Do you need help?'

She frowned. She wasn't a child. She hadn't been hurt. But when she finally tried to tug at her clothes with numb hands, he grumbled and set about unbuckling her belt, pulling off her boots, tossing everything in an unruly pile by the door. The knife he slid carefully out of sight.

A sob bubbled up in her chest again. His arms came around her, and she leaned against him and let him hold her, grateful for his warmth. Grateful for him.

No one else could hurt her quite so much as Sylvian. But right now, she didn't care. Everything hurt anyway. What was one small comfort?

'Come on,' he said at last. 'You need to bathe.'

He helped her slip out of her clothes and held her arm as she stepped into the deep fragrant water, letting its warmth soak through her as she lowered herself to sit. Sylvian had averted his eyes, she realised. Maybe the scars and bruises disgusted him. Maybe he just didn't want to look at her now. She certainly wouldn't.

She huddled in the water, pathetic and aching.

Ranulf was gone. She'd thought Eninn was showing her how to get him back. But he'd just wanted the book. Or the ring. Or something else. She didn't even know what yet. Ranulf was gone.

The avaricious little sod had been no help at all.

'Sit back,' he said. 'Stretch out your legs. The water will help with the tension. I promise. Here, let me . . .'

He scooped up the water in his hands and let it run over her shoulders, then over her hair. He coaxed her to lie back, his touch soothing and gentle, never lingering, never too hard on her. He washed her with determination and gentleness. He rubbed suds into her hair, untangling it with his clever fingers and combing through it until it was clean.

Lyta closed her eyes and lay back in the water, wishing she could just float away. All that mattered was here and now, Sylvian washing her clean and the glorious scent of the water, the steam in the air and the warmth driving the ice from her heart. His supple, dexterous fingers worked the tired muscles of her neck and shoulders, eased her arms and legs, until she drifted in the quiet, almost lulled to sleep.

'There now,' he murmured, his voice so gentle it hardly sounded like him. 'You need to get out, Lyta. The water's going cold.'

She let him help her to her feet and wrap her in warm and fluffy towels. He set to work again once she stepped out of the water, drying her with a focused determination. No simple task this for him. He approached it like a quest, like he'd been given a royal decree, or had been commanded by one of the gods. It made her feel safe. Treasured.

He made her feel safe.

The nightgown was long and woven from fine silk, the type of thing she would never have bought for herself, even if she could afford it. Another gift from Beatriz, no doubt.

'There,' he said, and he smiled. An actual smile. Not a grimace, not a scowl, not one of those dark self-deprecating grins.

She ignored the grime left behind in the water. Because although he had washed her clean of it, that was only the surface, wasn't it? She was still the same person underneath.

The cold swept over her again, eating into her bones, breaking her heart. She closed her eyes and felt her body wilt.

'Oh no,' Sylvian told her. 'No you don't.'

Before she knew what he was doing he'd scooped her up again and carried her back into her room, settling her on the bed. He pulled the blankets up over her, but when he started to move away she grabbed his wrist.

'Don't leave me.'

Reluctantly, he sank to sit on the bed beside her. Just as she had sat with him when he'd almost died.

'You need to sleep,' he told her.

But Lyta shook her head. She didn't want to sleep. Sleep would bring dreams and she knew that all her dreams would be nightmares.

'Sylvian, stay with me. I need you.'

His mouth opened but no words came out. He just stared at her.

Perhaps he didn't understand. Perhaps he thought her brains were addled. But she didn't want to be alone. She wanted to feel his body against hers. She wanted him. Just him. And she had done all along. She'd let too much of life slip by her.

She was not going to give him up again. She needed his warmth, his love, or at least something physical that might pass for love, if you looked at it sideways, in the dark. She needed *something*. And he had been the one she had always wanted it from. She needed to know she was still alive, that she could feel.

'Syl,' she whispered and pushed herself up on shaking arms so she could kiss him.

His lips trembled against hers and then, as if a spell had been broken, he kissed her back, his mouth hot and demanding. He slipped his hand into her damp hair and smoothed his thumb along the sensitive line of her jaw until she shivered. A sound came from deep inside him, something between desperation and submission and he shifted around, pressing her back down onto the pile of pillows. He kissed her like she was the air he needed to breathe.

Lyta tugged at the hem of his shirt and slid her hands underneath it. He shuddered at her touch, every muscle tensing. On his knees on the bed beside her, he leaned in further, pressing his body into her grip.

And just when she thought he'd tear the nightgown off her, he pulled back.

His eyes were darker than ever, the pupils wide with need. There was no doubting his desire for her. All the years apart, all the time separated, never expecting to see each other again, had magnified everything. All that wasted time blaming each other. She saw all that in his eyes, felt it in his skin and her own heart thundered with the knowledge.

'Lyta,' he growled. 'We shouldn't.'

'Why not?'

He didn't have an answer for that.

'I want to feel again, Sylvian. I want to be alive. I want *you*.'

She saw him hesitate, saw him fight against it. And saw him lose that fight.

'You have always had me,' he whispered, and the ache behind the words left her stunned. 'You always will. I am eternally yours, Lyta. Made for you.' He kissed her again, then ran his lips down the sensitive skin of her throat, while his hands found her breasts and he teased her there as well. 'I always was.'

At her urging, Sylvian shed his shirt and she pulled the nightgown off over her head.

She smiled up at him, but he gazed at her so solemnly it stole her breath.

'What is it?' she asked, suddenly unsure herself. 'What's wrong? Don't you want to?'

'Of course I want you. But . . . are you sure?' he whispered, his voice rough with need. Still he held back. He needed to hear her say it, she realised. He'd never believe it otherwise.

'Yes,' was all she could say. It was all she could say for a very long time. He sank down between her legs and kissed her until she gasped it out loud, until it rang off the ceiling and she bucked and writhed beneath his mouth. His tongue tormented the core of her pleasure he had once known so well. And he still knew her. He knew exactly what to do, what she needed.

When she couldn't take any more, she pushed him onto his back and straddled him, taking his length into her depths. He filled her, body and soul, until there was nothing left but one being. He looked up at her, dazed with pleasure and need combined and she could see him grasping for some last measure of control.

'I'm no good for you, Lyta,' he tried to warn her once again.

'I can decide that for myself.' She tightened her inner muscles until he made a guttural noise of surrender.

'Not fair, heart,' he said, but there was something of a laugh underneath it. 'It's true though. I never was. Never will be.'

Lyta started to move in that lazy, steady rhythm she remembered would always undo him. Sylvian's hands closed on her hips, holding her close, digging into her skin as he came, arching off the bed beneath her, lost completely to her, even if only for this moment, and tipping her over the edge after him.

She slumped forward, her hair spilling across his chest, her face close to his. He shifted so he could kiss her again, a sated, languorous kiss, taking his time and exploring her. Lyta nuzzled in against him and held his gaze for a long time.

'What was that?' Sylvian asked.

He would always look as if he was half-hunted, expecting betrayal at any second. Even with her. Especially with her. It was her shame.

'We're alive, Sylvian. And here. Does there have to be more than that?'

But there was. They both knew it. She just wasn't ready to say it. Not yet.

His breath evened, his eyes closed, and he breathed deeply at last, his body relaxing against hers. Lyta lay there for the longest time, just listening to his heartbeat and his breath, wishing that this would last forever.

Knowing that it couldn't.

Lyta kissed Sylvian awake with single-minded determination, and they started to explore each other again, to lose themselves in each other. To feel, to live.

CHAPTER TWENTY-THREE

Sylvian

Lyta was gone when he woke up. He had known she would be but it was still a bleak disappointment. The other side of the bed was cold, which meant she'd been gone for some time. Sylvian rolled onto his back and let out a breath, closing his eyes again. He didn't expect to be assailed immediately with images of all they had done last night. Memories which would keep any soldier happy for years on the front.

He'd dreamed about her for longer than he cared to admit. He'd sought her in other places and never found her. It wasn't possible to replace Lyta.

Of course, she was gone. Like a spirit, like a ghost, like a dream.

Then he realised what was hanging around his own neck, banging his chest as he sat up.

The necklace had caught his eye last night, a metal disc and a white-gold ring, swaying with her as she moved on top of him, bright against her pale skin with its spray of freckles like motes of gold dust. A simple pendant representing the Trickster god and a ring.

The ring – he'd seen it before.

He just didn't know where. Not on Lyta. Lyta didn't have time for frivolities like that. It bore the mark of the love goddess's star. And Lyta had left both with him. Why?

Sylvian dragged himself out of the bed and pulled on his discarded shirt, making sure the necklace was tucked inside. As he was finishing dressing, a rap sounded at the door.

'Come in,' he said, making sure he was decent. He almost felt like himself again. Except for everything that had happened. Except for Lyta and her absence.

Beatriz opened the door, looking unusually flustered.

'Oh, thank goodness you're here,' she said. 'The king has sent for you.'

Sylvian gave a curt bow. 'Of course, I'll go at once. Thank you for—'

She took his arm, stopping him before he could make for the door. 'No, you don't understand. There's a company of guards outside. Royal guards. And three of the other bodyguards. Sylvian, it isn't a request. They're looking for you specifically. They were perfectly polite, of course, but still.'

'General Vasquez?' he asked. Beatriz shook her head. 'Who is in command?'

'My steward said his name was Captain Reyes.'

It wasn't a moment to laugh. 'Reyes', indeed. He wasn't even trying very hard to hide his identity. Francisco had never been subtle, but using the old Castilian word for king was a new low. He probably thought it was tremendously clever.

Beatriz was right to be worried. With that many people present, and no doubt armed, it did not look good. Even with 'Reyes' in charge.

'Well, we'd better go and see what he wants then.'

Vasquez was not going to be best pleased when she heard about this. Oh no, she was going to go off on one, but what could she do? It wasn't Sylvian's fault, but that was not going to matter, was it?

The king was lounging on a chair in Beatriz's courtyard, wearing the uniform of a captain of his own bodyguard. The uniform Sylvian should have been wearing. The men around him, Torren, Juárez and Montes, looked so profoundly uncomfortable that it would have been funny to see his comrades in such a state if the atmosphere hadn't been so tense. If they hadn't been here for him, grim as executioners.

They stood around the king, his brothers-in-arms, who he would have trusted with his life, gazing at him as if he were a threat. Every one of them was a trained and expert killer. If they came for him, he would fall.

And then there was Francisco.

A familiar reckless sparkle lurked in his king's eyes. It always led to disaster.

Beatriz made a small noise of shock as she recognised this 'Captain Reyes' as the king and fell into a curtsey at the same moment Sylvian dropped to his knees and bowed his head. If he looked pathetic, so be it. The alternative was losing his head completely.

'There you are,' the king said, with unexpected warmth. 'I said he wouldn't be far, didn't I? I told you we were overreacting, Montes.'

The royal bodyguards were all avoiding the king's gaze. They liked this even less than Sylvian did. They knew him as well as he knew them. There was something very wrong.

'I'm sure your Majesty would never overreact either,' Sylvian said, unsure how he kept the tremble out of his voice.

'Of course he does, Captain Chant,' said another, far more unexpected voice. A slim figure, also dressed in a guard's uniform, stepped out from the shelter of the copious plants beneath the gallery and Sylvian's eyes widened in alarm. 'He's known for it. Aren't you, my love?'

The queen smiled at her husband fondly. Any man would be so lucky to have that smile turned on them. Yet, she wasn't Lyta. And that realisation dimmed the queen's beauty in a way that until a few days ago Sylvian would not have thought possible. She was still radiant, but not . . .

Not Lyta.

Annika shouldn't be here. She was to be protected at all times. Francisco had been clear about that from the very beginning, had forced the bodyguards to swear oaths in blood as powerful as those they had sworn to him, just as binding. Sylvian had done everything the king asked of him when it came to her. Everything.

'Where's our book, Chant?' Francisco asked.

Oh. The book. How did he explain the book? 'There's been a . . . a *complication*, your Majesty.'

Silence swept the courtyard like a north wind, and Sylvian knew he had made a mistake. But what else could he have said? He couldn't lie.

Where was Lyta? Where were Kit and Ben? Why wasn't anyone here to help him explain?

'A *complication?*' Francisco's voice was waspish. 'You seem to be having a run of them. What kind of complication?'

The queen glided forward and laid a hand on Francisco's shoulder. She watched Sylvian for a long moment, frowning. He wilted under her gaze. Annika wanted the book and now the book was gone. She was disappointed. He didn't know what to say.

'My brother is dealing with it,' said Beatriz, and Sylvian's breath caught with relief. 'Your Majesties,' she added, a little too late for complete politeness.

'My Lady Beatriz,' Francisco purred. 'What a pleasure. Were you—?' He glanced at Sylvian with a smirk. 'I hope Captain Chant has been entertaining you well.'

Beatriz gave nothing away. Nothing. 'Captain Chant is a guest in my house. The laws of hospitality are as old as time. He follows them impeccably, as you would expect.'

The silence grew arctic again. The laws of hospitality were ancient and honoured, laid down by the old gods and goddesses themselves – and the king was currently pissing on every single one of them. But in Amberes, Francisco made the law, and he did not take kindly to being chastised.

'Where is your brother, Lady Beatriz?' asked Annika, with a wide – and entirely false – smile. 'I've heard so much about him, his intelligence and wit. I would dearly love to meet him.' The look of irritation she directed at Sylvian made him flinch. 'Oh, for goodness' sake, Sylvian, get up off your knees. You look ridiculous.'

She didn't say that very often. Annika liked to see him on his knees. She always had. Funny how he could see that now, as if a veil had been removed from him. What had happened to him? What had changed? Sylvian pushed the rebellious thought aside and obeyed with care. Francisco watched his every move like a hawk.

Who had been whispering in their ears? Who had been turning them against him? If he could just get them alone, he could explain. As long as Francisco didn't order his head taken from his shoulders there and then. It didn't matter how long they had known each other, what they had shared. If Francisco gave the command, his fellow bodyguards wouldn't even hesitate.

Beatriz smoothed down her skirts as though she had not a concern in the world. 'My brother is hard at work, your Majesties, in an undisclosed location for his safety. The book must be transcribed, as per your instructions.'

The book that had been destroyed. Beatriz really was the consummate diplomat, or the most accomplished liar. Perhaps both. But what would they do when Francisco and Annika learned the truth?

'There,' said Francisco. 'See? It's all in order.'

But Annika didn't seem convinced. She looked at Sylvian as if seeking confirmation.

'That was the plan, your Highness,' he reminded her. 'You suggested it, if you recall.'

The queen opened her mouth for a moment, thought better of whatever she'd been about to say and closed it. She fixed him with that frank, unwavering look he admired and feared. It was perhaps the most unguarded and honest he'd ever seen her. No glamour, no guile.

'Information reached my lord husband that *The Book of Gold* was being sold on the black market,' she told him.

'Where is the thief, Sylvian?' Francisco asked without giving him a chance to recover.

'I'm not entirely sure,' he replied, wishing he could lie. His vows prevented that. Francisco had seen to it.

'Lyta left early this morning,' Beatriz supplied. 'With her brother. Something to do with the printshop. I didn't ask for the details. Things such as trade really don't concern me. I'm sure you understand.'

Francisco smirked. 'And your brother went with them, no doubt. Have we just discovered this undisclosed location, Lady Beatriz?'

'Obviously his Majesty is far too clever for me,' Beatriz said, her expression unchanging.

Sylvian didn't believe that for a second. If she was giving away this information, she meant for the king to have it.

'I suppose I have no choice but to believe you,' Francisco said.

'Your Majesties?' Sylvian asked innocently. 'You *don't* believe us?'

It was a risky move.

Something softened in Annika. Her grey eyes grew wide, her voice breathy. 'Of course I believe *you*, Sylvian. But several individuals claim that *The Book of Gold* was offered on the black market just this morning. The book we have been assured would be passed to us. And your thief is nowhere to be found. Neither is the book. You can understand our doubts, surely?'

Lyta wouldn't try to sell the book surely. She was many things, but not a fool.

'Offered by whom?' Sylvian asked.

For a moment, he didn't think they would answer him. They weren't used to being questioned. Then Francisco relented. 'Lord Charles Alderton of Albion, I believe,' he said, his loathing clear. There was long enmity between them and between the two realms. Any encounter never ended well. When they had first arrived in Amberes, there had been a late night when the two of them had gambled after a ball. Some card game or other. The queen had retired early and Sylvian had been guarding her. He didn't remember who had been on duty, but once again the king had probably either involved them in the game or sent them out of the room. Francisco maintained the Albion lord had cheated, but who really knew? The king refused to discuss how much he had lost or how it had happened. He'd been in such a foul mood no one wanted to investigate. Even Vasquez had sighed and waved debate away. All that was injured was his pride, after all.

'Lyta wouldn't work with him,' Sylvian whispered. Would she? How much did he know about Lyta now? Times had been hard, she'd said. She'd had to make concessions, do things she didn't want to. But she'd never stooped so low as to work for Janlow. Surely she'd avoid Alderton as well. Hadn't she and Frida implied that they'd crossed him somehow?

'No such alliance has been made,' Beatriz told them, fixing all her attention on him now. Sylvian wanted to believe her. Desperately. 'Absolutely not. Ben would never agree to that.'

'It's not really up to your brother, is it?' asked Francisco. 'He cannot copy what someone else has taken.'

But no one could take it from his memory. Could they? A chill ran through Sylvian. Ben trusted Kit, but Kit had been compromised by the duchess. Who knew what she could do to him through that brand. And, as Sylvian knew only too well, Lyta would do anything to protect her brother.

Something was terribly wrong here. No Lyta, no Ben, no Kit for that matter. And no sign of Frida either. He'd woken up alone, wrung-out, having been well and truly fucked by the notoriously fickle love of his former life. Maybe fucked in more than one way.

Lyta and Frida were criminals. He'd let himself forget that. People might talk about honour among thieves, but his past was proof there was no such thing as that. They would do whatever it took to survive.

Gods, he was an idiot.

Beatriz suddenly looked very concerned indeed. Her brother was missing. And her brother was the only one with access to *The Book of Gold*.

'We'll find them, your Majesty,' he said with a bow. 'You have my word.'

'Your word?' Francisco gave a cool laugh. 'I wonder how much that's worth now. Not a lot. Not until that book is delivered into my hands. Understand?'

Shocked at the tone, Sylvian couldn't help himself. 'Why is this so important to you? What is in that book?'

The king rose to his feet. He stepped towards Sylvian, grabbing a fistful of his shirt and pulled him close, his voice just a breath against Sylvian's ear, a whisper. 'Everything, my friend. The power of the gods. All their secrets and more. And I must have it. *She* must have it. Your queen has need of it. That is enough.'

His passion shook Sylvian to the core. He pulled back, staring into the king's eyes, taken aback by the depth of his hunger, his determination. And it was all for Annika.

If Sylvian failed the king, he'd be lucky to be put to death. Otherwise the king's torturers had many ways of making a man wish for death. They'd make it last too.

'Majesty?' Beatriz asked, interrupting his thoughts. 'May I be of aid?'

The queen was sitting on a bench, her skin suddenly pale. She looked drained, unwell, but she lifted a hand wanly. 'I am tired, Lady Beatriz. That is all.'

'My Queen, you should rest. Your strength is waning and in your condition—'

Every pair of eyes turned sharply on them – expressions by turns curious, outraged, shocked and surprised.

'Condition?' the king asked, each syllable of the word like a shard of broken glass.

Tears welled up in the queen's eyes. Her hands knotted together in her lap. She nodded slowly.

Fuck, Sylvian thought. *Fuck my life and all of its horrific coincidences.* Francisco pushed by him, sweeping his wife into his arms, all thoughts of the book or Lyta thankfully pushed aside by this revelation. Sylvian retreated to Beatriz's side while the king fussed over his queen.

'Is it true?' he asked as quietly as he could.

Beatriz nodded. 'But it will be a difficult pregnancy. Such unions are not meant to be.'

'What do you mean?'

'Aspects, like Ben and I . . . we are not meant to bring new life into this world. Our offspring are too powerful. And very few people could have fathered that child – only a champion, someone chosen to do so. It may well kill her long before she comes to term.'

It. That did not sound promising. The king had been unable to get her with child and Sylvian himself . . . It had been duty. Only a couple of moons before they left Castille for the Brabantine and Amberes Francisco had chosen him . . . Ordered him . . .

No. This wasn't happening. It couldn't be happening. He'd done his duty, obeyed his king, he'd . . .

'She's a—?' The word stuck in his throat. An Aspect. A channel for the divine. It wasn't possible. Annika was a woman. He knew she was a woman, better than just about anyone.

'Why do you think people love her so completely, Sylvian? You've felt it. The need to serve her, to adore her. Why did you think she wants the book so badly? Francisco doesn't want it, not really, except to give it to her.' Beatriz's face lit with revelation. 'Oh, it all makes sense now. She's with child and she's desperate to keep it. She thinks the book will hold the secret to her baby's survival.'

'But she's— I—'

Beatriz squeezed his hand. 'Later. Now I understand why you were brought here, we must keep you safe. This just keeps getting more and more complicated. Ystara has never made things easy.'

'Ystara? The goddess? I thought only Eninn escaped. In the stories.'

Up until recently, he would have adamantly declared that all the old gods were just stories, that men made their own fates. Now he wasn't so sure. Coming back to Amberes had changed that.

'With his wit and his heart, yes. But he wasn't the only one to try. *Ystara threw her light into the sky and lit the far north for a single moment.*' The words sounded like poetry. 'It isn't literal. The northern kingdoms have protected her power for generations, in their bloodlines. And there were others. Gods who hid, gods who ran, gods who took other forms. The Church continued hunting them – and us of course. They used us to draw them out. But the child of an Aspect, in a royal line like that of Castille . . . that would be powerful indeed. What is she playing at?'

Sylvian remembered the white-gold ring on Lyta's necklace, marked with the single star of Ystara and set with a single, perfect diamond. He was a fool. Now he remembered where he had seen it before: Annika had given it to Francisco when they married and he had always worn it on a finger of his left hand, the one that was now bare. The ring was missing.

Because Lyta had it.

No. Because he had it. Lyta had put it on the chain around his neck. He could feel it, like an icicle against his skin, under his shirt.

'Be quiet now,' Beatriz said, as if she read his thoughts. 'Say nothing. It's your only protection.'

The ring or his silence? There was no way of knowing.

In that instant the guards parted, and the king came back into view.

'I'm taking the queen back to the palace. We will not see you again, Sylvian Chant, until you hand us *The Book of Gold*, complete and undamaged. Do you understand me?'

No title, no Captain Chant. His full name, like it would appear on a warrant. Oh, he understood, all right.

'Yes, your Majesty.' He bowed deeply and kept his gaze averted. Nothing he could add would help him here.

But Francisco wasn't finished. He strode towards him and grabbed Sylvian's chin in a vice-like grip. This man who had fought alongside him, been like his brother, who had raised him high and who he loved more than any man in the world. Francisco, who he would gladly die for, who he had apparently given a much wanted and necessary child, though no one would ever mention it. Francisco jerked his face up and studied him with a gaze so cold that it made something in Sylvian shrivel up and die.

'You either come back with that book or with the head of your thief lover. Otherwise, I will hunt you both to the ends of the earth. Don't chose her over me, Sylvian, or it'll be the end of you both.'

And then the king, the queen and all the guards were gone.

Sylvian staggered, but Beatriz caught his arm before he could fall, and a ripple of warmth and strength passed through him. She was trying to help, but he didn't need divine intervention right now. He tore himself away.

'Well.' Beatriz sighed, as if the wrath of a monarch was just a minor inconvenience. 'That could have gone better.'

Sylvian had had enough. He couldn't help himself. She might be the richest woman in the world, she might be an Aspect, she might have taken them in, and she might have saved his life, but it didn't matter to him right now. He was sick of being used.

By Francisco, by Annika, by Lyta, by their so-called gods, and now by Beatriz.

She had known about Ystara and the queen. She knew more than she was saying. She knew how he had been used and why.

'Explain,' he growled at her.

CHAPTER TWENTY-FOUR

Kit

The workshop had never felt so busy. Kit had all hands on deck, ready to start production of each octavo as soon as Ben could give them the text. There was no time to waste. And if his employees were confused by this sudden flurry, they didn't let on. Work was work and it meant pay. If he seemed distracted or secretive about what they were printing and who it was actually for . . . well, after the pamphlet fiasco they were not about to ask too many questions.

Jem watched over it all, the bindery ready when the pages were printed. Kit was using all the typefaces, every set he had, in order to produce this wretched thing as quickly as possible. The books would not be big and there would not be many, not initially. They just needed to get them done fast.

How long it took depended on Ben, who was sequestered in the upstairs room, furiously transcribing pages. Kit was afraid to go in. Ever since Ben had touched that bloody book, he had not been the same.

Sometimes he looked at Kit with different eyes. Sometimes his skin glowed gold and images of words or drawings passed over it. Sometimes he said things that made no sense, and the rest of the time . . . the rest of the time he looked scared.

Now Kit knocked on the door tentatively, as if approaching an animal in a cage.

'Come in,' Ben said, but in a way that suggested he was only half-aware of anyone else beyond the room, and only half-aware that he was speaking at all.

There were sheets of paper everywhere. Kit sucked in a breath and shut the door firmly behind him. Slowly he advanced towards the window where Ben was hunched over at the desk, scrawling so fast the quill scraped and screeched on the paper.

'How are you doing?'

Kit started picking up sheets, each one covered in uniform, delicate script. How was he writing like that and producing this? Kit crouched down and gathered more into a stack, all perfectly neat and legible.

And the words . . .

They were poetry. Once he started reading them, it felt like music in his mind, sweeping him away, helpless before it. He had to keep reading, had to take it all in, because if he could read it all, he knew he would understand at last. He would understand everything.

Ben's hand on his face made him look up. Kit found himself kneeling in the middle of his bedroom, mouth open, the sheaf of paper rustling in his shaking hands like dry leaves in the wind. Ben's eyes were no more than a hand's width from his, and his touch was so gentle against Kit's cheek.

'It's hard, I know. I'm sorry. There's so much.'

An understatement. What was this book? Was it dangerous? It had to be dangerous.

'What's happening?' Kit asked.

'It's divine power. I'm sorry. I didn't realise how much . . . I didn't know . . .' A shadow passed over Ben's face and his eyes darkened. 'Time is wasting. Are you ready? Is your machine ready? The scholar tells us that this is how the word is spread now. *Our* word. Do you understand? *Our* truth. And then we will be free.'

The scholar. Ben was talking about himself in the third person. That was never a good sign. But then, Kit knew that voice was not Ben's.

'Who are you?' Kit asked. 'I'm not doing anything until I know what is going on and who you all are. What have you done with Ben?'

'He is here. He is safe. Without him we would be lost to the darkness, so we will protect him.'

THE BOOK OF GOLD

Kit's mouth went dry. 'Are you demons?'

'Demons?' The voice laughed in bitter amusement. 'Oh, you wish we were merely demons, little human.' Ben's body leaned forward, menace rolling off it in a wave and it bared Ben's teeth.

Before it could do anything more, Ben jerked back.

'Kyron, no,' he said, and his voice was softer now, gentler.

Kyron. Now that was a name Kit knew. The warrior god, the killer, the blazing sword – one of the old gods.

They had been in the book. And now they were in Ben.

He swallowed hard. 'And you are?'

Ben shook his head, solemnity replaced the look of anger. 'I am wisdom, human child.'

'Nimyeh,' he whispered, and Ben smiled, a brilliant, glorious smile. Proud to be recognised, delighted to be acknowledged. 'Who else is—? I need to speak to Ben. Just Ben.'

'We should be hurt, insulted even,' said a third voice, but it was immediately interrupted by a fourth.

'This is not our place. Let the boy go, Ystara. Let him speak.'

Ben's body stiffened and he collapsed forward onto his arms. He panted for breath, his eyes wild. 'Kit? Kit, just let me . . .'

Kit didn't hesitate. He dropped the pages and held Ben close. 'It's all right. I'm here.' The scholar was trembling, his eyes wide, but undeniably his eyes again.

'They're so *much*.' That was one word for it, Kit supposed. Not one divine being but four, locked in his head, fighting for control and escape.

'Just breathe.' He let Ben burrow against his chest and held him tightly until the shaking quietened. 'Better?'

'For now. Gloir and Ystara are about the only ones with any reason left in them.'

Love. Forge and hearth. The warrior. And wisdom. Quite a combination to have swirling through his mind. As Ben nuzzled against him, Kit lost focus. He had to think about something else. Anything else.

'They were in the book?'

'Trapped there, who knows for how long. When do the stories say they vanished?'

Kit shrugged. The stories were never too specific about things like that.

A single word slipped from Ben's mouth, a whisper filled with pain and despair. '*Centuries.*'

He clapped one hand over his mouth, his eyes filling with panic again. 'But this . . .' Kit indicated the pages strewn around them. 'This will help them escape, won't it? This is what they want.'

'I don't think even they know what they want.' Ben winced. 'I'm sorry but it's true. You're all half-mad with confinement and pain and—' His eyes focused on Kit again and his hands closed on the printer's shirt. 'I sound like I belong in an asylum. Perhaps I do. When I studied the theories of a Nexus I never thought . . . Kit?'

Kit steeled himself, thinking of Lyta, imagining what she would say. No one crossed his sister. Especially not when she had someone to protect. 'We'll sort this out. But they need to back the hell off and let us work, instead of behaving like children.'

For a moment it was as if the air had been sucked out of the room. Kit had never considered what it might take to insult a god, let alone four of them. But this was obviously a contender.

The laugh that burst out of Ben's mouth was bright and high. 'Oh, I do like him,' said Ystara on a breath, and the next thing Kit knew, Ben's lips met his in a kiss.

The scholar jerked back, himself again, his face flaming red.

'I'm sorry,' he said. 'I didn't . . . That wasn't me. I wouldn't . . .'

Kit's heart plummeted. Of course he hadn't wanted to. He wasn't himself right now. How could he be?

'It's all right, Ben. Not your fault. I suppose I should be grateful Ystara likes me so much.'

Someone needed to, since everything was spinning wildly out of control. Maybe having a goddess on his side would help.

Then again, given what they'd experienced so far, maybe not. Eninn hadn't been much help to Ranulf or Lyta.

'She says . . . That is, they say, they agree they'll *back off*, as you put it. The work is done.' Ben gestured to the papers. 'I don't know what it means though. They're still in here. I thought, when it was finished, they'd leave me. I thought— I don't know what I thought. Everything is so confused.'

'Perhaps it needs to be a book. That was the plan, wasn't it? Copy the book and give it to the king. Then spread copies all over the city and—'

That had been Lyta's plan, but Kit wasn't so sure anymore. Reading just a page had rendered him helpless. Perhaps the book wasn't something to be shared, but contained. It had already proved dangerous enough to Ben.

His head hurt just thinking about it.

'Two copies,' Kit said at last. 'That's all for now. I'll send the others away and do it myself.' That way he could limit the risk. 'One copy for the king. One for . . . I don't know. Insurance. To make sure nothing happens to us.'

'How does one extra copy make sure nothing happens to us? Surely more than one—'

'One extra copy. We'll keep it safe until we know more. Until we see what it can do. Now, is your manuscript complete? Do you need to write more?'

Ben looked down at his hands, covered in ink stains, like blood under his nails and splattered across his flesh. 'No. That's why they let me go.'

Slowly, carefully, Kit gathered up the remaining pages and Ben put them in order. There weren't as many as he had thought and some only had a few words on them. Printing the book would be fast. No need for elaborate capitals or decoration. Just words, ink and paper. Quick and dirty, like a pamphlet. The kind of thing that had started all this.

Carefully, Kit began to read again, focusing on the text itself, on how he would format it, how it needed to appear, all the basic logistics of a new book rather than the contents. He knew that if he let them, the words would try to sweep him away again.

He wondered where Lyta was. She'd been so broken by leaving Ranulf behind, but he'd left her with Sylvian because . . . well, that seemed to be what she wanted and needed. Besides, he'd been trying to look after Ben and that was bad enough.

But his sister was Ennin's own. She was eternally lucky. She'd survive.

And this was the one part of this godforsaken mission he could do. This was his role.

Godforsaken. Hardly. And that was the problem, wasn't it? He almost laughed at the thought and then looked guiltily at Ben who stared at him, uncomprehending.

'All right,' Kit said. 'I'll get to work. You need sleep, Ben. And you lot, let him rest.'

Ben sat down heavily on Kit's bed and lay back, his eyes closing the instant his head touched the pillow. Carefully, Kit pulled the blanket over him.

'I mean it,' Kit told the errant gods. 'Please, stop tormenting him.'

He left the room, but as he closed the door behind him, he thought he heard another laugh, followed by what sounded like a shushing noise and a grunt of frustration, but he refused to engage.

CHAPTER TWENTY-FIVE

Lyta

Lyta came to with a thundering headache and the taste of blood in her mouth. She couldn't see anything through the thick material in front of her face, which smelled of straw and sweat, and she could feel ropes encircling her wrists.

Stay calm. Ranulf's voice came to her, whispering in the back of her mind. Ranulf. Her heart twisted, and her breath caught. It couldn't be Ranulf. If it was, it was his ghost. *Don't panic. If you panic you're dead. Think, Lyta. Think!*

Where was she? What had she—?

She's been asleep, wrapped in Sylvian's arms. Frida had woken her.

'I need your help. There's something at Haldevar's I have to show you.'

Frida. Where was Frida?

Lyta's hands were tied behind her back and she seemed to be sitting in a chair so there must be an interrogation in the offing. She set to work on the thick ropes cutting into her wrists, testing them, trying to wriggle free. There was some give, but not enough. She might loosen them eventually, but she wasn't sure how long she had.

'Frida? You there?' she whispered. No answer came.

Not good. Not good at all.

They'd made their way through the morning bustle of Amberes and now Lyta wished she'd woken Sylvian and brought him too. But her business with Haldevar had never been exactly legal, Janlow could still be sniffing around, and the last time he'd encountered Sylvian he'd almost killed him.

Gods, she wished she'd woken Sylvian now.

But oh no, not her. Had to sort everything out herself. She'd left him sleeping. Just to reassure him she'd be back, she had slipped her necklace around his neck. Her pendant and the ring safe in his keeping. Just an impulse really.

When they got to Haldevar's shop, as soon as she stepped inside the sack went over her head, and a cosh sent her into unconsciousness. She still had the splitting headache and the blood in her mouth to show for it.

Stupid. So stupid.

She needed to escape. Needed to get out of here. The next option was to tip the chair over and try to loop her legs through her arms so she could at least get the hood off and see where she was.

'There you are,' murmured a soft voice and Lyta's heart fell. Janlow. 'About time you woke up.'

His hand slid up her arm, knuckles brushing against the side of her breast until she flinched. Couldn't help herself. He laughed. The bastard laughed and she felt a fresh wave of pure hatred run through her.

After everything in Montalbeau, how could she end up here?

'Petrus,' she said, keeping her voice as flippant as possible. 'Can't talk right now. I'm a bit tied up.'

His laugh slithered over her skin and she fought not to recoil again. She didn't want to give him the satisfaction.

He pulled the hood off her head, which solved at least one of her problems. But it revealed a lot more.

The room was beautifully furnished, with high windows overlooking gardens and the Falconbrook canal beyond. A chandelier hung over her head, and a somewhat familiar portrait glowered down at her from its place behind the imposing desk.

She was in Alderton's office. In his mansion. Presumably surrounded by his hired guards, Janlow's thugs and the gods knew who else.

So not good in every way possible under the sun.

Blood had dried on the side of her face, matting in her hair, and her head throbbed.

'You always had a smart mouth, Lyta, but I'd keep it closed now or his Lordship may decide to shut it permanently. Now, don't go anywhere.'

Janlow laughed again and closed the door behind him on his way out, leaving her alone to wait.

Time was not on her side. Lyta struggled against the knots, hissing in frustration when they only tightened. Launching herself to the left did no good. The chair was too bloody heavy. The bastard had clearly done this before. She managed to rock it just a little.

Something jabbed into her side. The knife. Sylvian's dagger was still tucked into her belt under her shirt. Either they hadn't looked, or they'd been so sure of themselves that they hadn't bothered to take it. Everyone knew she didn't like weapons and never carried one.

She bloody liked this one though. It was now her favourite knife in the whole world.

Another awkward manoeuvre and she'd managed to hook the rope around the tip of the blade itself.

It wasn't going to be quick, or comfortable, but it was all she had. Silently she gave thanks for supremely arrogant men.

But luck wasn't entirely on Lyta's side. She could barely cut a strand at a time at this angle, and she was less than halfway through when the door opened again, forcing her back into stillness.

Alderton stalked to his desk. He was dressed simply enough, but his clothes were still made of the finest quality silks, wool and linen, expertly tailored to emphasise his strong physique. He sat down opposite her and Lyta forced herself to meet his piercing gaze.

For a moment she couldn't think. Everything froze, every instinct telling her to get away from this man.

Janlow had also returned. He walked to the far side of the desk, placing himself between her and the window.

'Mistress Cornellis,' said Alderton. He made her name sound musical, a trick of his accent she realised, but this was a melody which promised pain and suffering. 'You have been most difficult to track down.'

She licked her lips and stilled her breath. 'Well, a girl likes to keep her mystique.'

Alderton smiled, a slow and lazy smile that would have been attractive in any other circumstances. But not now. Not with that look in his eyes.

'You really are quite remarkable, I'll give you that. I might even have work for you. I can always use an operative with your talents.'

Janlow snorted and to Lyta's surprise, Alderton's expression hardened. 'Petrus, try to be civil. It's the least I ask.'

Janlow looked stricken. He gave a brief bow, almost polite. 'My apologies, my lord.'

Alderton shook his head. 'Don't apologise to me. Mistress Cornellis is the person you insulted.'

Lyta watched the struggle play out on Janlow's mortified face as he drew a mask over his obvious rage. 'My apologies, Lyta.'

Lyta couldn't help herself. Her smile was radiant and that just enraged him all the more. She might be tied up, bloodied and at their mercy, but she could still enjoy this one shining moment of his humiliation.

'Why thank you, Petrus,' she purred. 'Nice to see someone teaching you manners at last.' She turned her attention back to Alderton. He wasn't royalty, she knew that much. Minor nobility at best. But he was rich, and he was powerful. He traded mainly in secrets, that most valuable of commodities. He had powerful friends at home and in high places all over the world, and probably a lot of damning information about them. Still, if he wanted to play it polite she could do that. 'May I ask why you had me brought here? And where is Frida?'

The slow smile crept back, edged with cruelty.

'I'm here, Lyta,' said Frida from behind her. She moved forward then, free to walk unconstrained, and came to a halt just within her view, at the far left of Alderton's desk.

Lyta kept her face impassive and slowly started to move her hands again under the tails of her coat, working her way through the ropes strand by strand and praying that no one would notice.

Because Frida looked absolutely fine. Her arms were folded in front of her and she couldn't quite meet Lyta's gaze.

'You're not hurt,' Lyta said, unable to keep the accusation from her voice. 'Or tied up.'

'One does not need to tie up allies,' Alderton said. 'Something I believe we can discuss shortly. Master Janlow here has various plans for you, none of them to your advantage naturally.'

'Naturally,' Lyta echoed. She knew all about Janlow's plans for her. Why hadn't she woken Sylvian up? Why hadn't she told him where she was going? She was an idiot. But she'd trusted Frida. She had always trusted Frida. They'd been together through everything. But now . . .

A sob lodged in her throat. Lyta swallowed it down, furious with herself as she blinked back tears. She had to stay calm. She had to think. She had to get herself out of this.

Another strand of rope gave way, and another.

'Mistress Elwynn assures me that persuading you to work with us would be much more lucrative for all concerned. I am inclined to agree. You are an incredibly talented woman. And we have common enemies after all.'

Lyta stared at him. 'We do?'

'You humiliated the Duchess of Montalbeau. You stole a scholar from the Magister. Both are coming for you. You should have heard the demands the Church made of the king. I would never have thought they would risk excommunicating the King of Castille, but it's not without precedent. Great Henry risked their wrath and survived, albeit in an isolated condition. It's a reputation my countrymen have fostered and our queen maintains. You could say we are stronger than ever for it. Francisco may stand against them for the sake of Benedict Alvarez and his knowledge. But for you or your brother? No, I think not. In fact, it may be in his interest to offer you up in the stead of the son of House Alvarez.'

This was not good news. Playtime was over now and she needed to get herself out of here. They were going to come for Kit and Ben. That was all she needed to know. And if the duchess got her hands on Kit again, she'd make him suffer.

A few more strands of rope fell away. Thanks all the gods they hadn't tied her feet as well.

'And what are you offering?'

Alderton chuckled. 'Ah well, yes, that's the thing. It's not so much an offer, my dear lady. You have something of mine, something you took from this very room. I want it back. And then perhaps we can discuss how you will work off your debt to me. With information, with items acquired, with various tasks I will set for you.'

A lifetime of doing his dirty work? Not exactly a dream solution.

'I don't have anything of yours,' she told him. That at least was not a lie.

'No, perhaps not. They wouldn't have brought you here if they'd found it. You would have met an unfortunate end in that miserable little shop your fence used. Just like he did. Isn't that right, Mistress Elwynn?'

Lyta stiffened. But the words were already out and Frida was not denying it. Her former friend stared fixedly at Alderton's very expensive rug but slowly her gaze rose to meet Lyta's. It was impossible to recognise the woman there, the woman she'd laughed with, cried with and caused havoc all over Amberes with. Frida looked like a stranger.

'What did you do?' Lyta hissed.

She didn't even know this woman's voice. 'It's just business. Sometimes that's how it goes. You know that. We all have debts.'

'What did you *do*?'

Frida drew in a tight breath. 'Look, I didn't mean to. I thought he had it. I thought for sure you'd have given it to him to sell. I tried to talk to him, but he just kept denying it. I didn't kill him on purpose.'

Haldevar. Lyta tried to force herself to take a breath, to keep breathing. She'd killed Haldevar.

'*On purpose?* Do you hear yourself? I thought you *loved* him.'

Bile rose in the back of her throat and Frida's gaze burned into hers. She wasn't denying it. She wasn't denying anything.

'Enough,' Alderton snapped. 'Where's the ring, Lyta?'

THE BOOK OF GOLD

The change in subject made her crack. She didn't care about Alderton and his demands. Frida had betrayed her. 'What fucking ring?' she yelled.

Alderton pushed himself up, levering his arms on his desk to loom over her. 'The ring you took from my safe,' he said, as if elaborating would change her answer. As if she didn't know what he meant. 'White gold, marked with Ystara's star. The royal ring of the Vasa, which Annika brought south with her. The first time it has left the royal stronghold of Tre Kronor in five hundred years. The ring that will offer protection to the father of her unborn child. The ring that marks her champion.'

Lyta's mind whirled. That little ring? Eninn had wanted it so much he'd lied to her about using it to find Ranulf. Well, not a lie, exactly but not the whole truth either. She'd found him only to lose him for good. If it was so bloody special, why had Annika let it out of her sight? Why wasn't it safe on the king's finger? How had Alderton of all people got his sticky little hands on it? Not that any of that was important right now. She didn't have it. She'd entrusted her necklace to Sylvian, kissed him back to sleep when he stirred and tried to open his bleary eyes. And with it, the ring. She had entrusted it to him without so much as a thought. It had felt right. Like it belonged there.

'Shush,' she had whispered. 'I'll be right back.'

But she wouldn't be. Not now. He was probably already convinced she'd done a runner of some kind, deserted him, gone off gods knew where and at this rate he was never going to find out what had happened to her.

Eninn, help me. You got me into this. You'd better get me out of it too.

She didn't know if there was any point praying to him now Eninn had deserted her, but she was desperate.

'I don't have your ring,' she told him, calming herself. 'I don't know what happened to it. It's just a bit of gold.' She turned on Frida again. 'And you murdered Haldevar for that?'

Something flashed in Frida's eyes. 'I know you had it. I saw it in that bitch's lair, hanging around your neck. If you hadn't been busy

• 243 •

screwing Sylvian bloody Chant again, maybe you wouldn't have been screwing the rest of us over.'

And then she saw it, the flicker in Frida's eyes as she realised that the ring had to be with Sylvian.

The last bit of rope holding her hands together snapped and Lyta grabbed the chair, hurling it at Janlow. He ducked and the chair kept going, smashing through the window behind him. The knife was still jammed under her belt and she couldn't get to it as Frida flung herself forward. Lyta lashed out, kicking her friend in the stomach and driving her back. Then she fled for the window.

Something whistled past her head, thudding into the lintel, a throwing knife still quivering as she dived underneath it. As she flung herself out over the balcony beyond, a burst of pain impacted her right shoulder, spinning her around in the air. She barely managed to grab the ledge and almost wrenched her arm out of her socket as she came to a jolting halt, hanging over Alderton's canal-front garden.

Pain like a line of fire burst up and down her side. She couldn't keep in the cry of anguish as her arm spasmed. She dropped, landing heavily on the gravel.

No time to recover, no time to gather her wits. She ran like the hunted animal she was, the throwing knife buried in her shoulder stopping most of the blood escaping and leaving a trail for them to follow. She just had to make the water. And then . . .

She couldn't think. Just run. *Eninn help me. Eninn save me. Eninn get me the hell out of this.*

The water closed over her, freezing and black.

Just like Haldevar, she thought. Frida would probably claim this was an accident as well.

CHAPTER TWENTY-SIX

Sylvian

Beatriz strode through the streets of the city, still in her elaborate Andalusian blue gown and tiny silk slippers, wrapped in a voluminous cloak lined in shimmering satin, which drew attention far more than it disguised her. Sylvian had no choice but to follow. They were going to have every beggar and cutpurse in the city after them the moment they left her fancy neighbourhood and there was nothing Sylvian could do about it, because the Lady of House Alvarez was not going to let him go alone. She had made that more than clear. Her brother was in danger.

Nothing was going to stop her. Certainly not this city.

If Sylvian got her killed in an alley in Amberes, he would never hear the end of it – if he managed to survive himself.

But she was also an Aspect so the gods should be looking out for her as well. Or at least he hoped they would. Eninn had saved him, hadn't he? He'd fetched Lyta and Kit while Sylvian had been dangling from a beam in that stinking temple. Seems like they all needed a bit of help from the gods these days.

They were making for the printshop and had almost reached the bridge over the canal to Johannes port when Beatriz stopped in the middle of High Street. Like she'd seen something from the corner of her eye. Like someone called her. Someone Sylvian couldn't see.

Other voices started up at once.

'Lady, please, lady, help us. Coin for an old soldier.'

Five of them were closing in on her. Sylvian was instantly on alert, whereas Beatriz smiled and tried to help.

'Of course, just a moment. Sylvian, if you will.' She reached for her purse.

He squared up as if he was her bodyguard. The men took one look at him and his hand on the hilt of his sword before backing up. They waited obediently as she handed each a coin and then all but bowed to her. As he watched, she pressed a slender hand on each of their heads of dirt-matted hair and a pulse of something rippled through the air.

The wide plaza and the canal quays around Johannes port seemed to still, watching her, wary. Even the crane lifting cargo from barges and the oxen pulling the carts. Even the birds.

'My lady, we should—' he started to say, but then glanced towards the riverside, distracted by the glimpse of a blond head. Golden hair catching the light for an instant before it ducked out of sight. Just a moment, barely a glance in fact, from the corner of his eye. But Sylvian recognised him instantly. This boy was more than just another mudlark hunting for treasures in the river.

Beatriz lifted her head and her eyes grew keen. 'I see him too.' The smile was brief, almost relieved, but still shadowed by concern. 'He wouldn't be here without reason. We should—'

'We don't have time,' Sylvian said. But no one told Beatriz what to do and she pushed by him, her fine skirts swirling around her ever determined feet. 'My lady, Beatriz, please!'

She was as impossible as Lyta, but without even her fragmentary common sense. He hurried after her, glaring at anyone who he suspected was even thinking of talking to her. She was going to get mugged or worse dressed like that, flashing coin around and—

'Sylvian!' Beatriz shouted suddenly and the alarm in her voice made him forget all his complaints. He watched in horror as she ran to the edge of the quay, where the watergate met the walls and jumped into the mud below. She was out of sight in an instant and he broke into a sprint to reach her, almost tumbling off the edge in his haste.

Eninn waded barefoot in the shallows beneath the wooden jetty nearest the watergate, amid the detritus of Amberes, his trews wet up to the knees. He bent over something caught in the supports.

There was a body in the water, half-submerged, red hair clogged with mud and blood, an arm twisted awkwardly around one of the supports. A knife jutted from its back.

'Lyta!'

Sylvian hurled himself down into the water, hauling her into his arms. She was cold, but not too cold. There was life still in her, fragile and tentative but still there.

'Do something!' he yelled at Lyta's god. 'Help her!'

But Eninn fixed him with a glare of undisguised loathing. The air around them went cold and brittle, biting against Sylvian's skin. The water stirred menacingly around him.

Was Eninn jealous? There wasn't time for this.

'Enough,' he snarled. 'You help her. Now!'

The Trickster god's eyes narrowed. This was not a child, nor a boy on the edge of manhood. He was ancient and ageless. And he didn't think like a mortal either. Something inside him was wild.

Lyta was his chosen, his favourite, a thief almost as skilled as he was, just as chaotic. She was his through and through. Why wasn't he helping her?

Sylvian's voice broke as he rounded on the god again. 'She's done everything for you. What more do you want?'

'He's angry,' Beatriz murmured, her voice shaken. 'She denied him, blamed him for Ranulf's death. And he—'

Sylvian's rage tore itself free. 'What are you, a child or a god? Of course she blames you. She blames everyone, herself most of all. Can't you see that? If you want to take it out on someone, take it out on me. I couldn't save him for her.'

Eninn stilled, a preternatural calm settling over him, like a cat about to pounce. He stared at Sylvian, the mismatched jewels of his eyes aglow from within, studying the bodyguard in a new light. Then he reached out his hand.

The Trickster pressed his finger to Sylvian's chest. Beneath his clothes, the ring dug into his skin.

The ring? Was this about the queen's ring? What did Eninn want with that?

Sylvian almost sobbed in frustration. He couldn't lose Lyta. Not like this, and not because her god was in some kind of snot. He felt the rage inside him twist and writhe, felt it feed the monster in him that he only released in battle. He loved Lyta. He had always loved her, even if he would never say it out loud. To lose her now when he had just found her again, when he had finally given himself up to her, wholly and completely—

The feelings coalesced in his chest where Eninn touched him, where the ring burned against him, white-hot and brilliant. All his need and desire, all he felt for her, all his love. And something else answered, pulsing, weak. It had to be from her. Eninn forgotten, Sylvian pulled her closer and pressed his lips to hers. She was cold and tasted of blood, but a soft breath escaped her lips. His name.

As it did, Eninn said a few words. Just a whisper. Perhaps not even a real sound. But Sylvian heard it all the same, deep inside him, like an echo. 'See, my sister?'

Beatriz closed her eyes and staggered back, as something profoundly *other* filled Sylvian, like a star bursting inside his body, enveloping him and the woman in his arms.

It only lasted a moment, but it seemed to take eternity.

And then all was still, quiet. Water washed against their feet and gulls circled overhead, their mournful cries echoing over the city, the city which rushed back in to fill the silence, above them, behind them.

Sylvian looked down into Lyta's bright blue eyes.

'You shout too much,' she told him in the shakiest of voices.

'Lyta!' He kissed her again, his mouth determined.

But Lyta jerked away, muttering curses. 'Knife,' she gasped in obvious pain. 'Fucker threw a knife at me.'

Sylvian swore, cursing himself for forgetting. 'Can you stand? I need to get it out. Then maybe—' But Eninn was gone. Only

Beatriz stood there, her arms wrapped around her body, staring at them as if they had committed a mortal sin. 'What?' he asked impatiently.

She shook her head, her dark hair spilling around her face. 'Nothing. You're right. We need to get that knife out and close the wound. Eninn called on help from *elsewhere* to save her.'

'Where?' Sylvian asked suspiciously.

'Knife!' Lyta gasped at him, struggling. 'Remember the knife?'

'Here, hold her still,' Beatriz told him, all efficiency now. 'I can do it. Lyta, hold on.'

Sylvian turned her around in his arms and she slung her arms around his neck and shoulders. He held her tightly, and as Beatriz pulled the short throwing knife out of her, Lyta let out a howl of pain. Beatriz dropped the blade and pressed her hands to Lyta's back, her face furrowed in concentration.

He felt a wave pass through him, and that same something in his chest responded, pulsing white light. When it faded, Lyta had pulled back and was staring into his face in wonder.

'Your eyes,' she said softly. 'Sylvian, what happened to your eyes?'

'My eyes?'

'The colour. They're the colour of ice. Can you see? Are you—?'

Her shaking hands framed his face, pressing in on either side. 'Lyta, love,' he whispered. 'It's fine. I'm fine. Nothing's—'

Beatriz was staring at him too, not in shock but in fascination.

'What's going on?' he asked her.

'I'm not entirely sure. Your eyes are blue, a very pale blue. And now, look Lyta, the colour is changing again.' They stared at him, standing in shallow water below the quay. Lyta still held his face and Beatriz watched him like some kind of experiment. He didn't like the scrutiny. 'Back to brown,' she said at last. 'Fascinating. What did you do, Sylvian?'

'Nothing!'

Beatriz raised her eyebrows. 'Hardly nothing. You and Eninn together . . .'

Then he remembered the ring and pulled it out on the chain.

'That's what Alderton wants back, that ring,' Lyta told him. 'With the star.'

'Ystara's ring?' Beatriz murmured. 'A royal treasure indeed. So that's how. But where did you get it?'

Lyta had the good grace to look a little sheepish.

'I stole it,' she said quietly. 'From Alderton's safe, at his fancy party. Eninn wanted it.'

Beatriz shook her head. 'I'm sure he did, the greedy little brat. But Ystara must have been in on it somehow. Otherwise . . . What are they playing at now? Sylvian, whatever you do, don't take that off. Understand me?'

'Frida killed Haldevar for it,' Lyta warned him and he saw the flicker of agony in her eyes. The disbelief shook through him and knowing it was just a shadow of what she had to be feeling, he held her closer. 'She handed me over to Alderton. Over that. So don't let it out of your sight. No matter what.'

Slowly, he nodded in agreement and tucked it away again. Ystara, the Goddess of Love. It made no sense. Why should he carry her amulet?

'See, I gave it to you for a reason,' Lyta said. She was still pressed against him, her body flush with his, her hands on his face, the fingertips caressing his skin softly.

Unexpectedly he felt a smile pull at his lips. 'I'm sure you did. Whatever that might have been.'

'You called me *love*,' she whispered, almost teasing.

Sylvian felt his face heat. 'A slip of the tongue.'

In any other circumstance, Lyta would have taken the opportunity to say something filthy, he just knew it by the gleam in her eye. But instead she sobered. 'We need to find Ben and Kit. The duchess knows we broke into her vault, and she'll find them in no time. Kit's printshop is the obvious place. Alderton said she was coming after him and the Magister is with her. He wants Ben back.'

Beatriz's face paled. 'That must not happen.'

'They threatened to excommunicate Francisco,' Lyta said. 'That's what Alderton said. It would cut his whole empire off from the Church, just like they did with Albion.'

'That wouldn't matter to Francisco,' Sylvian said. 'He hates them.'

'But he needs them,' Beatriz replied. 'The Church Imperial still has power. They could side with his enemies, set up another claimant to the throne. It could mean years of war. And if they come for us . . . Even the king knows how that will end. You heard him, Sylvian. If we don't deliver a book to him soon, this will have been for nothing.'

He couldn't. He wouldn't. Not Francisco. Except he would. Sylvian knew he would. His last words ran through Sylvian's head, even as he tried to smooth a hand over Lyta's hair.

'You either come back with that book, or with the head of your thief lover. If neither, I will hunt you both to the ends of the earth. Don't choose her over me, Sylvian, or it'll be the end of you both.'

He pushed that thought away. He didn't want to face it.

'Come on,' he said. 'Let's get to Kit. He's going to need us, I fear. If the Magister and the duchess have joined forces, they will not be subtle.'

There were steps up onto the quayside not far away, and it was a relief to escape from the smell of the canal. Sylvian didn't know what had happened back there and he didn't even know what questions to ask anymore, but he couldn't help reaching for the ring through the material of his shirt.

Ystara's ring, the queen's ring. How on earth had Alderton got his grubby hands on it, and why had Eninn urged Lyta to take it from the safe? To bring it to him? He ought to return it to Annika and have done with it all. But Beatriz had been clear. Don't take it off.

They were almost at the Guild Quarter when they heard great Cissonia ringing out across the city. It wasn't the passing of an hour or a high day. There was no market or trade meeting. Which could only mean one thing.

Panic spread around them like a whirlwind, and the news came just as fast.

'Arm yourselves,' members of the city watch yelled as they raced by, heading for the south wall. 'Amberes is under attack. They've taken the King's Gate and the Almshouse Gate is under threat! All militia to your positions. Arm yourselves.'

Lyta stiffened and Sylvian knew with rising dread what she'd do. The King's Gate was a stone's throw from Kit's shop. He tried to catch hold of her. They needed to assess the situation. But the moment he grabbed Lyta's arm, Beatriz took off, running down the road while a tide of people moved against her, fleeing north, away from the rising smoke and shouts of anguish and dismay.

They were as bad as each other.

Sylvian met Lyta's panicked gaze. There was nothing he could say. He let go and they sprinted after Beatriz, into the heart of a battle for their city.

CHAPTER TWENTY-SEVEN

Kit

Two volumes, bound in goatskin stained blue, onto which Jem had insisted on tooling a design of leaves and flowers inlaid with gold, sat on the workbench. The two men looked at them as if they might bite at any moment. Kit had sent everyone else home as soon as he came down with the manuscript, but Jem had just given him one of those looks and ignored his orders. As usual.

'You finished them quickly,' Kit said.

'You seemed in a hurry. It's a simple enough binding, just wrapped around the block and stitched on the spine. I more or less had them finished anyway for those pretty drawing books Countess Ursel wanted bound for her children. They were the same size.'

Kit hardly dared touch them if he was honest. He had that feeling again, that creeping sense of something coming off the books, something demanding to be read, something that would swallow him up if he let it.

He wasn't even sure what to do now. Take them to Lyta, or to the king? He'd thought someone would have been here by now demanding they be handed over. But there was no sign of his sister or anyone else for that matter. And upstairs, Ben slept on, delirious with dreams Kit couldn't imagine. He needed to check on him, to make sure he was all right, but he hadn't dared leave Jem alone in the workshop.

They had hardly noticed the noise, but when the door opened and Molly burst in, the chaos outside shook them out of their stupor.

'There you are!' Jem's wife shouted. 'Gods, are you deaf? The alarm's raised. There's an army at the gates. The duchess and the Church Imperial. Some sort of alliance, that's what the watch said. We've got to get out of here.'

The duchess. And the Church. Neither was a good option. A spark of pain wriggled in Kit's lower arm, where she had marked him, and he knew—

He was looking at the reason.

He grabbed a coarse sack and in spite of Jem's protests, picked up one of the books and wrapped it, shoving the bundle into his friend's arms.

'Take this and hide it somewhere. I don't care where. Don't tell me. Just make it somewhere safe, understand? You and Molly need to get away.'

Jem staggered back. The other book lay on the workbench, beautiful and dangerous.

'What about you?' Molly asked.

He shook his head. 'I can't go. They'll burn the shop if there's no one to protect it. I can hold them off. I can't leave Ben.'

And they wouldn't stop coming. He knew that as well, but he couldn't tell the two of them.

'You can't fight off an army, Kit.'

'I'll lock the doors and hide then. Or try to bribe them. I don't know. Please, there isn't much time and that book . . . Listen Jem, I know I'm asking a lot. It's important. It's for the king and it's dangerous. Just get it to safety. I think they'll be after it. If they believe there's just one and they have it, then we may have a chance.'

'They? Who's *they*, Kit?' Molly asked, clinging to Jem's arm but not moving.

He had to make them leave.

'The soldiers. They're here for this book. And for Ben, I think. Just run, as far and as fast as you can.'

He almost bundled them out of the door and this time they let him. As he left, Jem looked back at him.

'I don't know what you've got yourself into, but stay safe, Kit. You and that man of yours. Don't hang around here to die in vain.'

'If they don't find us, they'll tear the city apart. It's bad enough they're coming here.'

'You don't know that. Kit, come with us.'

He shook his head. His arm was burning now. It was all the warning he needed that the duchess was coming for him and the book. They wouldn't have to take the whole city. The King's Gate was only a couple of streets away and the Almshouse Gate not much further. They only needed to get this far.

'Just go,' he said. 'Now.'

Finally sense got the better of them. Outside the air was heavy with smoke. Kit could hear shouts and screams nearby, and the clash of weapons.

What had Ranulf said? It worked both ways. She could reach into his head, but Ranulf had been able to reach back. But how? Kit cursed and locked the door, dropping a thick wooden bar across it. It wouldn't hold for long, but it was something. He needed more.

He eyed up his printing presses. They were huge oaken frames, heavy and solid. They were his livelihood and now his only hope. Barricades in their own right if used as such. Carefully, deliberately, he undid the bolts holding them to the ground. Climbing up he unscrewed their counterparts at the top and then holding on to the very top of the printing press, he swung down. The whole thing came after him like a tree falling across the room. Kit tried to draw breath, horrified at what he was doing. All that finely balanced machinery, his pride and joy.

Blinking back tears, he climbed up the next one, released it and seconds later pulled it down across its sibling. A barricade, he told himself. It would take time to get through that. It had to be done.

More, he needed more. He needed to block the whole room off, make it impossible to get inside and through it. He needed to block the doors. Bracing himself against the back of the presses, he managed to force first one, then the other towards the door, straining with the effort until sweat ran into his eyes. The cases holding the type collections came next, spilling drawers and all those tiny metal squares across the floor as they crashed down. The noise was deafening. He moved to the next case, nearest the door, pulling it over as hard as he could, to wedge it against the remains of his equipment already there. The crash sounded even louder this time and it shook its way through him. His work, his tools, his trade. Everything. How long would it take to repair all this? He ached with loss, like he'd cut away a part of himself.

The workshop was a scene of devastation. Kit blinked through the tears streaming down his face, forcing himself to keep going, to find something, anything else, that might act as a barrier, a booby trap or a weapon. But he'd run out of time.

They were already outside, feet thundering, angrily shouted orders. Someone started hacking at the door and the narrow windows smashed as weapons were turned on them as well. Too small to climb through, he hoped. Not that it mattered. He could only slow them down so much. They'd come no matter what.

He prayed for help, but the hope was fading fast. The watch would dig in and wait for reinforcements. He and Ben were on their own. He grabbed the remaining copy of the book and Ben's manuscript before he bolted up the stairs, locking the door behind him. A pathetic piece of wood and metal was all that protected them now.

'Ben?' he said, ashamed of the breathless quality in his voice. 'Ben, we're in trouble.'

Ben sat on the edge of the bed, glowing from head to foot, words drifting over his skin again, his eyes like molten gold. He didn't even look human anymore. Ben *was The Book of Gold*. Writing it out hadn't worked.

Kit's heart dropped like a stone.

Oh yes, they were definitely in trouble. In so many ways.

A crash downstairs told him that the invaders were already inside. On the roof opposite he saw a shadow move. An archer. They'd probably ringed the area to make sure he didn't climb out a window. They were trapped.

'Kit,' said Ben. 'Stand back from the door.'

He heard footsteps on the steps and the door vibrated with blows, like giant hammers thundering against the wood. Kit nursed the book against his chest, his one hope for negotiation as the door splintered and fell apart.

Men in black flooded the room, armoured and armed. Kit staggered back but before they could overwhelm him, Ben stepped in front of him, arms held wide and said something, words in a tongue that Kit couldn't hope to understand.

The soldier in the front simply fell to his knees, the axe tumbling from his hands as he covered his face and began to sob.

'Ben? What are you doing?' Kit shouted.

But Ben didn't answer. His voice grew louder, that strange sibilant language like a song now, warping the world around them. The other soldiers dropped next, some stumbling backwards and falling down the steps, ploughing into those below. Ben sang on, drawing out their pain and fears, driving them back in a frenzy of panic. Soldier after soldier screamed and cried out.

A crash brought Kit's attention to the floorboards underneath them. It was only a single layer of wooden planks over the beams below. He'd never needed more. The bare boards cracked and bucked as something punched its way through. Black and shining, hard and dreadful. An arm.

It grabbed Ben's leg and jerked, taking him off his feet and slamming him onto the ground. There was a dull thud, a crack and his voice fell silent. Kit tried to catch him, dropping the book and seizing his arms. But it was too late. Ben was dragged through the broken floor, torn from Kit's grip.

Kit dropped to the ground, staring down through the jagged hole into his workshop, where Ben was sprawled on the ground as dark figures gathered around him.

Then the floor around his own body erupted, implacable hands seizing him, and he was dragged down as well. He was slammed onto the workbench in the bindery, his arms and legs splayed out and the air driven from his lungs. He lay there twitching, gasping for long dreadful minutes until a face leaned over to study him. A face he had hoped never to see again.

Iseult, the Duchess of Montalbeau, smiled her thin, cruel and oh so beautiful smile, her eyes sparkling with malicious delight. 'Christopher Cornellis, how lovely to see you again.'

They'd come through the wall, Kit realised. Clean through the wall, taking out one of the windows with it. He'd never believed the workshop was particularly secure, but this was ridiculous. They must have used a battering ram.

Then he remembered the obsidian-clad arms coming through the floor and dragging him down, and thought, *Of course*, absently, with a curious sense of detachment that had to be born of shock. *Of course they had. They'd brought their own battering ram.*

He chanced a glance to the left and saw him standing there, a huge shape covered in stone armour. Who else had she trapped and enchanted in such a way?

'Like him, do you?' the duchess purred. She ran one finger down Kit's cheek and laughed. 'Maybe I can find a use for you as well, once we're finished here.'

No, Kit thought desperately, as a life wrapped in obsidian unwound itself before him, a life as her slave, with no will of his own. Slavery might be illegal under Castilian and Brabantine law, but who would stop her? Who had ever stopped her? *No, please no.*

She smiled, as if reading his thoughts. 'I'll make sure it sticks this time. Who knew that Benedictus had such talents. Did you, Magister?'

'We knew he had potential. Raw and untapped of course.' The Magister drew nearer, close enough to nudge the unconscious figure on the floor with his foot. 'But nothing like this. If I'd known I would have bound him myself. It's almost as if—' He peered closer as the words drifted like summer clouds across the side of Ben's cheek, beneath the blood and bruises left by his capture. 'Remarkable.'

'Where's my book, Christopher?' the duchess said, snapping his attention back to her. 'What have you done with it? Not the sad thing you left behind. The real book.'

He couldn't tell her. The situation with Ben was bad enough with the Magister there. He simply couldn't let her know what had happened.

'Allow me,' said the Magister. 'It's much quicker.'

Before Kit could pull away again, the Magister grabbed his head in an iron grip.

'The book was destroyed,' Kit blurted out. 'When we tried to take it.'

'I know that much. I saw what was left. What happened then?'

'Ben . . . Ben . . .' He couldn't. He had to fight it.

'Oh we know what Benedictus has done,' said the Magister. 'One only has to look at him. No matter. We'll take him back to the tower and from there we'll ship him back to the Caput Mundi, to face the judgment of the Imperator. All gods must be bound or destroyed, save the One, the embodiment of all Imperators. These pathetic few will be no trouble at all, I promise you, trapped as they are in a cage of flesh and bone. Perhaps we'll take his skin and make a book of him. Poetic, don't you think?'

The duchess laughed. 'Now, that is a treasure I would love to see.'

'You held such a treasure in your vault for many years, dear lady. But even your security failed in the end. Perhaps you should have given it to us when asked. As Francisco moves away from the light of the Church Imperial, it is better that we return to the more secure lands of our beloved empire. When there are no gods left to aid him, where else will he turn? It is inevitable.'

'You can't kill gods,' Kit interrupted before he could stop himself.

The Magister glared at him. 'Perhaps not in the human sense. But in every way that matters. They can be cast out into the Nether and the wandering ways, exiled and broken, their powers taken. They never find their way back. The Church Imperial has made it its mission to wipe them from the face of the earth.'

'A mission so very tedious,' Iseult cut in. 'Now, tell me where my book is.'

'There is no book, woman,' said the Magister. 'Don't you understand anything?'

The duchess glared at him but then focused her attention on Kit again. 'Really? Then why are we at a printer's workshop? For a man so obsessed with knowledge, Magister, you really are remarkably stupid.'

The moment of silence dragged on as the Magister absorbed her words.

'Tell her,' the old man commanded.

'Upstairs,' Kit gasped and fell back, his head thudding on the solid wooden table in defeat. The duchess let her hand stray down his chest, exploring his body while her soldiers scurried back upstairs and returned with the blue-bound volume. She took it from them, her gaze fixed on Kit, only looking away when she opened the book. The moments stretched out until she smiled. A cold and terrifying smile.

'Beautiful,' she murmured. 'Oh yes, this will do very well. Excellent work, Christopher, my pet. This is a masterpiece and I will use it well. So, are we in agreement, my lord Magister?'

The Magister took the stack of pages covered in Ben's neat script from his soldier. Glancing through them, he paused as she had paused, reading the secrets the scholar had spilled out there. But it didn't sweep him away as it had Kit when he tried. He was focused as a metal spike. 'Indeed. Our work here is done.' He handed the papers back to the soldier. 'Pack these safely. Make ready to leave.'

'Please,' Kit tried, finally free again. Free to beg like a pathetic fool. 'Please, just leave Ben. Leave him here. He can't help you. He can't even help himself. You have the book. You have the manuscript.'

But they knew what he was, what was inside him. They knew everything.

The Magister scoffed. 'He is beyond price. A source, a Nexus. I thought you knew about scholarship, Cornellis.' And then, Kit forgotten, he addressed his guards. 'Secure Alvarez for the journey.'

A surge of something brought Kit up from the table. 'No!' Before he got any further the obsidian warrior had pinned him down again, his fist closing on Kit's throat.

'Oh, sweet Christopher,' the duchess said as if addressing a recalcitrant child. 'You aren't staying here either. I'm going to find so many uses for you. But first, just to stop any further nonsense today . . .' She looked over her shoulder and her voice hardened. 'Someone get me a knife.'

The soldier behind her replied brusquely. 'Ma'am, the royal forces are closing in on our positions and the city watch have almost retaken the walls. We're running out of time. If we lose the gate—'

'Nonsense, Commander. Give me your dagger and hold his arm. I won't be a moment.'

An armed church militia man leaned in to whisper something in the Magister's ear. He listened impassively and then nodded.

'We will leave you to your entertainments,' he told the duchess. With a signal to his men, they left, taking Ben with them.

The Duchess of Montalbeau ignored them, her eyes still feasting on Kit, held down by the obsidian guard, helpless. A knife had been provided and she turned it this way and that so it caught the light.

'I presume your little scholar friend worked out how to block my runes. No matter. His writings tell me how to make it so much more effective. The original book only showed me what it chose to reveal to me, but now here it all is, ready to be read. You probably didn't intend that, did you? Remarkable. We have so much to explore, you and I. Shall we begin our experiments?'

Kit's throat closed. Ben hadn't been thinking as he transcribed the book and Kit himself was so used to printing the text without thought to the content. . .

Stupid. So stupid. Both of them. Letting the gods write whatever they wanted.

The line of pain as she sliced into his skin had him bucking and kicking helplessly against the heavy wooden table. His own reflection in the polished stone armour of the man holding him was a desperate, cornered animal. Kit had never thought of himself as a brave man, but not as a coward either. Now he begged. He begged endlessly. He didn't care. And neither did the duchess.

She finished on the arm she had previously marked and moved on to the other. She was faster this time around, and yet more thorough. She'd been enjoying herself in Old Steen. Now she did it with deliberate purpose. And there was nothing he could do to stop her.

CHAPTER TWENTY-EIGHT

Lyta

Beatriz ran faster than Lyta would have imagined, her cloak billowing like a banner, like an incarnation of Cissonia, the spirit of Amberes itself. Lyta saw people turn in wonder at the beautiful woman running towards the fight, unarmed, determination writ large on her features. Beatriz's effect spread through the panicked mob and by the time Sylvian and Lyta passed, a resistance was forming among the workers and tradesmen of the area. Almost as if, by running towards the danger, she made them realise what they might lose.

'Barricade the streets,' one of the masters of the Blacksmiths' Guild was yelling. 'Block off the alleys, now! They'll come no further.' Apprentices and journeymen raced to obey, others lending their strength. From the air, from the soil, from the sound of the bell, Amberes found the will to fight back.

The city watch were already engaged. Smoke filled the narrow streets, and up ahead the sound of swords clashing reached them, at the same time as Sylvian took the lead and spread his arms wide to stop the two women.

'Behind me,' he told them in a tone of complete command. He had that dangerous look and Lyta suspected he would slaughter anything in their path.

'We're only two streets away,' she told him. 'I know a shortcut.'

'I'm sure you do, but they're up on the roof. Look.'

Archers had taken position and when one of the city watch broke cover, a hail of arrows rained down on him. He didn't stand a chance. Beatriz lurched forward to go to his aid, but Lyta held her back.

'You can't do anything now.' Three other city watchmen crept towards them, looking to Sylvian for leadership. He waved them in behind him. They couldn't stay here. Sooner or later the soldiers up there would spread out, lock down positions. They had to move, and Lyta knew which way to go. 'Through here. Sylvian. Now!'

She dragged them both into the back door of a baker's, now deserted. The ovens were still blazing, the smell of burning bread thick in the room. Lyta coughed and covered her mouth as she ploughed towards the front, which came out across the street from the print workshop.

A scattering of bodies lay in the middle of Preachers' Street. A group of men on horses were just taking off, their livery a familiar red.

'Church militia,' Sylvian whispered. 'And those are the Montalbeau colours. Just her men left.' The guardsmen had followed him, their faces pale beneath ill-fitting helmets. Military or not, they were just boys, who had likely joined the city watch hoping to better their positions. They certainly hadn't expected anything like this. Everyone traded in Amberes. It made no sense to attack it.

But Lyta wasn't sure sense counted when it came to the duchess.

'You need to get a report back to the Rose Palace, understand?' Sylvian told them. 'Get word to General Vasquez and tell her Captain Chant is going in, that the church militia have pulled back to the gates and it's just Montalbeau now. Tell her where we are. Got it?' They nodded, clearly terrified but grateful for a task that would take them away from the front line. 'If you don't I'm going to die in there, so don't fail me.'

'Yes, Captain. You can count on us.'

He nodded solemnly. 'Then go. And watch each other's backs.'

Sylvian made a good leader, Lyta thought, clear and precise, encouraging strengths and accounting for weaknesses. The watchmen retreated as fast as they possibly could.

'Think they'll do it?' Lyta asked.

'We can only hope. I think they'll try. Can't hurt, can it? And maybe we'll get help. Right, you two, I need you to stay here and—'

'That's not happening,' said Beatriz in a voice like a queen's. 'My brother is in there.'

Lyta had to admire that, but Beatriz wasn't the only one. 'And so is mine. Forget protecting us, Sylvian. We've got to stop them. If they take Ben and Kit, everything we've done, and everything we lost, will be for nothing.'

He shook his head, as if exhausted with the two of them. 'Just try to stay behind me and don't get hurt. If you can get either Kit or Ben to safety, do it. And then run. Understand?'

'Yeah, right,' Lyta said. But she couldn't argue. It made sense. The only problem was, she didn't intend to leave Sylvian behind either. Not this time. Never again. 'Are you ready?'

He glanced back at her, and their gazes tangled together. 'Lyta, I mean it. I . . . I lose myself when I'm in situations like this. I may not stop. Stay out of my way.'

She knew the wildness that came over him when he fought. She'd seen it happen in the market square and in Montalbeau. Not on a scale that this situation would call for but when Sylvian fought that was what he became. The fight itself. A being made only to kill. And right now, that was what they needed. Didn't he realise that?

'It's all right,' she told him and pulled him to her so she could kiss his lips once more. 'Kill them all, love. I'll be all right.'

If he didn't get himself killed first. If that happened, she'd never be all right again. She'd already lost Ranulf, and Frida. She could be about to lose Kit. If she lost Sylvian as well . . .

Sylvian burst out of the door of the bakery, his sword a blur of light in his hand. Lyta had only her dagger and Beatriz to protect, but the Lady of House Alvarez wore a determined expression that boded nothing good. The soldiers rushing to engage Sylvian didn't stand a chance, not even managing a shout as they died, their weapons never touching him. Lyta scooped up a fallen sword for Beatriz but as she did, she saw the archer take aim on the rooftop above. Lyta didn't think, just pulled Beatriz out of the way. The arrow thudded into the ground at her feet, and hoping he'd take a second before firing again, she dived forward, through the gap in the wall, dragging the other woman with her. They tumbled into the ravaged workshop.

'Lyta, look out!' Kit screamed.

She rolled, bringing the sword up blindly and felt it swatted out of her hands by a force so powerful it left her arm numb.

Guards closed on the two women, but Sylvian hauled them off, putting them to the sword before they could react to his presence.

And then the obsidian guard stepped into view, engaging Sylvian with a fury that matched his own. He drew a sword from his back, a lethal thing half a body length at least, which most men would have to wield two-handed. A bastard sword for a bastard. Lyta scrambled back towards the steps upstairs, taking in the ruined roof and the sprawled body of her brother on the table, his arms covered in blood. She drew in a ragged breath and then made her decision. Darting across the floor, sliding under the clash of the men's blades, she tried to reach Kit. He tumbled off the table, towards her, his face etched with pain, fresh, bright blood painting his hands and forearms in scarlet.

'What did she do? Where's Ben?' Lyta asked.

'They took him, the Magister and his militia. They . . . They . . . She . . .'

He looked around with frantic eyes, his face almost savage.

'What did she do to you?' Lyta tried to grab his arms, but he pulled back, balling in on himself.

'Lyta,' he gasped, 'you have to get out of here. You have to get away from me.'

'From you, what are you—?'

A deafening crash sounded behind her, and Sylvian drove the obsidian guard back against one of the supporting posts by the stairs. He held him there for only a moment. Sheer brute strength forced Sylvian back. The man lifted him from his feet and pushed him the other way, straight into a wall, pinning him there.

THE BOOK OF GOLD

Ranulf. It had to be Ranulf. Somehow he had survived and the dutchess had enchanted him again. Lyta knew she shouldn't have gone back. She should never have believed . . .

'Lyta,' Kit tried again, his voice strange and twisted. Desperate.

When she looked back at him, he hit her, full force, snapping her head to one side and slamming her to the ground. Before she knew what was happening her brother had her pinned to the floor, his legs straddling hers, his hands on her wrists, holding them over her head, his blood turning them slick and warm. His face wasn't his own, nor his eyes. He looked like the men in the tunnel beneath Montalbeau, the ones who had killed Ranulf.

'Kit?' she gasped.

A voice cut through the sounds of their struggle. 'Enough,' said the Duchess of Montalbeau. 'Pick her up, Christopher. Maybe we can made use of her as well. If not, you can just snap her neck and have done.'

Kit obeyed, in spite of Lyta's protests, hauling her to her feet and twisting her arms up behind her back to the point of pain. She'd always known her brother was strong, but cruelty wasn't in his nature, and he had never turned on her like this.

'What have you done to him?' Beatriz asked, her voice trembling in horror. Lyta could see why. The duchess had a knife at her throat and a hand clamped on her shoulder, fingers digging into the woman's skin. 'And where is my brother?'

'The Magister has your brother. They're going to haul him back to Caput Mundi so the Imperator can flay the skin off his body to remake *The Book of Gold* and peel back all his secrets. A shame. All that knowledge wasted, but they don't care about knowledge, do they? Not really. Just power. But lucky me. Christopher here made me a copy of my own. I'll know everything they do – long before them. And you, dear lady, are going to help me.'

Beatriz's face fell to disbelief. 'I am never going to help you.'

'I didn't say *willingly*. But you're an Aspect and I know what that means. You're a conduit for divine power, aren't you? Just like Benedictus. I'm going to drink you down, all your magic, all your power.

My lady showed me how, through this very book. All the years I studied it, all the things I learned, but it was never enough. She never showed me everything. But now I finally have a transcription. Even the brief snatches I read so far are remarkable. I'll make Montalbeau strong again. I'll take back this miserable stain of a city and once I've killed that upstart king—'

'That's treason,' Sylvian cut in. The grip of obsidian on his throat tightened.

'Yes, well, what's a little treason these days? I hear it being mentioned about you as well, Sylvian Chant. And *you* I can make use of.'

A noise at the entrance brought a harried and dirty-looking soldier into view. 'My lady, we're being driven back. The king's soldiers are reinforcing the gates. Our way out will be cut off if we don't—'

She snarled at him and he scrambled out of her way. They were going to run, her men. They weren't prepared to die for her, not here, not today. Even Lyta could see that. They weren't like her prisoners, mindless and savage, living only to kill for her and her goddess. And if they stayed, they would die. The king was coming and he would not treat this incursion lightly.

'Let them go,' Iseult of Montalbeau raged. 'Let them run like the cowards they are. Where will they go? They'll be sorry for it later. I'll have protection. New warriors, loyal in all things. I just need enough magic to do it. And I have everything I need right here.'

Without hesitation she slashed the blade across Beatriz's throat. Blood gushed from the wound, and the duchess held the woman's spasming body against hers. Lyta screamed but Beatriz's open mouth couldn't utter a sound. Even Kit shuddered, the horror of it making him fight against the dark magic holding him captive.

The light in Beatriz's eyes dimmed. The front of her beautiful gown turned scarlet and then almost black. But still Iseult held her, throwing back her head as Beatriz's life and powers drained into her.

She pointed the knife at Sylvian, still held against the wall by the obsidian warrior, and as Lyta watched black smoke coalesced around him, tendrils snaking up his body. Ranulf released him, but the smoke held Sylvian, crystallising as it began to turn him into a creature like her husband.

'Ranulf, please, you have to help.' But he didn't even look at her.

Sylvian gasped for breath as the smoke burrowed into his mouth and nostrils.

Lyta struggled again and Kit lost his grip on her, his hands too slippery with blood to hold her. She had to believe there was something of her brother still in there, just as she believed Ranulf was there too. Hope was all she had left. She threw herself forward, but Ranulf grabbed her before she could reach Sylvian, his grip like the stone coating him.

'You broke free once,' she said. 'We freed you. Please, Ranulf. Please. You, me and Kit, we have to stop her.'

Ranulf hesitated. She couldn't see his face, or his eyes, could only see her own reflection in the gleaming surface of his face, covered in mud and blood. It wasn't fair. She couldn't lose them like this. Not all three of them.

The smoke had devoured Sylvian entirely now, and half his body was coated in obsidian. He couldn't even struggle anymore. Her eyes met his and he frowned.

'Lyta,' he whispered, but more vines filled his mouth before he could say anything more.

Not like this, she begged the universe. *Eninn, please, not like this.* Not with Beatriz dead and Ben doomed, not with Frida a traitor and her brother, Ranulf and Sylvian enslaved.

'*Eninn, please,*' another voice whispered, echoing her prayer. Beatriz's voice rippled through the air. And others. So many voices. They murmured around the room, up in the corners, under the broken equipment and through the shattered ceiling. '*Eninn, I petition thee. Eninn, I summon thee. Eninn, I beg thee.*'

The duchess laughed, giddy with the stolen power flowing in her veins. 'Eninn can't help you. Why would he? He's the Trickster. All he does is run and hide. He deserted the other gods when *The Book of Gold* was first made.'

'Ystara threw her light into the sky and lit the far north for a single moment but only Eninn escaped with his heart and his wit,' the voices said, rippling as if through deep water, resolving into a single sound once more – and it didn't sound like Beatriz. This was the voice of a young man, and it rose with grief and regret. *'Ystara doesn't like it when people try to steal her light. I should know. Ystara, forgive me. You were able to help him before because of the amulets. Do it again. I offer you what is yours. Sister, come and take it. I offer all freely. I offer my place for yours. Take it and keep them safe where I cannot.'*

Sylvian threw back his head and cried out as light burst from his chest, shattering the stone covering him like glass. He and the obsidian figure disappeared in a blinding explosion, and Lyta was thrown clear, colliding with Kit and taking him to the floor with her in a tangle of limbs.

CHAPTER TWENTY-NINE

Kit

Lyta and Kit crashed against the shattered remains of the printing press, tangled together as light flared, bright and terrible, the blow bringing him back to his senses.

Lyta curled against him. Her eyes opened, blinked and she sucked in a terrified breath.

'Lyta?' he whispered and saw her flinch.

'Kit? Is that you? I can't . . . Kit I can't see.'

His chest constricted and he held her close. There had to be a way out of this. The duchess had reeled back, but she wasn't gone. He could feel her magic reaching out to him again, feel her rage.

He wouldn't let her take him again. He couldn't. With Lyta helpless, he had to protect her. All the times she'd looked out for him, saved his skin, all the things she'd given up to make sure he was going to be okay. Like Ben had said, they were only the men they were because of Lyta and Beatriz.

Beatriz who lay on the ground in a pool of her own blood. Ben who was gone. Probably forever. This was Kit's fault. He should have fought harder. He should have found a way.

'Kit, talk to me,' Lyta whispered. 'What's happening?'

He pulled the knife from her hand and she shied back from him in alarm. He'd never thought anything he did could frighten her, but there was fear in her now. She didn't trust him. Couldn't trust him. His arms burned with his own blood and despite himself he felt that dark and treacherous serpent insinuating its way through him again. The duchess was reasserting her control.

'Lyta?' Kit said. 'Listen to me. She's using me. But Ranulf said it works both ways, remember?'

She grabbed his face in desperation, pulling him into her embrace. 'What are you saying?'

'I'm going to try something, but if I fail, if this goes wrong . . . Please,' he went on. 'Don't let her take me. You have the knife. Lyta. You know what to do. Please.'

'I am not stabbing you, Kit Cornellis!' He almost smiled. She was unstoppable, his sister. 'The king's troops are almost here. We just have to hold her long enough.'

He prayed she was right. 'But if it goes wrong, please Lyta.'

She blinked, squinting at him as if she was starting to see again. 'I think it's clearing. Just give me a—'

A wall reared up through his mind and Kit lurched back from Lyta as the duchess wound her will through him. He had to get away. He couldn't risk hurting his sister.

'Kit,' she cried. 'Hold on. Please.'

Shadows closed in on him like briars. Kit lashed out, trying to push them away. He needed a way to fight back. You fought darkness with fire. And help had to be coming. He could hear Cissonia's bell outside, ringing across the city. Lyta was right. They just had to hold on, just a little longer. He just had to slow her down.

He ground his teeth together as he pitched himself into a very different battle. Reaching out into the dark consciousness trying to overwhelm him, he formed his own will into a spear of light and threw it at her.

The duchess jerked back, more with surprise than alarm. Then she caught herself and let out a slow, mocking laugh. 'You? You ludicrous man. You have no idea what you're doing.'

'But I do,' Lyta whispered. 'Hold on, Kit.'

She moved like a shadow on the ground, low and swift, sliding under the binding table and coming up beneath the duchess as she advanced on Kit. Lyta slammed the blade into Iseult of Montalbeau's stomach.

The dark pall closing in on him shattered. For a moment everything went still, and then, to Kit's horror, the duchess just smiled.

'You think that will do it? Stupid girl, I have all the healing powers of the gods in me.'

The duchess reached down and closed her hand over Lyta's, jerking the blade out and dropping it. With a swift and brutal move, she kneed Lyta in the face, sending her back against the wooden table leg, and advanced on her, clearly intent on dealing with Lyta herself this time.

No! Kit surged to his knees and flung his hands out, forcing himself into the darkness of the duchess's soul, illuminating it from within. He thought of Ben, of the glow beneath his skin, of the wild magic that coursed through him. His heart sang with the memory of him. He thought of Beatriz, the way the world glowed around her, the way she made warmth wherever she went, the light and the comfort of her presence.

There, beneath the darkest shadows, it shimmered like a pool of golden light, the magic from which the duchess was fuelling all her dark arts.

'Stop it, Christopher,' she snapped. 'I'm warning you now. I'll make you pay for this.'

But Kit didn't stop. He wouldn't stop. He couldn't. He knew that now. No matter how much he wanted to be respectable, to stay out of trouble, no matter how often he had tried to push Lyta away, he was a Cornellis as well, and every bit as stubborn as his sister was. He might want a different life, but he wasn't actually that different, not deep down. He had always tried to obey the rules, but if the rules were wrong, or corrupt, or used by people like the duchess against the common people of Amberes, someone had to do something about it.

Like a weaver who had found a loose thread, Kit grabbed the duchess's magic, and he pulled.

And something answered. Something which took all he was and swallowed it whole.

As if the string had been suddenly cut, Kit collapsed into the floor. He tried to push himself up again, but all of his strength was gone.

His arms shook and his vision swam sickeningly as he tried to focus on the duchess.

Iseult's eyes were wide in shock and horror. The wound in her stomach blossomed again, blood seeping through the fine material. So much blood. She dropped to her knees, clutching at her clothes, trying to staunch the flow. It oozed through her fingers, far more than there should be.

A figure rose behind her, wreathed in light and godly power, blood still drenching her neck and chest, dark hair falling loose around her flawless face. She looked like a goddess in that moment, one of death and sacrifice. One reborn.

'It works both ways,' said Beatriz in a voice that rippled and sang. 'Darkness and light. Healing and death. Clever Kit worked it out.'

'This isn't...' The duchess scrambled to face Beatriz. She coughed and black blood burst from her mouth. 'What have you done?' Her skin burst out in sores and open wounds, and she doubled over, gasping for breath.

'Turned it all back on you. Everything I've ever healed. Every time I've ever helped another live. You can have their deaths, all of them. And my own. Not nearly as much as you deserve.'

'But you—' Iseult hissed, barely able to form words. 'You're a healer. You're *kind*.'

Beatriz smiled, the most chilling expression Lyta had ever seen in her life. 'Never mistake kindness for weakness, Iseult.'

Iseult, the Duchess of Montalbeau, gave one last whine of despair, her eyes turning to blood as she twisted and writhed in agony, and then finally, she fell still.

The darkness infecting Kit turned to ash, crumbling away at last.

CHAPTER THIRTY

Sylvian

Blinding brightness tore through Sylvian's mind, shattering the obsidian around his body and banishing the shadows choking and binding him. The man he had fought was hurled back, ripped away from him to crash down against the solid wood of the press, slumping there even as Sylvian slid to the floor, lost in the blinding light.

A woman stood over him. Jet-black locks fell around a heart-shaped face, and as his eyes adjusted, he feared it was the duchess. But there the resemblance ended. Her eyes were pale as glaciers in the far north and her mouth a perfect rosebud, but her skin was a deep brown, which spoke of sunshine and the blistering heat of the far south. She was a study in paradoxes. The woman studied him for a moment and that was when Sylvian realised he could see through her to the shadowy reality of the printshop beyond. But it was like looking up from the depths of a pool, as if in drowning she had come to rescue him.

'Well, you can't stay here,' she told him in firm and solemn tones. 'My brother has made a grand gesture. And probably a terrible mistake. As usual.'

'My lady?' His lips felt numb as he spoke.

'Your lady,' she mused. 'Yes, probably. We'll get to that later, I think. Get up, Sylvian. There is still work to do.'

Ystara. Who else could it be? She was beautiful, but also harsh. People imagined the Lady of Love would be gentle, but he knew differently. She glowed from within, like a fire. Fire warmed, comforted and kept away the dark. But it also hurt, consumed all it touched, burned everything to ashes.

'My lady,' he tried again. 'Why are you here? You were—'

'Trapped with the others. Eninn took my place to save you and yours. His pendant and my ring side by side around your neck made it possible, my champion. As it was possible for you to save your Lyta, once you accepted your love. Look at you.' She sighed, as if deeply disappointed in him. Or perhaps just sorry for him. 'You really are in a state.'

'But I—' He blurted out the words before he thought about it. 'I serve Kyron the Warrior. I always have. I kill people, lady. It's all I'm good at. Death and violence.'

Ystara reached out with one hand, her touch gentle as she cupped his chin and lifted his face, turning it this way and that to study him.

'It's not the only thing you're good at. You think people don't kill for love, Sylvian? They do far worse than you have ever done, my sweet boy. Now, Lyta needs you. Ben and Kit need you. My little brother – who thinks he knows better than anyone in this reality, and is, as I've said before, usually wrong – needs you. You have many duties. People you have bound yourself to protect. That's love too, isn't it? Wake up, my champion. We have work to do.'

She sounded like a general. Something in him snapped to attention, unable to help himself, and she was gone.

Body aching, head pounding, Sylvian found himself in the wreckage of the printshop. A broad-shouldered stranger slumped against the broken frame of the press, the obsidian shattered around him.

Everything came back to him in a rush.

'Lyta!'

Her voice sounded shaken from the other side of the workbench. 'Here, we're here. Are you—? Is Ranulf—?'

Ranulf.

Sylvian felt it like a blow to the chest. She had thought it was Ranulf. She was still trying to save Ranulf, even after – after everything.

'It— It isn't him, Lyta.' He didn't know if she could hear him. His voice couldn't manage more than a whisper.

'Move, Sylvian,' said Beatriz in tones that were not to be argued with. 'Get out of the way. Let me see to him.'

Beatriz was alive? Even as he moved his protesting body out of her way, the room filled with armed men and women wearing city watch livery, shouting orders, holding each of them in place, weapons drawn. Rage boiled in him, dragging him to his feet. He didn't have a sword – he'd lost that somewhere in the fight – but he could take one in seconds.

Slowly he straightened, ignoring the orders to stand down from the hysterical guards. They had taken one look at the destruction around them and decided that whoever was still in here had to be the enemy. Perhaps they weren't wrong. His eyes darkened and he drew his lips into a wolfish smile. The nearest guard blanched. The ones still clogging the entrance backed up in panic.

'Oh yeah, he's in here all right,' called a voice from outside and Montes stepped inside, the Cordovan warrior ducking to clear the broken window. 'Might have guessed given the state of the place.'

The general followed him, Vasquez's neat form somehow taking up more space than the warriors who accompanied her.

'Stand down, Sylvian,' she ordered. 'It's over. You lot,' she nodded at the city watch who, frankly, looked ready to wet themselves. 'Outside. We'll deal with this.'

They scattered and Sylvian found himself facing five of his fellow royal bodyguards and the general who led them.

'Where's the king?' he asked. 'Is he safe?'

Vasquez gave him a look which branded him an idiot. 'You think we just danced off down here and left him alone? He's fine. On his way, of course, probably furious he's missed the fight. He's pissed off, Sylvian. Really pissed off, so you'd better have an excellent excuse for all of this.'

Before Sylvian could answer someone else spoke. 'We don't have time to explain,' Kit said. Only he didn't sound like Kit anymore, not the wary young man trying to make things right. This voice was determined and would brook no dissent. 'The Magister took Ben, and we have to stop them. They're going to kill him, Sylvian. They're going to take back the book from his skin. They said—'

Juárez leaned in and whispered something in the general's ear. 'The infamous Christopher Cornellis,' she said with a nod of understanding. 'So this would be your sister Lyta?' Lyta still huddled on the floor, covered in mud, blood and the gods alone knew what else. Next to her was the ravaged corpse of the Duchess of Montalbeau. That did not look good either. 'Did you do this?'

No one lied to the general. She had that peculiar way of making people tell her the truth. Not magic like the Magister. Nothing so sordid. Just sheer force of will.

'Some of it,' Lyta admitted cagily, knowing better than to own too much of the chaos that surrounded her.

'General,' Sylvian said as respectfully as he could muster, trying to smooth over everything disrupted by the Cornellis siblings. 'We have to go. If they take Alvarez beyond our borders . . .'

'If you leave now the king will have your head, Chant. He's said as much. He'll take it as treason. He wants the book, and her.' She pointed at Lyta. 'You've really pissed him off.'

For once, Lyta had no smartarse reply. Sylvian would have counted it a miracle under any other circumstances.

Beatriz looked up from her ministrations, her voice shaking with anger as much as exhaustion. She still bristled with power. 'If my brother is harmed, General, your king will have more things to worry about than his own petty—'

Vasquez frowned. 'Lady Alvarez, threats to the royal personage—'

Sylvian reached out for Lyta's hand and pulled her to her feet. 'We have to go.'

Vasquez let out a world-weary sigh. 'Half our troops are going to be coming after you. The Magister and his militia are fleeing to the Scholars' Tower, on the road to Luttich. Juárez has our horses at the end of the street.'

Her leave to depart was unspoken. His brothers-in-arms stepped aside in silence, the way out open. Sylvian knew it was the only chance he was going to get. And he had to take it.

Kit was already outside, making down the street, but Lyta hesitated. 'Beatriz?'

Still tending to the fallen warrior, the Lady of House Alvarez glanced at her. She looked pale, exhausted, with shadows under her eyes. She might have been able to make threats, but Sylvian doubted she could do much more than that right now. Still, she'd give Francisco a nightmare of a time. 'Get my brother back, Lyta. I'll deal with the king when he finally arrives.'

Sylvian didn't need to tell her that such an action was as perilous as anything they were about to attempt. An army was coming after them. They just had to reach the Magister and Ben first.

He nodded his thanks to Vasquez and the others, and raced for the horses outside. Juárez had moved to block Kit, but when he saw Sylvian, he lifted his head in understanding and stepped aside.

'Sylvian, he's going to lose his mind if you go,' said his fellow bodyguard. 'You know that, don't you?'

Something caught in Sylvian's throat and he nodded. 'I don't have a choice. Not now.'

'We'll do what we can.'

Which would be nothing. But the sentiment was appreciated. Juárez stepped back, letting them past. Kit vaulted into the saddle, ready to go.

Sylvian wanted to stop, to check Lyta was all right, but there wasn't time. Grabbing her by the waist he hoisted her up onto her mount. She took the reins, holding them too tight in her hands until her knuckles went white.

'Do you know how to ride?' he asked.

'I know how to hang on,' she replied. 'That's enough.'

He had to say something. Anything.

'I'm sorry it wasn't him, Lyta. I'm—'

Lyta shook her head. 'He died to save us,' she told him firmly. 'He didn't want to live like that again. If she'd brought him back, enslaved him a second time—' She swallowed hard, clearly unable to go on. 'We have to go. Now.'

He squeezed her hand gently and then released her.

The remaining horse was his. The stallion whickered and pawed at the ground, ready to be off.

He caught a glimpse of Juárez shaking his head in dismay. So did Lyta.

'Sylvian,' Lyta called, and he looked back at her. Her grief was masked again. You'd never know it had been there. 'Whatever happens, we're with you. *I'm* with you.'

He nodded and dug in his heels, the warhorse responding in an instant, taking off at a gallop for the Almshouse Gate.

The Magister had too great a lead. Sylvian realised that as soon as they were out on the open road. There was no way they were going to catch him before he reached the tower, and even if they did it would be the three of them against armed church militia on a holy mission. No, he needed to think, to formulate a plan. There would be no second chances.

He slowed his mount as they neared the edge of Amberes' lands.

'What are you doing?' Lyta called as she drew level with him. Her horse appeared to be following his, which was a relief. Kit slowed down as well.

'Up ahead,' Sylvian said. 'There's a copse of trees overlooking the road. They'll be waiting for pursuit.'

'How do you know?'

'It's what I'd do. The Magister will head on with Ben, but that's a deathtrap.' He nodded towards the landscape ahead. 'I need you to do exactly what I say.' She opened her mouth to protest, of course. '*Exactly*, Lyta.'

'Fine,' she growled. 'But we don't have time.'

'If we don't do this right, we're not going to have any time at all.' He dismounted and they followed suit. 'You're going to make yourselves look helpless. Easy targets and no threat.'

'You're using us as bait?' Kit asked, only slightly incredulous.

'If we're lucky there won't be many of them. We only need three.'

He handed Lyta the reins of his horse and then reached up behind his neck to take off the necklace. He slid the ring off and put it on his little finger. Perhaps he should have been surprised to find it fitted perfectly, but then again perhaps not. He beckoned to Lyta and when she bent down he slipped the necklace with Eninn's pendant back around her neck where it belonged. Bemused, she let him and when he brought his lips to hers, she kissed him back.

'What's that for?' she asked.

Sylvian smiled. 'Luck.' Behind them, Kit gave a growl of disgust. 'All right, just ride through slowly. Keep your eyes on the road. And if you hear something try not to react.'

'What do you mean *something*?'

'Lyta, just do what I say. For once.'

'Once,' she agreed. 'This once. That's it, Sylvian. The only time.'

Sylvian found their would-be ambushers with no problem at all. They hadn't even hidden their tracks. He took out the first in silence. The second and third were distracted when Lyta and Kit stopped in the road and had a very obvious argument. He came upon the fourth in the nick of time, with arrow drawn, obviously having decided to use the pair as target practice. The whole sorry affair was over quickly and with his own form of quiet efficiency.

When he met them at the other side of the trees, having assured himself that this was all the Magister had left behind to block the way, he dumped the uniforms and armour he'd stripped from the bodies and Lyta looked at him as if he had lost his mind.

'I'm not wearing that.'

Sylvian cocked an eyebrow at her watermarked leather outfit, which was caked with mud and blood. 'These uniforms are how we get in. You're not exactly dressed for the occasion.'

Kit on the other hand was already setting to work finding clothes to fit his broad frame. A dark determination had seized him, the strain of his worry showing in his face, the lines around his eyes and the grim set of his jaw.

'Are you going to be all right?' Sylvian asked.

Kit strapped a sword to his side. To Sylvian's knowledge he'd never lifted one before. 'I have to be,' he replied. 'There isn't anyone else, is there?'

'And you can use that?'

Lyta's brother nodded. 'Not like you, maybe, but well enough.'

'Lyta?' There was another sword there for her, but she tapped the dagger at her belt.

'I've still got my stabby best friend. I'll stick with that. Are you two finished? We've got a job to do.'

Sylvian mounted, strapping the other sword to the saddle by his leg, just in case. 'Another job. You keep dragging me into criminality, Lyta.'

'Well, what did you expect coming back here, Captain Chant? Ready?'

She urged her mount forward, and they had no choice but to follow her towards the tower.

CHAPTER THIRTY-ONE

Lyta

Night had crept in by the time they reached the gates of the tower, and they tagged onto the rear of a group of militia limping back from the incursion into Amberes. Getting through the gates was easy after that and Lyta felt unease crawl up her back. She wanted to grab her pendant and pray to Eninn, but that was impossible through the armour pressing close around her chest.

No women joined the church militia, nor the ranks of their scholars. They were kept at home, secluded and, as far as she was concerned, enslaved. She'd always known this, but it had never been quite so obvious to her as it was here, in this bleak place.

The courtyard was a flurry of activity, with several more elaborately armoured men barking out instructions to those around them.

'Man the walls. The godless Castilian bastards will be here in no time for vengeance, and we have to be ready.'

To Lyta's horror, Sylvian strode right to the nearest one with an aura of purpose. 'Commander, we have information for the Magister himself. Where can I find him? It's of the utmost operational importance.'

The man looked Sylvian up and down. 'The Magister is sequestered with his prisoner. You can give me the message and be about your business, soldier.'

But Sylvian didn't move. He glared at the man as if he might commit murder there and then and ask forgiveness later. 'My instructions were to tell the Magister alone.' The tone screamed 'Don't you know who I am?' And to Lyta's surprise, the man before him instantly backed down. Perhaps he decided the risk wasn't worth anything it might gain him. Perhaps he was just too busy. And stupid.

'In his chambers in the main tower. I presume you know where *that* is.'

The sarcasm wasn't lost on any of them, but Sylvian ignored him. 'Thank you, Commander. Your assistance will be noted.'

He turned away sharply, gestured to the two of them to follow him, and took off across the courtyard on his long legs. Lyta and Kit fell into step beside him.

'That was a risk,' she murmured.

'It worked. Don't knock it.'

The tower itself was almost deserted. In the library the scholars were packing books and scrolls into crates, and no one looked at them as they passed. They were making ready to retreat. Lyta couldn't believe it. The Church didn't back off. They ruled half the world, even if they let little kings and lordlings think differently. It was an empire all by itself, the greatest of empires. But the tower was just a small outpost, a pocket in enemy lands, and this time, faced with Francisco and his army coming out of Amberes, they were making ready to desert their stronghold. What did that mean?

Was Ben more important to them than their foothold on the edge of their world?

No, not Ben perhaps, but the gods locked inside him. Destroying them would further the mission the Church had set itself a thousand or more years ago. No gods but the Imperator Eternal.

And Eninn was in there too now, or so Ystara had told Sylvian, swapping places with her so she could use the ring to save Sylvian from the duchess's enchantment.

Which made no sense because the one thing Eninn knew how to do was look after himself. He was the one who had escaped, leaving the other gods to be trapped in the book in the first place. Everyone knew that. Since when had he learned self-sacrifice?

It didn't matter. Miserable little feral god or not, he was her god, and Ben was her friend. Her brother loved him beyond reason, though he might not be ready to admit that yet. And besides . . . she would not let the Magister win.

The thought of him still sent a chill through her.

She put her head down and followed Sylvian.

The stairs led them upwards to the chamber where Lyta had been brought when she had been captured. As they approached, the militia guards at the door hailed Sylvian, but he didn't pause. Instead, he drew his sword and killed them with brutal efficiency, before flinging open the door, not caring what might be on the other side. There wasn't time to care, she told herself.

Ben hung by his arms from chains attached to the ceiling, cruel iron manacles digging into his wrists. He was naked, his body aglow with golden light, symbols and signs moving over his bare skin like a magic lantern show. The mosaic of the eagle beneath him seemed to shift and move as if alive. He illuminated the Magister on his throne, who looked transfixed by what he saw. He was alone in the room, his guards dismissed.

Papers were still burning in the brazier beside him. The manuscript, Lyta supposed. He didn't need it when he had Ben. And he clearly didn't want anyone else to have it.

He started as they entered, standing up in outrage. Kit slammed the doors shut behind them and lifted the bar into place while Sylvian approached, bloody sword in hand.

Slowly, the Magister took his seat once more, composing himself.

'So, you've come to see the end. Marvellous, isn't he?'

Kit muttered something obscene and almost hurled himself forward, but Sylvian stopped him with a single raised hand.

'Get Ben down. Make sure he's unharmed.'

Unharmed, that was a joke. His eyes were still closed and he seemed broken and lost. All the same, Lyta and Kit moved to obey. The sooner they could get him out of this the better. Lyta wasn't going to bother looking for a key. She already had her lockpicks to hand. Kit boosted her onto his shoulders and she set to work.

'You've fallen in with bad company, Captain Chant,' the Magister said. 'A veritable circus act it appears. How would they have fared in the games of old in Caput Mundi? In the truth of the blood and sand?'

'You'd be surprised,' Sylvian replied smoothly and Lyta felt an unexpected surge of pride.

The lock gave way with an audible click and Ben crashed to the ground, still trapped in his stupor. Lyta and Kit dropped beside him, trying to wake him. To no avail. This was not good, not good at all.

'Did she really murder the duchess?' asked the Magister, toying with his ruby ring. So word of that had gotten here ahead of them.

'More of a group effort,' she heard Sylvian reply.

'Your king will be pleased. To be honest, so am I. A dreadful woman with ideas far above her sex. Like that one behind you. Needs taking down a peg or two if you ask me.'

'I—' Sylvian hesitated, his voice choking in his throat. 'I don't—'

The Magister pushed himself onto his feet. *Damnation*, Lyta thought. They'd forgotten what he could do. The way he could twist words and minds. He peered at Sylvian who stood, frozen and confused.

'Not doing terribly well, are you, Captain? Let me explain. The last time we were here, you kissed this ring. You let me bless you. It's not something to be done lightly. Deference like that implies subservience, you see. And now I demand that. Drop the weapons, if you please.'

Sylvian's hands spasmed and the scars on his forearms flared horribly bright, as if etched in molten metal. He gasped in pain and fell to his knees, his sword and knife clattering to the ground before him.

'I was hoping to learn more from Benedictus, but I've learned enough for the moment. Further study will be needed. But for now . . .'

He waved his hand and an unseen force seized Lyta and Kit, hurling them back against the walls and dropping them. Ben's body blazed like fire as the Magister approached.

'Time to put an end to this, I think. Little gods who have spent too much time in the wild need to be brought to heel. Show yourselves.'

He made another complicated movement with his hands and his ring blazed like a beacon. Swirling golden light burst into the air and spilled out into a circle around Ben's crumpled form. Three figures appeared and Lyta knew at once who they were, who they had to be.

Kyron wore the skull of a great elk as his helm, the antlers spread wide like wings. He dressed in leather and fur and the sword strapped to his back was a monstrous thing. His hands were huge and gnarled, his arms like the branches of ancient trees, and his eyes blazed with rage. Beside him stood Gloir, neither male nor female, but somehow both, with their leather apron and their hammer in hand, dark skin streaked with molten gold, decked in a multitude of earrings, bangles and necklaces. And Nimyeh, tall and slender as a silver birch sapling, her white-blonde hair tumbling down her back and the owl crown on her head. Old gods. Ancient gods.

Slumped at their feet was a fourth. A scrawny adolescent boy with golden hair, curled up as if in pain and bound in chains. They had gagged him with metal too, which cut cruelly into the sides of his mouth.

'Well?' said the Magister. 'Have you discussed my offer?'

The three gods standing over Eninn glanced at each other. They looked almost guilty, but in agreement. As if a terrible decision had been reached.

Lyta didn't like that one bit.

Movement caught the corner of her eye. Kit crawling to reach Ben.

'We have,' said Nimyeh at long last. 'For our freedom we will help you.'

'What?' Lyta exclaimed in horror. 'What are you talking about?'

'Power,' said the Magister with a sneer. Nimyeh dropped her gaze in shame. 'That's what they are. Beings of pure power, but locked away what can they do with it? I've offered them freedom in exchange for a simple thing. It's better than this miserable existence. What happens when a god is killed, do you imagine?'

Lyta shook her head. She had to keep him talking. If Kit could reach Ben. If he could wake him, then perhaps the scholar would know what to do. Perhaps Ben would be able to talk sense into them. Because this sounded all kinds of wrong. Every instinct she had screamed that.

'I don't know. You have a god funeral? A god murder investigation? Tell me, Magister, if you're so wise.'

He paused, considering her words. Then he laughed. Not a proper laugh. It was a brief exhalation, mostly scoffing. 'Perhaps I won't have you executed immediately, Mistress Cornellis. Perhaps we'll take you back to Caput Mundi as well and make an exhibition of you in the circus after all. There might be some amusement in that.'

Great, she thought. *A plan.* But even a plan like that was something, so long as it didn't involve immediate death. 'I aim to please,' she lied and gave him her most dangerous smile.

'I'm sure you do. When a god dies, power is released, power which can be taken and used. Our Imperators of the past have each of them killed gods to achieve their own godhood. To conquer a people you first must defeat their belief in their deities, and themselves. Since the August One, gods have fallen before us and entire civilisations have followed. In some places we leave pockets of them to grow. In others we confine them for safety. Like animals. Livestock. It has served us well. But the current Imperator is old and he grows weak. He should have finished this years ago, but he thought he knew better. And he was deceived by this Trickster god.' He said the last words as if describing the worst scum of the city.

Eninn. Gods, he really hated Eninn. Of course he did. Eninn was chaos incarnate in many ways and the Church Imperial was all about order and control.

'And now,' the Magister went on, 'we have him. Time to make him accept his fate.'

'He was always foolish,' said Kyron, his deep voice rumbling through the stone of the floor, walls and the ceiling overhead. 'Too trusting. A child, really.'

'But that's the problem,' Gloir cut in, their whole demeanour less certain about this turn of events. They rubbed one glowing hand over their face. 'He's just a child. He always has been and always—'

'He deserted us,' Nimyeh reminded them.

'Then why is he back? This is not right,' the God of the Forge and the Hearth said. 'You know it is not right.'

'We agreed,' Kyron said. 'Our freedom for his. A simple trade after so long.'

'*You* agreed. If Ystara was here, she would vote with me. And it's not a trade. It's a sacrifice. We know all about sacrifice.'

The ground rumbled, rocking Lyta on her feet.

Ben stirred as Kit pulled him into his arms, holding him close, whispering words to him no one else could hope to hear. But Ben shook his head. There was nothing he could do to control them now. The gods were free, if only in that small circle of fiery light.

Eninn lifted his head. Whatever the other gods had done to him, he looked so pale and helpless that Lyta felt her heart lurch inside her. His eyes met hers, one blue and one green, all hope lost in them.

'We will cast him into the Nether,' said the Magister. 'His power will pass to me and I will free you. I will become the Imperator and together we will rule this land. You will be restored. And your followers will flock to you once more. Your servants and priests will worship you, sacrifice to you as of old.'

'Don't listen to him,' Lyta yelled. 'He might compel the truth, but he lies as easily as water flows around a rock.' She didn't know where the words came from, but she had to make the three of them understand. 'He isn't going to free you. He'll trap you again and use you to sustain his power forever. Don't be the idiots you always were.'

The Magister strode towards her and seized her by the scruff of her neck. Without another word, he reached inside the chest plate she wore and pulled out Eninn's pendant.

'His servant, of course. With his lies in her mouth. What a surprise. Another trick from the Trickster.'

As Eninn tried to rise again, Kyron brought his foot down on his shoulder, crushing him into the floor.

TheMagister grinned down at Lyta and then let her go. She stumbled back, holding the precious pendant in her hands like it was all she had left.

'Enough of his tricks. We are agreed. Open the way and throw him through.'

In the midst of the circle, something tore. Reality wrenched itself apart. Beyond it there was nothing. A terrible emptiness. A void.

Lyta had heard whispers of the Nether in the oldest stories: the wandering ways, the place where gods went to die, a prison without mercy, an existence without hope. Just endless torment. By entering, the gods were stripped of all power. And there was no way back. Only gods could open the way, but the Nether would devour whatever they sent through.

'No,' she gasped. 'Please, no.'

For all his faults – and there were many – Eninn was still her god. Only Kit meant more.

But they weren't listening to her. She was just a mortal, just one woman, and they hated Eninn with centuries of resentment.

'Stop this,' another voice shouted, and she saw Sylvian finally move, the ring on his hand aglow with its own silvery light.

Kyron seized Eninn by the hair, almost casually dragging him up from the ground and before anyone could stop him, he hurled the boy-god into the Nether.

There was a scream, which Lyta didn't understand at first had come from her. And then she was moving as Kit roared her name, surging up from the ground, trying to stop her.

Eninn fell alone into the darkness.

'Lyta! Don't!' Sylvian's cry echoed around her, his voice distorted and hollow as it tried to follow her where he could not.

Icy cold needles raked over her skin as she plunged through the rip in the world. Lyta hurled herself after her god into the Nether and the wandering ways, and the fissure snapped shut behind her.

CHAPTER THIRTY-TWO

Kit

One minute Lyta was there, the next she was gone. The roar of denial that broke from Kit's mouth brought him up off his knees, still clinging to Ben, dragging him up as well.

Sylvian already had his sword in his hand and was starting forward, intent on running the Magister through where he stood.

But the Magister shimmered like light falling on water and flung his arm out towards Sylvian, the simple motion driving him back with the same unseen force that had attacked Kit earlier. Sylvian slammed against the wall. The light around his hand fluttered and went out, and suddenly in the circle of gods another figure took form. A dark-skinned, dark-haired woman with pale and endless eyes, dressed in silver robes, dropped to her knees with a cry of dismay. Chains hung from her body, dragging her down. She looked up at the others.

'What have you done?' she gasped. 'You fools. You've betrayed us all.'

Kyron drew his weapon, ignoring her, the great sword dwarfing her. 'You are as much a thief as our brother, Ystara. That mortal was my servant and look at him. Helpless and weak thanks to you. Defeated by magic. But I will take him back and make him strong again. A warrior. My champion instead of yours. Now, Magister, fulfil your debt. Release us.'

The Magister released a thin laugh into the silence that followed. 'I think not. Let a thing like you roam free? Never. I bind you away in that pathetic prison of flesh and I'll keep you safe until I need another sacrifice.'

He seemed to examine himself, as if he was flexing new muscles, while Kyron staggered back in shock. The Magister began to speak, words in an ancient language that made the air shake and tremble.

'Eninn and Ystara are the only ones with half a wit left,' Ben mumbled against Kit's chest. 'Even Nimyeh, once she gets an idea in her head, is completely inflexible. I tried to warn them. I tried.'

'I know you did, heart,' Kit murmured back to him, holding his fragile body close. He was shaking, his strength completely gone. How he was still conscious was a miracle in itself.

'He's going to close the spell, lock them in me again. Kit, I don't know if I can . . . If I can stand it. I don't know.'

'Hold on for me. We've got to find a way to help Lyta.'

'The wandering ways are endless. There's no path back. It's all my fault.'

No it wasn't. Kit knew exactly whose fault it was, and that wasn't Ben. The Magister stood before them radiating stolen magic and power. Even as they watched he closed the circle holding the gods. They reached out, shouting, pleading, threatening, but to no avail. In the blink of an eye, they vanished once more.

'Are they—?' Kit asked.

'Inside me again. Burning away, raging, screaming. Oh Kit, I can't. They're like rats in a sack, clawing and biting each other, and me, in an effort to get out.'

Kit held him tighter. 'Talk to them, Ben. They listened before.'

'They listened to *you*.' A pained smile touched the corners of his lips and Kit longed to kiss him there.

'Right then, listen to me again. All of you. If you don't cooperate you're trapped in there forever. And that's only if they let Ben live. If this madman decides to kill him, I don't know what happens to you.' He caught that thought and what it might mean. He'd lose Ben. Lose him forever. *Please no. Gods, please no.* He didn't even know who he was praying to. The gods he'd met were useless. 'Let Ben use your magic. Help him. For once in your miserable existences, do the right thing. Please.' He added the last word, because even trapped they were still gods, beings of unimaginable power. Creatures of magic.

And he was trying to boss them around like he would apprentices in his workshop.

'You are Cornellis,' the Magister snapped. 'The printer. Have you been behind this all along? You came here to take Benedictus from us once before. Perhaps I should thank you for that. None of this would have been possible if you had not.' He laughed again. The bastard actually laughed. 'Come here.'

The unseen force wrapped itself around Kit's body, dragging him away from Ben who slumped back to the ground, overcome by the magic raging inside him.

The Magister examined Kit, his gaze piercing, his presence more so. As he narrowed his eyes a spike of something cold and invasive drilled itself into Kit's mind.

'Look what she did to you. Almost succeeded too. I can use this. Oh yes, I can use this. She buried the hooks deep in you. For all her weaknesses and corruption, she had talent, our dear Lady Iseult.'

He pushed further, the fresh cuts on Kit's arm catching fire with unnatural light. Kit gasped in a breath which scraped down inside his throat, and his lungs ached as if barbs sprung up inside him. But the pain in his head was the worst, as if the Magister was in there himself, tearing and biting. A scream built up, dammed inside him, unable to break free. If it did, Kit feared it would shatter him completely.

The Magister grabbed a fistful of Kit's hair, wrenching his face up. His mouth fell open with the pain he couldn't voice.

'You should be grateful, Christopher. We'll make use of you. Teach you the ways of true obedience, just as I taught Benedictus.' He paused, gazing down at Kit as if he craved something more. 'There's something else to you, isn't there? Beautiful, like your sister. Rose gold and alabaster. Such a combination.'

Kit tried to recoil and the grip tightened again so that he almost tore the hair from his head. 'Oh don't be like that. It's better for you this way. You get to stay with him. Loyal to me, of course. Eternally loyal, unquestioning, willing. So we'll need to still that brilliant mind of yours, burn out some of the independence and—'

He clenched his other hand into a fist. The scream broke free of Kit at last, echoing off the walls, off the stone. He howled in white-hot and blinding agony as the Magister unleashed his newfound godly powers to remake Kit from the inside out, tearing through his mind, burning him, searing away what made him a free man.

Golden light burst around them like a comet in the night's sky, and Kit slammed down hard onto the floor. He lay there helpless, chest heaving, the Magister's grip on him broken, like he himself felt broken. But even as he regained some measure of who and what he was, as he opened his eyes he saw something else drift by him, the sun in all its glory taking the shape of a man.

A bare foot stopped beside his face, a figure crouched, and a hand reached down to stroke his sweat drenched hair. The touch was tender and gentle, and so familiar.

There were no ghostly words floating on his skin this time. He was so bright it hurt to look at him, but Kit couldn't tear his eyes away. He'd blind himself for good before he did that. Ben smiled. And it was truly Ben's smile. Kit felt a surge of relief.

'What are you? No, I forbid this,' the Magister babbled.

'You forbid?' Ben asked. 'How would you do that?'

'Benedictus, remember who you are.'

'Who I am?' Ben straightened, leaving Kit to take another step forward. 'I know who I am.'

Who was he? Kit would like to know that himself right now. Not just Ben. Not his Ben. Not shining like a new star, not advancing on an enemy of power like the Magister without a single care. This being was so much more. And yet . . . it was Ben. The smile, the keen eyes, the strength. It was more fundamentally Ben than Kit had ever seen him.

The Magister regained some measure of his confidence. 'Remember who *I* am then. Remember how happy you were here, in the library, with your studies. We can offer you that again and more. The chance to study the greatest texts of all ages. The chance to visit our finest libraries, to learn all there is to learn. Every secret, Benedictus. Everything. You're a Divine Nexus, the very thing you sought to study. You draw the power of divinities to you, uncover them, make them part of you. The power within you is untold. The things you can do.'

Ben tilted his head to one side, as if trying to solve a conundrum of some kind. He did that when he was lost deep in thought, like he needed to get another angle on the problem in order to solve it.

'Ben,' Kit whispered and poured all the love he had into that single name.

Ben shuddered, as if he heard, as if he still recognised Kit's voice.

Except that the Magister was using his powers of persuasion now. He'd succeeded twice, once to trap Ben in his power and once with the gods themselves. He would try again. He'd keep trying. He wanted nothing so much as to control Ben Alvarez.

'Think of what I can offer you. Remember. You can learn all you would wish to know, explore every possibility. Think of the freedom if you simply join—'

'That isn't freedom,' said Ben, in a soft voice, a lover's voice. He stretched out his hands, flexing those long, beautiful fingers, examining them the way he would read some ancient script. 'The gods are not trapped with me. They are safe. Welcomed. Home. You, on the other hand . . .' Ben's voice darkened, rippling with Kyron's energy all of a sudden. 'You trapped a vulnerable boy, tricked him, bent his will to yours. We remember all that you did to him. As he remembers.' Then he lifted his head high and his voice was his own again. '*I* remember.'

He took another step forward and the Magister retreated until he crashed into his throne. He didn't look so confident anymore. His face had fallen to a mask of fear. He moved his hands again, clearly attempting to summon his magic, but this time nothing happened.

'What have you done?' he whispered. 'What have you done to me?'

Kit couldn't see Ben's smile now, but he could hear it in his voice. And it was Ben's smile, Ben's voice. Ben, so clever, so quick, so willing to learn and adapt to something new.

'What you're so fond of doing. I've bound you. And now, we judge you. Gods and mortals, Nexus and champion. Sylvian, your duty, please.'

The sword seemed to come out of nowhere, a blur of light and death combined. It passed through the Magister's neck without impediment, and his head fell with a thud, the look of horrified surprise caught forever on his face.

It rolled towards Kit who, in a moment of panic, kicked it away into the corner. He hauled himself to his feet and flung himself at Ben, pulling him into an embrace. Ignoring the glow, ignoring the strength which flowed through him, the warmth and otherworldliness. It was still Ben. His Ben.

And something else as well. Something other. He couldn't dwell on that. Not now.

'What happened to you? What did they—?'

His legs went from under him. Ben brought his arms around Kit and held him up, cradling him close. 'We came to an agreement, as you so wisely suggested.' He smiled again, that same, soft familiar smile. 'And because you said *please*.'

The laugh sounded like Ystara. But also like Ben. His Ben.

'Ben, I thought . . .' Thought he'd lost him, thought the Magister would enslave them both, making him no more than a thing with a heart made of metal and stone, just rose gold and alabaster like he'd said.

Ben kissed his mouth, softly, gently. Kit melted against him, holding him as if clinging to a rock in a storm. Ben's voice was a whisper.

'Rose gold and alabaster,' he said, as if he had picked the image directly from Kit's mind. 'Like a statue, or an icon. That's how he saw you, but you're so much more than that. It's going to be all right, Kit. I promise.' Ben's lips moved against his as he spoke. This time Kit kissed him back, pouring all his relief into every touch. He was alive. He was there. That was all that mattered in that instant.

Except . . .

'Where's Lyta?' Sylvian said, his voice cutting through their relief. The guard was pale, the arm holding the sword trembling. He was staring at the bare patch of floor where the rift in reality had opened onto the Nether, where she had vanished. 'Bring her back, Ben.'

His voice shook like the winter wind that tore through him. Still a warrior but one on the edge of breaking with loss.

Ben's body tensed and when he replied, he spoke with unbearable sorrow. 'I can't. No one can. The Nether and the wandering ways are endless. They're gone.'

Sylvian's eyes, black as the endless night of the Nether, widened in horror and grief, then rage flooded them instead. He lifted the sword again, advancing on the two of them. Without thinking Kit tried to push Ben behind him, but it was like trying to move a standing stone.

The ring on Sylvian's hand caught the light, white and shining. He was Ystara's champion, empowered by her power, and he had just lost the woman he loved.

'Bring Lyta back now.'

CHAPTER THIRTY-THREE

Lyta

The darkness was complete, the cold like the worst winter's night, and something akin to starvation gnawed away inside her, but Lyta forced her eyes to open anyway. There was nothing there, nothing around her, except for the figure of Eninn, curled up in a ball floating in front of her. In the Nether.

She reached out her hands, caught him effortlessly and drew him against her.

He stirred, his eyes opening. 'Lyta?' His voice echoed strangely in this empty place. But it was his voice. And though she couldn't remember actually having heard it out loud before, she knew it as intimately as she knew her own or Kit's. She'd dreamed it perhaps, or imagined it. Because he'd always been with her. All her life.

He looked the age Kit had been when their mother had died. When everything had first fallen apart, and she'd had to take charge of it all to save them both. He looked as lost as Kit had back then, and it broke her heart all over again.

'I'm here,' she murmured and held him close. His eyes, so beautiful, like two jewels in the endless darkness, glittered with unshed tears. Stars reflected in them.

But there were no stars here.

'*You* shouldn't be here,' he told her. 'You should be back there with Sylvian and Kit, where you always wanted to be. Safe. Lyta.' He sighed her name as if it was a prayer and she smiled.

'Couldn't let you go without me. Where's the fun in that, Eninn?'

He stared at her for a long moment, his expression of shock almost comical. And then his lips quirked just a little. 'I do promise endless adventures, don't I?'

She tried to return the expression. Bravado. That was what they both needed. They thrived on it.

'How could a girl resist a tempting offer like that?'

There were stars in his eyes, or maybe they were tears.

They drifted down until their feet touched sand and she found herself holding his hands loosely in her own. Sand, she realised, not nothing. Looking up she saw a night's sky full of stars, and off to the left great rocks jutted from the earth like teeth.

'Where are we?'

Eninn gazed around himself in wonder. 'I remember this place. From the beginning. This is where it started. Where I started. Look.'

A shadow slipped along the base of the rock and darted across the opening, skimming over the sand. Then it was gone. She waited a moment longer, but nothing happened.

'That's it?' she asked in disbelief.

Eninn laughed at her lack of awe. He seemed to be coming back into some semblance of himself now. As if she was remaking him, or simply reminding him of who he was. Eninn the Trickster. Her friend. 'I didn't say it was an impressive beginning.'

'Can we go back?'

He shook his head with a sudden solemnity which surprised her. Eninn was cunning and delight, not given to gravity. 'I can't. You, on the other hand . . . I think you have to. You can't stay here. Look, you're making it real. Can't have the Nether and the wandering ways turn real. That isn't the point.'

'I'm what? How?' She looked around at the landscape still forming around them, the grasses moving in a breeze, the clouds above them, the smattering of stars still lighting up the sky bit by bit. She knew those stars. Legends said they were formed from the severed tail of a great dragon, long before humanity walked the earth, or dreamed, or believed in gods. Perhaps Eninn knew the truth.

He squeezed her hand before releasing her. 'You humans are amazing. You just believe things into being. You didn't like emptiness, so you brought us land and sky.' He pointed to the stars spread out over their heads, a river of light flowing across the night. 'Next thing you know . . . Look!'

Fireflies burst out of the foliage that hadn't been there before and spiralled around the two of them.

'You can't stay here, Lyta. You're making a new world where there should be nothing.'

'I'm not leaving you alone here,' Lyta told him. She wouldn't. It would be like abandoning Kit. She couldn't do it.

'I don't think you get a say. But if anyone could rescue me, it would be you, Lyta Cornellis. Once upon a time some other god would have made you a queen. Or an empress. They would have made you, at the very least, a legend.' He shook his head. A scruffy-haired, adolescent, helpless before her and their fate. 'Alas, you only had me.'

It was Lyta's turn to laugh. 'What would I have done being a queen or an empress? I can't rob my own treasury, can I?'

Eninn cocked his head to one side and grinned. Such a trickster expression. It made her heart sing again. 'You'd be surprised. Now, you need to imagine a door.'

'As simple as that?'

He gestured the burgeoning world around them. 'Apparently, for you. Who knew?'

Lyta pulled a face. 'I think I liked you better when you didn't talk, Eninn.' She focused her mind on the rocks and imagined an opening. It took form, almost like a cave but with carved stone pillars on either side of the darkness and a lintel above it. Spirals and diamond shapes peppered the rock surface, cut into the stone by a loving hand in honour of their deity.

Eninn frowned then, reaching out his long clever fingers to trace the shapes and patterns. His mismatched eyes gleamed with recognition. 'I remember this place. I think . . . I think I lived here. How do you know this Lyta?'

She shrugged. It was like she had always known. Like it had been in her dreams for as long as she could remember. Like him.

'You must have shown me.'

But he shook his head. 'This is a secret place, a sacred place. There's more to you than anyone knows, Lyta Cornellis. I don't think even you realise it.'

'Well, I wish you'd explain it to the world. Maybe it would listen to you and stop shitting on my life. Come on.'

She grabbed his arm, tugging him after her.

'No, I have to stay here, I told you.'

'I have decided to believe differently,' she told him in those older-sister tones Kit always said would be the death of him. 'Come on, Eninn. Enough arguing.'

She pulled him through the door after her.

'You can't!'

'Watch me,' she told him and pushed her way through. The world tore around her, the Nether peeling back to reveal that miserable chamber in the tower, where Sylvian, Kit and Ben staggered back from the new rip in reality.

'Lyta, stop!' Eninn called, but she clung to him grimly and pulled him through with her. 'You can't. This isn't how—'

And then he was gone. She staggered forward and fell, gasping for air, without her lost god.

Kit reached her first, with Sylvian only a step behind, though when her brother swept her into his arms, the warrior took an awkward step back.

'What happened to you? What did you do?' Kit asked.

Lyta's heart plummeted as she fought back tears of frustration and loss. There was no sign of Eninn. Nothing at all. She couldn't show them her pain. Wouldn't. It couldn't be real.

Instead, she glared at the three men and hid behind her trademark smart mouth.

'Kit, your boyfriend is glowing. That's not right. Tell him to stop.'

Kit relaxed a bit, relieved to find her mostly herself. But she couldn't tell him that she wasn't. That everything had changed. That Eninn who had always been with her, was gone.

She'd thought, just for a moment, that she'd won, that she had cheated whatever celestial forces governed the gods and their demise.

But she hadn't.

The body of the Magister slumped across his throne. She couldn't see his head. 'Who did that?' Sylvian awkwardly raised his hand, still without uttering a word, staring at her like she was some kind of divinity herself. She hummed her approval. 'Good work. We should get out of here. I have a bad feeling about—'

The crashing outside the door brought them all shuddering back to some kind of reality. It sounded like a battering ram and as if in answer to her thought, the doors bucked inwards, shattering before a force that they had never been made to withstand.

Royal guards flooded the room and Lyta realised that Francisco had come. Who else could it be? The Magister had dared to invade his city, flouted his law and his security, after threatening him. Kings always answered fire with fire.

And Francisco of Castille, Aragón, León and the Greater Brabantine believed in scorched earth tactics. Break something of his, no matter how small and insignificant, and he'd burn your world to the ground and sow salt amid the ashes.

His bodyguards appeared first, the men she'd seen with Sylvian. The king himself came through the doors like a man enraged, took one look at the fallen magister and then turned on the motley assortment of survivors before him.

'What on earth have you done?' he thundered.

Sylvian knelt down on one knee, dropping his sword at his feet. 'Majesty, we—'

'I'm going to have to explain all this to the Imperator and it is not going to be pretty. You, Lyta Cornellis, what happened?'

The fact he was completely ignoring Sylvian was not a good sign. She glanced at Kit and Ben. Kit had thought to take off his cloak and give it to the scholar. And thankfully Ben seemed to have got the glowing under control. He just looked like a rather thin and delicate man from the far south who had been through hell.

'They kidnapped Ben,' she said, frantically trying to work out how much he would believe. Francisco struck her as a practical man, not given to fantasy or imagination of any kind. Annika might believe her about gods and magic, but not her husband. And unfortunately Annika was probably safe back in the Rose Palace. 'So we came after him and— Look, we may not have meant to have killed the Magister but—'

Francisco crossed his arms in front of him, incredulous.

'You didn't *mean* to kill a prince of the Church, *but* . . .?'

She paused, trying to work out what to say. 'I mean, no one is actually sorry, are they?'

For a moment she thought he might explode. He stared at her like he was trying to work out whether she was entirely real, or if he had actually heard her say those words.

And then he roared with laughter.

Not a pleasant sound at all. It made her profoundly uneasy. Nobody else moved a muscle or cracked a smile. His bodyguards, the men Sylvian had served with, and the general who led them, looked grim as executioners.

'Your honesty is refreshing, I must admit,' he said at last. 'Right, the three of you can go. You'll be wanted for questioning, so we can get this story sorted out before there are too many questions, but you're right. No one is going to miss the old bastard and he did invade my city first. If they want to make trouble over that, I'll deal with it. But they'll probably be as glad to see the back of him as I am. Time to get out of here because I have sappers ready to reduce the whole thing to rubble so no jumped-up cleric thinks to try something like this again. Seigneur Alvarez, your sister is raising hell back in the city demanding your return, so you'll need to see to that. Put some clothes on first.' He grinned, as if finding a naked man in the midst of all of this was part of a huge joke. 'Lady Beatriz also presented me with the book you made, Master Cornellis, but it will not do.'

Kit stared at him, mouth open. It was like seeing his hackles rise all at once. 'Why not?'

Lyta flinched. After all this and Francisco wasn't happy with the book? She just didn't need Kit getting himself imprisoned again because his professional pride had been dented.

Francisco waved a hand at him. 'I cannot present it to the queen in that state. It has— What was splattered all over it, Vasquez?'

The general cleared her throat, still watching Sylvian. 'The duchess, your Majesty. Parts of her anyway.'

'Yes. Such a mess. You'll have to do it all again. Properly this time. We'll want copies on vellum as well, hand-illustrated I think, to present to neighbours and friends. The most beautiful books the world has seen. You can do that, can't you? You have the time. And copies on paper for the masses as well naturally.'

Kit shuddered, his face a mask of horror. And Lyta knew he was going to argue. 'But—'

Gods and goddesses, Kit, not now. Just promise anything and we'll sort it out later.

Ben cut him off before she could find the words. 'Your Majesty, it would be our honour.' He must have learned the smooth diplomatic voice from his sister. 'Typis Cornellis produces the finest books in the city, as you know, and far quicker than the likes of Plantin or Silvius. I will personally oversee the translation and editing, if he will have me. It will take time, of course, but we are more than willing to dedicate ourselves to the work. We should discuss the costs, and the outlay however. The rebuilding of the workshop alone . . .'

The king nodded, but the enterprise had been decided as far as he was concerned. Lyta could see that. His mind was on something else already. 'Of course. We'll see to financing. Whatever you need, Alvarez, Cornellis.'

Lyta tried to breathe evenly and calmly because every nerve inside her was still screaming. Something was wrong. Something was terribly wrong.

Sylvian hadn't moved. He hadn't got off his knees or lifted his eyes from his king's feet. He hadn't tried to speak to him again. He was waiting, like a man expecting the axe.

THE BOOK OF GOLD

Finally, Francisco glanced at him. 'Sylvian Chant, you're under arrest for high treason. I'll save us the bother of a trial, shall I? I already know your guilt.'

He drew an oversized sword from the sheath on his back. It reminded her of the weapon Kyron had wielded.

Lyta, the voice in the back of her mind warned. And she knew it. Eninn. It had to be Eninn. *You have to save him. He's Ystara's now. We made a deal, my sister and I. I owe her.*

Of course she had to save him. But not for any god.

'What do you mean, *treason*?' Lyta interrupted.

Francisco glared at her, his good humour gone now. 'Exactly what I said, Mistress Cornellis. He was given a choice, bring me the book or your head. Instead, he ran. Now take my mercy and leave him to me.'

He'd come with her and Kit even knowing what it would mean for him. That was what the scene with the general had been about. Lyta stepped deliberately between Sylvian and the king, her heart pounding on the inside of her ribs.

'I don't think so, your Majesty. I believe there's been some kind of misunderstanding here. You have the book, albeit in a simpler form than you perhaps anticipated. And I know it's just a copy but I'm sure we can work something out if we just stop and think.'

How, she didn't know. She also suspected that stopping and thinking was not Francisco's strong point. He needed someone to do that for him, that much was clear. Someone like Annika.

But Annika wasn't here. She was . . .

'Where is the queen? Can we not appeal to her mercy?'

He studied her, as if trying to fathom what on earth possessed her. No one stood up to him. Clearly.

And then it came to her, the exact words Alderton had used back in the study.

The ring that will offer protection to the father of her unborn child. The ring that marks her champion.

It had protected Sylvian. Ystara had broken the obsidian and—

Oh Eninn, she thought, and her eyes slid to Sylvian. He didn't meet her gaze. He didn't move. But his shoulders stiffened and he looked so ashamed. If she could have reached out and killed him herself in that moment she might just have done it.

Think, said Eninn, in the back of her mind, as clearly as if he stood beside her and whispered in her ear. *Think, Lyta.*

Because she had to think, or she was going to lose everything. She was going to lose Sylvian for good. Not again. Dear gods, not again. There would be no coming back from this. She was out of miracles.

'Fine, well, I'll just take the ring back to the Rose Palace and explain to the queen you changed your mind when you gave it to him, will I?'

Francisco's eyes narrowed. 'What?'

It was like dancing across thawing ice on the city canals. One wrong step and she was going to get them all killed. She had to keep going.

'You *did* give it to him, didn't you? Because how else would he have got it? And with it, the blessings of Ystara. He's her champion, and the champion of the queen. That's the only reason we're still alive after all this. Sylvian and the blessings of the queen's beloved goddess. Isn't that right? Ben can surely tell us. He can ask Ystara and speak for her, but that's it. You had to have given Syl the ring. Because of the pregnancy.'

The looks from Kit and Ben weren't encouraging either. They both knew how dangerous a line she was walking, but she didn't care. To save Sylvian . . . He was hers at last and she would not lose him. Not to a man like this.

'Lyta,' Sylvian said in a low, careful voice. 'Everyone knows that the child is my lord king's. She is his wife. To say anything else would be treason indeed.'

She breathed in, and out again. And plunged onwards. 'Oh dear, well if that's the case, why did you give Sylvian the ring, my lord king?'

The sword hung from Francisco's hand, its tip scraping against the floor. 'My queen's ring?' he murmured, his tone suddenly even more dangerous.

'Well, you treasure it. And you *definitely* wouldn't have lost it to Lord Alderton after he conned you in a card game, would you? Just like I *definitely* didn't *accidentally* take it from his safe at a party one night. Definitely not. I'd never do anything like *that*. So you *must* have given it to Sylvian, as her champion. Don't you see? So he could be her champion in your place. I mean, you're the king. If anything were to happen to you, as king . . . well, that would be a disaster. Sylvian only represents your power. He always has. It's what the queen would want, to protect you above all, even herself. Because of *course* the queen knows who the father of her child *is*. Doesn't she?'

The sound of the sword stopped abruptly.

'He's her champion on my behalf?' he asked. Actually asked. He looked so bewildered, because she had just laid out exactly what had happened, and he was the last one who would want that story out in the world. Because if Annika ever found out he'd gambled away her precious ring, or killed the father of their child out of pointless jealousy . . .

Lyta nodded encouragingly at him, her eyes wide with feigned innocence, her mind sparking in a thousand directions at once, and the Trickster god laughing away in the back of her mind.

'Sylvian is mine. He loves me. He always has done. If you need me to beg for his life I am more than happy to do so.'

Francisco's brow knotted in confusion. 'Didn't you marry someone else?'

'A technicality. Syl was always mine. Weren't you?'

Sylvian's eyes shone as he finally looked up at her. 'Yes,' he replied without hesitation, without any guile whatsoever. 'Yes, Lyta. Always.'

The words reverberated through her like Cissonia's bell, pure and sincere. The ring glowed with Ystara's light, illuminating him again, testifying to the truth of it. Lyta swallowed hard and looked back at the king. Because she had to. Because she could not afford to lose now. Lose now and she lost everything.

The king was still staring at her, as if trying to work out who or what she was, as if he could recognise the trickster in her eyes. And yet Lyta knew she had never said anything more truthful in her life.

Francisco drew in a breath and exhaled slowly. For a moment he clenched his jaw, then released it and his expression grew speculative. He was turning over his options in his mind, she realised, his thoughts as slow and thorough as a meat grinder. Finally, he nodded and then, impossibly, he smiled as if it really was all just a joke. As if nothing had happened at all.

'Her champion. Of course he is. Get up on your feet, Captain Chant. A misunderstanding, that's all. Must have been a lingering trick of the Magister's dark arts. You saved us again, Sylvian, by executing him. Perhaps we should leave this place. And if what you both say is true, I believe you can keep my bodyguard out of trouble in future, Lyta Cornellis.'

The king marched from the room without waiting for an answer, his guards following him.

Lyta breathed again and ran to Sylvian. He wrapped his arms around her and buried his face in her hair. She pressed her face into his chest and fought not to shake, not to collapse against him.

'Lyta,' he breathed. 'You take such risks, my love.'

He kissed her, focusing on her lips as if all the world depended on showing her how he felt with that single gesture. And she let him, falling into him and never wanting to stop. He was hers, then, now and always.

Love. That was a powerful word. Especially from someone like him, with all of Ystara's power behind it. That was something to unravel another time. Not now. It was far too much for now. Perhaps she should have said it back. But she didn't.

'I can't believe that worked,' she whispered as they parted.

Sylvian moved as if to kiss her again and then hesitated, still holding her, shaking slightly. No, not shaking. Laughing.

'Are you sure it was just you that came back and not Eninn as well?' he asked.

'Funny you should ask that,' she admitted. She had heard his voice, warning her, guiding her, more clearly than ever before. Something had come back with her. 'Something else to figure out. But right now, didn't he say they're going to demolish this tower? We should get out of here before he realises he could solve all his problems by keeping us in here when he does and apologising to Beatriz and Annika for the terrible mistake later.'

Because kings, when you got down to it, were still kings. And she didn't trust him an inch.

CHAPTER THIRTY-FOUR

Kit

The workshop looked like a strong gust of wind would blow the whole thing to pieces. Most of the front wall had been reduced to rubble. Every window was broken, the door no more than kindling, and inside was a scene of devastation. Blood smeared the floor and the walls. Holes punched through the ceiling, revealing the dark attic above. The printing presses, the cabinets and their drawers lay around like a giant toddler had torn through the place scattering toys in its wake. Most of the precious type had been ground underfoot.

Kit and Lyta stood in the jagged hole in the wall and stared inside.

'It could be worse,' she told him.

Kit closed his eyes, forcing himself to stay calm. He pinched the bridge of his nose. 'How?' he asked. 'How could it be worse than this?'

'Someone removed the bodies. And nothing caught fire. And the roof is still in one piece. There, that's three things.'

Three things. He had exactly three things going for him.

'There's that,' he sighed, resigned. 'Want to help me tidy up?'

She sighed dramatically. 'Don't you have actual apprentices for that sort of thing?' But all the same, she started forward with him, picking through the debris, trying to work out where to start. The gods alone knew where his apprentices were. And his friends. He hadn't had word from Jem and Molly. He only hoped they were safe, and that the other book was hidden.

It took both of them to lift what remained of the printing presses. He might be able to repair the worst of it, he decided eventually. Because he couldn't afford to replace them.

'Where's Sylvian?' he asked after they had worked in silence for a time. They had righted the cases and put the drawers back in. Now Lyta was picking up the pieces of type.

'I don't know. Still at the palace. He was summoned when we got back to the city, before the general cornered us. The queen wanted to see him.' When Kit winced, she caught the expression. 'Not like that. At least I hope not. She's his queen and he's her champion and— Look, I don't want to think about that. Not yet.'

'That was yesterday. Have you spoken to him about it?'

'No,' she said. 'And I might not. What does it matter? It can't be undone now.'

'But what if—?'

'Please, Kit. Don't.' And that was that. He knew his sister and if she didn't want to have a conversation, then that conversation would not be had.

'What are you going to do now?'

'I don't know.' She sighed, focusing on the pieces in her hand. 'How do you even tell these apart? They all look the same.'

He took them from her and sorted them in silence.

'How are you so fast at that?' she asked.

'Practice.'

'You'd make an excellent sleight-of-hand man, you know.'

Kit sighed because of course her mind went there. 'No. I really wouldn't.' There was nothing he wanted less than to get further involved in crime with his sister.

'What about you and Ben?' she asked at length.

Kit had not been looking forward to answering that question. 'I don't know if there is a *me and Ben*. He's a noble, Lyta. He's back home with Beatriz, the Lord of House Alvarez or something. I don't even know his proper title. And he's a Divine Nexus. Full of gods. They're still in him. Maybe I don't even know who Benedictus Alvarez really is.'

He hadn't meant to say it all, but the words rattled their way out of him as if the Magister was still there, forcing the truth from him against his will.

And it was true. He didn't know Ben. Or what Ben was now. Perhaps he never had. There had been that quiet, shy scholar, afraid of his own shadow. And that determined, inquisitive man who asked too many awkward questions. And the divine, golden creature in the tower.

But for a moment Kit had thought . . . He'd hoped . . .

He pushed it away and went back to work. This was all he had: the shattered remains of his trade and craft.

The sound of someone clearing their throat behind them made Kit turn in alarm. Ben stood in the broken doorway, dressed in clothes that marked his position and his status more clearly than anything Kit had ever seen him in. He looked like something from a royal court portrait, his slender frame clad in the finest materials, cut to perfection. His hair had been styled and his face shaved.

Beatriz had been busy.

'I don't know about Benedictus Alvarez,' he said softly. 'But I'm still Ben. And I think we ought to talk, Kit.'

There was a long and agonised silence. Lyta broke it, of course. Lyta had never met a silence she couldn't batter into submission.

'Right, well, I'm going to go somewhere else. Anywhere else. Kit, don't be stupid. And you . . .' She couldn't hope to tower over Ben, but she still made a valiant attempt. Her hands waved around him as if taking in a multitude. Which she was really. 'If any of you hurt my brother, you'll have me to deal with. Understand?'

Ben studied her resolute face solemnly. Then a small smile tugged at his expressive lips. 'Yes, Mistress Cornellis,' he replied formally.

'Especially you, Ben. I have a god too. And Eninn does not play fair.'

Kit couldn't see his sister's face and was glad of that. His skin heated with embarrassment.

'I understand, Lyta,' Ben said.

She nodded and Ben moved aside to let her leave.

Oh gods, she was leaving and they would be alone and . . . Kit threw himself after her, reaching the door as she strode down the street outside.

'Wait. Where are you going?' he called.

'I don't know. To steal something. Or fuck some shit up. Cause mayhem anyway. Have fun, Kitten. I intend to.'

Kit groaned and let his head hang.

Ben's hand touched his tense shoulders carefully. 'She's joking.'

'I'm glad you think so.'

'How are you, Kit? You never came back to Beatriz's house. I mean, *our* house. I mean . . .' His voice trailed off into embarrassed silence.

He was standing so close that Kit could feel the heat from his body, and the scent of soap and perfume drifted around him. He turned to face Ben and instantly regretted it. Those eyes, all the colours of autumn, glowed from within with such intelligence that he was lost.

He had to force himself to back away. He needed to work. The king was expecting him to print the book again. He still had to find Jem and Molly and get the other copy back. And the workshop was still a disaster.

'The general had questions for Lyta and me,' he said at last, barely suppressing a shudder at the memory, because it had stirred up a host of others. It had just been a simple room in the barracks, barely more than a cell, but at least they hadn't been dragged off to Old Steen he supposed. A healer had been summoned. There had been food, baths and a change of clothes. And relentless questions from a woman almost as determined as his sister. They had been there all night. He picked up another tray and tried to ram it back in the case, but it was off on an angle and it jammed.

Ben still didn't get it. 'Yes, she questioned Beatriz and me as well.'

The drawer wasn't budging. Kit shoved it again, the whole cupboard rocking back with his frustration. 'Let me guess, she came to your house yesterday evening or this morning. At some decent hour anyway. You sat in that lovely first-floor parlour, with the books and the lanterns and all, and had refreshments. I'm sure it was very civilised.'

Finally the drawer jolted into position and slammed back into the case with a crash.

'*What did they do?*' Ben asked in an entirely different crisp, cold voice. And there it was, Kit thought. Now you could hear the aristocrat in him.

The scholar was no more. This was Seigneur Benedictus Alvarez, and Kit didn't even know who that was. Ben was gone. They were back in the roles they were born to and that would have to be that. The man he'd met had been enchanted, and Kit, like a fool, had thought that was really him. But it wasn't. It couldn't be.

Kit sighed, leaning on the wood, trying not to break apart with the pain inside. 'It's fine. We're fine. But they only let us go this morning and frankly, I'm exhausted. It was a long night.' Not that he could have slept in the barracks room with Lyta pacing and swearing.

And anyway he didn't have anywhere else to sleep anyway. He glanced up at the ragged holes in the ceiling again. He hadn't even dared go up there yet.

Ben's arms came around him before he knew what was happening. He froze, unable to bring himself to shake off the unexpected embrace. 'It's not fine. I didn't know. I swear, Kit, if I'd realised—'

It felt so good to just be held by him. Just for a moment longer. But it couldn't last. It wasn't real. It couldn't be.

'I've got to work,' he said. 'I need to get this place back together and—'

He pulled away, almost made it across the room before he saw the splattering of blood still smeared across the floor where the duchess had fallen. His stomach heaved. He'd have to look at that every day. And remember. Remember what she almost made of him.

'Not here,' Ben said softly. 'You don't have to be here.'

Kit growled, a savage sound from deep in his chest. 'Where else, Ben? This is all I have. All I have left.'

This time Ben just took one of his shaking hands in his own and held it firmly. His hands were so much stronger than they looked. 'Kit Cornellis, you have a commission from the king himself and an unlimited budget, remember? We're going to transcribe the book again and this time I'm going to translate it properly. I have control of it now, and the gods are willing to cooperate rather than try to escape all in one rush. They've promised. So we're going to go and view a rather nice workshop up off Lombard's Street, not far from the Golden Angel Press. It has a suite over it too, not just an attic. And—'

Kit ground his teeth. 'I don't need charity.'

Ben laughed. Actually laughed at him. Typical. Just bloody typical. 'You certainly do not. And you won't get it from me. My sister has the key to the vault. But like I said, you have a commission from the king, remember? Here, I made him write it down.' He took out a letter from his jerkin and handed it to Kit, who held it like it might explode. He didn't open it, just stared uncomprehending at Ben who was still talking. 'Well, I say *him*, but some unfortunate clerk did the writing while Francisco complained. But the upshot is the same. Typis Cornellis has a royal licence and a royal commission. He wants a number on vellum with hand illumination to send to other royal courts and the great libraries. The finest leather bindings, gilt inlay and all the rest. He wants a host of volumes on paper as well for everyone else. Only the very best of everything.' Kit read the letter carefully. Everything Ben said was there, as promised. He'd been too busy in that tower room praying that they'd get out of it alive. He hadn't paid attention to the king's demands.

'But this will cost a fortune. I'll have to get extra presses and hire artists.'

'And you will need a brilliant scholar to edit the text so it doesn't bring you to your knees as soon as you try to read it this time.'

He sounded amused. And not a little bit smug.

Kit glanced up at him over the top of the letter and narrowed his eyes. He kept his voice deliberately flat. 'Yes, but where will I find one?'

A fraught silence stretched out between them, only interrupted by a sound like laughter on the breeze from somewhere far away. Kit knew that laughter now. The gods had not gone anywhere. They were listening to every word. In that awful moment, Kit feared he'd said the wrong thing and cursed his quick tongue.

Then Ben seemed to shake himself. His eyes sparkled playfully and he bowed, fluid and elegant, as if they had just met each other at the start of a courtly dance. 'Benedictus, Seigneur of House Alvarez at your service, Master Cornellis. I have studied in Salamanca and Paris, not to mention Valladolid. I can translate any language of the scholarly world and I . . .' His expression faltered and the confident voice quietened, hesitated. All that noble bravado bled away. 'If you'll have me. Kit?'

A nobleman to the core, Ben was everything Kit guarded himself against, everything he distrusted. But he sounded so unsure as he said those last few words. More like the timid scholar Kit had first met in the library of the tower. The one who had so enchanted him from the start that he'd found himself helpless with the need to protect him.

Kit sighed, giving up the fight, and reached out for him. Ben folded in against him, pressed to his chest and made a sound that was something between relief and surrender.

'I'll embarrass you,' Kit warned him. 'Every day. All the time.' Ben lifted his hands to Kit's face, his fingertips tracing shapes on his skin which made him shiver. 'You can probably trace your lineage back fifteen generations, my lord Alvarez. I don't even know who my father was.'

For a moment Ben just frowned, studying him, so solemn and intent. He had never looked more beautiful. When he finally replied, there was a glint of amusement back in his eye.

'More than fifteen generations, I'll have you know. But lineage is vastly overrated. Stop arguing with me, Kit Cornellis. Don't you know who I am?'

Ben kissed him, his mouth tentative and his touch so gentle. Kit couldn't stop the moan which ripped itself from his chest this time, but the sound was lost somewhere between them. He did indeed know Ben Alvarez, he realised. Knew him like he knew his own heartbeat. Like he knew how to breathe.

And all he wanted was to know more.

CHAPTER THIRTY-FIVE

Lyta

The bell of Cissonia was ringing out the noon hour over the many towers of Amberes. It was time to have a break from work, to eat and rest in the bright sunshine, which flooded the city, driving away the shadows of the last few weeks. Lyta had made it as far as the Great Market, drawn towards the Rose Palace because that was where he would be. If he was still in there, and hadn't been sent off to some far-flung land or locked up in a desolate pit. She didn't know. She'd last seen him as they'd reached his barracks and the general had issued orders which took him in one direction and the guards surrounding her and Kit in another, sweeping them along with the tide.

The queen wanted to see him. And that was that.

For a while Lyta had thought he would come for her, storm in and take her and Kit out of there. He was hers, he had said. Always had been and always would be. But he hadn't.

And he wasn't. Not anymore.

He's fine, said Eninn for the hundredth time. *Ystara always looks after her own.*

And maybe she did – until it was time for them to give their lives in a grand romantic tragedy, or die in an act of self-sacrifice. Being Ystara's champion was not for the faint of heart.

Especially when her Aspect was a queen, and he was her champion, and he'd sworn to protect her. When his life depended on it.

But there was nothing faint about Sylvian's heart.

Lyta turned onto the market itself, and there in front of the coffee shop she saw a familiar figure, pouring the thick black liquid into two glasses.

Frida raised her hands, empty of weapons, gloved, her dark livery marking her clearly as a servant of Lord Alderton now. She'd even tied her hair demurely at the back of her neck. She looked like a new person, stirring cream in her glass. She gestured to the other seat and Lyta took it.

'Frida,' Lyta said.

'Hello, Lyta. It's good to see you.'

'Is it? How are things?'

'Same old, same old. I'm hearing some wild rumours.'

'I'm sure you are.' There were more rumours swimming around than fishes. 'What's the latest?'

'That the queen has a job for you.'

That was news to Lyta. The queen had whisked Sylvian away. No mention had been made of Lyta. 'Not that I've heard.'

'I see. Well, be careful. She wants something and she's a Vasa. Royalty can't be trusted. Ever. She's a foxier one than she lets on.'

'Aren't we all.'

Frida's voice softened and she leaned in, all concern. 'Lyta, you have a huge problem—'

'Yes, and it's called her Majesty.' A problem in more ways than one. Sylvian was gone. She'd thought they were okay now, that they would work something out. Not settle down or anything but . . . *Something*. But then Annika had snapped her fingers and off he went. She'd thought he'd come back for her but instead, she and Kit had been turfed out in the dawn's light and sent on their way without so much as a thank you. 'I get it. Are you trying to warn me off or something? You don't need to. No one wants me near royalty.'

'It's nothing to do with me. Or my employer. I just thought you'd want to hear it from a friend first, that's all.'

Also news. *Careful*, Eninn warned. As if she needed warning about that. 'Still my friend then?'

For a moment Frida's eyes glittered. Her voice softened. 'It was a lot of money. You would have taken it too if he'd offered.'

Lyta swallowed down a thousand replies. 'I'm sorry you think that,' she said at last.

'Look, I left you the knife. I should have taken it but I didn't know how things would go and I wasn't about to leave you helpless in there.' Frida sipped at her coffee, her eyes darting around the square. 'He'd have me gutted if he found out. As it is he thinks Janlow screwed up and, boy, is he paying for it. Which is endlessly entertaining of course. You'd love it.' When Lyta didn't grin, Frida's face fell. 'I . . . I wouldn't ever have let him kill you.'

For a moment Lyta wanted to believe her. Haldevar probably had, for all the good it did him. And she could still feel the sting of the throwing knife in her back. Janlow wasn't that good. And Frida was . . . Lyta swallowed hard, looking at a woman she hardly knew anymore, pieces of her heart falling away in despair. Frida had killed Haldevar, whether it was an accident, as she had claimed, or not. The upshot was the same. She'd killed the man she supposedly loved while trying to find that ring. For money. And she had sold their friendship for the same coin.

Lyta felt Eninn bristle inside her – trickster he might be, but never traitor. Frida stared, really stared at her.

'What happened to your eyes?' she asked.

Lyta blinked. 'Nothing. Trick of the light. Well, I have places to be.'

She started to push herself up to her feet and Frida grabbed her hand, stopping her. 'You lied to me too. Lied about the ring and about the plan. You could have got us all killed in there. You—'

'Are we done?' Lyta asked, snatching her hand free. It felt tainted. Like everything else.

The sound of marching feet made her glance over her shoulder, a detachment of royal guards coming their way. When she looked back at Frida, the woman was gone, a half-empty glass the only sign she'd ever been there.

So that was that.

Lyta slid to her feet. No point in running. There was nowhere to go. Besides, she had been waiting for this.

Sylvian was resplendent in his uniform, stiff and formal, the model of the perfect royal bodyguard. She'd been wondering when this would happen, when her lover would vanish back into his profession. When she'd know for sure she had lost him again.

She'd been waiting for it. But it still hurt.

'Lyta Cornellis,' he said with authority, and the men behind him halted and snapped to attention. Why had he brought so many guards? Did he think she'd run?

Perhaps she should. Eninn's smile pulled at her lips, twisted with her pain. It would serve Sylvian right.

The captain approached her alone. Not just Sylvian, definitely not Syl. Captain Sylvian Chant, royal bodyguard and queen's champion. He stopped within an arm's reach, while his men spread out to encircle them.

Lyta couldn't help herself. She reached out and flicked at the medals attached to Sylvian's uniform contemplating lifting the new one. He closed his hand on her arm and her eyes fell on the ring instead. She wouldn't take that. It had saved him too many times. She couldn't afford to put him at risk. Not now, not ever. Despite his martial appearance, his touch was surprisingly gentle. It was the only thing that gave her even a sliver of hope. His touch made her shiver inside.

'Lyta,' he said softly, so his companions couldn't hear, and the reluctance in his voice was all the warning she got. 'The queen wants to talk to you.'

Oh. That was going to be awkward. She frowned, thinking about Frida's warning and pulled back from him. He didn't seem to react, his hand falling to rest on the hilt of his sword indifferently. Not a threat. Not really. She hoped.

She found herself checking on Eninn, but he didn't respond this time. Nothing of interest to him here, not yet. And no warning for her either. That was *interesting*.

'A job or a discussion about you?' she asked as casually as she could.

He had the good grace to look horrified. 'Gods, I hope it's just a job. She wants me there too.'

Lyta smiled, because what else could she do? And in the back of her mind where he curled up and slept, she thought she heard the Trickster give his soft laugh like an echo.

'Maybe she has tips and needs you there for demonstration purposes,' she suggested, just to see his face turn scarlet. And to remind herself that he was still human. And perhaps somewhere, still her Sylvian.

He stepped in closer to her again, his voice still low, but more like his voice again. A ripple of something twisted inside it that set those little tremors inside her off again.

'Lyta, this is serious. Don't say things like that. Especially not in the royal court.'

Of course it was serious. When was anything not serious anymore? She didn't need court etiquette guides from him. 'What happened to "I'm yours, Lyta"?'

He winced, just a fraction, guilt flickering in his dark and endless eyes. You'd only see it if you stood where she was, close enough to touch. 'I deserve that.'

But he didn't back down either. Captain Sylvian Chant straightened, his eyes hard as obsidian. She hated that look.

So not so much *hers* anymore. Well, everyone had to do and say whatever was necessary, in order to survive.

'Never mind,' she told him.

Sylvian moved faster than she anticipated. He grabbed her shoulders as if to shake her but instead he just held her firm, like he couldn't let go, staring at her with such ferocity that she froze, heat pooling in her stomach. The look stole her breath.

Treacherous desire flared in her chest, burning too brightly to last.

But he belonged to the queen, didn't he? Now more than ever, she knew that.

His voice was a soft rumble of warning. 'You're going to get us both executed, you know that? Probably without even trying.'

No putting it off any longer. The queen wanted to see her. Frida said Annika had a job for her. All she could do was see where this would go. And hope that along the way, she could steal Sylvian back.

'Lead on then, Captain Chant. We don't want to keep her Majesty waiting.'

He fixed her with a dubious look, which was strangely more like him, more like the man she knew now, than she could have hoped to see. 'You aren't going to run?'

Neither of them believed in happily-ever-afters, she knew that. Not anymore. They were realists and life in Amberes was hard. Tangled as they now were in the affairs of kings and queens made it even harder. But there was a maybe in there somewhere. If they could find it. There was more to come. There had to be.

Lyta grinned the reckless grin she had inherited from her feral god.

'Maybe,' she told him. 'Think you can catch me?'

Author's Note

I have always loved books and libraries. They are a core part of my life, my livelihood and my interests. Rare books and book-bindings fascinate me, as does the origins and development of western printing and the revolution it sparked. Don't ask. I will go on forever. You have been warned. Amberes and the world of The Book of Gold were inspired by so many aspects of the marvellous, dangerous and often wild world of early modern printing and bookbinding, and by the real Amberes, the 16th century city of Antwerp, home to one of the greatest printers of them all.

The Book of Gold started, fittingly enough, with one very special book – namely the Plantin Polyglot Bible aka the Antwerp Polyglot bible aka the Biblia Regia aka the King's Bible, and the accompanying book of biblical studies with its incredible maps and illustrations. Want to know exactly where the Tower of Babel was? It has you covered. I work in a library of rare books and we have a precious copy of the set. It has fascinated me from the start. The bible was produced by the great humanist publisher Christophe Plantin in Antwerp in the 1570s and edited by the biblical scholar Benito Arias Montano. (And yes, I shamelessly stole their names.)

My interest in these beautiful volumes led me to research the rather chaotic story of its production which involves accusations of heretical pamphlets printed by Plantin, bribes to stop rioters destroying his premises during the infamous massacre, the Spanish Fury, all kinds of censorship issues, paper shortages, rampant corruption, a desperate search for and production of speciality typefaces, the entire print run being lost at sea so they had to start again, near bankruptcy on several occasions, another shipwreck after which Montano had to travel from the west coast of Ireland to Antwerp in disguise, and finally when everything was finally finished, Montano being charged with heresy by a rival and tried by the Spanish Inquisition. He survived, was exonerated and was eventually coaxed out of a hermitage when Philip II offering him the coveted post of librarian of the fabulous El Escorial, the royal library near Madrid. Philip II awarded Plantin the title *Prototypographus*, the First Printer, in recognition of his work.

The inspiration for The Book of Gold lies in the early days of printing in Europe, when a massive transformation occurred in how information was spread. It led to the democratisation of knowledge, putting it in the hands of whoever could read. Literacy soared and new ideas were born which would transform the world, giving birth to the modern era. The role of a printer was a dangerous one. Licences were required because both Church and State kept a stranglehold on knowledge. Translation was a potentially heretical subject, while a secret market in forbidden books stretched across the world, centring largely in Antwerp, because all of the world's trade routes met there, a place full to the brim with printers' workshops and a burgeoning humanist movement exploiting those connections. But not all in the trade played fair. Industrial espionage was common, as was the practice of accusing rivals of heresy and sedition. For example, the famous Wicked Bible of 1631, a copy of the King James Bible containing the exhortation "Thou shalt commit adultery" is now thought to have been sabotage by a rival printer. The printers Robert Barker and Martin Lucas were called to the Star Chamber, fined £300 (equivalent to about £54,000 today) and deprived of their license, effectively destroying their business.

I visited Antwerp, and went to the amazing Plantin-Moretus Museum, home of the Polyglot Bible, because I *had* to. It was like a pilgrimage. The more I learned about the city in the late 1500s, and

AUTHOR'S NOTE

this incredible printer who revolutionised science, medicine, geography, philosophy and any other area of learning you can think of, the more the story took form. Situated on the gorgeous Vrijdagmarkt, in the original building with its symbol of the golden compass, the museum is a magnificent piece of history in itself, and still has original typesets, woodblocks, and printing presses. The amount of fangirling was frankly embarrassing. I almost cried. Really.

I couldn't get the tale of the Polyglot bible out of my head and I kept thinking, all this would make a wonderful novel. But while I'm happy to rummage around in history for the juicy bits, I'm not a historian. My imagination tends to run away with me far too much for that. I like to fill in the blanks and if there's no evidence for what should go there, I make it up. Shamelessly.

But the story, real and imaginary it would not leave me alone.

In October 2022, at the Irish National Science Fiction Convention, on a panel about research, we were asked what story, or fact from history did we want to put in a book but had not yet found the story for it. I recounted the tale of the Plantin Bible, at length, and something obviously triggered in the tangle of information at the back of my mind. The next morning I woke up with these characters, their conflicts, and a heist (obviously) ready to go, and The Book of Gold was born.

When writing fantasy, we build up layers and layers of our new world from the flotsam and jetsam of reality. Amberes grew out of the lost Antwerp of the 16th century, when it was the crossroads of the world, the first really modern city. I used old maps, visited sites and touched the remains of the city walls. We even took a tour of the canals, which are now underground, aka the sewers. But honestly it felt like magic, like it was meant to be. A quest. The Book of Gold is the book of my heart.

The world of Amberes is a mixture of reimagined history and magical fantasy, but at its heart is a found family of common people who come together to save each other when faced with impossible threats from the great and powerful, and a vast resource of divine magic trapped inside a mysterious book. I wasn't keen on

AUTHOR'S NOTE

writing about kings and nobles. This was always about craftsmen and scholars.

And crime. Because Lyta. Nothing was going to stop Lyta.

It has been a magnificent adventure which often felt more like uncovering a story than creating one. I can't wait to find out what happens next.

But as mentioned above, I am not a historian and never will be. Just a writer. The factual inaccuracies, mistakes and the made up bits are all my own.

Acknowledgements

No book, no matter how magical, happens on its own. Although we often wish they would write themselves, and sometimes as in this case it feels like they mean to, so many people have contributed to the creation of The Book of Gold. It really is the book of my heart and to have it be a reality is a dream come true.

Thanks to the wonderful group of people who make up Octocon, the Irish National Science Fiction Convention, past, present and future, who have supported me for so long, and where the question "what historical fact do you want to put in a book but haven't yet?" had me recounting for a captive (unfortunately for them) audience the many adventures of the Plantin Polyglot Bible. Sorry about that folks.

Thanks also to my many friends in writing including: Sarah Rees Brennan, Kate Pearce, Kari Sperring and Jeevani Charika for their thoughtful and insightful critiques which really helped shape this story and its world; C.E. Murphy, Susan Connolly and Sarah again, for brainstorming and talking me off several ledges; all the Naughty Kitchen (Alison 'Serendipity Biscuits' May, Janet Gover, Sheila McClure, Kate Johnson, Queen Immi Howson & Jeev again) for the constant support, and endless fun. And for Feral Bob!

Thanks as always to everyone at Mulcahy Sweeney Associates, especially Sallyanne Sweeney and Edwina de Charnace, and to all the magnificent team at Hodderscape for making the book of my

ACKNOWLEDGEMENTS

heart a reality, especially Molly Powell and Sophie Judge. I am also grateful to Micaela Alcaino for the beautiful cover art.

I am also deeply thankful for the Plantin Moretus museum and the National Print Museum in Dublin.

Finally thanks to my family, who have been dragged on trips to many libraries and print museums, who have heard a thousand rare book stories, who have profited (!?!) from my bookbinding experiments, and who still put up with me. Diarmuid and Emily, you can now cook your own pizzas so they don't end up quite so burned when I get distracted by something old and shiny.

And Pat, you are still and will always be my hero, in every book and in every lifetime.

Just in case I have forgotten anyone, which is entirely possible, you too!

About the author

Ruth Frances Long writes romance and fantasy from the heart which often strays into weird and wonderful liminal places. In 2015 she won a European Science Fiction Society award for *A Crack in Everything*. She also writes as Jessica Thorne, was longlisted for the RNA Romance Fantasy award in 2020, and wrote a tie-in novel for the music festival Tomorrowland. She lives in Ireland and works in a specialized library of rare & occasionally crazy books. But they are mostly under control.

WANT MORE?

If you enjoyed this and would like to find out about similar books we publish, we'd love you to join our online Sci-Fi, Fantasy and Horror community, Hodderscape.

Visit hodderscape.co.uk for exclusive content from our authors, news, competitions and general musings, and feel free to comment, contribute or just keep an eye on what we are up to.

See you there!

HODDERSCAPE
NEVER AFRAID TO BE OUT OF THIS WORLD

@HODDERSCAPE   HODDERSCAPE.CO.UK